Au

Annie's Legacy

Also by Ken McCoy

Hope Street
Cobblestone Heroes

Annie's Legacy

Ken McCoy

First published in Great Britain in 2001 by
Judy Piatkus (Publishers) Ltd of
5 Windmill Street, London W1T 2JA
email:info@piatkus.co.uk

A catalogue record for this book is available from the British Library

ISBN 0 7499 0567 0

Set in Times by
Action Publishing Technology Ltd, Gloucester

Printed and bound in Great Britain by
Mackays of Chatham plc, Chatham, Kent

To Dean, Jane, Matthew, Angela and Thomas. With fond memories of all the grief you lot have caused me over the years. But I wouldn't change any of you.

Thanks to Val, for all her bright ideas; and to Judith Murdoch for once again pointing out the error of my ways.

Part One

Chapter One

August 1953

'Sixpenny, please.'

The girl held out a threepenny bit and three pennies and relinquished them to the conductor as though it was all she had left in the world. The bundle in her arms moved and whimpered, causing her to glance up guiltily at the man, who smiled good-naturedly.

'It's all right, love. We don't charge for babes-in-arms, especially when they're not the size o' two penn'orth o' copper. Yer first, is he?'

He took a sideways glance at the girl's face and realised from her age that it perhaps wasn't the most intelligent of questions. She gave a faint nod as he clicked off a blue ticket.

'First – and last,' she said suddenly, as much to herself as to him.

He handed her the ticket, then leaned over to take a look at the child. A tiny pink face peeped out from behind a knitted blue matinée jacket. Dark, liquid eyes looked back at him, seeing him but having little memory of him once its gaze had returned to its mother.

'Blimey! He's fresh outa the oven.'

The girl looked away, sharply.

'Sorry, love, didn't mean to offend. How old is he?'

'It's a *she*.'

There was no emotion in her small voice. She looked down and crooked her little finger in the baby's mouth. It sucked at her, hungrily.

'She's ready for a bit o' breakfast,' grinned the conductor. 'Mind you, me and her both.'

His top middle tooth was missing which added comedy to his genial face but it didn't impress the girl who looked away, not wanting this conversation. She wished she wasn't the only passenger on the bus so the conductor could bother someone else. Thankfully he took the hint and sat on a seat near the door to count his meagre takings. The journey continued in silence. He was probably okay, she thought. But then again her life had been destroyed by a man who looked okay. Best not to trust any of them.

The conductor glanced up at her, his eyes quickly returning to the job in hand as she somehow seemed conscious of his stare. What was the mother of a newborn baby doing on the early bus? Pound to a pinch she wasn't married. Not at her age. She didn't look any older than his daughter who had only just left school. Fourteen – fifteen at the most, her face was pale and drawn as though she'd been poorly. He stole another glance – no, as though she'd been crying. Bit of both perhaps.

A fragile beauty crouched behind her wan features. Her lifeless blonde hair was clipped back by assorted hair slides. Frightened blue eyes, guarded by wire-rimmed NHS glasses, searched the world rushing past the bus window, as though scared of what was out there. She was not very tall, maybe five foot two, slightly built and wearing a cheap, floral-print dress that fitted where it touched and a dark green knitted cardigan with a large white envelope poking out of one of the pockets. There was a plaster on her bare left leg that wasn't quite big enough to cover the livid graze it was meant to protect and on her feet were a pair of well-worn plimsolls, recently whitened with the dye running over the rubber welt. The baby was wrapped in a yellow woollen blanket with BRMH DO NOT REMOVE printed on it.

They were out in the country now, with stops few and far between. No one was waiting at these, which was only to be expected at this time on a Sunday morning. Through the window she saw the spire of a distant church rising above the heavy summer foliage as the bus snored slowly up a long hill. Its appearance seemed to create a conflict of decisions within her. She hadn't worked out her plan in any great detail, she just had an ultimate goal. The method of arriving at this goal was now down to providence. The church steeple looked providential to her. Divine providence. God had got her into this mess by allowing her to be born – He could get her out of it.

'Excuse me, what church is that?' she asked suddenly, half turning in her seat to look at the conductor, and pointing out of the window at the same time. Her voice was as frail as her body; it had the resigned note of someone who just didn't care what the world did to them any more.

He followed her pointing finger. 'Er – Beckhall Church, love.'

'Oh,' she said, disappointed. Then another thought occurred to her. She turned round again. 'I mean, has it got a proper name?'

The man shrugged, not understanding the question at first. Then it came to him. He stroked his chin, making an audible rasping sound. Shaving for the early shift on a Sunday was a bit of a waste of time.

'I went to a wedding there once,' he remembered. 'I think they call it Saint Catherine's. In fact, they definitely do. I remember now 'cos me wife's called Catherine only she's not a saint – but don't tell her I told yer.'

She didn't return his grin, which faded quickly when he realised his humour had fallen on stony ground.

Catherine. She ran the name across her thoughts and smiled thinly, nodding to herself. Approving.

'Can I get off here, please?' Her manner now was that of a timid schoolgirl asking leave to go to the toilet.

''Course yer can, love.' The conductor rang the bell,

causing the driver to look into his mirror. People rarely got off here at this time on a morning. He nodded at his mate and drew the bus to a halt. The girl carefully placed her ticket into the used-ticket slot, as though not wishing to contravene any rules, and stepped off, stumbling slightly as her leading foot landed on a large stone. The conductor reached out a steadying hand. 'Careful, love!'

But she had already regained her balance and looked embarrassed at her own clumsiness.

'Mind how yer go.'

She didn't seem to hear and walked on. The conductor stood on the platform and stared back at her dwindling form until the bus turned a corner and she was out of sight, but for some reason not out of his mind. Shaking his head he sat down, oddly uncomfortable, feeling she needed help and that he should have known what sort. His wife would have known.

The church spire was obscured from view now and she tried to remember exactly where it was. There must be a turn off leading to it. The quiet country road was bounded by high, unkempt hedgerows of beech and privet and hawthorn, twittering with early birds. Leaning drunkenly into the hedge was a sign which presumably had once said *BECKHALL 1 ml*, only some wag had replaced the BE with FU. It confused the girl as she couldn't remember what the conductor had said the village was called, but she knew this road must surely lead to the church.

A skylark hovered above her in the pale blue, early-morning sky, seemingly matching her pace, but she didn't hear its song so it flew off to seek a more appreciative audience. The church clock began to strike and she knew she was heading in the right direction. She counted the bongs until they stopped at six. Every step was increasingly painful. Her eyes searched the road ahead for somewhere to sit and rest. A mile was a long way in her condition.

The road crossed a narrow river by means of a hump-backed stone bridge. The copings on the parapet wall were missing here and there, the reduced height providing a welcome seat for the girl. Hugging her infant to her, she gazed over her shoulder into the running water. She liked running water, there was something comforting and pure and honest about it. Words that didn't sit easily with the life she'd had so far. For a brief moment she sat and enjoyed the happy sound of the river.

There was also something dangerous about water. She shuddered and looked away. Drowning was the most horrible of deaths. Struggling for air that wasn't there, lungs bursting – and then what? No one had ever come back to tell. Someone was whistling and being told to shut up and not scare the fish. She chanced another look and saw a line of fishermen spaced all the way up one bank, their lines curling downstream with the flow. Coloured floats were bobbing cheerfully, one almost beneath her. Natural politeness forced a smile from her in response to a wave from the nearest of the fishermen, a young man of about her own age.

Encouraged by her smile he shouted up to her, 'Nice day for it.'

He was chastised once again for disturbing the fish and turned to the man standing one place up river, saying something inaudible but obviously uncomplimentary. For a brief second the girl wondered why shouting should scare fish. Did fish have ears? She'd never seen a fish's ears. Then the thought had gone. Not enough of a diversion to cheer her – to distract her from what had to be done.

The young fisherman wondered if she was from the village. If so he'd make it his business to enquire as to her identity before much longer. From where he was standing she looked a bit of all right. A bit on the skinny side maybe, and a couple of years younger than him, but there was definitely something special about her. He was thirty yards away but he felt an attraction. The baby must be her brother or sister, or some child she was minding for a neighbour. He considered risking the wrath of his companions once again by giving her another shout, maybe to ask for a date. You got nowhere in this world without a bit of cheek.

'Keep yer eyes on the job, lad. Look at yer float.'

The warning came from the man he'd just had words with. The girl glanced down at his float which was being pulled beneath the surface by a captured fish. The young man dragged his attention away from her and transferred it to the job in hand and proceeded to reel in his catch, his first of the day. By the time the fish was wriggling into his keep-net, the girl had gone. He looked up at the bridge and shrugged away his disappointment. His neighbour grinned and made a disparaging remark about the young Lothario to the man next up the line.

The girl's eyes were now fixed on the rutted road as she took care not to stumble. She had little thought for her own well-being but she had to protect her precious burden.

The rest had been welcome, she'd have stayed longer had she not become the centre of attention. The strength was ebbing from her limbs once again, then the first sight of the spire fired new life into her. Not much further to go. She could see the church now. Built in pale, weathered limestone, solid and old and reliable. Reassuring. Rich people would go to a church like this. Decent people, nice people. Her brow was damp with perspiration despite the early-morning nip in the air. She looked down at the baby sucking frantically at her finger.

'Not just yet, my darling, not just yet.'

Her failing strength just carried her to the wooden bench opposite the church. *In Memory of Wilfred Eames* was carved on the back. It was rustic and unsafe-looking, but it would have to be on the verge of collapse not to take her weight. She sat down, her breath coming in short bursts which slowed as her resting lungs required less oxygen. The same skylark seemed to spot her and renewed its serenade, hoping for more appreciation this time. But the songbird's performance was curtailed by a kestrel which moved into its air space to hover menacingly as the frightened lark flew off. She squinted up at the hovering falcon, but she was a town girl and wouldn't know a kestrel from a cuckoo. The bird, having spotted its breakfast, dropped like a stone from the sky, taking the girl's gaze with it until it passed behind the church, transferring her focus to the clock. Twenty past six. No people disturbed the tranquillity. Putting the baby to her breast, she felt more contented than she'd ever been in her short life. But it was a contentment tempered by what she had to do. There was no other way, she knew that. God knows she'd tried to think of a better way out. But when there's no one in the world who believes in you, no one you can trust or rely on, nowhere to go to get away from the horror of it all, what alternative do you have? She'd needed protection and she'd been offered scorn and derision. Not even Miss Bulmer had believed her. *He'd* got to her already, primed her for what to expect, and he was a very plausible man so Miss Bulmer really wasn't to blame. She shouldn't have threatened him that she was going to tell her favourite teacher, that was a stupid thing to do. Jimmy Johnstone might have made a difference to her life, but providence had seen fit to dictate otherwise. Jimmy had been her last hope. Her only hope.

The weathered sign outside the church read:

Saint Catherine's RC Church, Beckhall
Sunday Mass 9 a.m.; 11 a.m.
Parish Priest: Fr John Barrett, DD

She nodded her approval of the church's being Catholic. With any luck the priest would be a person of integrity. Surely he wouldn't let her down like all the others? Catholic priests didn't let people down. She wasn't a Catholic herself but she knew that much. She looked down at her daughter, sucking away contentedly.

'What d'you think about becoming a Catholic, my darling?'

They'd probably call her Catherine, after the church. Why not? It was as good a name as any. She'd been calling her Doris, after Doris Day in *Calamity Jane*, her favourite film of all time. Catherine was a much more fitting name for a Catholic girl. She'd certainly never heard of a Saint Doris. A rare, amusing thought came to her mind, but failed to make her smile: Saint Doris of Deadwood.

The whole parish would take an interest in her daughter's welfare. That would keep the authorities on their toes. Oh, yes, there was nothing better for keeping the authorities on their toes than people who lived in places like this.

With her free hand she extracted a pencil and a small writing pad from her cardigan pocket. Pity about the pencil, but the other letter was written in proper ink from a Parker fountain pen. There was an irony here. It was the pen *he'd* given her; imagine his face if he knew what she had written with it! The first letter was written in her best handwriting, which was a lot better than most – as was her grammar. Whoever read it would know it had been written by an educated person which would, of course, add further weight to its contents.

It was a struggle to write with her daughter at her breast, but she took her time. It had to be legible. Then she took the large envelope from her pocket; inside was another smaller, sealed envelope, alongside which she placed her note. She then sealed the large envelope and wrote *Fr John Barrett, DD* on the front. Putting it back in her pocket, she nodded off and was woken by the ringing of the seven o'clock bell. Her baby was fast asleep at her breast. She drew the infant gently away from her nipple, smiling as the child's mouth continued to open and shut, reluctant to be taken from such a comfy place. Buttoning up her dress, she focused her eyes on the Mass times. First service nine o'clock. Two hours. Would her daughter be okay for two hours? It'd probably be less. People would start arriving well before then. They'd no doubt open the church at eight o'clock – just an hour away.

She looked down at her sleeping daughter and felt her resolve weakening. No – she'd weighed up all the pros and cons and this was by far the best thing to do. The first part of her plan had begun to form in her mind even before the child was born, the minute she'd walked through the door of Barrack Road Maternity Hostel where she'd been packed off to give birth to her bastard child. Their words, not hers. The maternity hostel for unmarried mothers was an environment bordering on hostile, manned by so-called care assistants ill-suited for work in any NHS maternity hospital because of incompetence or bad attitude or both. But for all the lack of compassion, there was a rough honesty about the place. No false smiles and lies. No dreading being alone in bed and waiting for the door opening. She'd swap that for a foul-mouthed nurse any day of the week.

She had anticipated the immense love she'd feel for her child and had told herself that such feelings were to be ignored at all costs. Her baby would have no chance of a happy life with her as a mother. Keeping the child just to satisfy her own maternal instincts would be the ultimate self-indulgence. Anyway, if they caught her and took her back to the home they wouldn't let her keep her baby.

This and other reasons had determined the second part of her plan. Her ultimate goal.

Fingering the envelope in her pocket, she wondered if she might be burdening her daughter too much. Was she being unfair? To hell with unfair! Life had been unfair to her. This is how it had to be. Switching off her confused thoughts she stood up and almost ran across the road, under the lych-gate and up the worn flagged path to the church door. Finding it open surprised and alarmed her. Someone must be inside. Her plan had been to leave her child in the doorway, but if possible it would be so much better and safer to leave her inside.

She stole a glance through the door. Empty. That was right, she remembered, vaguely. Catholic churches never locked their doors. Holding her child up to her cheek, she entered warily, creeping past the church notices and the empty collection trays. Her lips pecked softly at the baby's face as she moved quietly down the central aisle towards the altar, glancing nervously up at the Stations of the Cross carved on the walls to either side of her. A blue-and-white Virgin Mary smiled benignly down upon her with one hand raised as though saying, 'Hello, Annie, thanks for dropping in.' The lady on flower duty had been in the night before and left a vase of carnations and roses beside the unlit candles on the Lady Altar. Those on the cleaning roster had left the church dust-free and smelling of lavender furniture polish, but one of them had inadvertently left a cigarette-end on the stone baptismal font. This would ordinarily earn the woman a chastening rebuke, but the priest would have other things to think about this morning. High above, in the vaulted roof, a trapped sparrow fluttered about among the oak timbers, looking for a way out. Something Annie Jackson had been seeking for some time now.

Beneath her quiet feet the wooden block floor was worn concave from a hundred and thirty years of shuffling shoes. She arrived at the low wooden communion rail and wondered if she dare step over it and approach the altar. Why not? In for a penny, as they say. Her heart was pounding, partly from fear of being discovered and partly from dread of her imminent loss. Kneeling down in front of the altar, she laid her sleeping daughter gently on the floor and placed the envelope beside her. Then, with hands clasped and eyes dripping tears, she looked up at the huge crucifix behind the altar and whispered, 'Please – I hope I'm doing the right thing.'

With an effort of will she didn't know she had in her, Annie turned and ran back up the aisle, stopping at the end and wanting to look back. But she knew she mustn't.

The second part of her plan would be nowhere near as difficult as this.

Chapter Two

March 1945

'Hip-hooray, we are free,
Free from the gates of mizzeree
No more school, no more stick,
No more flippin' arithmetic . . .'

Annie began the song and it was taken up lustily by her two companions.

'No more English, no more French,
No more sitting at a wooden bench . . .'

The inclusion of French was a bit ambitious as the singers were only seven years old. It was a school-holiday song passed down by older kids. The three of them skipped along in time to their singing. Spring was only a fortnight away and the end of the war wasn't much further off. Brian Gibbons' gas mask banged against his hip in the cardboard case bearing his name and address. His two companions had discarded theirs as the urgency wasn't being impressed upon them quite so much nowadays. Now that Adolf was on the run.

They skipped down the centre of Lowtoft Road as this bit had been recently surfaced with tarmac and was easier on their Wellington-booted feet than the wide cobbled channels to either side. Few cars hampered their progress. A council dustcart lumbered past with no one on its rear platform. All three of them jumped on for the free ride, jumping off as it swung into Ashley Avenue and laughing at the dusty fist shaking from the driver's window. Two days of rain had eased off in time for their exit from Lowtoft Junior School. A week's half-term holiday lay ahead, better known as 'Teacher's Rest'.

'Teacher's Rest, Mother's Pest,' Annie's mam had said when told of the impending holiday. She said that every half term, as did every other mother.

Annie's boots had been chafing at her legs. She stopped to turn down the tops, rubbing at the sore, pink circumference just below her knees.

'I'm gonna put some Grasshopper Green on this when I get home,' she announced.

'What's that?' enquired Movita Lunn, Annie's best friend.

'Ointment – cures everything in the world.'

'Our Maureen's got nits. Does it cure nits?' asked Brian.

'Prob'ly. Cured me mam's elbow.'

The boy nodded, impressed. The skipping and singing resumed until they arrived at an iron lamp-post where a man had leaned a short ladder against the projecting arm.

'Watcher doin', mister?' inquired Annie, chirpily.

'That's fer me ter know and you ter find out,' grinned the man, lighting the gas mantle.

'It's not dark yet,' pointed out Brian. 'Yer not s'pposed ter light 'em till it's dark.'

The man closed the glass window and came back down his ladder.

'Nay, I'm not Captain Marvel. I can't light 'em all up at once.'

Annie understood the logic behind his answer; she was the only one who did. Brian cupped his left hand inside his right armpit and squeezed with his right arm, producing a farting sound. The man hadn't seen how he did it.

'Watch it! Yer'll blow me blinkin' cap off doin' that.'

This produced screams of laughter from the three children who skipped on down the road, all of them trying to emulate Brian's brilliant trick but only Annie meeting with any success. She'd try it on her mam when she got home. Her mam could do with a laugh.

Brenda Bacup spotted the happy trio as she came out of Mrs Holmes' shop with a twist of lemonade powder in her hand and a packet of stolen cigarettes in her cardigan pocket, as ordered by her older brother. Brenda didn't understand camaraderie of the sort enjoyed by Annie and her pals. She had no friends to speak of, only kids who hung around with her because she was big and aggressive. She wetted a fat finger between her lips, stuck it into the paper cone and brought out a fingerful of yellow crystals which she stuck in her mouth. Her quick brain tried to think of a reason to chastise Annie, whom she hated. Mainly because she was quite pretty and very popular, qualities Brenda would never enjoy.

Annie and her friends stopped at a chalked set of hopscotch squares on the flagged footpath. She bent down to pick up the stone with which she intended to start the game when a blow from behind sent her sprawling to the floor, tearing a hole in the elbow of her gaberdine coat and grazing her forehead. She lay there for a few seconds trying to gather her thoughts. At seven years old she was entitled to burst into tears, but she fought them back. Only softies cried for nothing – and crying didn't mend a torn raincoat. Instead she got to her knees and looked up at Brenda.

The girls were the same age but there any similarity ended. Annie was small and slender whereas Brenda was twenty pounds heavier and several inches taller. Masses of tight ginger curls spiralled away from her freckled face, unbrushed and unwashed. Mean eyes, one green one brown, were buried deep beyond freckled cheeks puffing out either side of a broad, snub nose, below which her top teeth projected beyond rubbery lips like a row of unloved gravestones. In many ways Brenda Bacup was a girl who deserved such a face. She stood over Annie and gave a scowl which would have frightened most people, young or old.

'I warned yer I'd get yer, Jackson. Next time, yer do as yer told.'

'Warned me what?' enquired a bemused Annie, examining the tear in her coat. 'Look what yer've done – me mam'll go mad.'

'I warned yer not ter go showin' off in t' test,' snarled Brenda.

It was the first Annie had heard of this warning. Not that she'd have heeded it anyway. 'It's not my fault yer a bit thick,' she retorted, tenderly touching her grazed head.

The hand that had sent her to the floor knocked her over again, stinging Annie's ear.

'Ow!' she yelled. 'Leave us alone. I haven't done nowt.'

Movita Lunn stood uncomfortably by, watching but not daring to help. Brenda Bacup was not someone you messed with, unless you were Brian Gibbons. He flung himself at Brenda, only to be swatted away like a fly. She returned her attention to Annie.

'I warned yer last week – it's yer own fault fer takin' no notice.'

'I never heard yer.'

'Are you callin' me a liar?' Brenda grabbed Annie by her long blonde hair and tried to pull her off the ground.

'Ow! Give over. Anyroad Jacky Naylor beat yer as well, why don't yer pick on him?'

Brenda had no answer other than to draw her fist back in readiness to thump Annie again. Brian was on the ground rubbing his sore head. Movita stood quietly, too scared to intervene.

'Hey! What's goin' on?'

The lamplighter had seen the disturbance and now pushed Brenda to one side. Seeing Annie on the floor, he turned and glared down into the bigger girl's face, flinching slightly as Brenda returned the glare with fifty per cent interest.

'Why don't yer pick on someone yer own size, yer flamin' bully!'

Brenda ignored him. She looked down at Annie and sneered, 'I'll get yer next time, Jackson.'

'Go on, clear off afore I rattle yer flamin' ear 'ole for yer,' threatened the lamplighter, sincerely hoping he wouldn't be taken up on his threat. Brenda's ear 'ole wasn't something he relished rattling.

Brenda strolled off, sticking two fingers up over her shoulder and kicking Brian in the ribs as she passed him. The man pulled Annie to her feet.

'She'll come ter no good will that one,' he said. 'You mark my words. Are yer all right, love?'

Tears weren't far away but Annie didn't want her friends to see her crying. She set her mouth and blinked her eyes dry.

'Me coat's torn,' she announced, examining the tear. 'Me mam'll go spare.'

'Do yer want me ter come back wi' yer and tell 'er what 'appened?' offered the man.

Annie shrugged, her eyes on the ground, reluctant to display any sign of weakness. She took a deep breath before replying, 'No, thanks, mister,' then turned to go, her two friends joining her. Movita nodded her thanks to Annie's saviour.

'Yer ought ter tell on that Brenda,' said Brian. 'She's allus pickin' on yer. I were gonna bray her meself, but she caught me off balance.'

'Give over,' scoffed Movita. 'Yer couldn't fight yer way out of a paper bag.'

'I didn't see you steppin' in,' he muttered.

'Are you kidding?' Movita's auburn ringlets swirled about her head as she turned to face Brian. 'I'd sooner fight Joe Louis.'

'I'll get her back meself,' said Annie, her voice trembling. 'You just wait and see.'

They arrived at the junction with Carrcroft Road where Brian went his own way with a brief 'See yer' to the two girls, who waved and walked on. Movita put a comforting arm around her friend's shoulder and told her not to worry about Brenda who was a big fat ginger turd. Annie decided to change the subject, think about something else to take her mind off unpleasant things. She'd do that a lot in the coming years.

'Shall I ask me mam if yer can come round for yer tea?' she enquired. 'If I 'ang me coat up quick, she'll not see I've torn it.'

'What yer having?' asked Movita.

'Bread an' slap,' said Annie, her smile returning. Slowly at first, curving her lips, then lighting up her eyes before spreading all over her face. 'But if yer come round she'll make us summat nice so yer won't go telling yer mam we never have nowt proper to eat.'

'Awright – shall I come in with yer, then she won't be able ter say no?' suggested Movita.

'Yeah,' agreed Annie. 'I'll tell her yer'd only be havin' bread an' slap at your house, then she'll definitely make us summat nice.'

'Has she got any eggs?'

'I think so. We had three left this morning an' she cleans for Mrs Ramsgill on a Friday so she'll have had her dinner there – unless Mrs Poot's been round and borrowed 'em for her Yorkshires. She's allus doin' that and she never brings us any back. Me mam says we've ter make allowances 'cos Mr Poot's not all there.'

Brenda Bacup was almost forgotten as they joined hands and skipped in unison towards Annie's house in Fogerty Row. There were four Fogertys – Street, Terrace, Avenue and Row – all with back streets and all built around the turn of the century. Their red-brick walls were now dulled by fifty years of soot, deposited by the many tall chimneys projecting from the foundries and factories, fracturing the Leeds skyline. The idea was to send the smoke so far up that it wouldn't want to come back down in a hurry. But the law of gravity is not a law to be ignored with impunity. What goes up must come down, and down it had come, on to the houses and into the lungs of the very workers who'd sent the smoke up the chimneys in the first place.

Annie's hair was clipped back behind her ears with yellow and red hair slides and bounced on her shoulders as she skipped, her blue eyes sparkling with fun once again. It took a lot to get her down. A lot more than Brenda Bacup anyway. She was the apple of her dad's eye. He'd last been heard of just after Christmas, somewhere in Belgium, where he was 'well' according to the latest cryptic missive his wife Olga had received from the War Office. Olga had been having a bad war. Not hearing from her husband for five months hadn't helped, but there were plenty in the same boat as her so there was much mutual sympathy to be had. Movita's dad had been classed as unfit for military service due to his being epileptic, although there was some scepticism locally as to the truth of this. 'I've many a time seen him *paralytic* outside the Plasterer's Arms,' Olga Jackson once grumbled over the railings which separated the Jacksons' back yard from old Mrs Poot's next door. Mrs Poot had nodded her agreement. She thought all the men should do their bit, like her Horace who'd been bayoneted by the Boers and returned home a shadow of the man she'd married.

The girls skipped past the street signed Fogerty Row without sparing it a glance and turned down the next street, Back Fogerty Row. Front streets weren't for kids coming home from school. They were for visitors and for having your photo taken on the front step. The back street was for everyday use. They were lucky to have a back street; many of their pals lived in back-to-back houses with the lavvies six doors away in the communal yard.

A bicycle was propped up on one pedal against the stone

kerb outside Annie's house. From her back yard emerged a uniformed, nose-picking telegram boy with a bag slung over his shoulder. He paused to finish ransacking a nostril, examined his findings, rolled it into a ball and flicked it at a passing dog before mounting his bike and riding off, whistling, unaware of the misery he'd just delivered.

'What's he doin' at your house?' wondered Movita.

Annie said nothing. Charlie Fricker's mam had been given bad news about her husband by a telegram. Annie's pace quickened and Movita allowed her to walk into the house first. She didn't follow as arranged but instead hung around in the yard, smiling over the low dividing wall at Mrs Poot who'd also seen the telegram boy and was waiting at her own door to see what it had been about.

'It's probably nowt nor thummat,' reassured Mrs Poot, her diction distorted due to her teeth being left on the scullery shelf. 'I onth had one wishing me Happy Birthday.'

The grey-faced old woman uncrossed her arms, hitched up one of her pendulous bosoms and ran a tidying hand through her sparse white hair, a habit she'd acquired when it was worth the trouble.

Movita nodded and waited for her friend to emerge with an invitation to tea. Five minutes went by with no sign of Annie.

'Give 'er a knock – 'appen she's forgotten yer there,' urged Mrs Poot, who knew by now that bad news had befallen her neighbour and wanted to know the extent of it so that she could pass it on.

Movita walked to the half-open door and gave it a tentative knock. A kettle steamed unheeded on the scullery hob, the noise not quite drowning the sobbing coming from the room beyond. Annie came back to the door. The sparkle had gone from her face, replaced by confusion.

'Yer won't be able ter come for tea,' she said. 'Me dad's been killed.'

Annie closed the door and Movita turned to go. She

looked across at the woman next door who was already hurrying out into the street to do her duty and pass the bad news on. At least her Horace had come home so she was better off than some.

Chapter Three

The following months held many black days for Annie. Her mother, Olga, had reacted badly, worse than she'd anticipated considering the circumstances under which she'd married Alan Jackson. Annie desperately missed not having her dad's homecoming to look forward to and was secretly jealous of all the kids whose dads had lived through it all, even Movita Lunn whose father had been at home all the time.

'It's the worst time of me life,' Annie confided to her friend as they sat side by side at the VE Day street party, two months later. Movita put her arm around her pal and murmured words of comfort. Kitchen and dining tables had been brought out into the centre of the street and covered with an array of table cloths. For the last few weeks ration coupons had been 'put to one side' in hopeful anticipation of such an event, thus providing a feast wasted on stomachs accustomed to far less. The partygoers were mostly women and children. Servicemen lucky enough to be at home were made more than welcome but most of the men who, for a variety of reasons, hadn't fought stayed away. Dogs circled the tables, snapping up playfully thrown buns, slices of ham and spoonfuls of jelly (a popular event). Raucous voices accompanied Vera Lynn singing 'There'll Be Bluebirds Over the White Cliffs of Dover' from a wind-up gramophone and a row of paper Union Jacks fluttered noisily above their heads. Olga and Mrs Fricker hadn't joined the revellers and Annie had only been persuaded out because Movita had said she'd prefer to go to Annie's street party than her own. Her dad had already celebrated himself into oblivion and her mother was standing watch over him, ready with a harsh word and a clenched fist.

'Me mam says yer've not ter worry 'cos things'll get better, you'll see.' Movita's mam was well-meaning, but wrong. 'Me mam says she'd rather me dad 'ad been killed than be allus getting' drunk an' bein' a useless owd bugger.'

Annie understood the logic behind this. 'I suppose me dad's a hero, isn't he, getting killed an' all that?'

Movita nodded. 'Me mam says it's better to be a dead hero than a live pisspot.'

The two girls indulged in a bout of mutual consolation as Vera Lynn gave way to George Formby, causing the party-goers to sing along to the plunking of imaginary ukuleles.

Olga was never told the exact circumstances of Alan's death, just that he was 'Killed in Action'. A man from the War office had been round with the news, unaware that the telegram boy had already beaten him to it. A mistake in the system apparently. It hadn't been possible to bring Alan's body back, but he'd been buried with full military honours somewhere in Belgium.

Theirs hadn't been a marriage made in heaven but he'd done the decent thing by her when she fell on with Annie; Olga certainly wouldn't have married him otherwise. Him with the gappy grin and ears like a taxi with its doors wide open. In truth, Annie's dad could have been one of three and she'd only 'been naughty' with Alan the once, so he wasn't exactly the hot favourite, more of a ten-to-one outsider.

He'd been a carpenter, working on the new Queen's Hotel in Leeds City Square. On the day it was officially opened by the Earl of Harewood, Alan had been one of the few workmen selected to bring their wives or girlfriends and mingle with the hierarchy. He'd thought it an ideal opportunity to impress Olga, a young seamstress he'd admired from afar for quite some time. Drinking champagne and standing within nodding distance of the noble earl had impressed Olga enough for her to drop her knickers for Alan round the back of St George's Crypt later that evening.

The other two possible parents, including Alan's best pal, Maurice Feather, had made themselves very scarce indeed when they'd found out she was pregnant. Alan had come forward of his own accord, unaware of the other suspects, truly believing he must be the father – and who was she to disillusion him? She was quite a catch, with or without a bun in the oven. Maurice, invalided out of the RAF in 1944, had been round to offer his condolences when he'd heard of Alan's death and Olga had made a bit of a play for him.

'Yer do know that Alan wasn't really Annie's father, don't yer?' she'd confided over a bottle of milk stout. 'And I don't suppose yer'll need three guesses as to who is.'

Maurice hadn't been back since.

Annie managed to steer clear of Brenda Bacup's bullying until September of the following year, when she fell foul of her again. Annie, Movita, Brian Gibbons and Norman Newton had been to the horse chestnut trees in Gledhow Valley woods and came back with a pillowcase full of conkers. Brian and Norman had done most of the work, being the ones who climbed the trees and shook the conkers down, so Annie and Movita took on the sales job.

'Conks, ten a penny,' shouted Movita, as she and Annie moved around the school playground at morning playtime. Chalked cricket stumps had been partially rubbed off the lavatory wall and replaced with goalposts, against which a game of 'shots in' was in progress. Grimy faced, short-trousered boys, mostly with legs too skinny to support their socks, gathered round to make purchases from

Annie, who was carrying the goods and conducting the business. Business was brisk as the only other competitor was Kevin Bacup, Brenda's younger brother, selling at seven a penny.

Brenda appeared at speed from behind the two girls, shouldering Movita aside and pushing Annie with all her might. Both the bag and Annie fell to the ground, scattering the conkers across tarmac to the delight of the many children who rushed to pick them up. Annie got to her feet and squared up to Brenda.

'I told yer not ter go round sellin' conks,' said Brenda, menacingly, wiping her runny nose with her sleeve. 'Our kid's t' only one allowed ter do that.'

'Yer never said nowt of the sort,' protested Annie. 'Anyroad, we're sellin' 'em cheaper than your kid.'

'Not now yer not,' smirked Brenda, looking round at the children happily gathering the scattered conkers. 'Yer givin' 'em away fer nowt.'

'Well, in that case, they won't want ter buy any off your kid then, will they?' retorted Annie.

Brenda hadn't thought of this. Kevin was selling on her behalf, earning a miserly commission. Up to now he hadn't sold any and his sales prospects looked bleaker still. Angrily, she dragged her arm across her runny nose.

'Ugh – yer've got snot on yer sleeve,' commented Annie, to loud laughs from the onlookers.

Brenda swung a heavy hand against Annie's face and knocked her to the ground.

'I'll do yer fer this, Jackson,' she snarled.

A circle of fight fans had gathered. 'Knock 'er 'ead in, Silversleeves!' someone shouted, generating more amusement and giving birth to a new nickname for Brenda. Annie's supporters added similar shouts of encouragement and derision. Brenda's jeering cronies joined in on her side as Annie got to her feet once again.

'Kill her dead, Brenda!'

Annie, her face white with rage and determination,

hurled herself at the bigger girl, fists flailing wildly, but to no avail. Brenda held her in a headlock and punched her in the face until blood oozed down on to her school frock. The bell rang to signal the end of playtime and the crowd scattered and ran to the entrance. Brenda paused to deliver one last blow, then stood back to gloat.

Annie wiped the blood from her mouth and glowered at her persecutor. 'I'll get yer back – jus' you wait an' see.'

Movita put a protective arm around her friend as Brenda ran into the school.

Mrs Backhouse the bellringer, tall, stern and bilious, spotted the girls and motioned with her free hand for them to approach her. 'What happened to you, Jackson?' she enquired, no hint of sympathy in her voice.

'I fell, miss.'

Movita's mouth opened and shut, desperately fighting the desire to tell on Brenda. But if Annie didn't want to, it was up to her.

'Come with me, we'd better get you cleaned up before you go into class.'

The teacher had a fair idea of what had happened but she was aware of the code of honour which prevailed among the children. If anything it made teachers' lives a bit easier.

Annie grew a little older and a little wiser and the memory of her dad faded until she couldn't picture his face. There were photographs of him, but these lacked animation and try as she might she couldn't remember how he'd looked when he laughed or spoke to her or smoked a cigarette. His memory became a black-and-white, one-dimensional image standing beside the clock on the mantelpiece.

> Remember, remember the fifth of November,
> Gunpowder treason and plot.
> I see no reason why gunpowder treason
> Should ever be forgot.

Children learned the rhyme at school the same as they learned their multiplication tables: parrot fashion. Whether Guy Fawkes was a hero or a villain was completely immaterial to the youngsters, who began the ritual several weeks before the big day. 'Chumping' was the name given to it in Leeds, other towns and cities had different names, but they all meant the same thing: collecting wood for Bonfire Night. Stuffed Guy Fawkeses would lean against walls on busy streets, outside cinemas and ideally, outside pubs. Kids would shout 'Penny for the Guy' and grown-ups would smile and remember their own childhood and happily hand over the odd coin or two which would be spent on fireworks.

On November 5th a huge wigwam of wood would be erected in even the narrowest of streets whilst many a distraught householder searched the district to try and locate his stolen backyard gate before it went up in flames. Dads would light the fire and mothers would bake parkin and supply chestnuts and potatoes for roasting in the embers. As the fire burned on into the night it would be kept alive by the addition of unwanted sticks of furniture, and husbands returning from the pub would howl in dismay when it was discovered that the burning stick of furniture was only unwanted by the wife who had seen her chance and taken it.

But for many kids, the best night was the night before – Mischief Night.

People were supposed to observe tradition and turn a blind eye to the harmless mischief perpetrated by roaming bands of kids who would spend a happy couple of hours knocking on doors and running away, lugging dustbins into the street and posting dog turds through letter boxes. Inventive juveniles would devise more dangerous pranks than these and Annie sensed a devious plan lurking in Brian Gibbons' mind when she opened the door to his knock.

'Are yer comin' out mischiefin'?' he enquired. More accomplices hovered by the gate. Annie had her coat on in a second.

'Don't gerrup ter nowt daft,' warned Olga, as her daughter stepped out of the door.

'Where's Norman?' enquired Annie, wondering where Brian's constant companion was.

'Scarlet Fever. He's in Seacoft Hospital.'

'Oh 'eck! Is he gonna be all right?'

'I suppose so.'

'You might've caught it off him.'

'Have I 'eck!' Brian looked worried; antibiotics weren't widely available yet.

'Anyway, what're we doin'?' enquired Annie. Brian shrugged.

'Go on,' said Colin Wigglesworth. 'Tell 'er – tell 'er yer barmy idea.'

'Tell me what?' said Annie, who wasn't struck on Colin Wigglesworth.

'It's norra barmy idea,' protested Brian. 'I bet it'd work.'

Annie impatiently pushed him. 'Bet what'd work?'

Colin answered for him. 'There's a steamroller parked on Florence Street. Brian reckons he can start it up an' drive it.' He looked scornfully at his friend. 'Yer only trying ter do summat better than your kid.'

'No, I'm not,' protested Brian, whose elder brother had stolen old Mrs Poot's knickers off the clothes line the previous year and hung them from the lightning conductor on top of Paradine Hill Methodist Chapel.

'Yer can get locked up fer nickin' steamrollers,' pointed out another wary gang member.

'I'm not nickin' it – I'm only movin' it,' explained Brian.

Annie thought the idea was silly, but she took Brian's side against the others. He could be a bit daft, but she liked him best.

'Yer could park it outside t' Bughutch,' she suggested. 'Yer know, that big side door where they all come out. They'd not be able ter gerrout then.'

The Bughutch was the Western Cinema on Florence Street. The roller was parked only a few yards down the street from the exit door. The boys laughed at the idea. It had great appeal. Annie was always coming up with good ideas, which was why they allowed her into their gang.

'Well, it's better than hangin' knickers out,' said Brian. 'Anyone can hang knickers out.'

Annie agreed. She'd felt sorry for Mrs Poot. Knickers were personal items and it was rotten of people to snigger at her for something that wasn't her fault. They strolled on and passed a row of houses with empty milk bottles on the steps awaiting collection by the Craven Dairies.

'Hey!' said Colin, who had little faith in Annie's over-ambitious plan. 'Why don't we pee in them milk bottles?'

Annie wrinkled her nose in disgust. 'I'm not peeing in milk bottles.'

'Yer couldn't anyroad – 'cos yer 'aven't gorra willy.'

'Don't be so rude, Colin Wigglesworth.' Annie looked at Brian. 'How're yer gonna start it up?'

'Easy,' he said, mysteriously, happy to have a supporter.

'He reckons his uncle showed him,' said Colin, scornfully.

'He did an' all,' insisted Brian. 'He took me ter work once an' showed me 'ow ter do it – 's easy.'

The gang arrived beside the unguarded machine and looked up at it in awe.

'It's a bloomin' big steamroller,' observed Colin. Grunts of agreement came from the others, including Annie.

'It's not actually a steamroller,' said Brian. 'It runs on diesel. Steamrollers are a lot bigger 'n this.'

More grunts; this was plenty big enough for a gang of ten and eleven year olds. Colin folded his arms and looked at Brian.

'Go on then,' he challenged. 'Start it up.'

Brian hesitated. He was wishing he hadn't mentioned it now. But Colin wouldn't let go.

'What're yer waitin' for? Christmas?'

They all sniggered apart from Annie. Brian didn't want to lose face. He walked slowly round the machine before stopping beside a metal box located at the back. Inside was a starting handle. He took it out and strode around once again before inserting it into a round hole in the engine cover.

'It starts t' donkey engine,' he explained knowledgeably. 'Then that fires up t' main engine.'

Everyone was impressed apart from Colin. 'Go on then,' he goaded.

The rest of the gang joined in and Annie felt sorry for Brian. She knew he wouldn't be able to start it up; he was always full of bravado but not much action.

'I'm goin' ter,' he muttered. 'Don't worry.'

His face contorted as he heaved at the handle, trying to turn it without success. This was his way out.

'It won't turn.' He injected a note of disappointment into his voice.

'Yer mean, yer daren't do it!'

'It won't turn,' insisted Brian. 'You 'ave a go if yer don't believe me.'

Colin folded his arms. 'Nay, it were your idea. You said yer could do it. Don't go askin' me.'

'I'll help you,' volunteered Annie. 'Colin's prob'ly not strong enough.' She stepped forward and faced Brian, placing her tiny hands between his.

Colin felt slightly emasculated at Annie's barb. The others grinned at her getting one over on him. She stood facing Brian and gritted her teeth, pulling with all her strength as he pushed. The handle moved, slowly at first, than faster and faster until their hands jumped off it and the handle fell out. There was a high-pitched whining noise under the roller's bonnet then the main engine rumbled into life, vibrating the road beneath their feet and causing some of them to step back warily. Brian looked triumphantly at his handiwork, his apprehension suddenly forgotten as he climbed through the sliding window into the cab.

'Come on,' he said, as he clambered inside. 'Anyone for the *Skylark*?'

A door opened across the street and a substantial woman stood in menacing silhouette against the light from the room behind her.

'Clear off, yer little bleeders!' she called out. 'Afore I tek the back o' me hand ter yer!'

Colin and the other gang members took to their heels. Brian squatted down in the cab and Annie hid behind the rumbling machine. The woman seemed satisfied that she'd scared the gang off and closed the door. Brian looked out through the cab window. He'd come this far and was determined to show Colin up now.

'Come on, Annie – I'm gonna gerrit movin'.'

Annie hesitated. This was by far the most daring thing she'd ever been involved in but Brian's wide grin erased her fears and she was climbing in beside him as he spun the wheel that released the brake. The roller jerked forward, he grabbed the steering handle and tried to guide it in a straight line. They were all over the road.

'I thought yer said yer could drive it!' she complained.

'Nay, give us a chance,' he protested. 'I've got ter get used to it first.'

'Yer'd better get used to it quick, we're nearly there.'

Brian spun the handle and turned the front roller towards the large double doors of the cinema exit. Then he twirled the brake wheel, but there was no response.

'Oh, 'eck! I can't stop it!'

'Switch t' engine off!' advised Annie with some urgency.

'I don't know how ter!' There was panic in his voice.

Brian was still gamely trying to stop the machine when the front roller battered down the cinema doors and they entered the auditorium. People screamed in horror and clambered backwards over the seats behind as the rumbling behemoth demolished the two front rows. The steering handle turned of its own accord and sent them into the screen just as Johnny Weismuller's Tarzan was stabbing to death a fierce rubber crocodile. Brian was frozen with fear as the roller slowed then stopped against the back wall. Sparks were flying, there was dust and mayhem all around and the screen was draped around the machine as Annie clambered out of the side window.

'Come on, Brian, yer barmy beggar!' she urged her shocked friend.

Within seconds they were both out, clambering around the back of the wrecked screen and scurrying to join the panicking patrons. Both of their faces were white with shock.

'Are you okay, kids?' asked an usherette who was trying to maintain some semblance of order.

'Yes, thanks,' said Annie.

'Are you with anybody?'

'No, we came on us own.'

The film was a U-certificate so this was plausible, but Annie wasn't sure. She dropped her eyes to hide the guilt written all over her face. People all around them were asking for refunds so the two of them took the opportunity to slink off. Later, Brian suggested joining the queue to get their money back, but a furious Annie dragged him out of the building. Colin Wigglesworth and the gang were waiting for them at the end of Florence Street as a police car and a fire engine raced past.

'I said yer were bloomin' barmy,' said Colin smugly. 'Yer'll get into right bother fer this.'

'No, we won't,' said Annie. 'Nobody knows it were us. And yer'd better not say nowt ter no one or we're *all* in bother.'

'We weren't goin' ter say nowt anyroad,' protested Colin. 'Were we, lads?'

The gang nodded. They were green with envy over the kudos Annie and Brian would earn if word of this got around. The following day's *Yorkshire Evening Post* told of a gang of youths who had been frightened off by a householder, but not before they'd started up the roller and sent it on its way.

'Tell yer what, Col,' said Annie as the gang trooped homewards.

'What?' said Colin.

'It were better than peein' in milk bottles.'

Poverty was a great leveller in the 1940s and the line between honesty and theft depended on your point of view. Brian Gibbons drew the line a bit further down the page than most. To him, Bretheridge's jam factory was just asking for it. His reputation as a local brigand had burgeoned after the steamroller incident and he felt it incumbent upon him to maintain that reputation. Annie went along with them that day, but Movita chickened out. She was all right was Movita, but she did tend to chicken out. The two of them were out walking when they chanced upon Brian and Norman in Lowtoft Avenue. Norman still looked pale after his recent illness.

'I thought you'd got Scarlet Fever?' said Annie.

'I did – nearly died three times,' he boasted.

She wrinkled her nose in disbelief.

'I did – you ask me mam,' insisted Norman.

'Wotcher doin'?' asked Annie.

A secretive gleam lit Brian's eye. It was Sunday morning and there was never much doing on a Sunday. Norman Newton nudged him. 'Don't tell her, she'll only blab.'

Annie gave Norman a push that had him staggering backwards. 'Who says I'll blab?' she snorted. 'I've never blabbed on no one.' She turned to Movita. 'Have I?'

'No, she's never,' confirmed her friend who would much rather have had Annie to herself that morning than share her with these two rough lads.

Annie quite liked Brian. Not as a boyfriend – he was a bit too plain and common to be her first boyfriend. But he was a good pal who wouldn't let you down.

'We're off ter t' jam factory on Compton Street,' revealed Brian, who had an undisclosed affection for Annie.

'It's shut today,' said Movita. 'Come on, Annie.'

Brian tapped the side of his nose and smirked, mysteriously. 'All the better.'

Annie's curiosity prevented her from following her friend. Movita stopped in her tracks, annoyed.

'Why is it better?' asked Annie.

'Come wi' us and we'll show yer.'

It was a choice between Movita and a Sunday-morning adventure. To Annie there was no contest. She looked at her friend and asked, 'Fancy goin' with 'em?' She already knew the answer.

'They'll only get us into bother,' prophesied Movita.

'We'll be makin' some money,' tempted Brian. 'Lots o' lovely dosh.'

'Come on,' Annie urged her friend.

'No – I've got to go home.'

'Okay,' said Annie who considered she'd done her duty by Movita in inviting her along. 'See yer later then.'

Movita stalked off in a huff and Annie joined the two boys as they headed for the jam factory. Each of them carried a shopping bag. From inside his bag, Brian took a small canvas sack.

'Here, you can use this.'

'What for?'

'It's yer swag bag,' he laughed. 'We're off ter nick some jam jars from Bretheridge's yard.'

Annie looked puzzled. 'What d'yer want jam jars . . .?' Then the penny dropped and a wide grin came over her face. 'Yer crafty monkeys!'

'We'll take 'em back tomorrer,' explained Norman with a grin. 'Ha' penny a jar for empties. We've done it loads o' times.'

'What if somebody catches you in the yard?' enquired Annie, impressed at the simple audacity of the plan.

'We'll get told off fer trespassin',' said Brian.

'We've been told off afore,' grinned Norman.

Annie laughed out loud, infecting the others, and the

three of them set off at a happy gallop towards the scene of the crime.

Compton Street was deserted as usual, with the exception of a ragman's horse that had strayed from a piece of waste ground where it had been tethered for the night and was chewing the grass growing between the cracks in the pavement. The ragman in question had got so drunk the night before that he'd forgotten where he'd tethered his transport. The three children spent some time yanking up grass and feeding it to the horse before Annie, with a leg-up from Brian, climbed on the sad-looking animal's back. It felt warm and velvety beneath her. She leaned forward and stroked its neck.

'Dig yer heels in,' urged Brian. 'That's how yer make it gallop.'

'I don't want ter make it gallop,' said Annie. 'I'm all right as I am.'

The horse moved around with its head close to the ground as it grazed for the sparse fodder. Norman grew impatient and gave it a slap on the rump. The horse lifted its head and shook its neck, blowing a loud raspberry through its nostrils, causing the two boys to laugh loudly.

'Leave it alone,' protested Annie, who was nervous now. She'd never been on a horse before. Not even a seaside donkey. It was as though the horse suddenly became aware of the thing on its back. It kicked its hind legs backwards and set off at a gallop along the cobbled street, with Annie clinging desperately to its mane, bouncing high in the air with every step and landing painfully on the horse's broad back. The boys screamed with laughter and Annie with fright. She let go and fell to the ground, rolling over and over before coming to a halt against the kerb. Brian arrived and looked down at her, concerned.

'Are yer okay?' he asked.

She sat up and assessed the damage. Her dress was torn, which wouldn't please her mam, and her knee was grazed. ''Course I'm not okay,' she grumbled. Norman Newton arrived, his grin still intact. Annie got painfully to her feet and kicked him on his shin.

'Ow! What were that for?'

'For slapping the horse on its bum!' snapped Annie. 'That's what frightened it.'

'There were no need ter kick me,' he complained, hopping on one leg. 'They ought ter sign yer up fer Leeds United wi' a kick like that.'

Brian laughed and led the way to the yard. The horse was nowhere in sight. Bretheridge's stored all the returned jam jars in crates which were stacked in the yard. They didn't feel it necessary to employ a security man because who besides themselves would want empty jam jars? A philosophy which Brian and Norman entirely agreed with. In the two boys' opinion, Bretheridge's might just as well have left the yard gates open. The surrounding wall was only ten feet high, which was nothing to climbers of their calibre. They'd been stealing jam jars for weeks, just a few at a time so as not to raise suspicion, then taking them back the following day. It was easy money and well worth the risk. Brian and Norman scaled the wall in seconds and were soon sliding back the bolt on the gate to let Annie inside. But leaving the gate wide open was a mistake, as was Brian's next act of bravado as he tried to impress Annie.

One particular pile of crates was stacked against the wall and almost as high.

'Bet yer can't climb up them crates,' challenged Norman.

Brian studied the pile with a practised eye. Annie looked up from her jar collecting. ''Course he can't. It'd topple over.'

'Bet yer a tanner I can,' said Brian, winking at Annie. Had she not been there to impress, he probably wouldn't have bothered.

'Yer on,' said Norman.

They both watched as Brian gingerly climbed the fifteen crates stacked on top of each other. Annie had one eye on the gate, ready to run for it if they were caught. The other two could make their own arrangements. If they were nabbed it was their own fault, acting daft like this.

Brian triumphantly reached the top and began to beat his chest.

'Come down, yer silly sod!' shouted Annie. But Brian couldn't resist giving his Tarzan the Apeman call.

The ragman's horse, which had returned to the street, pricked up its ears at Brian's call and broke into a trot which had turned into a gallop by the time it swerved into Bretheridge's yard.

Brian was still gloating to Norman and singing 'I'm the King of the Castle' when the horse hit the pile of crates. Brian's singing wavered as his jam-jar tower toppled and him with it. He disappeared beneath it all with a great crashing and tinkling of broken glass. Annie and Norman stood rigid with horror. There was no sign of their friend. Annie cut her hands on the broken jars as she tried to get to him.

'Go get somebody!' she yelled to Norman.

The boy set off at high speed, not knowing exactly which somebody he was supposed to get. Annie could see Brian now. There was a lot of blood about. A second pile of crates looked set to topple, having been disturbed in the crash. She grabbed her pal's arm and pulled him clear, using every ounce of strength in her skinny body. The second pile came crashing down, just missing them both as a breathless Norman arrived back with a young woman.

'I'll get an ambulance,' she said, after surveying the scene for a second.

Annie knelt down over Brian. Blood was pumping from a gash in his leg. 'We need to stop this bleeding Norman,' she said, urgently. 'Gimme yer shirt!' He took it off and handed it to Annie who ripped it up and spun it into a long length of material which she wrapped around Brian's leg.

'Find us a stick!' she yelled.

Norman went frantically scrabbling round, wishing

Annie could be more precise with her instructions, then returned with a short piece of wood which seemed to meet with her approval because she took it off him and wound the tourniquet tight. The young woman returned but kept her distance as Annie stemmed the flow of blood from Brian's leg.

'I've phoned for an ambulance,' the woman said nervously. 'Is . . . is he all right?'

'I don't know, missis,' replied Annie. 'He's bleeding a lot and I think he's knocked out.'

'Perhaps that's as well,' she said, inadequately.

The police arrived first in the form of a hefty constable who rode into the yard at breakneck speed on a large black police bicycle which narrowly missed Annie before crashing to a halt in the pile of smashed crates. The fallen policeman got to his feet and hopped around the yard on one leg, cursing violently and clutching his other knee, from which protruded half a jam jar.

Shortly afterwards the clanging ambulance screeched to a halt and two ambulancemen rushed in and laid a stretcher beside the constable, trying in vain to persuade him to stop hopping about and get on. It was only the young woman's persistence that diverted their attention to Annie and Brian, and their eyes lit up at having a proper patient to deal with, not some clumsy copper whom they now completely ignored.

'Will he be all right, mister?' asked Annie, who was having her hand bandaged by one of the ambulancemen. The vehicle in which they were travelling was now racing towards St James' Hospital with its bell clanging and light flashing.

'Don't know yet, love, but if he is, it's thanks to you. Where did you learn to make a tourniquet?'

'It showed yer how ter make one in last week's *Schoolfriend*. Didn't say nowt about having ter rip yer shirt up, though.'

'I notice it wasn't your shirt you ripped up?'

'No, it were Norman Newton's. His mam'll play hell with him.' Annie grinned.

Brian opened his eyes and looked up at her. 'What's happening?' he moaned.

'Yer in an ambulance. Yer fell off them crates, yer barmy sod.'

Brian grinned. 'Great!' he whispered. 'Norman owes me a tanner. Hey, I've never been in an ambulance before . . .' Then his cheeky eyes went still. One of the ambulancemen frantically ripped his shirt open and banged at the boy's frail chest. A trickle of blood ran out of Brian's mouth and Annie knew her pal hadn't made it. She stared down in deep shock as Brian looked back at her through lifeless brown eyes. The ambulanceman was sobbing with frustration now and had to be pulled away by his colleague who said, 'It's no use, Mick, the lad's gone,' before gently closing Brian's eyes for the last time.

It was a toss up whether Annie would finish up a hero or a villain after such an event. She was never asked how the three of them had got into the locked yard. It was assumed that, by some oversight, the gate had been left open and she saw no advantage to anyone, especially herself, in clarifying the situation.

Mrs Gibbons had been taken away by a nurse after collapsing at the hospital on hearing the news. Her daughter Maureen and eldest son, Barry, now stood motionless beside their father who had his head buried in Olga's shoulder.

Hospital life went on around them as they mourned the dead boy. Beside Annie sat a young woman smoking an illicit cigarette, her leg encased from toe to hip in plaster, liberally adorned with signatures and the most obscene comments which might well have fascinated Annie were her mind not miles away. Could she have done anything to prevent the accident? She wasn't sure – which didn't stop her from feeling guilty.

'I'm ever so sorry, Mr Gibbons. He were such a nice lad, were your Brian.'

Olga looked at her over Mr Gibbons' heaving shoulder and shook her head slightly as if to tell Annie that words are pretty useless at times like this. A shoulder to cry on and someone to moan at are all anyone can actually provide.

Annie felt even worse when Mr Gibbons broke away from Olga and came over to her.

'They told us what you did, Annie,' he said, between deep breaths, taking her hand. 'How yer pulled him out and tried to stop him from bleedin' – he were a daft little beggar, were our Brian, but by heck, we thought a lot about him!'

'So did I, Mr Gibbons,' said Annie. 'And yer right, he was a daft little beggar, but he were a right laugh, were your Brian!'

Such odd words of consolation made Mr Gibbons smile despite his grief; he leaned over and gave Annie a kiss on her forehead that made her dissolve instantly into floods of tears. He stepped back, concerned. 'I'm sorry, love, I didn't mean to upset yer!'

'It were all my fault, Mr Gibbons,' she sobbed. 'I should've stopped him!'

'Nay, yer couldn't have stopped him, lass.' Mr Gibbons could somehow handle things better being the consoler rather than the consolee, the boot being on the other foot so to speak. 'When our Brian got summat into his head, nowt could stop him. I suppose he were acting the goat, was he?'

Annie shook her head hurriedly in defence of her dead pal. 'Oh, no – he were just standing on the top of a pile of crates, pretending ter be Tarzan.'

'Acting the goat,' concluded Mr Gibbons.

'We shouldn't have been there,' confessed Annie.

'Kids are always where they shouldn't be,' excused Mr Gibbons, 'especially our Brian.' He was determined not to place any blame on Annie, who in his opinion was a heroine.

But Annie didn't agree.

Chapter Four

Like all kids, Annie's primary schooling was geared up to the one big day which would determine the course of the rest of her life: scholarship day.

She had arrived at school early. The green double-decker bus which was to take the pupils of Standard Four to Brookland Park High School to sit their City Scholarship exams was already parked outside the school gates. The driver leaned against the warm bonnet of his bus, smoking a Woodbine and exchanging pleasantries with a group of young mothers who had just dropped off their children prior to going off to a variety of part-time cleaning jobs to make ends meet.

The school itself could have done with a good clean. Like all the buildings in the area it was a victim of industrial grime, solidly built towards the end of the nineteenth century when the government finally accepted responsibility for the elementary education of children.

Around fifteen per cent of the children were expected to pass and go on to continue their education in a grammar school with a view to acquiring the much-vaunted School Certificate. Surprisingly, Brenda Bacup was one of that fifteen per cent; despite her behaviour and demeanour she was a bright pupil. Annie was standing by the bus holding a coiled length of rope. She'd skipped to school with it and was wondering who she could trust to look after it while she went off to sit her scholarship. Brenda Bacup had also arrived early. She had stolen two packets of cigarettes the day before and had kept one for herself. Her older brother had started smoking when he was ten, so why shouldn't she?

Some of the children were already clambering aboard the bus, but Brenda made a detour towards the girls' toilets at the far side of the playground, her fat legs splaying out beneath her grey, patched and pleated skirt. As she sauntered past Annie, she curled her lip.

'Hey, Jackson – me dad's takin' us ter Butlin's at Easter.'

It was a lie. Brenda's father was the last person in the world to take his family on holiday, but that was beside the point. Brenda knew full well what had happened to Annie's dad. When she got no reaction she retraced her steps and looked down at the rope in Annie's hand.

'What yer gonna do wi' that – 'ang yerself? I would if I didn't have a dad ter take us ter Butlin's.'

Grinning at her own joke she went on her way. She fancied a 'sly drag', to quote her brother, to get the day off to a good start.

It had been two and a half years since Annie's last run-in with the class bully, during which time the need for revenge which festered inside her had been unrequited. It might have remained so had Breda kept her big mouth shut that morning. Annie watched her every step and saw her take a packet from her cardigan pocket as she entered the old brick building. Curious, Annie set off in pursuit.

The toilets were deserted, as Brenda had expected them to be at that time on a morning. The odds were that no one would pay a visit before morning playtime so she was all right for a few minutes at least. The bus wasn't due to leave until ten-past nine which gave her a good ten minutes for a smoke. She entered what the older girls would have called 'cell seven', the last cubicle in the line, the only one with a working bolt on the door. Annie followed her into the toilets when she heard the bolt being slammed into place. A definite plan had formed in her mind. She wrinkled her nose slightly as she always did when entering that place. A fug of stale body waste hung in the air, blamed by the girls on the boys, whose toilets were on the other side of the wall. The boys of course blamed it on the girls and many scatological insults were hurled over the wall each playtime.

Tiptoeing to the outside of Brenda's toilet door, she silently looped the skipping rope around the handle and tied both ends around the handle of the adjacent door, pulling the rope tight and making sure the knot was secure.

Ten minutes later, Annie sat gazing intently through the bus window, her eyes fixed on the entrance to the toilet block as the bus driver got into his cab. Miss Leeney had been up to the top deck and called out the register. When it came to 'Bacup', Annie had hidden her head behind the boy in front and shouted, 'Here, miss.' None of the other kids seemed to notice, they were all too full of their own thoughts and worries. The importance of this day had been impressed upon them constantly for the past six months. Annie smiled to herself at the thought of Brenda finding herself locked in the lavvies on scholarship day. She'd be hammering on the door, screaming to be let out, but the toilets were well out of earshot.

Brenda Bacup didn't sit her scholarship that day – or any other day. Mrs Backhouse's incontinence had taken her short just fifteen minutes from morning break and instead of waiting for Mr Glossop to vacate the staff toilet she decided to use the girls'. As she crossed the yard at an urgent lope she heard Brenda's shouts.

Brenda didn't expect a teacher to come into the toilets. Normally, teachers wouldn't be seen dead in the girls' lavvies, so her language became quite ripe when she heard someone outside.

'Can you open this bleedin' door!'

Mrs Backhouse was shocked to hear such language from

such a young voice, but the need to relieve herself was greater than her desire to reprimand whoever was in there. She took up occupation in a cold cubicle a few doors away so her functions wouldn't be heard, a foot wedged against the boltless door, just in case.

'Are yer deaf or summat?' called out Brenda. 'I'm supposed ter be taken me bleedin' scholarship this morning' n' somebody's locked me in.'

Mrs Backhouse clung to her seat with horror. She lived in a cloistered world with her curate husband. This was language of the gutter and completely foreign to her. On the peeling door in front of her was an obscene drawing of a smiling man with a penis as big as his body. Underneath was written the name of Mr Glossop, the headmaster, alongside an arrow pointing upwards to eliminate any doubt as to who the deformity belonged. Mrs Blackhouse's shocked eyes darted around the whitewashed walls. More obscene graffiti and drawings of male genitalia. Meanwhile Brenda was becoming even angrier at the lack of response.

'Is it you out there, Jackson? 'Cos if it is I'll kill yer when I gerrout!'

No answer.

'It is you, isn't it, yer bastard? I'm warnin' yer. Remember t' last time I belted yer? Well, it'll be ten times worse if yer don't lerrus out.'

Mrs Backhouse had heard enough. She finished what she had to do then came out and fumbled with the rope, still not revealing her identity. The language from within grew ever riper.

The ten-year-old girl was angrily puffing at a cigarette when Mrs Backhouse finally opened the door. They stared at one other for a shocked second, the cigarette dropping from Brenda's mouth. The angry teacher took a pace forward, grabbed the girl by the ear and dragged her, screaming, from the toilets.

'Right, young lady. We'll see what Mr Glossop has to say about this.'

As she spoke, the toilet door image of Mr Glossop passed fleetingly across her thoughts, making her tighten her grip on Brenda's ear.

When Annie and the rest of the scholarship group returned to the school late that afternoon, Brenda was sitting outside Mr Glossop's office as a heated discussion took place within.

'Who's owd Glossy talkin' ter?' enquired an inquisitive girl of Brenda.

'Me mam – she's playing 'ell 'cos he won't let me sit me scholarship. Somebody locked me in t' lavvies this mornin'.'

Eventually a hard-faced woman in a hairnet and Fair Isle cardigan emerged from the headmaster's office. She knocked Brenda off her chair with a hard slap to the side of her head. The look in her eyes betrayed no hint of love for her daughter.

'Yer brainless little shit! I don't know why I bleedin' bother wi' yer!'

She stormed off down the corridor as Brenda struggled to her feet, cursing volubly. This provoked a howl of amusement from the pupils now gathered around her. Gradually they all moved off, leaving Annie on her own, facing her old tormentor.

'I told yer I'd get yer back,' she said quietly, so that only Brenda could hear.

Chapter Five

Four years after the death of Olga Jackson's husband, Leonard Spode became her benefactor. He was the owner of Spode Fashions, which he ran from a converted bus garage round the corner in Nightingale Street. He'd come out of the army and set up his business with just £75 demob money plus another hundred left to him by his recently deceased father with whom he hadn't got along. But the old man had had no one else to leave it to and at least Leonard had redeemed himself by serving King and country.

Olga had been a machinist with Hector Ripley's before the war, but they'd closed down. She'd tried various cleaning jobs, worked on the school dinners and in the local Thrift Stores, but she needed somewhere nearby so she could be home in time for Annie's coming back from school. Spode Fashions fitted her requirements ideally; in fact, Leonard Spode had been decent enough to call round and visit her at home to interview her for the job. Annie had been on her best behaviour and had made a good impression on her mother's prospective employer. He'd had a mixed effect on her.

'He wears scent,' she confided to Movita Lunn on the way home from school the day her mother started work. 'He smells like a woman.'

'Mebbe he's a poof,' said Norman Newton. 'Poofs wear scent.'

'Me dad wears some smelly stuff after he's had a shave,' said Movita, who, like Annie, wasn't sure what a poof was but didn't want to show her ignorance. 'He reckons it dun't 'alf sting. Mebbe that's what Spodey had on.'

'Mebbe,' conceded Annie. 'He stands right near yer when he talks to yer – an' he's right tall.'

'I hate it when they do that,' sympathised Movita. 'Mrs Backhouse does that when she's tellin' yer off.'

'I hate Mrs Backhouse,' agreed Annie. 'She smells an' all.'

'She's got rubber knickers,' explained Norman Newton. 'It's 'cos she can't stop peein' hersen.'

'Give over – who told yer that?' said Annie, scornfully. 'Yer come out wi' some right stuff, you do.'

'It's right – our Lizzie told me. She saw her in t' girls' lavvies last week, pullin' 'em up.'

Both Annie and Movita knew of Mrs Backhouse's occasional visits to the girls' toilets and that some of the doors had a tendency to swing open at embarrassing moments. But they also knew about Norman's fanciful imagination.

'Right,' threatened Annie. 'I'll ask your Lizzie – and if yer telling lies, yer for it.'

'Anyroad, me mam reckons Spodey's a poof,' commented Norman, kicking a tin can into the road.

'Does he wear rubber knickers an' all?' laughed Movita.

'I'm just tellin' yer what me mam said,' grumbled Norman. 'Me mam says I 'aven't got ter touch him wi' a ten-foot barge pole.'

'What would yer do with a ten-foot barge pole?' enquired Movita. 'Stick it up his bum?'

'Aw, no, he'd like that,' said Norman. ''Cos he's a poof.'

This went some way to explaining what a poof was, and the three of them were still sniggering when Brenda Bacup ran past, hurling an expletive at them which none of them picked up. She'd been shocked by the consequences of Annie's revenge, but her threats of retribution had been met with a determined, 'I'll ger yer back a lot worse next time!'

As Brenda couldn't imagine anything worse than losing a place at grammar school she decided not to risk finding out what Annie had in mind.

The scullery door was already open when Annie arrived home. Her mother had made a special effort to be there when she got back at quarter-past four. The two-up, two-down terrace house was furnished as well as any in Fogerty Row. Alan Jackson might not have been Clark Gable in the looks department but he'd been a good breadwinner in the short time they'd been married. The back room was where they lived, the front room reserved for best. Two worn moquette easy chairs sat on a square of carpet and faced the now empty hearth of the cast-iron Yorkshire range, above which a mantelpiece supported a large wooden clock, a photo of Annie's dad, a spill vase full of home-made paper fire lighters and a Coronation tea caddy which contained the rent money and ration books. A cheap dining table, four unmatched chairs and a dresser completed the furnishings. In the front room was a three-piece suite and a china cabinet, bought in instalments just before Alan had been called up, which was lucky as a man from the War Office came round and arranged to pay off all outstanding debts for them. His Majesty didn't want his soldiers worrying about how their wives were managing while they were away fighting. Hilda Outhwaite from number seven had a house full of stuff on tick, all paid for when her Walter got called up.

'Well?' inquired Olga.

'Well, what?'

'Well, how did yer get on? Yer got yer scholarship results today, didn't yer?'

'Oh, yeah, I forgot – me an' Movita passed. We're both goin' ter Brookland Park.'

Olga screamed with delight and hugged her daughter. 'Well done, love!' She danced around the room, making Annie laugh.

'Right, we're celebrating,' announced her mother. 'How does poached egg on toast and rice pud sound? Mr Spode gave me a sub on me wages, so can yer nip round ter t' Co-op for a small white loaf?'

'We've still got 'alf a loaf left in t' pantry,' said Annie, who'd been learning home economics the hard way.

'I know, but I thought we'd 'ave some fresh, just ter treat ourselves. Get a quarter o' best butter as well.'

Olga handed Annie a two-shilling piece and squeezed her daughter's hand in hers. 'And I'd thought we'd go to t' pictures tonight for a bit of a treat. *Brief Encounter's* on at the Regal.'

Annie looked up at her mam and smiled. 'That'd be great, Mam.'

'Right, that's settled then,' said Olga. 'And don't forget ter give us Divi number. What is it, so I know yer know?'

'Nine, nine, eight, three, oh.'

'Good lass – an' bring me some change.'

Olga glanced in the mirror over the dresser as her daughter dashed out of the door. The past few years had drained the vivacity out of her. Thirty-three years old and she looked nearer forty. Angling one of the side mirrors she examined her face. Oh, God! Her Vivien Leigh profile was gradually being eroded. In a few years she'd look more like the Wicked Witch of the West. Ten years ago she'd had the pick of the crop. Young men used to fall over themselves to take her out and she'd done her best not to disappoint any of them. It had been great while it lasted, but all good things must come to an end.

The local Co-op was experimenting with a new 'serve yourself' arrangement and Annie found herself behind the bread and confectionery, listening to a conversation on the other side between two unseen women from the next street who were hovering over the milk and dairy products.

'I reckon she started this mornin' – I were told it's a sweat shop, that's why I didn't bother. T' job were mine if I wanted it, but I allus say yer better off at Burton's than these twopence-ha'penny places. Yer know where yer stand wi' Burton's.'

'At least she'll not have ter worry about him chasin' her round t' machines!'

'I don't think that'd have bothered Olga. She's had ter go without for a long time now. It's only human nature, innit?'

'I don't think it's Spodey's nature.'

'Why? D'yer think he's a bit – yer know?'

Although Annie couldn't see, she knew the 'yer know' would have been accompanied by a meaningful nod. For some reason these two words always were.

The second woman laughed. 'Well, a man of his age not married – I mean ter say, it's a bit funny.'

'Happen he's just got more sense. I wish *I'd* had more sense.'

'Aye, me an' all.'

The conversation had largely passed over Annie's head, although she knew they were talking about her mother.

Olga had switched on the wireless, hoping to catch a bit of music to accompany their meal. A recording of a speech Churchill had just made in America came booming across the room.

'*From Stettin in the Baltic to Trieste in the Adriatic, an Iron Curtain has descended over the Continent* . . .'

'Now that reminds me,' she said, pouring out the tea. 'These curtains could do wi' a wash. I don't want 'em to end up like Hilda Outhwaite's. She hasn't washed hers since the Relief of Mafeking.'

Annie glanced momentarily at the offending curtains as she stirred a lump of strawberry jam into her rice pudding.

'Mrs Rossington were in t' Co-op, talking ter another woman. She reckoned it's a bit funny Mr Spode not bein' married at his age.'

Her mother coloured slightly, having a fair idea what Mrs Rossington had meant. Annie remembered the conversation with Norman.

'Norman Newton says his mam says Mr Spode's a poof.'

She waited to see if this might elicit a more detailed definition of the word. She figured there was more to it than a man who liked having barge poles thrust up his bum. Her mother's reaction showed no prospect of enlightenment, so she continued, 'He says she wouldn't touch him wi' a ten-foot barge pole.'

'Irma Newton needs ter mind what she says,' retorted her mother, sharply. 'Mr Spode'll be putting food on our table, which is more than her Larry does. He's been demobbed over three years now and he hasn't even looked for a job.'

'Norman reckons he's got shell shock.'

'Shell shock?' snapped Olga. 'Yer dad got shell shock – he were shocked so much it damn' well killed him. Larry Newton should be thankful he came home in one piece.'

She was in tears. Tears of anger and frustration – and even tears of sorrow at the memory of her Alan who, if nothing else, had been good to her and had loved her. She dabbed her eyes with her pinny. Annie was mortified to have upset her mother for no reason. She got up and went round the table.

'Sorry, Mam,' she said, contritely. 'Were it my fault, for talkin' daft again?'

'I don't know, love. We've all ter do us best. There's plenty besides me who's lost their husbands.' She gave Annie a bright smile. 'Finish yer pudding, I'll be all right. I'm not lettin' nowt spoil things for us. You passin' yer scholarship's t' best thing that's happened in a long time.'

Annie made a mental note to tell Norman Newton that his dad should be grateful for coming home in one piece and not to moan about shell shock. She missed her dad, but didn't say much about it. Her mam had enough to put up with.

Chapter Six

Leonard Spode's face grinned down at Annie from the poster beside Lester Street chip shop. 'Vote Spode X' – a simple message designed not to confuse the unsophisticated voter. His image now sported the inevitable daubed on Hitler moustache and fringe, but he was still the only candidate with a photo on their poster. Annie was vaguely impressed, she'd never known anyone who had their face on a poster and now she was about to meet Mr Spode – if he was there, that was. She hadn't actually seen him since he'd been round to their house just before her mam went to work for him, two years ago.

Spode Fashions had moved premises, out of the converted bus garage and into the ground floor of Haley's Mill – seven thousand square feet of humming machines. Olga had been made up to charge hand and was now earning good money. Spode was an appreciative employer and turned out a good product. Business was booming and his entry into local politics seemed a logical next step.

Annie entered her mother's place of employment and knocked on a frosted glass, sliding window. A blurred image on the other side pushed it open, revealing a middle-aged, efficient-looking woman whose manner was less formal than it might have been with a potential client, which Annie, patently wasn't.

'Can I help you, dear?'

'I've got a message for my mother, Mrs Jackson – Olga.'

The woman's face brightened. 'You must be Annie. Wait there a tick, I'll get her.'

Just then the man from the poster, albeit minus the Hitler moustache and fringe, came into the office beyond the small window and did a double take of her.

'Is everything all right, Mrs Greenhalgh? he asked, politely.

'The young lady's come to see Olga.'

An enquiring frown knitted his brows. 'Don't tell me – you're Olga's daughter?'

Annie nodded, slightly flattered to be recognised by such a famous man.

'Good Lord – it doesn't seem two minutes since you were just a tiny tot. How old are you now?'

'Thirteen.'

She was too young to recognise the odd look in his eyes. The last two years had seen Annie transformed from a gawky child into a confident teenager. Brookland Park's teachers were fanatically keen on proper pronunciation and Annie's flat Yorkshire vowels were being gradually rounded. A door opened beside her, releasing the sound of whirring machines and radio music to which a few women were singing along. Olga stood there, anxious.

'What is it, love?'

'Movita's invited me for tea, I wondered if it was all right?'

'Good grief, love, yer've come to work just ter tell me that?'

'Well, you weren't at home and I thought . . .'

Olga placed an apologetic hand to her mouth. 'I'm sorry, love, I should have told yer this mornin'. I'm doing an extra hour tonight, we've got a rush job on.'

'Is it okay then – for me to go to Movita's?'

'Just so long as yer back no later than eight.'

'I will. Thanks, Mam.'

Olga gave her daughter a peck on the cheek before

disappearing again into the noisy machine room, closing the door and shutting out the sound. As Annie left, Spode watched her through the small window, then summoned Olga into his office.

'Hey, Annie – yer'll never guess who's asked me out?'

'Who?' enquired Annie. She was still a little out of breath from running to get home in time. It was twenty-past eight but her mother didn't seem too concerned.

'Leonard – Mr Spode. Well, to be honest I think he wants me to help him with his campaign, but he's taking me to a posh restaurant.'

'Why would he want you to help him? You don't even vote for his party.'

Olga shrugged. 'I allus vote for the best-lookin' bloke. It's as good as owt. Make us a cup o' tea, love, while yer on yer feet.'

Annie went into the scullery and called out over her shoulder, 'Good job Bessie Braddock didn't have to rely on you then.'

Her mother laughed. 'Actually, I think he wants me to help because I've got a bit of a gob on me. That's what politics is all about, yer know. Them wi' the biggest gob gets the most votes. Stands ter reason. Yer not gonna vote for somebody what can't stand up for hisself, are yer?'

She shouted the last sentence so that Annie could hear her over the hissing of the tap as she filled the kettle.

'Where's the matches?' called back Annie. 'It's okay, I've got them. Mam – I wish you wouldn't put used matches back in the box. So, what are you going to be doing? Making speeches or kissing babies?'

Olga laughed. 'Don't know yet. I suppose he'll tell me ternight. One thing I know for certain, it's not a romantic date – he's not the romantic type.'

Annie put the kettle on the hob and lit the gas ring. 'So I've heard,' she said, blowing out the match and noisily kicking open the new-fangled pedal bin to dispose of it. 'I've heard he likes his vice versa.'

'Annie Jackson!' scolded her mother, suppressing her amusement. 'Where'd yer get that sort of talk from?'

Her eyes followed Annie as she walked back into the room to await the kettle's boiling. There was an indefinable but delicate beauty about her daughter. Perhaps it wasn't a face destined to adorn a magazine cover – Annie's beauty came from within. Her features were sharp but with a symmetry that pleased the eye. Her skin was fair and unblemished and her eyes wide and deep blue. She wore her fair hair tied back in a pony tail, the fashion of the moment. Now that summer was upon them it would become streaked with blonde from the sun. Very soon, young men's heads would be turning in her direction and Olga would have to be on her toes.

'Leonard's just not very demonstrative in that respect,' she said. 'It doesn't make him a . . .'

Annie raised her eyebrows, questioningly.

'You know what I mean,' said her mother.

Annie and Olga stood beside Leonard Spode as the Returning Officer announced the results. His attempt to disguise his broad Yorkshire accent failed miserably. Spode's count was the last to be announced.

'Leonard Harthur Spode – three thousand, one 'undred and heleven . . .'

The remainder of his announcement was drowned in cheers, none louder than Olga's as her boss's victory was declared. Annie joined in, quite enjoying the reflected glory. At the victory party in the Free Trades Hall later that evening, Spode danced with her, complimenting her on the way she responded to his tuition so effortlessly.

The floor cleared as the Johnnie Dalmour Quartet went off for a ten-minute beer break. Spode led Annie back to her mother, nodding his appreciation to a few applauding sycophants.

'Well, Olga,' he smiled, 'I've taught her the waltz, the foxtrot and the quickstep. She knows as much as me now, only she's already a damn' sight better.'

Annie was flattered by such a compliment, especially as it came from a man of importance.

'Happy Birthday, Annie.'

There was a wide smile on Spode's face as he entered the house, uninvited. Olga thought it was okay for him to walk in and out as he pleased, but Annie wasn't too sure. One hand was behind his back and he leaned forward, thrusting his cheek into Annie's face. He'd taken a sartorial step up since his election and today wore a well-cut, dark blue suit and military-looking tie.

'Give us a birthday kiss, I've got a little present for you.'

She hesitated.

'Go on,' urged her mother. 'It's not like you to be shy.'

Annie pecked him on the side of his cheek, recoiling slightly at the strength of his after-shave.

Like a magician producing an impossible bunch of flowers from thin air, he brought his hand from behind his back and presented her with a leather school satchel. Annie knew it was the best money could buy. Only one other girl in her class had one like it and she was fee-paying, not a scholarship girl like Annie. Her eyes widened.

'Thanks, Mr Spode – it's really lovely.'

'I think you know me well enough to call me Uncle Leonard.' Spode winked at Olga, who smiled her approval. Annie said nothing as she unbuckled the straps to examine her present.

'Look, Mam, it's got a geometry set inside!'

Further investigation produced another shout of, 'It's a Parker fountain pen!'

'With a gold nib,' said Spode, smiling at her excitement.

'Well,' said Olga. 'I think that deserves another kiss.'

'Now then, Olga,' he said. 'You don't want to be embarrassing the birthday girl. Oh, by the way, I've got tickets for the Empire on Friday to see Guy Mitchell. I know he's a certain person's favourite.'

The smile on Annie's face widened at this. A picture of the young American singing star hung on her bedroom wall. She stood up and ran to the door.

'Where yer goin'?' enquired her mother.

'I'm off to tell Movita. She'll be ever so jealous, she loves Guy Mitchell!'

Spode and Olga laughed as Annie ran out of the house.

'That seems to have brightened her day up,' he observed. 'How about me brightening yours? I thought we might get our glad-rags on and have a night out.'

'What – tonight? I'd need to arrange a baby-sitter and everything.'

'Baby-sitter? She doesn't look much like a baby to me. Anyway I'll have you back at a respectable hour.'

'Well, that doesn't sound much fun.'

'You can always invite me up to see your etchings when I bring you home.'

Olga slapped him playfully. 'Mr Spode, you naughty man!'

Fumes of Friar's Balsam diluted in a bowl of hot water were assailing Olga's nose when a knock came at the door. She called out to Annie from beneath the towel shrouding her head and the bowl: 'That'll be Leonard – can you go, love?'

Annie answered it and looked up at Spode in disappointment. He wore a different suit, dark grey with a stripe, and new-looking. A man with two best suits; she was impressed.

'My mam's got a bad cold,' she said, unhappy with his gaudy tie. Poor taste for a councillor.

'He dose that,' shouted her mother, releasing the fumes into the room as she pulled the towel off her head.

'I know tha—' began Spode, then smiled as he heard Olga saying the same thing. Annie saw it as more of a smirk than a smile. He shouted through the doorway past her, 'I got your message, Olga. I just thought I'd pop round to see how you are.'

'Come in, Leonard,' she shouted. 'But don't come anywhere near be unless yer want this cold.'

'I was looking forward to the theatre,' he called out from the doorway. 'I won't come right in. There's no point in both of us suffering – Guy Mitchell will just have to wait for another day.'

'Our Annie were right lookin' forward to it.'

'Pity, that,' sympathised Spode. Then, as if the thought had just struck him, he said, 'Tell you what – why don't I take Annie? To be honest, I quite fancy seeing him myself.'

'That's ever so good of yer, isn't it, our Annie?'

Annie had mixed feelings about her and Spode going without her mother, but the lure of Guy Mitchell overcame any misgivings. 'Yes,' she said. 'That'd be smashing.'

Spode looked at his watch. 'Right then, that's settled. It starts in half an hour but I've got my car outside, so we're okay for time.'

'I'll go and get my coat,' said Annie, with mounting enthusiasm. 'I'll not be a minute.' She ran upstairs, hoping his expensive suit wouldn't show up her Leeds Market coat.

Throughout the evening Spode was a model of good manners and generosity as Annie sat excitedly through the show. She'd never been to the Empire before. From their seats in the front stalls she laughed at the comic in his loud-checked suit making disparaging comments about the tall, gormless-looking stooge standing beside him. A conjuror had her gasping with disbelief as he produced an owl from under a handkerchief. She felt sorry for the bird which sat on a perch looking miserable throughout the rest of the act. Then the lights dimmed and an unseen voice set her heart racing with excitement. She'd never seen a real live star before.

'Ladies and gentlemen – would you please give a great

big Yorkshire welcome to . . .' the audience went quiet in anticipation '. . . MR GUY MITCHELL!'

The band, augmented by the two bassoon players who always travelled with Mitchell, started up as the star bounced jauntily on wearing a white suit and red waistcoat. Within seconds he had the audience singing along, no one louder than Annie. Spode smiled down at her, concealing his embarrassment masterfully and pulling a half-pound packet of liquorice allsorts from his pocket. If the sweets were meant to keep her quiet they failed miserably. She knew every one of Guy's songs, much to the amusement of the star himself who came down the steps and into the auditorium, trailing the mike lead behind him.

'The other half of my double act seems to be sittin' right here in the audience, folks,' he laughed, to great applause. 'What say we bring her up on stage?'

The applause grew louder as he leaned over and took Annie's hand. Her heart pounded as he led her up the steps on to the brightly lit stage.

'What's yer name, darlin'?'

'Annie.'

'And is that yer daddy down there, Annie? The guy that's glowing with pride – or is it embarrassment?'

The audience laughed at this. Annie shielded her eyes against the lights until she could see Spode smiling broadly back up at her.

'No, that's Mr Spode, he's my mother's boss. She's got a cold.'

Spode's grin widened, happy that she'd mentioned his name.

'And does Mr Spode have a first name or ain't you on first-name terms, with him bein' yer mom's boss an' all?'

More laughter from the audience. Annie thought she was in heaven, on stage with the man of her dreams.

'He's a councillor,' she said, hoping this might impress Guy. 'Councillor Leonard Spode.'

A mixture of friendly boos and hisses came from the

audience. Spode stood up, grinning and shaking his fist at them, provoking louder boos. But he was happy with the publicity this would bring him. Any association with show-business was always a vote catcher. Guy Mitchell returned his attention to Annie.

'What's yer favourite song, darlin'?'

Annie didn't hesitate. '"She Was The Roving Kind".'

The band struck up even as she was speaking. The singer bent down beside her and shared the microphone, duetting with her and grinning his appreciation as she played her part. What she lacked in musical talent, she more than made up for in enthusiasm. The duet finished to rapturous applause and the star escorted her to her seat. He walked back up the stage steps genuinely captivated by the young girl he'd met so briefly.

'I won't come in,' said Spode as the car pulled up outside Annie's house. 'Don't want to risk catching a cold from your mother.'

'Thanks for taking me, Mr Spode,' she said politely. 'It was the best time ever.'

She leaned up and kissed him on his cheek. He smiled and squeezed her bare knee, his hand moving fractionally upwards before he removed it. 'My pleasure, love. There'll be plenty more trips like this when your mam gets better.'

Annie got out and walked through the yard to her door, then felt an uncomfortable sensation. She turned and saw him staring at her with an odd expression on his face. It turned to a smile as soon as he saw her looking back at him. He waved then pressed the starter, easing the black Humber out of the street.

'That you, Annie?' called out her mother from upstairs.

'Yes.'

'How d'yer go on with him?'

There was a note of self-interest in Olga's voice which her daughter didn't pick up on. Annie went into her mother's room and sat beside the bed, eyes still glowing with the excitement of the evening.

'It was brilliant, Mam. The best night I've ever had. Guy Mitchell got me up on stage to sing . . .'

She related every detail to a smiling Olga, who was keen for her daughter to really get to like Spode, for whom she had long-term plans. Both facially and financially he was a vast improvement on Alan – although she did miss her husband's gentle manner. She smiled to herself. Can't have everything; she'd have to settle for looks and money. Two out of three wasn't bad.

The following February the King died, plunging the nation into a mourning tempered by the knowledge that the country now had a bright young Queen to reign over them. Norman Newton wasn't impressed.

'What's wimmin know about rulin' a country?' he muttered to Annie as they made their way to the Clock cinema to see *The Man From Planet X*. It wasn't Annie's choice but Norman was paying, so he figured it was only fair that he should choose.

'What's wrong with women ruling the country?' she enquired.

'She'll not last two minutes, that's what. She'll allus be washin' her hair when she should be out rulin' an' stuff.'

'It'd do *you* no harm to wash your hair now and again,' countered Annie, who had no strong feelings either way about the royal family.

'Supposin' we had ter go ter war – what good would she be then?' he challenged. 'Standin' there wi' her head under t' tap?'

'About as much good as King George, I imagine,' said Annie. 'He didn't do any fighting. That were left up to men like my dad.'

'And mine.'

'Has your dad still got shell shock?' enquired Annie. Norman grinned.

'Me mam says he's got job shock now. He's workin'

down at West Hunslet Foundry. Reckons he were safer in Germany.'

Annie looked at her friend and wondered what love was like. It was supposed to hit you in the eye, turn you to jelly and all that stuff. Norman Newton didn't do any of that to her, he'd never be any more than a pal. He'd try and kiss her in the pictures and she'd go along with it more out of curiosity than anything else. It was a skill she needed to acquire for when the right person came along.

The next few months saw Olga's ambitions come to fruition. Spode now took her out on a regular basis, their trips interspersed with family outings when Annie accompanied them.

'He's all right but he's always touching me,' she said to Movita as they studied for their end-of-term exams in Movita's house.

'Touchin' you – how d'you mean?'

'Oh, don't get me wrong, he means no harm,' said Annie. 'He probably doesn't even know he's doing it. Some people are like that. When I'm sittin' next to him in the car he keeps squeezing my leg when he's talking to me.'

'Squeezing? Does it hurt?'

'No – nothing like that. I just think it's a bit embarrassing, that's all. Trouble is, if I said anything he'd be mortified.'

'Men are so stupid,' said Movita.

'That Norman Newton wants ter keep his trap shut an' all,' grumbled Annie. 'He reckons his mam saw my mam drunk in the Ashley Arms.'

Movita made no comment. She's heard the same from her own mother.

'Norman says his mam says she saw you in the Ashley Arms last Saturday with Mr Spode – and you were drunk.' Annie only mentioned this in order that her mother would confirm her belief that Norman Newton's mother was lying.

'Irma Newton hasn't got no room ter talk,' retorted Olga, angrily. 'Next time yer see their Norman, ask him to ask his mam about that Pole I saw her knockin' around wi' when her Larry were off fightin' fer King and country.'

Annie made a mental note of this; she was getting a bit sick of Norman's constant remarks about her mother and wouldn't mind having something to throw back at him. She'd have felt more reassured had her mother flatly denied the accusation, though.

Olga studied Leonard as he brought the drinks to the table. He wasn't a bad-looking bloke – tall, dark and now with a pencil moustache which he hoped gave him a look of Errol Flynn, only this was wishful thinking. But as a lover he was less than enthusiastic. Maybe it was her. Maybe she hadn't got it anymore – it certainly wasn't through lack of trying. Still, he was kind and attentive and generous – especially when it came to plying her with drink. Irma Newton had been right – she'd been absolutely plastered that night in the Ashley Arms.

'Just this one, then I'm on to fruit juice,' said Olga. 'I'm beginning ter get a reputation as an old soak.'

'Nonsense,' protested Spode. 'You just know how to enjoy yourself, that's all. Don't let the killjoys spoil your fun.'

'If you say so, Councillor,' laughed Olga, gulping down the double gin and holding out her empty glass. He joined in her laughter.

'Blimey!' he said. 'I should learn to keep my mouth shut. You'll have me in the poorhouse at this rate.'

And all the time he laughed and joked he studied her in the way a spider would look at a fly as he wove his web, only Olga wasn't the fly he really wanted to trap.

It was the luck of the draw that found Leonard Spode sitting on the Leeds Education Committee, and being in the right place at the right time that saw him elected chairman within his first year of office. Few successful businessmen found time to sit on the council. This made Spode a much sought-after individual, a man who made things happen without the artificial power of a union or the civil service behind him. A self-made man.

It was within the remit of the council to grant a licence to a retailer to sell school uniforms for the various secondary and grammar schools in the area. The council didn't profit much from this as the idea was to ensure the children got their uniforms at a reasonable price. Certain children of low-income parents were given generous but discreet discounts to ensure they were dressed as well as the more fortunate pupils. Uniforms were the great class leveller within schools.

Towards the end of his first meeting as chairman he dropped his bombshell.

'I had a disturbing anonymous telephone call to my house last night,' he announced, gravely. 'The caller was accusing this very committee of corruption. I was told this corruption goes back several years, back to well before I joined the council. But this doesn't absolve me from any blame if it's still going on.'

'Well, I for one have no idea what this person was talking about,' protested George Robertshaw, the vice chairman. 'What sort of corruption?'

'Accepting bribes in exchange for the granting of a licence for the sale of school uniforms.'

The gasp from the committee members sitting around the long, polished oak table was audible.

'Impossible,' snapped a lady councillor. 'Such matters are discussed and voted upon. We'd all have to be corrupt in that case. Illingworth's have had the sole retail licence for over twenty years, they're above that sort of thing.'

'And do Illingworth's have any competition?' asked Spode.

'Now and again someone else puts in a bid. The licence only comes up for renewal every three years.'

'But Illingworth's bid is always the highest?'

'Well, the highest bid isn't the be all and end all. Illingworth's are good, well-established and reliable. That counts for a lot.'

'So Illingworth's have been outbid and still been granted the licence?'

'Well, yes, but . . .'

'And what about the manufacturers?'

'It's up to Illingworth's who they buy the uniforms from. They place their own orders in accordance with the specifications they get from us.'

'So they've pretty much got it all sewn up – if you'll pardon the pun?'

'Mr Spode, to say there's been corruption is simply preposterous . . .'

'I am aware of that, madam,' he said, loftily. 'But I'm also aware that mud sticks.' His stern expression softened. 'Look, ladies and gentlemen. As you all know, I'm in the same business myself and these rumours have been flying round the trade for some time now. Personally I don't believe a word of it. You've been giving Illingworth's the licence purely out of convenience – and why not? They're good at what they do, so why change a good thing?'

The rain sighing beyond the tall windows of the Council Chambers did nothing to lift the dampened spirits of the chastened councillors. Nods and murmurs of agreement passed around the table. Leonard Spode sat back and lit a cigarette as, one by one, heads tilted his way expectantly. His voice hardened.

'But we do need a change now and then to keep people on their toes and to show the voters that we're not complacent about such matters.' He looked slowly around at the worried faces. 'We should nip these rumours in the bud before they get out of hand. The licence is up for renewal in a month's time. I suggest we seek an alternative supplier.'

The nodding and murmuring became more emphatic this

time. Resigned to the inevitable change, they didn't care who got the damn' licence so long as their own positions remained secure. Spode suppressed a smile. The anonymous phone call was completely fictitious, but it had served its purpose.

'I propose we advertise in the newspapers for tenders from interested parties as soon as possible. That should forestall any trouble-raking editor who's thinking of putting these rumours into print. All in favour?'

The show of hands was unanimous.

The following day Spode became a sleeping partner in Rawnsley's Outfitters. The directors and shareholders remained old Herbert Rawnsley and his son Michael, who was gradually taking over the reins from his father and finding it a struggle. Spode, in exchange for an interest-free loan to them of ten thousand pounds, became entitled to a third of the nett profits plus a generous salary for his role of consultant and business adviser.

The other two were more than happy to have him as a partner, in view of his promise to assure Rawnsley's of the licence to sell school uniforms. A licence which was granted to them five weeks later.

The move took Illingworth's by surprise and left them with three thousand pounds worth of unsaleable stock on their hands, plus orders to their suppliers for another two thousand pounds. Orders that had to be paid for, even if they couldn't sell them, such was their complacency in assuming the licence would be renewed. Illingworth's marketing director rang the council department up the day after they got the bad news.

'I'm just checking that we'll be allowed to sell off our stock.'

'I'm sorry, sir, we couldn't allow that,' said the officer, looking up at Spode who was standing beside him.

'But that's daft! What are we supposed to do with them? Give them away?'

'I'm sorry sir, but that's not our problem. You no longer have a licence to sell them.'

'Who got the licence then? If it's that bastard Spode, I'll have the council's guts for garters!'

'I am allowed to disclose that information, sir. It's Rawnsley's Outfitters.'

'Rawnsley's? Well, they're a decent enough firm. Happen they'll cover our costs.'

Herbert Rawnsley, the chairman and founder, played little part in the running of his company. His son Michael, who had formed the unholy alliance with Spode, had gradually taken the helm and now ran things single-handed. He took Spode's advice as to how to handle Illingworth's when they rang, cap in hand.

'I'm sorry but we've already placed orders with our own suppliers,' he lied. 'We don't need any more. If you'd only rung yesterday . . .'

'Good God! You've been quick off the mark. Your supplier wouldn't be Spode Fashions, would it?'

'You're right – it wouldn't.' Another lie. 'Our suppliers are our own business.'

'And what am I supposed to do with all our unsold stock?'

'I'll send someone round to make you an offer.'

Rawnsley's outfitters bought all Illingworth's stock at cost less seventy-five per cent. Illingworth's toyed with the idea of giving their stock away rather than be treated like this, but business sense prevailed and they took their loss with bad grace.

Chapter Seven

Spode felt uncomfortable holding Olga's hand as they meandered through the early-summer crowds thronging Blackpool's Golden Mile. But it was what couples did. He drew the line at wearing a 'Kiss Me Quick' hat but, persuaded by Olga, settled for a two-shilling 'Stetson' to match her 'Annie Oakley'.

Olga mistook his discomfort for nervousness, understandable enough in a man about to pop the question. She'd already said 'yes' in her mind and just wished he'd get on with it. They reached the comparative quiet at the end of the South Pier before he stopped and pulled her to him. Her heart raced in anticipation.

'Olga,' he said, hesitantly, 'I've been meaning to ask you something.'

She feigned a look of surprise. 'Oh?' she said, wanting to squeeze as much romance as possible out of this moment. She wanted it to become a precious memory, unlike Alan's proposal, which had begun with the words, 'Yer not, are yer?'

'I . . . er . . .' mumbled Spode.

She was dying to help him out, but resisted the temptation. He changed his mind and turned away. 'No,' he said. 'I'm being silly.'

She held his arm. 'Leonard – let me be the best judge of that.'

He turned back to her, took a deep breath and said quickly, 'I just wondered if you wanted to come and live with me?'

She was taken aback. '*Live* with you?'

'Sorry,' he said. 'It's a bad idea – forget I ever mentioned it.'

'You mean, just *live with you*, nothing else?'

Spode shook his head, not understanding her question. 'I don't know what you mean? What else is there?'

'Well, there's Annie for a start. I couldn't just leave her.'

'You wouldn't have to – she can come as well.'

They began walking back down the pier, the incoming tide swishing below the slatted boards beneath their feet.

'Leonard, let me get this straight. You want me to come and live with you, over the brush . . .?'

He shushed her into silence as her words attracted the attention of a passing elderly couple, who went tut-tutting on their way.

'Oops!' grinned Olga, holding her hand to her mouth. then she took his hand and stopped him.

'See how shocked people would be if I came to live with you without us being married.'

The word 'married' jarred Spode's nerves. 'I don't really care what people think,' he said.

'Well, I care what people think – especially where Annie's concerned. And you're a councillor. You've got to care what people think or you won't stay a councillor for very long.'

There was truth in her words. Leonard Spode wasn't exactly a dedicated councillor, it was only a means to an end for him. Before very much longer he hoped there would be bigger fish to fry. But she was right, living in sin with Olga and Annie would be bad for his image. How come he hadn't thought of that? Probably because his common sense had become blinkered by the real reason for his friendship with Olga.

'So would you come and live with me if I – er – if I married you?' he said at length, as though voicing his thoughts.

'Leonard, is this a proposal? Because if it is I can only give you three out of ten for being romantic.'

'What?' He was miles away.

'Oh, never mind.'

She let go of his hand and pushed her way through the crowds, annoyed and saddened by the way things had turned out. Not quite sure why she was doing this, he set off after her and caught her by the exit gate.

'Well?' he asked.

'Well, what?' she snapped.

'Will you marry me?'

His voice had gone up a few decibels and was heard by several passers-by, who stopped to hear her answer.

'If she says no, I'm available,' cackled one old woman.

'Yer bloody welcome to 'er,' cackled her even older husband. 'In fact, I'll give yer ten bob ter tek 'er off me 'ands.'

Olga stared up at Spode, who was becoming increasingly embarrassed by the whole situation. No way had he intended proposing to her. All he'd wanted was a union of convenience – not this. Olga led him clear of the curious crowd who went on their way, disappointed. This was the best offer she was ever likely to get.

'If you're serious, the answer's yes' she whispered, only half expecting him to sweep her up in his arms in delight.

'Good,' he said. 'That's settled then.' He put his arm around her and led her to the Pleasure Beach where they celebrated with a ride on the Big Dipper. That evening he took her to the Tower Ballroom to watch Reginald Dixon rise from the stage playing 'I Do Like To Be Beside The Seaside' on his Wurlitzer.

'I expect that won't be the only organ rising tonight,' Olga said, hopefully. But she was to be disappointed – and not for the last time.

* * *

August 1952
As it was the second time around for her they settled for a quiet wedding at the register office and a drink with a few friends at the Ashley Arms afterwards. Leonard drank in moderation, but Olga drank like a woman trying to forget something. Or somebody. The differences between Alan and Leonard had been becoming more apparent each passing day, but she still married him. God! – who else would have her? At least he could give her and Annie a good home. They were to move out of Fogerty Row and join him in his four-bedroom detached in Weston Grove. Perhaps she was sacrificing something but it still seemed worth it.

Annie looked up at the house the morning they moved in, determined not be overrawed. It was a substantial dwelling with large, stained-glass bay windows, a porch and a brick garage – and a brand new tarmac drive flecked with white granite chippings on which Spode parked his brand new Jaguar.

Most of their own furniture had been sold to a second-hand furniture man for less than fifty pounds. They'd kept Annie's bed and a few 'bits and bobs', to quote Olga, such as the radio, the clock and the Coronation tea caddy.

A young boy of around thirteen who had been mowing the front lawn stopped what he was doing and stared unblinkingly at the newcomers. Spode walked over to him, thrust a handful of change into the boy's hand and patted his shoulder.

'That'll do for today, Ronnie,' he said. 'Call back next week to finish the rest off.'

The boy shrank from his touch. Someone else who can't stand him, thought Annie.

'Watch 'im,' muttered the boy out of the corner of his mouth as he trudged past her.

Annie had neither the time nor the opportunity to ask him what he meant, but made a mental note to have a quiet word the next time he came to the house. She never saw him again.

'Well? What d'yer think?' enquired Olga, awaiting Annie's appraisal of their new home.

'I quite like the drive.'

'She quite likes the drive!' Olga shouted to Spode, who was opening the garage door.

He gave one of his broad, empty smiles.

'It'll make a nice change for her.'

'And me,' said Olga.

'We could do wi' a lock on the bathroom door,' Olga informed her husband a few weeks after settling in. A bathroom was a luxury she wasn't used to. It was early evening and Leonard had poured them both a drink while Annie was rummaging through her satchel for her English homework.

'Oh, yes, and just who do you think you might be locking out? There's only me and Annie in the house.'

'Well, I don't want either of yer barging in on me when I'm sitting on the toilet, thanks very much.'

'If you shut the door we'll know someone's in, won't we, Annie?' he winked at his new step-daughter, seeking her agreement. Annie made no comment.

'By the way,' he announced, conveniently changing the subject, 'I've put my name forward as a candidate for the forthcoming election.'

'Forthcoming election?' echoed Olga. 'You've only been in a year.'

'Not them elections – I'm talking about a real election, the Parliamentary by-election. I assume you heard about Harold Norwood popping his clogs?'

'Yer what? Yer mean you're thinking of becoming an MP?' She laughed, which annoyed Spode.

'What's wrong with that?'

'Well, being a Town Councillor's one thing, but I can't see *you* as an MP.'

'I see – and why not?'

Over the last few weeks an edge had begun to creep into

his voice that Annie hadn't noticed before he married her mam.

'I don't know, it seems a big step, that's all,' commented Olga, wishing she'd kept her mouth shut.

'Do you think I'm not good enough?'

'I never said that, Leonard.'

'Not everybody's as thick as you, you know.'

Annie froze, awaiting her mother's reaction. She wasn't used to domestic arguments but sensed one was in the offing. Olga managed to control her tongue.

'Steady on, Leonard,' she said, placatingly. 'I were only saying, that's all. No need ter get yer knickers in a twist.'

'Don't you dare talk to me as though I'm some sort of idiot!' he snapped. 'Just remember where you come from and where you are now.'

Annie felt her mother had every right to be angry, but Olga showed remarkable self-control. She walked over to the corner bar and poured herself a brandy which she drank with her back to him, looking at the reflection of her infuriated face glaring back at her from the mirror behind the bottle shelf. Spode quickly switched on his empty smile and looked down at Annie, who glowered up at him.

'I think we've just had our first marital tiff, and in front of the girl too. Shame on us.'

'First and last, eh?' said Olga, her emotions now under control.

Spode joined her at the bar and poured himself a whisky. 'I'll drink to that, my love.'

But Annie couldn't detect any love in his voice. She remembered what it sounded like; she thought about her dad constantly. Something else she thought about was the amount her mother was beginning to drink. Until meeting Spode, Annie had never seen her drunk. Now it was becoming a regular occurrence. It was almost as if he encouraged it.

Ethel Greenwood poked her head around the door to the

boss's office, hair in curlers enshrouded in a headscarf. Tonight was Mecca Locarno night. Taking a half-smoked Senior Service from her mouth, she smiled at him. No make-up apart from lipstick on her lips and teeth.

'Olga not in today, Leonard?'

'No,' replied Spode. 'She's not too good this morning.'

'She were not too good last night from what I hear.'

'Now then, Ethel. You're speaking of the woman I love.' There was more than a hint of sarcasm in his voice. 'She just had a couple too many, that's all.'

'Do you want me ter take over while she comes back?'

'You do that Ethel – and Ethel . . .'

'Yes.'

'I think we can make that arrangement permanent. Olga's retired.'

Ethel closed the door and went back to her machine. Faces turned to look at her. Questioning.

'Hey, you lot!' she shouted, her face cracking into a great grin. 'Get yer bleeding 'eads down. Yer looking at the new chargehand.'

'What happened to Olga?'

'Retired,' she announced. 'She were as drunk as a skunk in t' Ashley last night. Nearly got 'ersen thrown out.'

Heads nodded and shook in equal numbers. 'I'm surprised he bleedin' stands for it,' commented one of the cutters. 'If he'd played his cards right he could have had me.'

The laughter was eventually drowned by the sound of machines whirring into life. Olga had lost all her friends the minute she took up with Leonard Spode.

October 1952

Olga was fast asleep on the settee when Spode walked in. A smell of cooking drifted through from the kitchen where Annie was clattering pots and pans. Her having to make the evening meal every night was becoming a bit much, but with the state her mother was constantly in, she had no choice. Spode wouldn't be best pleased if he came home to an empty table.

He walked up behind her and put his hands on her waist, making her jump slightly.

'How's your mam?' he asked. Annie wrinkled her nose. His aftershave was as pungent as ever, despite his not having shaved for several hours.

'Dead to the world. She was fast asleep with a glass in her hand when I came home. I wish she'd stop drinking.'

'Don't worry – I'll put my foot down,' he reassured her.

'I wish you would, Uncle Leonard. She looks ever so poorly nowadays.'

He gave Annie a gentle slap on her bottom. 'We'll sort her out between us. We don't want anyone from the Social coming round, saying she's an unfit parent, do we?'

The thought had never occurred to Annie. In a couple of months she'd be fifteen. Fifteen-year-old girls didn't need much looking after.

'What are you making for tea?' he enquired, his bottom-slapping hand returning to her waist.

'Oh, just sausage and mash, that's all.'

'How d'yer mean, that's all? It's my favourite. Cooked by my favourite girl.'

She smiled self-consciously and moved away from his touch. 'I'll bring it through in a few minutes,' she said.

Annie was in her bedroom doing her homework. She grimaced at the sound of raucous laughter coming from below. Drunken laughter, her mother's laughter. So much for Uncle Leonard putting his foot down.

Olga held out her glass for Spode to fill up. The top buttons of her blouse were undone, showing her bra and her sagging cleavage. 'Hey! I do hope yer not trying to get me drunk so yer can have yer wicked way wi' me, yer naughty boy. Because if you are, yer going the right way about it!'

She screamed with laughter at her own coarse humour as he generously replenished her drink. He turned his eyes away from the wrinkled skin between her breasts.

'The girls at work were asking after you.' His smile didn't extend beyond his teeth. 'I told them you were too pissed to come in.'

Olga screamed with laughter again. 'Yer didn't? Yer rotten sod! Just for that yer can give me the bottle, I've got a reputation ter keep up.'

'That's right, you have. You're the local drunk, aren't you? As well as the local whore. Tell me, who's Annie's real dad? From what I hear it could be one of many.'

She frowned, trying to unscramble her intoxicated brain enough to make sense of these insults. Then she saw him smiling and she smiled back.

'Don't be rotten ter me, Leonard. Gimme a drink.'

Spode allowed her to take the bottle of gin from his grasp and winced as she put it to her mouth and took a deep drink. A gulp like that would have sent his head spinning. He looked up as Annie walked into the room, then quickly snatched the bottle away from Olga.

'That's it,' he said, firmly. 'No more.'

He shrugged at Annie who looked at him then down at her mother, grinning inanely back at her.

'I thought I'd have a bath – does anyone need the bathroom for the next half hour?' Annie addressed the question to Olga.

'No, my dear. If I need to – erm – relieve myself, I shall pee all over Leonard's gera – geranerums.'

She screamed with laughter once again.

'Go ahead,' said Spode to Annie. 'If she needs to go, she can use the one in the side porch.'

Annie nodded and turned for the stairs. The downstairs toilet was not her mother's favourite place. It reminded her of the outside lavatory in Fogerty Row.

Annie had had a bath every other night since they'd moved into this house. She poured shampoo into the water as it ran from the hot tap, then knelt beside the bath and swirled it round with her hand to make bubbles. As usual she left getting undressed until last, keeping one eye on the door as she did so. She wished Spode or – or Uncle Leonard as he preferred to be called – would have a little more consideration for her privacy. Three times since she and her mother had moved in he'd just walked into the bathroom while she was having a bath. He'd knock first and ask if she was decent. Once she'd said she was on the toilet, which had done the trick, but being in the bath apparently didn't count. The first time he'd walked in, picked up a towel and walked out without giving her a glance as she sat there, arms shielding her budding breasts. The second time he'd rummaged in the bathroom cabinet, looking for a bottle of aspirin. That time he'd turned to look at her and asked if she'd seen them.

'No,' she'd said.

He turned and walked out, complaining of a splitting headache, even evoking her sympathy. Perhaps she was overreacting, not wanting him to see her in the bath. Different people had different ways. The last time he'd sat on the toilet lid and asked how she was going on at school. Her guard was down but her arms weren't. Her breasts weren't for his eyes. He'd chatted for a couple of minutes before leaving.

'She's fallen asleep.'

Annie looked up, startled, as Spode's smiling face appeared round the bathroom door.

He entered and sat on the toilet lid without taking his eyes off her. She crossed her arms over her breasts as usual, shielding herself from him.

'She's beginning to worry me, you know,' he said. 'I'm really frightened in case someone finds out and reports her to the authorities.'

'Authorities?' queried Annie. 'What would they do?'

'They might put you in a home for a start. I mean, I'm out at work all day, I can't look after you.'

He took a step towards her when he saw the concern on her face.

'It's all right,' he was kneeling beside the bath and rolling up his shirtsleeves, 'I won't let it happen. I'll lie if I have to. But you and me have got to stick together – agreed?'

Annie nodded her head, uncertain what she was agreeing to. She wished he wasn't here, though, this was incredibly embarrassing.

'Do you know what an alcoholic is?' he asked.

'It's a person who drinks a lot.'

He nodded, eyes drinking her in as she fastened her frightened gaze on the tiled wall in front of her. Wishing she had no breasts to hide from him and hoping the soap suds were obscuring her thickening pubic hair. She was slim but shapely; her pale skin still had the purity of the childhood she was just leaving behind. Spode's pulse quickened.

'It's more than that,' he said. 'It's a person who can't stop drinking and I'm afraid your mother's reached that stage.'

He picked up a piece of soap and rubbed her back. 'This is the bit I can never reach,' he said, in a voice half an octave higher than usual.

His trembling hand ran down her back and into the water, just touching her bottom.

Annie went rigid with shock. 'It's okay, Uncle Leonard, I can manage, thanks,' she said, faintly.

'Nonsense, wh-what are step-dads for?' There was a febrile tremor in his voice as he anticipated what was to come. The beads of sweat on his forehead were not caused by the steam from the bath.

'It's – it's important that you and I get very close so we can protect your mother from herself.'

His words made little sense to Annie. She was petrified with a mixture of fear and embarrassment, wanting him to go but not daring to tell him. He picked up a flannel and rinsed the suds from her back. His other hand picked up the soap and rubbed it awkwardly over her shoulder as his breathing quickened.

Olga awoke courtesy of a retching, bilious surge rushing up from her bowels into her mouth and sending her running blindly upstairs to the bathroom. She had forgotten Annie was taking a bath, her drunken state and the urgency of her predicament had removed all memory of that.

Had she been a little more sober she might have noticed her daughter sitting in the water with her arms folded across her breasts and a look of acute distress on her face.

Had Olga's befuddled brain not been so focused on the toilet bowl she might have noticed her husband kneeling beside the bath, swiftly bringing his hand from beneath the water just in front of Annie with a mixture of guilt, frustration and annoyance on his face. She might also have noticed the tell-tale bulge in his trousers – a bulge she herself had rarely managed to induce.

Spode got to his feet and backed out of the room, cursing his ill luck, leaving Annie weeping in the bath and her mother vomiting noisily down the toilet.

Annie lay in bed, staring into the darkness; her world was upside down. Where there had been safety and security there was now danger. She was living in a dangerous place and there was nowhere else to go. Tomorrow she'd tell her mother, who would make everything right. They'd probably have to move back to Fogerty Row but it was better than staying here with *him*. Her pillow was damp with tears as Spode came into her room and sat beside her bed, words of false comfort oozing from his mouth.

'I hope I didn't embarrass you earlier on? Did I embarrass you? Oh, dear, it seems I did.'

She had her back to him, her heart thumping, not knowing what to do if he started again. He was too big and strong for her.

'I was only trying to be a proper dad to you.'

His voice dripped sweetness, cloying and sickening. She

could gauge his unwelcome proximity by the strength of his aftershave.

'Dads do that, you know, bathe their children. I bet your dad used to wash your back?'

Annie could never remember her dad bathing her. It was so long ago. Anyway, she was a young woman now, it was different. She was dead sure her dad wouldn't have done what Spode had just done.

'Please, I don't want you to do that again.' Her voice was weak.

He put a hand on her shoulder, causing her whole body to stiffen in anticipation.

'I've upset you,' he said. 'I call tell. Look, I've got to see to your mother now.'

He stood up and made for the door. Annie lay hunched and stiff, willing him to go. He turned round.

'I don't want you upsetting her with your silly schoolgirl imaginings. I know how you girls can put two and two together and make five.' His voice was harsh now.

Annie was in tears now as the realisation struck her. It would be her word against his – who would her mother believe?

'Do you hear me?' he rasped. 'Your mother's ill, she's an alcoholic. She's not to be upset by any of your stupid stories. You don't want to end up in a home, now do you?'

He closed the door and left Annie weeping in the dark.

Chapter Eight

Just as the knock came on the door, the telephone rang. Spode picked it up and turned to his election agent, Malcolm Lindis. 'You get the door, will you, Malc? It'll be the bloke from the *Yorkshire Post*.'

Lindis opened the door and welcomed the reporter into the house. Spode waved them both into the living room as he spoke loudly down the phone. '*Thanks . . . thanks very much. I'll pass the message on to Annie. She'll be really mad that she missed you . . . and you. Hey! Send us a couple of tickets the next time you're over here. Honest? . . . Great. All the best, Guy.*'

His bemused secretary at the other end of the line shook her head. Had her boss gone mad? Spode replaced the receiver and turned to his visitor. 'Sorry about the shouting but it was a transatlantic call, you know what the lines are like.'

'Transatlantic?' said the reporter, his notebook already in his hand. 'Anyone interesting?'

'Well – not unless you're a pop music fan. It was an American singer, Guy Mitchell. Young Annie got on stage to sing with him when he came to Leeds Empire.'

'I remember that.'

'Do you really?' said Spode, who himself remembered the article word for word. 'Anyway, he'd somehow got word I was running for Parliament and rang to wish me luck.'

'How on earth did he find out?' wondered the reporter.

Spode smiled and picked up a school photo of Annie. 'I think a certain little bird might have mentioned it in one of her many letters to him. They correspond regularly, you know.'

The reporter's pencil was scribbling furiously. He drank Spode's whisky and wrote a couple of mundane pages concerning the candidate's hopes and ambitions for the constituency, which were much the same as his opponents' only Spode somehow didn't seem as believable as the rest of them. Still, the Guy Mitchell angle would ensure he got better coverage. As Spode well knew. After the reporter had left, Malcolm confronted Spode.

'I tried to get hold of Guy Mitchell myself yesterday for a quote I could pass on to the papers, but I was told he was down with laryngitis and wouldn't be speaking to anyone for a week.'

'Really?' said Spode. 'And what the hell's that got to do with anything?'

He was given three columns on page two under the ponderous sub-head: *Guy's girl's step-father enters election race*. Unfortunately they'd favoured a photo of Guy Mitchell over the one he'd given the reporter of himself.

Olga turned her face away as her daughter came into the kitchen. She stared at the electric kettle, the first she'd ever owned, waiting for it to whistle – a sound which used to amuse her. Spode had gone to the factory, Saturday mornings being one of the few times he could spare to attend to his proper job now that the by-election was looming. It was two weeks since the bathroom incident and he hadn't been near Annie. She'd just had her first bath in all that time, his absence encouraging her to take the risk. Her ear had been constantly tuned to the sound of his car coming into the drive, and a chair had been wedged beneath the door handle for good measure. There was a bolt on the toilet in the side porch, which was handy as she had no intention of ever using the bathroom toilet. Not while he was around. Her precautionary measures plus his now impeccable behaviour had lulled her into a sense of security. Perhaps he'd realised his mistake and would never do it again; perhaps everything would be all right now. The state of her mother's face told her differently.

Olga knew she'd be unable to hide from her daughter for very long so she turned to face her.

'Mam!' cried Annie, concerned to see the livid bruising down the right side of her mother's face. 'What happened?'

Olga turned away again as Annie walked round her to get a better look.

'It was *him*, wasn't it?'

Her mother hung her head and emptied the boiling water from the kettle into the teapot, her trembling hand sending some of it on to the Formica worktop.

'Damn!' she cursed. Picking up a half-smoked cigarette from an ashtray, she took a deep drag then broke into a loud, throat-scouring cough, sending tears streaming down her pale cheeks. She wiped them dry with the sleeve of her dressing gown.

'Uncle Leonard - Spode - he did this to you, didn't he?' challenged Annie. 'I heard you arguing last night.'

Olga looked at her daughter through defeated, lachrymose eyes. The drink had eaten away at her from the inside. Taking away her strength, her self-esteem and her courage.

'It was my fault, love, I've nobody but meself ter blame.' Her voice was heavy with shame.

Annie gripped her mother's shoulders. 'Mam, he hit you. How can it be your fault?'

Olga placed her hands on top of Annie's. 'Sit down, love. This needs some explaining.'

She sat down. Olga's hands were now shaking uncontrollably as Annie held on to them, drawing her mother down into the chair beside her.

'I got drunk,' said Olga. She laughed thinly and shook

her head. 'Hey! No surprise there. I must have said summat out of place and he lost his temper. I know it weren't a nice thing for him ter do but it must be a right sod havin' ter live wi' a drunk like me.' She took another drag on her cigarette before crushing it out between her nicotine-stained fingers and tossing it into a large glass ashtray on the coffee table.

'He'd no need to hit you,' said Annie, stoutly. 'He's a pig and a bully and we should tell the police.'

Thus determined, she moved towards the phone, intending to tell the police the whole story, not just the bit about her mother.

'Don't!' called out Olga, urgently.

Annie stopped with the telephone in her hand.

'Honest, love,' pleaded Olga. 'It's all right. I'd rather yer didn't.'

Annie turned and looked back at her mother in disbelief.

'Ringin' the police could cause us a load o' bother,' warned Olga. 'It'd be the end of all this for a start.' She looked around the well-appointed kitchen. 'He's only done it the once, love – just the once.' She repeated her words as if to convince herself that what he'd done was in some way excusable. 'And I did give him good reason,' she added, as if to emphasise the point.

'He did it to me as well!'

Annie blurted it out without thinking. Olga looked shocked.

'You what? Leonard hit you? When did this happen?'

It was time for Annie's tears now, pouring down her face in great cathartic streams as she prepared to unburden herself.

'Well, he didn't actually hit me . . .'

Olga's face softened with relief. It wasn't as bad as she'd thought. 'Oh, thank God for that, love.' She squeezed Annie's hands. 'He's not a bad feller – he's just not very good wi' women, that's all. Some fellers are like that. They just don't know how ter go on.'

But Annie had come this far and she wasn't going to stop

now. Despite the look of relief on her mother's gaunt face she had to know the truth about this man.

'Mam – he messed about with me when I was having a bath!'

The shocked look returned to Olga's face.

'Messed about? What d'yer mean, messed about?'

Annie took a deep breath. 'It happened about two weeks ago. You'd had a lot to drink and I went up for a bath.'

Olga frowned, trying to recall the incident, then shook her head. The drink had fogged her memory.

'He came into the bathroom when I was in the bath and . . .'

Anne dissolved into sobs, her face buried in her hands. Olga pushed her hand beneath her daughter's chin and gently forced it up.

'Annie – what're yer saying?'

'Mam – his hands were all over me. Down my front, between my legs, everything!'

Olga withdrew, stunned. If this was true her marriage was over for sure. It definitely wasn't in her best interests for it to be true. Could Annie have got it wrong? Spode had never struck Olga as a sex maniac of any kind. Quite the opposite in fact. She stroked her daughter's hair.

'When exactly did this happen?'

'You should know when it happened, you were there!'

Olga felt a paradoxical sense of relief at this. She most definitely had *not* been there, she'd certainly have remembered something like that. Annie had got it wrong.

'How d'you mean, I was there? If I'd been there I'd have remembered.'

Annie looked into her mother's eyes. 'Mam, you were drunk. You came into the bathroom to be sick. If you hadn't come in, I don't know what he'd have done.'

Olga tried to cast her mind back to the time in question. There'd been so many nights when she'd thrown up, one just blurred into another.

'Oh, love,' she said, lamely. 'I don't remember, honestly.'

Annie nodded her understanding. 'You were very drunk. He came into my bedroom later and told me not to tell you. Said you'd be classed as an unfit mother and I'd be put into a home.'

Whatever blood was left in Olga's face drained away. 'He said that?' Spode had mentioned that very possibility to her the previous night, just before he hit her.

'Can they do that, Mam? Put me in a home?'

Olga took her daughter in her arms. She'd never felt so useless. 'Yer nearly fifteen, pet. I don't think they can do much once yer get ter sixteen. Certainly not after yer've left school.'

'That's two years off.'

'I know, love. It's not that long.' She sat back and held Annie at arm's length, studying her. Both faces were wet with tears.

'Has he done anything or said anything since?' she asked, shaking her head in hopeful anticipation of the answer.

To Olga's relief Annie shook her own head. 'I've kept out of his way,' she said. 'This morning was the first bath I've had since that night.'

'I thought yer were beginnin' ter smell a bit.'

Annie attempted to laugh at her mother's joke, but failed. 'What are we going to do, Mam?' she asked.

Olga sat and thought for a long time as Annie stood up and poured them both a cup of tea. Olga had drunk hers before she arrived at a decision. The base of the empty cup rattled from her trembling hand as she put it down on the table.

'Look, love, he's only hit me the once and he's only messed with you the once. Happen he's learned his lesson. So I reckon the best thing is ter say nothing an' see how he behaves over the next few weeks. We've a lot ter lose.'

'So has he,' Annie reminded her, disappointed at not

being able to ring the police. She needed to purge herself of this man and that seemed a good way to do it. 'If any word of this gets in the papers, his chances of becoming an MP'll go up in smoke.'

'I doubt if the papers would print something like that,' said Olga. 'Not without a bit of proof.'

It didn't seem much of an argument to Annie, but she knew better than to pursue it. 'In the meantime, Mam,' she said, 'could you try and not drink so much?'

'I'll try, love. Honest ter God, I'll try.'

'Apart from my mam you're the only person in the world that knows,' confided Annie, handing the shared cigarette back to Movita, who looked shocked at her friend's revelation. Her own dad wasn't beyond lashing out at her mother now and again but he'd always regretted it. Mrs Lunn could give as good as she got in the fisticuffs department. Movita's dad was an inadequate, epileptic drunk, but no child molester. The conversation was taking place in the toilets where the girls of Brookland Park High congregated to smoke illicit cigarettes and pass on items of scandal, gossip and sex education.

'If he does it again,' said a determined Annie, 'I'm going to ring the police, I don't care what happens to me.'

'Why don't you tell him that?' suggested Movita. 'Mebbe it'll make him think twice before he tries to touch you again.'

'Mam reckons it's best not to mention it. Best to leave well alone. The election's in a few weeks. If he becomes an MP he'll have to behave himself. Mam reckons he'll not dare put a foot wrong then.'

There was a long, contemplative silence as both girls puffed on their cigarette and reflected upon their lives.

'We're moving to Sheffield,' announced Movita, matter-of-factly.

'Sheffield? You never told me.'

Movita shrugged. 'I didn't know myself until last night.

My dad's been offered a job with a steel company; there's a house goes with it. He reckons it's a golden opportunity. With him being an epileptic piss-artist, he doesn't get many golden opportunities.'

'He could be a beer taster for Tetley's,' said Annie, hiding her disappointment at the prospect of losing her best friend.

'He could, couldn't he?' laughed Movita. 'Hey – d'you know what he calls the gents' toilets?'

Annie shook her head.

'The Used Beer Department.'

'Right,' smiled Annie. It wasn't funny enough to mollify her feeling of desolation. In many ways Movita was the only person she could confide in when things went wrong. Annie had plenty of other friends but no confidantes. She and Movita had been best friends ever since she could remember. All she had now was Norman Newton, who was supposed to be her boyfriend. She wished Brian were still alive. She could have relied on Brian, daft as he was.

'Are you still going out with Norman?' enquired Movita.

'Yeah – he keeps wanting to, you know – but I won't let him.'

'You what? All the way?'

Annie grinned and blushed. 'Give over – I wouldn't let anyone go all the way. Nobody from round here anyway.'

Movita nodded her approval. 'There's nobody from round here I fancy that much. Still – there might be someone in Sheffield.'

'When are you moving?' asked Annie.

'Six weeks – just after Christmas.'

'Will you write to me?'

'I might phone you. We'll have a telephone.'

'I'll phone you one week,' decided Annie, 'and you phone me the next. That way they won't notice the bill.'

A shaft of light opening on to the bedroom wall opposite her bed stirred Annie into wakefulness. Someone had come into the room.

Who is it?' she asked, without turning round. She was dreading the answer.

'Only me, my pet.'

Her heart started to pound. It was *him*.

'What do you want?' She was trying to keep the fear out of her voice.

'I think we ought to talk.'

'Talk? What about?' She still hadn't turned round. 'Can't we talk tomorrow? I was asleep.'

'This is important.' He sounded irritable. She turned over and saw him standing in the doorway in his dressing gown, silhouetted against the landing light. 'It's to do with your mam.'

'Mam? What about her?'

He sighed and sat on the edge of the bed. She moved as far away from him as she could, without falling out of bed. 'I'm worried about her. I think I might have to have her committed before she does herself any harm.'

'Committed? How do you mean, committed?'

He paused for dramatic effect. 'Into a psychiatric hospital.'

'Psychiatric . . . you mean a nuthouse? Mam isn't nutty, she just drinks too much, that's all.'

He placed his hand on her shoulder. Annie shrank back with revulsion.

'You don't see things from my point of view,' he whispered, his mouth close to her ear. 'All I'm doing is trying to help. I want to do the right thing by both of you.'

'How can having Mam locked up in a loony bin *help* us?'

'It might save her life. You want to save her life, don't you?'

'Yes, but . . .'

His hand returned to her shoulder. 'Believe me, if there was any other way . . .'

His dressing gown fell open and it was awfully apparent that he wasn't wearing anything underneath. His eyes followed her gaze down to his hardening penis. She was frozen with shock.

'Aha!' He grinned. 'Don't tell me a pretty girl like you has never seen one of these before?'

Annie didn't answer. Her breath was coming in short bursts. He took her hand and pressed it against his erection. Suddenly she came out of her frightened trance and pulled her hand away.

'Get away from me, you dirty man! Get away or – or I'll tell!'

Her voice was hoarse with horror and fear. He stood up and withdrew to the door, his face contorted with rage.

'Don't you dare talk to me like that, you little slut! Just remember who you are – the daughter of a whore! I'll turn you both out on to the streets as soon as look at you!'

He stormed out of the room and into his own bedroom as Annie collapsed tearfully into her pillows, weeping fitfully, then lifted her head as she heard her mother screaming in fear and pain.

'Thank you for seeing me at such short notice, Mrs Roundtree, but it is urgent that I speak to you.'

'I gathered as much, Mr Spode. And might I say how refreshing it is that a man in your position is willing to give up his spare time in order to attend to the welfare of his daughter.'

'Step-daughter,' corrected Spode.

'Even more commendable.'

He looked at the certificates and trophies dotted around the headmistress's study and nodded his approval. 'Brookland Park High appears to have won many honours over the years.'

'We pride ourselves on being one of the best Grammar Schools in the West Riding,' gushed Mrs Roundtree.

'In the whole of Yorkshire, if your reputation's anything to go by.'

'Do sit down, Mr Spode. I hear you're running for Parliament?'

'Yes, indeed, Mrs Roundtree, and I hope I can count on your vote?'

'Sadly I don't reside in your constituency, otherwise you'd be most welcome to it.'

He smiled and crossed his legs, allowing the sleeve of his elegantly cut grey suit to ride up over his new gold Rolex. Mrs Roundtree looked across at him with approval. Tall and not too heavy, middle age had taken nothing away from his good looks. His dark hair was streaked with grey along the sides, giving him a distinguished appearance. She'd always hoped her own hair would do the same when the inevitable grey arrived, but like most red heads was doomed to the salt and pepper look. The headmistress returned his smile. Most of the fathers of her scholarship girls were working-class. Leonard Spode looked for all the world like a parent of one of her fee-paying students.

'How may I help you, Mr Spode?'

He switched off his own smile and leaned forward in his chair. 'I'm desperately worried about Annie,' he said, sounding concerned.

'Oh, dear.' Mrs Roundtree opened the manila file she had in front of her. 'Are you talking about recent weeks?' she asked.

'Yes, I am,' he replied. 'Over the last few weeks she's been acting very strangely and I was wondering if you'd noticed anything odd about her behaviour at school?'

'Well,' she began flicking through the file, 'ordinarily Annie is a model pupil of above average ability.' She closed the folder and looked at him. What she had to tell him wasn't written down, she'd only produced the file for effect. 'After you rang, I had a word with Miss Bulmer, Annie's form mistress. She tells me Annie's demeanour has been more morose of late – and she's normally such a cheery young lady. Popular with her friends and teachers alike.'

'But not of late?'

'Apparently not. Might I ask what she's been like at home?'

He sighed, as though reluctant to divulge what was on his mind.

'I can promise you that whatever you say will not go beyond this study.'

'Thanks,' he said. 'Although I don't suppose it'll do any harm to appraise Miss Bulmer of the situation.' He took a deep breath. 'Annie's been stealing money from me. She doesn't know I know, but believe me, she has.'

Mrs Roundtree's expression grew intent as he continued.

'She's also been lying to me about where she gets to on a night.' He held out his hands and shrugged. 'I'm a busy man, Mrs Roundtree. I haven't got time to be chasing after young girls. I believe she's become involved with a gang of local youths. You can imagine my concern.'

'What about Annie's mother? What does she think about it all?'

His face grew grave and he looked at the floor. Mrs Roundtree would have heard rumours about Olga's drinking. Spode knew he didn't have to be the first one to broach the delicate subject. Her already knowing would add invaluable credence to his lie.

'Look, Mr Spode. I – er – I do know about Mrs Spode's drink problem.'

'Oh, my God! Is there anyone who doesn't?'

'It's not widely known, but I make it my business to check on such matters.'

'Yes, of course you do. I would expect no less from a woman of your standing.' He examined his manicured fingers, unstained by nicotine and uncallused by manual work. 'I came here to ask for your help,' he said, quietly. 'Perhaps you're not in a position to do anything. After all, it's your job to educate. Moral guidance should be up to me. But if there's anything at all you can do, I would be most grateful. She's a fine young lady and I don't want her to . . . you know.'

Follow in her mother's footsteps were the words on the tip of Mrs Roundtree's tongue, but she kept them to herself.

'We'll do what we can, Mr Spode. Like you say, it will be as well to appraise Miss Bulmer of the situation.'

He held out his hand. 'I can't ask for any more, Mrs Roundtree, thank you very much.'

Through a supreme effort of will, Olga had remained off the drink for a whole afternoon. She wanted to be sober for once when Annie came home from school. Marrying Leonard Spode had been mistake, she knew that now. There was barely a square inch of her body that didn't bear a bruise. He hadn't hit her in the face since that first time. She'd covered up for him then, telling people she'd bumped into a door. But people weren't stupid – and neither was Spode. Olga knew Annie wasn't safe and was planning their escape.

Her daughter could barely raise a smile as she came in from school. Gone was the cheery young girl who'd got her mother through the shock of losing Alan. The glow had left her cheeks and the sparkle from her eyes.

Olga took Annie's hands. 'We're leaving him,' she announced.

'When?' was all the girl had to say. She didn't need chapter and verse as to why, she already knew why. Although her mother didn't know about the incident in the bedroom, Annie hadn't wanted to burden her with that.

'Tonight. He's got a council meeting after tea. He won't be home till late.'

'Where will we go?'

'I've got some money saved up. We can stay in lodgings for a few days until I get a job.'

Spode had had a drink or two when he arrived home. Alcohol improves the humour of some people. Leonard Spode was not one of them. He sat down at the table with fists clenched either side of his knife and fork as he waited for Olga to serve him his meal. The three of them ate in sullen silence, broken eventually by him.

Glaring at them from under thunderous brows, he told them, 'The authorities are keeping an eye on you two. I've had to tell them, it's my civic duty.' His eyes bored into Olga's, who dropped her gaze. 'One more slip from you, you whore, and I'm having you locked away for good.'

He leered at Annie. 'That's right, *whore*. Has it ever occurred to you that you don't look a bit like your late daddy?'

'What're you talking about?' enquired Annie.

'Please, Leonard, don't do this,' begged Olga.

'"Please, Leonard, don't do this",' he mimicked. 'I'll do what I damn' well please in my own house!' he roared. 'And I'll not have a whore like you telling me what to do.'

Olga stood up and left the table. Spode sprang after her and dragged her back by her hair.

'Come back here when I'm talking to you.'

'Leave her alone, you're hurting her!' screamed Annie.

He hurled Olga to the floor. 'There's where she belongs,' he sneered. 'In the gutter.' Then he turned to Annie and thrust his face right into hers, the whisky on his breath mingling with the scent of his aftershave, spit spraying on to her face.

'If Alan Jackson's your dad, I'm the Queen of bloody Sheba!'

Within an hour of Spode's leaving for his meeting, their cases were packed and waiting in the hall. A knock came on the door. Annie had been wondering whether to ask her mother about that 'Queen of Sheba' jibe but decided against it. He'd revealed his true colours and rising to his bait would have been a minor victory for him; she didn't want that. But it didn't stop her from being curious.

Olga shouted down the stairs to her 'That'll be the taxi. You go, love. I'll not be a minute.'

Annie opened the door and stepped back in horror as Spode stepped inside, his face ugly with rage. He'd heard Olga calling from upstairs so he contemptuously pushed the girl aside and took the steps two at a time.

'There's a taxi outside,' she heard him shout, angrily. 'It wouldn't be for you, would it?'

His words were punctuated by the sound of heavy blows. Olga was bleating in pain and terror.

'You take one step outside that door and I'll have you committed – d'you hear me?' he ranted.

Annie ran up to help, but the damage was already done. Spode had backed out of the bedroom and was blocking the stairs, Olga's purse in his hands. He was counting the contents, his face livid with rage.

'You thieving slut! Where'd you get this money?'

He went back into the bedroom where she was sobbing in pain. Annie followed him and jumped on his back, her slender arms around his face. He hurled her over his shoulder on to the bed beside her mother, then thumped Olga viciously in the stomach before storming out of the room.

It was quite a while before Olga could speak. Her face was stained with tears as she and Annie clung to each other.

'I think he's broken summat, love. I can hardly breathe.'

'I'll get an ambulance,' said Annie, desperately worried.

She went to the top of the stairs and looked down at Spode who was in the hall sitting on one of the suitcases.

'Good job the meeting was called off, eh?' he sneered up to her.

'Mam needs an ambulance, you've broken her ribs, you . . . you bloody coward!'

The insult seemed to wash over him. 'She's putting it on like she always does. Never believe what a drunk tells you.'

Annie proceeded down the stairs. 'I have to ring for an ambulance.'

He stood up and blocked her path.

'If your mother leaves this house she goes straight to a

mental hospital. You mark my words, young lady. I've already warned them,' he lied. 'They're only waiting for my say so.'

'But she's in pain. She needs to go to a hospital.'

Spode's face twisted into a rage at her defiance. He grabbed her by her upper arm, hurting it as he thrust his face into hers. 'I know all about you, you little slut. Like mother, like daughter. If she goes to a hospital, it's one of my choosing, and you know what that means.'

'Leave it, Annie. I'll be okay.'

Annie looked up at her mother, leaning on the balustrade on the landing.

'Are you sure, Mam?'

'I'll be okay, love.'

Olga turned to go back into the bedroom and eased herself on to the bed, her world destroyed by this evil man. Annie turned to face Spode.

'You're a wicked, stupid, lying . . .'

He hit her with the flat of his hand, knocking her to the floor with blood pouring from her nose. Spode knelt beside her, his mouth spraying angry spittle over her as he spoke.

'Listen here, you little slut! You obey me or I'll have your mother committed and you sent to a bloody reformatory! And don't think I can't.'

Annie curled up in tears. There seemed to be no escape from this man.

The Guy Mitchell connection just edged Spode into first place on election night. After a recount he beat the second-placed man by seven votes. Still, a win was a win and he became Leonard Spode, MP.

The declaration was made just after midnight and he invited a few people back to his house for a victory celebration. Annie was already in bed when they arrived and had mixed feelings about the note of triumph in the voices coming from downstairs. *The foul pig has won.* She knew there was a good side to it. He'd be away more and would definitely have to watch his step now he was in the public eye. Maybe she and her mother were safer. The noises from below kept her awake for quite a while until she fell asleep.

Olga was already fast asleep on a sofa. Her new celebration frock, bought by Spode, covered the strapping on her broken ribs. She'd kept the pain anaesthetised with constant drinking. Her husband had won that particular battle. He looked contemptuously down at her as she snored gently, and took an empty glass from her hand.

'Why did you marry her?' enquired Malcolm, who'd caught the expression on Spode's face.

'I needed a wife.' Spode shrugged, taking the drink his agent was offering him. 'And she served her purpose. With my not being married there were some damaging rumours going round about my – er – sexual preferences. Rumours that could have ruined my political career before it started.'

Malcolm grinned. 'About you being a shirt-lifter? I heard that myself. Good move, Leonard, we'll make a politician out of you yet.' As he moved away he turned and looked back.

'You're not, are you? You know.' He waved a limp-wristed hand.

Spode looked at him evenly and tipped a measure of whisky down his throat. 'Even if I was there'd be nothing for you to worry about, you ugly little bugger.'

Malcolm laughed, happy with the answer. His man was completely amoral, a useful quality in a politician.

Spode stood unsteadily at the door with his agent who was being picked up by his wife. He was the last to go.

'Wish I had a wife who was useful,' he commented as Mrs Lindis arrived in the family Rover. She returned his wave with a smile.

'I don't think madam can ride a bloody push bike – much less drive a car,' grunted Spode, looking back at Olga who hadn't stirred from her slumber for over an hour. 'Just look at her, eh! Pissed as a newt on my big night.'

'You've had a few yourself,' commented Malcolm.

'To which I am perfectly entitled,' retorted Spode. '"To the victor the spoils" and all that. But what's she won, eh? Bugger all, that's what she's won.'

He acknowledged Mrs Lindis' shouted congratulations then closed the door. It had been a good day for him. The first of many. He poured himself a large malt and sat down opposite his sleeping wife to go over the events of the day and contemplate his glittering future.

'You won't be part of it, you hideous old hag.' He tipped the drink down his throat and poured himself another. 'Imagine you thinking a man like me could ever love you. God! You stupid woman. Couldn't you see what I was doing?'

His mind travelled upstairs to where the main reason for his marrying Olga lay fast asleep. Spode grinned. He had the two of them right where he wanted them. Terrified to cross him lest he sent Olga into a nuthouse and Annie into care. Time to reap his rewards.

Olga snorted on, deaf to his insults as he finished his drink then made his way unsteadily upstairs. Annie was sound asleep as he pushed open her door. Her golden hair tumbled across the pillow, lit by the landing light.

'Hello, Annie,' he whispered loudly.

She didn't hear him and slumbered on. Her lack of response encouraged him to approach her bed. It took him longer than usual to remove his trousers but still Annie slept on. She had her back to him as he climbed in beside her. He could see that the hem of her nightie had ridden up the back of her thighs. Putting his arm around her, he clutched clumsily at her breasts, bringing her instantly awake. She gave a scream which he stifled with his hand.

'It's only me – Uncle Leonard. I'm an MP now, you know. What d'you think of that, eh? Your Uncle Leonard an MP.'

Annie could feel his erection pressing against her

bottom. Her nightie was up around her waist and there was nothing between her and him. Overcome with a wave of horror and revulsion she tried to cry out but her voice was mute; all her strength had been driven away and replaced by rigid fear. Then he was inside her, hurting her, thrusting at her with loud animal grunts, his hands inside her nightie grabbing frantically at whatever was available. She couldn't breathe and thought she would choke to death with terror.

This time it was Olga's bursting bladder that brought her staggering up the stairs. But too late to help her daughter. She'd taken to drinking beer in the hope that she wouldn't get drunk quite as easily. Glancing through the open door of Annie's room, she took a step past, retraced it, blinked her blurred vision into focus and gasped with horror at the sight of her husband raping her daughter.

'Leave her!' She flung herself on him, beating at him with flailing fists. 'Leave her, you foul bastard!'

But Spode had passed the point of no return. Annie, semi-conscious with the shock of it all, vaguely felt him surge inside her, accompanied by the sound of her mother screeching obscenities. Spode withdrew and turned to defend himself. He grabbed Olga by her wrists and forced her backwards through the door. She kicked him in his uncovered genitalia, causing him to yelp like a dog in pain as both of them staggered backwards. In his agony he tried to push her away from him but she held on and pulled him backwards down the stairs.

The noise of them both plunging down the polished wooden steps, screaming with rage and fear and pain, brought Annie to her senses. Sounds of pictures falling off the wall, the hall table being knocked over as the two of them reached the bottom. Then the human sounds were gone and all was eerily quiet apart from the solitary banging of something hard and heavy rolling down the wooden stairs, step by step, until it reached the silent carpet at the bottom. Followed by an ominous nothing.

Still sobbing, Annie slid from the bed and went to the top

of the stairs. She could just see her mother's legs sticking out from beneath Spode's body. She flew down and heaved him off Olga, listening at her mother's mouth for signs of breathing, searching her wrist and her neck for a pulse without success. Frantically Annie tried artificial respiration as she'd been taught at school, interspersed with hugging her mother and imploring her not to die.

Spode moaned and blinked his eyes, looking up at Annie with blood oozing from his nose. The sight of him lying there, trouserless, with the instrument of her terror lying flaccid and unthreatening between his pale legs, sent a rush of rage and revulsion flooding though her. Beside her mother's head lay a large, cut-glass flower vase, sturdy enough to have survived the fall down the stairs. Annie picked it up and brought it crashing down on his head with all the strength at her disposal, knocking him back to oblivion where he belonged, before she collapsed, weeping uncontrollably on her mother's body.

The phone had been ringing for a while before Annie got to her feet and picked it up. This was perhaps the help she needed. She held on to the receiver with trembling hands. It was Malcolm Lindis.

'Leonard – sorry if I woke you up but I can't find my wallet and I wondered if . . .' His voice tailed off as he heard Annie weeping at the other end.

'Olga? Are you okay? Could you put Leonard on?'

'My mam's dead.' Annie's voice was tiny.

'Annie? Annie, is that you?'

The phone had dropped from her fingers as she looked back at her mother. She didn't hear him tell her he'd be round in a few minutes and not to ring anyone else before he got there.

'She's in a state of shock, officer,' Malcolm said to the police sergeant who was kneeling in front of Annie's unfocused eyes. 'She's hardly said a word since I got here.'

'What exactly has she said?' enquired the policeman.

Malcolm shrugged. 'Nothing that makes sense. As far as I can tell, Leonard and Olga were acting the goat and fell down the stairs. They were both a bit drunk.'

The sergeant looked back at Annie. 'Is that what happened, love?'

Malcolm was inwardly pleading with her not to blurt out the truth which she'd told him earlier and which could well land her in jail for attempted murder or worse. This way, if his man were to pull through, his reputation at least would be intact. Annie remained mute and impassive. She'd taken in what Malcolm had said and was hoping her step-father would die. Saying nothing was the easiest way out.

'She's obviously in shock, Sergeant,' remonstrated a doctor, pushing the policeman to one side and peering into Annie's face. 'She needs to get to the hospital as soon as possible. You can interview her tomorrow.'

The sergeant stood up. 'Well, I don't think there's anything to be gained from questioning her now. It looks like a dreadful accident.' He looked at Malcolm. 'Were they very close?'

Malcolm nodded, sadly. 'They've only been married a few months. Everything was going right for them. He'd just won his Parliamentary seat, you know, that's what the celebration was about.'

'I heard,' said the policeman, who had voted for the other man. He led Malcolm out of Annie's earshot. 'I couldn't help but notice his trousers were down. God knows what they were up to.'

Malcolm had prepared a plausible answer for this. 'Olga could be quite, er, amorous when she'd had a few,' he explained, confidentially. 'Perhaps it's better not to ask Annie about that – unless, of course, you have to.'

The sergeant had worked out the probable scenario himself. Malcolm had confirmed his suspicions. No point making police work any harder than it already was by making something out of nothing.

'Aye, yer right,' he said. 'No doubt the poor lass will have seen the – er – the state of him. No need to upset her more than we have to. It was obviously an accident, open and shut, I'd say.'

'What are Mr Spode's chances? Any idea?' enquired Malcolm as the doctor helped Annie to the ambulance.

'We won't know for sure until we get him to hospital, but he doesn't look too good. Could even mean another by-election.'

Chapter Nine

Although the Halifax Road Children's Home was locally known as t' Orphanage, most of the resident children had living parents, although the fathers' identity was often a mystery. Annie was one of the few genuine orphans. When the house mother referred to her as 'Orphan Annie' she was told by her new resident, in no uncertain terms, that she would never respond to such a title. This got Annie off to a bad start.

'Well, pardon me for trying to be friendly,' snapped Mrs Laycock, whose aspirations to be a kind and loving house mother had been dashed over the years by the damaged children sent into her care. She was a stern-browed woman whose objective now consisted of simply doing the job while preserving her own sanity.

'Take no notice of her,' advised a youth who had witnessed the confrontation, after the house mother had gone. 'She's a pain in the arse but I've had worse.'

Annie needed a friend. She smiled at the young man. Without taking his hands from his pockets, he introduced himself.

'I'm Jake Parker, only everybody calls me Nosey.'

'Is that because you are?'

'Don't be daft – it's Nosey as in Nosey Parker. If I was Jake White they'd call me Chalky or if I was Jake Clark they'd call me Nobby or if . . .'

'I'll call you Jake,' interrupted Annie.

The youth grinned. 'Fair enough. Haven you gorra nick-name?'

'No, just Annie, Annie Jackson.'

'I could call yer Jacko, if yer like?'

'I prefer Annie.'

It was a purpose-built hostel on the fringe of a council estate still under construction. Ten children of varying ages lived there in the care of Mrs Laycock and a couple of part-time helpers. Annie shared a room with a girl called Doreen who was two years younger and rarely said a word. Most of the kids had been abused in some way. Officially, Annie was the only one who hadn't. None of the children spoke of their abuse, but it was there, in their eyes – in their mistrust of adults and to a lesser extent, their mistrust of each other. Annie and Jake formed an instant bond, though not a boyfriend/girlfriend bond. Because of events in both their lives neither was ready for such a relationship. She'd packed Norman Newton in the last time he'd 'tried it on'.

Annie had her fifteenth birthday in the home. Spode was still in hospital with a fractured skull, but was over the worst. Annie confided in Jake although he kept his own secrets to himself. She suspected his abuse had been far worse and more prolonged than hers. He was fourteen and a struggling pupil at a local comprehensive school.

Annie's biggest worry was what would happen when Spode came out of hospital. Would he want her to go and live with him? Jake reckoned it was too late for her to accuse him of rape now. She should have done it straight away.

'Mind you, even then it wouldn't have done yer any good. Yer a kid, nobody believes kids. Fellers like him can wriggle out of owt. Haven't yer got any aunties or uncles or grandparents or owt?'

'No . . . there was just me and my mam, really. My grandma Jackson's still alive, but she's gone doolally and she's in a home. I've got an Uncle Ronnie, but he lives in Canada and I've never seen him. Could be dead for all I know.'

It was Sunday afternoon and they were in what Mrs Laycock called the sitting room. Half a dozen mismatched dining chairs, two old settees and a fairly modern gramophone, left to the home in someone's will. Unfortunately they didn't leave any records to play on it. Annie and Jake were on their own, the sitting room was rarely used.

'Yer could run away,' he suggested.

'Don't think I haven't thought of it. If I had some money to get by on for a while, I'd be off.'

'I could come wi' yer,' he offered. 'I've run away before.'

'We still need money.'

Jake nodded. 'I'll think o' summat,' he said. 'There's allus ways an' means,' he said, mysteriously.

'I'm not stealing,' said Annie, quickly.

'Who said owt about stealin'?'

'I'm just saying, that's all.'

Jake abandoned a certain plot he'd been hatching and turned his mind to more honest ways of making money. 'I suppose we could go carol singing,' he said. 'What're yer like at singing?'

'I once sang on stage with Guy Mitchell.'

'Yer never!'

'I did. He got me up out of the audience. I might not be tuneful, but I'm loud.' She drew a fond thought from her memory and smiled. 'My mam used to say I sounded like a cow in labour.'

Jake could only make partial sense of the analogy, but he didn't want to show his ignorance. 'Me too,' he grinned. 'I can play a mouth organ though.'

A clatter of feet in the hallway had them both turning round. Four of the younger children had returned from Sunday School choir practice. Annie and Jake had resisted all attempts to persuade them to go. Sunday morning service was more than enough for them. Both bore an unspoken grudge against God for allowing them to be treated the way they had been. Mrs Laycock's voice came from upstairs.

'Come on. Let's hear yer then,' she shouted.

The children hesitated, looking uncertainly at each other. Then Annie heard one of them counting the others in. 'Silent Night' began in perfect harmony, a small boy singing descant. Annie was mesmerised, Jake's brain was working overtime. As the last note died sweetly away, his plan was formulated. Mrs Laycock clapped loudly and was still clapping when she poked her head round the door.

'Hear that?' she said, sharply. 'That's what happens when yer put yer mind ter doin' summat. Mind you, I might as well be talkin' ter t' wall as talk ter you two.'

Jake grinned at Annie after the woman had left. 'I've got an idea,' he said.

The children were reluctant to go along with the plan as put to them by Annie.

'We want you to come carol singing with us to get some money for Mrs Laycock's Christmas present.'

'On the other hand,' suggested Jake, 'we could buy ourselves Christmas presents wi' the money.'

This idea had their full support. It was probably the only chance they had of getting something they actually wanted. Dependent on charity as they were, the presents they got were usually books, things for school or clothes. This was their chance of getting themselves a proper present.

'Right,' said Jake. 'We'll start ternight. I'll work out a route and we'll all meet here at half-past six.' He tapped the side of his nose. 'And not a word ter no one.'

Four heads nodded and Jake grinned at Annie. 'All we've got ter do is mime and collect the brass.'

'What about you playing the mouth organ?' she suggested. 'Do you know any carols?'

'I can play "Old MacDonald Had a Farm".'

‘That’s near enough,’ she laughed.

Jake’s organisation was impeccable. He took his charges to a grid of terraced streets where the doors opened out on to the pavement and his choir could sing to two houses at once, thereby doubling the take. His collection tin with a convincing home-made label was a master stroke.

‘We’re collecting for the Halifax Road Children’s Home,’ he announced, every time a door was opened. ‘These children belong there. It’s to give them a good Christmas.’

Money was happily handed over. Encores were sung for an extra threepence and the collecting tin became heavy in Annie’s hand.

‘Why don’t you tell them we belong there as well?’ she enquired.

‘Sounds greedy if yer collecting money for yerself. Nobody likes a greedy bugger.’

Annie admired the psychology of this. In just an hour and a half they made nearly two pounds. Jake led them home and gave each delighted chorister five shillings.

‘Same time tomorrow,’ he said. ‘And remember,’ he tapped the side of his nose, ‘say nowt ter nobody.’

The following night they did a twenty-minute session outside all the working men’s clubs in the area, six in all. The take went up to two pounds seventeen and six. Three half-crowns for each of the four choristers . . . they’d never been so wealthy. Annie felt guilty at her and Jake taking the lion’s share.

‘Don’t be daft, we’re management,’ he argued.

‘You might be. I’m just collecting the money.’

‘I know,’ he grinned. ‘But it’s that face o’ yours, innit? Yer’ve got one o’ them faces what makes ’em cough up a bit more brass.’

‘Have I?’

‘Yeah – yer’ve got summat about yer. Has no one never told yer?’

‘No.’

'Well, you 'ave. Summat special.'

'Oh.'

It was inevitable that Mrs Laycock would find out. Her face was set in stone and her arms akimbo as they returned after their fifth lucrative night.

'And where do you think you've been?' she demanded.

'Carol singing,' said Annie, defiantly.

'I know very well you've been carol singing. I also know you've been collecting money for this place. You know that's against the law, don't you?'

The four younger children hung their heads.

'I've just had a woman round ter give me some money. She said she couldn't find her purse when yer knocked on her door, so she brought it round later.'

Annie glared at Mrs Laycock. 'Since when was carol singing against the law?'

'Collecting money under false pretences, that's against the law,' snapped the house mother, looking at the collecting tin.

'What false pretences?' persisted Annie. 'We told everyone we were collecting for the home and that we were from there.'

A sneer came over Mrs Laycock's face. 'Well, if yer collectin' money for the home yer'd better hand it over. As I'm in charge, I'll say what's done wi' it.'

Jake took the youngest boy by his shoulders and positioned him in front of their house mother. The boy's eyes were glued to the ground. He daren't look up.

'Kevin,' said Jake, 'remember when I first suggested us goin' carol singin' – what did Annie say we should do wi' the money?'

The boy was too nervous to reply but one of the other children remembered. 'She said we could buy Mrs Laycock a Christmas present.'

The house mother glared at them all in disbelief, then lifted Kevin's chin and stared into his worried eyes. 'Yer know what happens ter little boys what lie, don't yer, Kevin?'

Kevin wasn't sure what happened, but he knew it wasn't anything good so he nodded. 'Yes, Mrs Laycock.'

'Is it true then?'

Kevin thought for a while, then nodded again. 'Yes, Mrs Laycock. That's what Annie said all right.'

There was a long silence. Jake took the tin from Annie and handed it to Mrs Laycock. It contained about two pounds. The night's takings.

'We've done ever so well,' he said. 'We've been makin' four or five bob a night. There must be nearly two quid in there.'

Still suspicious, she took the tin from him. She knew something wasn't quite as it seemed, but she couldn't put her finger on it.

'I'll only take half of it,' she said. 'The little 'uns can share the other half between 'em.' She looked at Annie and Jake. 'Not you two, though. I reckon it were them what did all the singin'.'

'That's right,' agreed Jake, cheerfully. 'Me and Annie can't sing for toffee. Merry Christmas, Mrs Laycock.'

Annie watched the house mother usher the smaller children back into the home, then took Jake's arm. 'Jake Parker, that was brilliant! If you weren't so ugly, I'd kiss you.'

'And if you didn't have a face like a cow's arse, I'd let yer.'

'Ah, you can't say that because you once said there was something special about my face.'

Jake turned and looked at her. Seriously at first, then his expression lapsed into a broad grin. 'Don't be such a bighead, Annie Jackson.'

In all her life Annie had never liked anyone as much as she liked Jake.

Christmas came and went. There was a party with games and balloons and fancy hats. Annie and Jake took a back seat. They were the oldest and far too mature for such silliness. Each spent their carol-singing money on the other.

Annie bought him the most expensive harmonica two pounds could buy, with a button on the side for changing key (or something), and Jake bought Annie four Guy Mitchell records to play on the gramophone in the sitting room. Running away was postponed until the spring. They would go together, maybe head for Liverpool and stow away on a ship heading for America.

In the meantime another worry had presented itself. Annie hadn't had a period since being raped by Spode. Movita, who was studying human biology, said it was understandable after all she'd been through and Annie found it convenient to agree.

She invited Jake to see in the New Year in her room. Strictly forbidden, of course, but she wanted someone to talk to and to say 'Happy New Year' to. She let him in to her room at eleven o'clock. On her only table was a candle, a bottle of cider and four mince pies she'd stolen from the kitchen. Jake found her preparations amusing.

'I've never been to a society dinner before.'

'Watch it, or it might be your last.'

'Sorry.'

Annie had an ulterior motive for inviting him to her room. Up until then he'd never spoken of his past. He knew all about hers and had been a rock to lean on whenever she'd felt down.

'Jus' remember, Annie,' he'd say, 'they're all bastards except you and me. But we're better than them. Just you wait an' see.'

She handed him a mince pie and poured him a teacupful of cider. 'I suppose you'll be leaving school when you're fifteen?'

He grinned. 'Not much choice. I don't spend much time there as it is.'

Annie couldn't understand this. School to her was a haven from an otherwise sad life. He read her thoughts.

'Learnin' an' me don't get on,' he explained. 'Nobody in our 'ouse could read nor write an' I'm no better. All t' teachers 'ave given up on me.'

'What? You can't read or write?'

'I can write me name an' read a few old words, but not much more.' He saw the look of concern on her face and grinned. 'Hey, don't you worry about me. I can allus get a job on t' buildin' sites or mebbe in a garage. Yer don't need ter read an' write in them jobs. I'm good at football as well,' he added. 'Might get a trial wi' Bradford City.'

'But, Jake, you're very bright. I can tell by just talking to you. You should learn to read and write.'

'It's a bit late now,' he pointed out. 'I'm leavin' school at Easter. Then I'm leavin' this place.'

'And I'm coming with you.'

'I know – we'll 'ave ter start makin' plans.'

Annie nodded. 'How long have you been in homes?' She'd never delved into his past before.

He paused for a long time then looked up at her, his eyes suddenly distant and frightened. As if there were things out there he didn't want to remember. Annie reached across the table and placed her hand on his. Then he blinked and smiled.

'Since I was nine,' he said.

She looked at him, hoping for more information. He shrugged and obliged. This was the first time he'd unburdened himself to anyone. The first time he'd met anyone who mattered enough to talk to about it.

'Me mam had this boyfriend who were a bit of a nancy boy. He used to . . . yer know, muck about with me on a night when I were in bed. Me mam knew about it, but she never did nowt. Well, she did actually, she used ter lock me under t' stairs when I cried. Her idea o' bein' a mother.' The memory registered in his eyes which became sad and distant. 'They'd go out on a night an' get drunk, next thing I know he'd be in me bedroom. It were happenin' all the time. He said if I told anyone about him he'd kill me, so I used ter knock off school in case anyone asked how I got me bruises.'

'Bruises?'

'I sometimes used ter lose me rag an' call him "arseface" – he'd knocked seven shades o' shit outa me.'

'You shouldn't swear so much,' Annie scolded, gently.

'Sorry.'

He told the story with no hint of self-pity, just giving the facts. Snow was falling outside by the time he stood up and walked to the window. Annie joined him. Together they watched the falling snowflakes glow as they came within range of a street lamp, settling on the ground, hiding all the dirt and grime beneath their pristine purity. Annie wished she could cover over the grime of her own life as easily. Jake continued his story.

'One night, just after me tea, I must've said summat I shouldn't so they gave me a good hidin' an' locked me under t' stairs. Then they went out an' left me there. I were only nine.'

Annie felt her heart going out to him as he went on with his story. 'They left me there all night, then t' followin' mornin' I heard 'em both go out. I were hungry by then – and thirsty. So I started kickin' at a wooden panel. I knew I'd get into trouble but I didn't care by this time. Anyroad it broke an' I managed ter crawl out.'

He grinned at Annie. 'I were bloody hungry, I can tell yer. I made meself three jam sandwiches and drank a full pint o' milk. Then I nicked some money outa t' rent tin an' buggered off.'

'Good for you,' said Annie. 'What happened then?'

Jake smiled here, the memory of the next part wasn't at all unpleasant. 'I got a bus out into t' country. It were summer so it weren't cold or nowt. I found this old empty 'ouse in t' middle o' nowhere an' lived there. I did all right for meself,' he said, proudly.

'Anyroad, t' police caught me after a couple o' weeks. I told 'em what he'd done ter me an' said I'd run away again if they sent me back ter live with him. Nobody could prove nowt so they put me in a home.'

'So he got away with it then?'

Jake nodded. 'He called me a liar.' Then he grinned. 'Trouble is, I am – only not about that. Him and me mam split up. She reckons it were my fault, so she never comes near me. Not even at Christmas.' He paused for a long time then said, 'Not that I'm bothered.'

'How many homes have you been in?'

'This is me sixth. I keep gerrin' kicked out for makin' trouble. The only trouble wi' me is I don't like fellers messin' wi' me. I had enough o' that with arseface. No matter what home they send yer to, there's allus a bleedin' nancy boy who thinks he can mess around wi' yer.' He looked at her and grinned. 'I'd kick up a fuss but they'd never believe me.'

'You should have gone to the police.'

Jake shook his head at her naivety. 'I did go to t' police, but I were a kid. The police don't believe kids. I told t' women from t'council when they came ter visit, anybody who I thought might believe me. But nobody did.'

'What about the other children? They could have backed up your story.'

'It doesn't work like that. They were all scared ter say owt. They used ter just kick me out before somebody started believin' me. It suited me. I knew one day I'd end up somewhere like here.'

'Like here? So you think this place is okay, do you?'

Jake shrugged. 'Best I've been to. Mrs Laycock's gorra gob on her like t' Mersey Tunnel, but she's all right.'

Annie studied his face by the light of the street lamp outside. Behind his teenage acne was a pleasant face. With clearer skin he might even progress to becoming handsome. A recent scar above his left eye betrayed his propensity for fighting. Boys like Jake would always need to fight their corner. Despite his outward bravado, the memory of his mother had brought him close to tears. A thought struck Annie.

'I could teach you,' she said.

'Teach me what?'

'I could teach you to read and write.'

He considered her offer as he munched on a mince pie. It was a good offer. Secretly he'd always wished he'd paid more attention at school. He knew he wasn't the dunce they made him out to be, but didn't know how to prove them wrong. Annie was offering him a chance.

'Fair enough,' he decided, a little ungraciously. 'Yer on.'

'We'll start tomorrow,' said Annie. 'It'll be your New Year's Resolution – to learn to read and write.'

'New Year's Resolution? I've never made one of them before. What about you – have you made one?'

She went quiet, a picture of Spode uppermost in her thoughts. 'Oh, yes,' she said. 'I've made one all right.'

In the room below she could hear Mrs Laycock's radio as the old year drew to a close.

'I think it's nearly twelve o'clock,' said Annie.

The chimes of Big Ben from below confirmed this.

'Happy New Year, Jake,' she said, holding out her arms to him. They stood up together and he returned her embrace nervously.

'Happy New Year, Annie.'

She kissed his cheek, lightly. 'You've got to kiss and make a New Year's wish,' she said.

He thought this over for a second then kissed her fully on her lips. They were still embracing when the door opened.

Mrs Laycock had made her way upstairs after hearing more than one set of footsteps moving about in Annie's room. The thought of someone having more fun than her on New Year's Eve annoyed the hell out of her. Leaving the chimes of Big Ben booming out on her radio, she crept up the stairs and quietly opened Annie's door. She and Jake were locked in an embrace in the middle of the room.

'Jake Parker, get out of here this instant, you dirty boy!' she shouted, angrily. Annie held on to Jake's arm and stood her ground.

'He's not a dirty boy,' she said firmly. 'He was giving

me a New Year's kiss. That's not being dirty.'

'That's all I was doing, honest, Mrs Laycock,' confirmed the embarrassed youth.

'Yer know the rules as well as anyone – and rules are made for a purpose. Out, my lad, or yer'll feel the back of my hand.'

She was a substantially built woman and such a threat was not to be taken lightly. Jake half turned to Annie.

'Now!' snapped Mrs Laycock.

After he had gone the two of them squared up to each other. Annie was seething. 'That wasn't fair,' she complained, bitterly. 'He was only being friendly.'

'It's how friendly – that's what bothers me. I've a reputation ter keep. So first thing tomorrow I'm having you to the doctor's for a pregnancy test.'

'What?'

'You heard.'

'I heard, but you can't make me go.' Annie was in tears.

Mrs Laycock suddenly sighed, as if she'd used up all the anger at her disposal. 'Annie, I *can* make you go – and I will.'

Annie went to the door and held it open. 'Please leave, Mrs Laycock. I think you're the most awful woman I've ever come across.'

The house mother was upset at this. Maybe she'd gone too far; she'd never been called 'an awful woman' before. Christ! What sort of an ogre was this place turning her into?

'Well, I'm very sorry yer feel like that,' she said, subdued. 'It's not me what makes the rules – but it's my job ter see they're kept.'

Annie said nothing but pushed the door shut with a bang the second the house mother left. Perhaps having a pregnancy test would do no harm. It would relieve her of a nagging doubt if nothing else.

She breathed on the window to melt a hole through the film

of frost, then rubbed it clear with her fingers before peering through at the shivering, skeletal trees and the hoary lawn that comprised the bleak back garden of Halifax Road Children's Home.

'Who's the father?' Mrs Laycock's voice came from behind. 'As if I didn't know.'

'That's right, you don't know,' said Annie without looking round. 'In fact, I've never come across a woman of your age who knows so little.'

'It's that Jake Parker, isn't it?'

'No.'

'Who is it then?'

'You wouldn't believe me if I told you – no one would.'

'Oh, yes, and why wouldn't I believe you?' sniffed Mrs Laycock. Her decision to send Annie for a pregnancy test had been justified, but she felt no satisfaction at the result. The idea had been to try and shock Annie into keeping to the straight and narrow; she hadn't thought for a minute that the test would be positive.

'Was it a member of the royalty what got yer up the spout? Happen the Duke of Edinburgh's been putting it about?'

Her sarcasm stemmed from disappointment in a girl she'd actually grown to like. Although it would never have done to show Annie that; it might smack of favouritism.

'You wouldn't believe me, Mrs Laycock, because I'm a fifteen-year-old girl in trouble. All I can say is that it wasn't of my making. I've done nothing wrong.'

Mrs Laycock assumed an arms akimbo stance, annoyed that Annie wouldn't turn round. 'Nothing wrong? You've dropped your drawers for some dirty man. If there's nothing wrong with that then God help us all.'

'Your right about the dirty man bit, Mrs Laycock. But as for the rest of it, you couldn't be more wrong.' She turned to face the house mother but looked straight through her. The woman couldn't hurt her now. 'Anyone with a grain of intelligence should be able to figure out what happened to me, so there's no point me trying to explain it to you.'

Mrs Laycock stared at her, wondering whether or not to relent. But showing such weakness would make a rod for her own back. Others would be tempted to exploit it.

'One more thing, Mrs Laycock,' continued Annie. 'Jake Parker has been sexually abused by the staff of every home he's been sent to except this one. I know you're too stupid to believe it, but it's true. For the first time in years he felt safe here. The odds are that it will start again now that you've kicked him out of here for doing nothing.'

Mrs Laycock stared at her. No way could she allow herself to believe such nonsense. Perhaps seeing her mother killed had mentally unbalanced the girl. If so she was in the wrong place. As were most of her residents. She looked at Annie again and saw the truth in the girl's face. With her conscience now riddled with doubt and guilt, the house mother left the room, leaving Annie to her thoughts.

She was pregnant by her step-father. Of all the things that had happened to her this had to be the worst. Somehow she must find someone to confide in. Jake had been moved to another home as soon as the news broke. The doctor couldn't be absolutely precise as to how far along she was, but it could have happened the first week she'd moved into the home, making Jake the prime suspect.

Movita was shocked when Annie rang her with the news. It had taken Annie all her time to stop her friend going to the police.

'No, Movita, it'd make matters worse. Who'd believe me?' she argued. 'They'd say I was only accusing him out of spite because he killed my mother.'

'No one's saying he killed your mother.'

'They might think I think he killed her.'

'Did he kill her?'

'Yes.'

'Look, Annie, if there's anything I can do to help - God, it's a pig being so far away at a time like this!'

'I wish I had you here,' said Annie. 'I don't know who to

turn to. Jake was lovely but they've sent him away.'

'Sounds as though you and Jake hit it off together?'

'We did, but not like you mean. He was a good friend to me. Movita . . .'

'What?'

'They think he's the father.'

'Oh, heck! The pips are going. Annie, try Miss Bulm . . .'

The line went dead but Annie caught the name. Miss Bulmer was her form teacher at school. She had a soft spot for Annie.

'So, I leave you alone for a couple of weeks and you get yourself pregnant!'

Leonard Spode stood in the doorway, moving momentarily to one side to let Doreen out. Annie's room mate certainly didn't want to be part of this confrontation.

He supported himself with crutches which drew Annie's eyes down to his bandaged, shoeless foot. His face was still hospital pale with a livid scar across his forehead between two short lines of tiny dots which Annie found herself counting. She knew this scar was her contribution to his injuries. Ten stitches – not much considering the effort she'd put into the blow. He'd raped her, made her pregnant, killed her mother, and this was how she'd repaid him. Ten stitches weren't enough, nowhere near enough. She held him in her gaze, disgust and hatred spilling from her eyes.

'You made me pregnant and killed by mother,' she said, simply. 'You're a rapist and a murderer!'

The accusation took him aback. He'd been told the father was one of the residents. For the life of him he couldn't remember exactly what had gone on that night. He vaguely remembered getting into Annie's bed and maybe trying it on with her but the drink and the fall and the bang on the head had blurred his memory. Was she telling the truth? Had all his careful planning come to fruition and he'd been too damn' drunk to know anything about it? Christ! The trouble he'd gone to and all he'd got was one drunken screw he couldn't even remember. He remembered who'd hit him on the head, though.

'I beg your pardon?' he said.

'I think you heard.'

'Mrs Laycock's right, you're mentally unbalanced. Must run in the family.'

This slur against her dead mother sparked Annie's temper. 'I'll get you back for this,' she shouted, advancing on him. 'I'll tell anyone I think might believe me.'

'That's no one, including me.'

'Miss Bulmer, she'll believe me. She'll make things difficult for you – and Mr Lindis, he knows what really happened.'

The mention of his agent's name took him aback slightly. He recovered and pointed to the livid scar on his forehead. 'If anyone's going to get into difficulties,' he threatened, 'it isn't going to be me. I saw who did this and a word in the right ear could see you locked up for attempted murder.'

'I should have killed you like you killed Mam. I should have killed you for what you did to me.'

He sneered in her face. 'Yes, my dear, perhaps you should, but you missed your chance.'

Annie collected herself. She'd let him get to her, which was wrong. All the fear she'd ever had of this man had been washed away by the immense tide of loathing she now felt for him.

'Mr Spode,' she spat his name out, '*I will get you back for what you did. Just you wait and see.*'

The tone of her voice sent a shiver down his spine. He tried to laugh but the sound that came out was more of a grunt. He turned and walked out of her life.

Gloria Bulmer gave Annie a smile as the girl approached her along the school corridor, a smile that lifted Annie's dejected spirits. Miss Bulmer was a life-belt bobbing about in the black ocean of her despair, her only hope. Mrs

Laycock, who was supposed to be in charge of her welfare, was acting like Snow White's step-mother. There was no point confiding in her. And no point telling all and sundry, only to become a laughing stock. She had to choose her allies carefully.

'Hello, Annie.' There was a measure of sympathy in the teacher's voice that was rare in Annie's life. 'How are you coping?'

'Not so good, miss,' she admitted. 'Miss, I wonder if I could have a talk to you – please?'

The teacher seemed to be expecting this. It was lunchtime and the staffroom would be occupied. She looked through the glass door of an adjacent classroom.

'In here,' she said.

Annie followed the teacher into the empty classroom where Miss Bulmer turned to face her. She was very pretty and quite young, and to counterbalance this had tied her dark hair back and donned unnecessary spectacles in an attempt to make herself look bookish. Miss Bulmer, Annie's only hope, was a popular and energetic teacher of History and English.

'I understand you're pregnant,' she said gently, sitting on the corner of the teacher's desk and taking off her glasses.

Annie was taken aback. The people in the home weren't supposed to tell anyone yet until her future had been decided.

'Who told you?'

'Your step-father was here yesterday. He told me everything.'

'I doubt that, miss.'

Miss Bulmer walked to the door and looked up and down the corridor before taking a packet of American cigarettes from her pocket and expertly flicking one out.

'I know you smoke.' She smiled. 'But excuse me for not offering you one, I quite like my job.' She lit up from an old lighter which took several attempts to ignite. 'He seems a very nice chap to me,' she went on. 'I expect he'll do well as a politician.'

'He raped me, miss. That's why I'm pregnant.'

If Annie's intention was to shock the teacher, she failed. Gloria Bulmer blew smoke over Annie's head, her cheerful blue eyes suddenly sad.

'I was hoping you wouldn't say that, Annie. I was hoping he was wrong about you.'

'Wrong, miss? How do you mean?'

'He told me you might say something like that.'

'But it's true, miss.'

'Annie, I thought you and I were friends. Don't play me for a fool to suit your own ends.'

Annie was crestfallen. 'I'm not, miss. He raped me the night my mother was killed. She pulled him off me and he pushed her down the stairs.'

'So you think he killed your mother?'

'He *did* kill my mother, miss. Please, you've got to believe me!'

Miss Bulmer frowned and drew deeply on the cigarette. 'Have you any idea of what you're accusing him?' Even in a crisis she was careful not to end a sentence with a preposition, especially before a pupil.

'I'm just telling you what happened, miss.' Annie saw her only hope drifting away, creating deep resentment within her. Why should she have to plead with people? She was the victim in all this. 'You're like all the others,' she added, resentfully.

The teacher was slightly offended at this, although she wasn't sure who the 'others' were. She wanted to believe Annie, but had seen a change in her over the past few months. A change brought to the school's notice by the so-called wicked step-father. There was another big question mark over this story and it was time to confront Annie with it. She dropped the cigarette on the floor and crushed it under her foot. Annie watched these movements in sullen silence, their eyes meeting after the teacher had picked up the incriminating tab-end and dropped it in a waste paper basket.

'Annie,' said Miss Bulmer, 'just listen to yourself. You're telling me he raped you and killed your mother, but at the time you didn't see fit to mention it to anyone. What do you take me for?'

'I thought you were my friend.'

'I am your friend but there are limits. I just cannot believe you wouldn't have said something at the time it was all supposed to have happened instead of waiting until now. Annie, I know you – you wouldn't have been able to contain yourself. I know *I* wouldn't. Good heavens, if something like that happened to me I'd have told everyone who could hear me, but you didn't say a word.'

'But I did, miss,' she remembered. 'I did tell someone.'

'Oh, and who was that?'

'Mr Lindis, he's Spode's agent. Before the police came I told him what had happened and he said not to tell anyone or I'd be accused of attempted murder.'

Annie story was sounding more and more far-fetched to the teacher. She sighed.

'Attempted murder? Annie, why would you be accused of attempted murder?'

'Because I hit Spode with a vase and knocked him out, miss.'

Gloria Bulmer's head was spinning now. She held up her hands.

'Right,' she decided. 'If what you say is true there's only one course of action. You must get hold of Mr Lindis and get him to confirm your story.'

'*Then* will you help me?'

'Yes, Annie, I'll help you all I can. Ring me at home tonight and let me know what's happening.'

Malcolm Lindis was struggling with his conscience. He'd just heard that Annie was pregnant and didn't need to put two and two together to work out the reason why. He was now wishing to God he hadn't rung Spode's house at that inopportune moment and got himself involved. Annie was bound to tell the police the truth and she'd want him to back her up. God! What a mess. She'd want him to admit to the police that she'd told him about the rape and that she'd kept quiet about it on his advice. Never mind Spode's career, his own career was up the spout. Not to mention his freedom.

When the phone rang he somehow knew it was her. His hand hovered over the receiver for a second before snatching it from its cradle.

'Hello!' he said. His throat was dry and it didn't sound like him.

'Could I speak to Mr Lindis, please?'

It was Annie. He could say Mr Lindis was out and would ring her back. It would give him more time to think.

'Hello?' she said, wondering why he hadn't answered.

He cleared his throat and took a determined breath. Whatever you're going to do, Lindis, do it now.

'Speaking,' he said.

'Ah,' said Annie. 'It didn't sound like you. Er – this is Annie Jackson.'

'Hello, Annie, how are you?'

'Pregnant,' she said bluntly.

'Oh, I am sorry.'

'And we both know who the father is.'

'Do we?'

'Leonard Spode,' she said. 'I should have told the police there and then what happened, but you told me not to.'

'Annie, what on earth are you talking about?'

He'd made up his mind how to deal with it: wash his hands of the whole business. There was silence from Annie's end as she began to realise what she might be up against.

'Mr Lindis – when I told you about Spode raping me, you told me not to say anything or I might be accused of attempted murder. And now, because I didn't say anything at the time, no one is going to believe me. But they will if you tell them what I told you.'

'Annie, when I got to you, you were delirious. I couldn't

make head nor tail of what you were talking about. I can't go making up stories just for your benefit.'

'But, Mr Lindis ...' She was stuck for words. 'So you're not going to help me?'

'Of course I want to help you, but I'm not going to lie to the police.'

'Oh, I see ... Mr Lindis?'

'Yes.'

'In many ways this makes you as bad as Spode. I hope you get what's coming to you.'

A chill went down Lindis' spine and he wasn't at all sure he'd done the right thing.

Annie picked up the phone again and dialled Gloria Bulmer at home.

'It's Annie,' she said, faintly.

'Yes, Annie. Have you spoken to him?'

'He ... er ...' Annie was fighting back the tears. 'He won't help me, miss.'

It didn't surprise the teacher. Try as she might she couldn't see any substance in Annie's version of events. It was high time the girl stopped trying to fool everyone.

'Look, Annie,' she said, gently. 'You're angry at Mr Spode because you think he was responsible for your mother's death, and you're trying to get back at him. I don't know, maybe if it had happened to me I'd do the same. Who knows how we'll react in such circumstances? But it's not fair on him.'

Annie was now totally defeated. There was nowhere else to turn. She shouted down the phone at Miss Bulmer, who was no longer her friend: 'But it's never happened to you, has it, miss? So you don't know what you're talking about. I'm telling you the truth!'

Without waiting for a reply she put the phone down on an uncomfortable Gloria Bulmer.

Annie's parting shot weighed heavily on Malcolm Lindis' mind. *You're as bad as Spode. I hope you get what's coming to you.* He sighed as he turned his car into Spode's street. If Annie's accusations were true he didn't want to be bracketed with a rapist. He been called many things: ruthless, hard-nosed, unfeeling. His integrity had been called into question more than once, but that was the name of the game. His job was to guide people on to one of the green leather benches in the House of Commons. Many of these people would otherwise have difficulty finding their way to a decent seat in the pictures. He frequently had to be unscrupulous, but it was wrong of him to condone rape. At the time it had seemed a good idea for Annie to keep quiet until it became clear what she was letting herself in for. Okay, it was in his interests too that she kept quiet, and if she hadn't rung the other night he'd have swept the matter into a dark corner of his mind.

However, there was an outside chance that Annie was lying. He needed to remove that doubt before he made his next move. Whatever that would be.

Spode's Jaguar was occupying the drive so he left his Rover by the kerb and walked across the lawn to the front door. Spode opened it, a walking stick in his hand and a broad beam on his face.

'Malcolm, great to see you, come in.'

He entered, his glance flickering down to the spot where Olga had died, with Spode's half-naked body lying across her. How could the man be so bloody cheerful, standing right there, where it had happened?

Malcolm Lindis followed the politician through into the living room, where he and Spode had spent many hours planning the election campaign. He couldn't fail to notice the absent wedding photograph of Leonard and Olga which had hung on the fireplace wall. Annie's recent school photograph, various ornaments and bits and pieces which had belonged to Spode's late wife, were also no longer on show. All evidence of his dead wife and her daughter had been removed from the room. What sort of bereaved husband and step-father would do such a thing?

Over a glass of whisky they went through the usual small talk about business, Leeds United and the weather. No mention of Olga or Annie. Malcolm thought this was either callous or too painful for Spode to talk about. Something told him it wasn't the latter, but if it was, it was just hard luck, Malcolm wanted to talk about it.

'I went to Olga's funeral,' he said.

'So I heard,' replied Spode. He tapped his leg, which was still in plaster. 'Couldn't manage it myself. Sent some flowers though.'

There was a long silence as Malcolm chose his words. 'I was the first here that night,' he began. 'You were unconscious and Annie was crying her eyes out. Olga was ...'

'Dead,' Spode finished his sentence for him. 'Bit of horseplay that went wrong. Both of us were drunk.' There wasn't a hint of regret in his voice, he could have been talking about next-door's cat.

'That's exactly what I told the police,' said Malcolm. 'Almost verbatim in fact. Only I made it up because you were still unconscious when the police arrived ... Annie, who saw it all, told me a completely different story.'

'Did she really? And what did that lying little slut have to say for herself?' Spode threw his whisky down his throat and poured himself another. Malcolm stood in front of him and looked him straight in the eye.

'Leonard,' he said, challengingly, 'she told me you'd raped her and Olga dragged you off. The two of you were fighting and fell down the stairs.'

Spode dropped his gaze and sat down heavily in an easy chair, his face reddening. He took another drink.

'And which version do you believe, Malcolm?' He almost spat the words out.

The truth was now crystal clear to the agent. An innocent man would have denied such an accusation instantly. He felt a sudden loathing of this man. This rapist he'd just helped to win an election. His voice mirrored his feelings.

'What? You mean between Annie's version and the

version I made up for you – the one you found it convenient to go along with? It's hardly a difficult choice, is it?'

Spode got to his feet and squared up to him. 'Get out!' he roared. 'And don't make accusations you can't prove or I'll destroy you, Lindis.'

Malcolm backed away, convinced now that he'd made the right move in confronting Spode. What his next move was to be, he wasn't sure. Spode was right, neither he nor Annie had any proof that a rape had been committed. He had to tread carefully or he might end up a lot worse off than Spode.

The following night, Thursday, was Malcolm Lindis' Rotary night. As usual it was held in the function room of the George Hotel at the top of Tunnel How Hill. He left at midnight, slightly the worse for drink after celebrating his selection as chairman elect. His intention was to walk home, in fact he'd assured his concerned companions that he'd be doing just that, but it was freezing outside. A taxi would have been a sensible solution. He stood in the pub doorway, wondering whether or not to go back inside and ring up Fairway Cabs. His Rover stood temptingly in the car park. What were the chances of being stopped by the police? None if he drove carefully. The battle against common sense was lost.

The road back down was steep and winding, unlit for a mile until it reached a built-up area. Malcolm didn't get that far. His brakes failed at the first sharp turn, sending his car plunging through a stone wall and over the edge of Midgeley's Quarry. No one saw the accident. Mrs Lindis assumed he'd stayed the night at a friend's house as he often did. She planned giving him a telling off for not ringing her.

His car was found the following morning by a couple of quarrymen. It was assumed that Malcolm must have died instantly. A blood test showed him to be way over the limit. The mechanical report on the car's roadworthiness was filed away without being brought up at the inquest. A brake pipe had come adrift, but this was dismissed as being inconclusive. It could have happened as a result of the one-hundred-foot plunge.

Chapter Ten

The time she spent in the Barrack Road Maternity Hostel might have been the loneliest of Annie's life had it not been for an unlikely friendship. Movita sent her a couple of letters, but for reasons best known to herself she stopped writing. Out of sight, out of mind probably. This hurt Annie more than she cared to admit to herself. Had the situation been reversed, no way would she have abandoned her friendship with Movita, despite their living in different towns. She read about Lindis' death and felt odd at having spoken to him just a few days before he died, but she felt no pity for him. He'd done her no favours.

Jake rang just once, telling the woman who answered the phone that he was Annie's Uncle Ronnie. Annie picked up the phone wondering why her uncle should be ringing her.

'Annie, it's me, Jake. I'm not supposed ter contact yer, so I told 'em I were somebody else.'

'Hello, Uncle Ronnie,' she replied, going along with his subterfuge. 'How nice to hear from you.'

'Everybody reckons I'm the baby's dad.'

Annie looked down at the woman who was listening intently to this conversation despite having her nose in a magazine.

'So I heard,' she said. 'I've told everybody that's not the case.'

'It's him, isn't it?' said Jake, not attempting to hide the disgust in his voice.'

'Yes,' said Annie. 'It can only be him.'

There was an awkward silence. The woman beside Annie had correctly guessed at the topic of conversation and was hoping for juicy revelations. Annie realised this.

'Can we talk about something else?' she said.

The woman's disappointment was noticeable as she turned over the pages in exasperation.

'Hey!' Jake said. 'Listen ter this. Yer know when I said there were a nancy boy in every home?'

'Yes?' Annie's heart sank. Was it starting again for him?

'Well,' went on Jake, 'the other kids had warned about this bloke called Hardisty. They reckoned he liked pretty boys like me.' Jake used the term without conceit. He knew what he looked like, he could look in a mirror with the best of them.

'Anyroad, what I did, I nicked some green indelible ink from school an' kept it in me pocket. A few days ago he collared me and told me ter come to his room 'cos he wanted ter talk ter me, private like.'

Jake was laughing to himself at this point, making Annie laugh too although she didn't know why yet.

'When he got me inside, he got all smarmy wi' me, like they do. He said he thought I looked lost and needed a cuddle. Next thing I knew he's got his . . . er . . .' He paused, aware that Annie didn't like him using bad language. 'He got his wotsit out . . .'

'What's a wotsit?' she teased.

'Yer know – that thing what I've got and you haven't.'

'Oh, right.'

'Anyroad, he told me ter hold it for him. I grabbed it with one hand and poured the ink all over it. He didn't realise what I were doin' at first so I managed ter empty nearly all the bottle on him.'

'What happened then?'

'Yer what? I shot outa that room like shit off a shovel.

Straight ter t' warden's office ter tell him what I'd done. He called me a troublemaker like they all do, so I said it were easy ter prove, all he had ter do were look at Hardisty's wotsit.'

'And did he?'

Jake laughed again. 'No, he was as bad as Hardisty. He gave me a crack round me head, so I ran off ter get the police.'

'I thought the police didn't believe kids?' said Annie.

'They did this time,' chortled Jake. 'I went into the cop shop an' put the bottle of ink on the counter. It were a woman copper what I spoke ter. I said if she wanted to know where the rest of the ink was she should take a look at Mr Hardisty's dick. Then I told her what had happened. When the cops got to Hardisty's room he were panickin' like hell, scrubbin' his dick wi' a Brillo pad an' soap. He were cryin' like a big kid when they took him away. They took the warden away as well.'

Annie screeched with laughter. This was revenge of the sweetest kind. It didn't make up for all the misery Jake had had to endure from these awful people but it gave her hope that one day Spode would suffer a similar fate.

'I'm learnin' ter read,' said Jake.

'Really?' Annie smiled at this.

'Yeah. I asked one of me teachers an' he said if I really wanted to, he'd give me extra lessons after school.'

'That's brilliant. You must stick at it. The trouble with you is you're too dumb to realise how intelligent you are.'

'If I was intelligent, mebbe I'd know what yer talking about.'

Annie giggled. 'Just promise me you'll stick at it. You could go to university if you put your mind to it.'

'Give over – learnin' ter read'll do me.'

'Promise me you'll give it a go?'

'Okay, I promise . . . Annie?'

'Yes.'

'If yer want ter tell everybody that I'm the father, it's okay by me.'

'I couldn't do that. You've your own life to lead.'

'Okay.'

Did Annie detect a hint of relief in his one-word reply? 'When you've learned to read and write, I want you to send me a letter.'

The woman raised an eyebrow. Fancy having an uncle who couldn't read or write.

'You'll be the first person I write to,' promised Jake. 'I've still got a bit of green ink left.'

'I'll look forward to that,' she giggled. ''Bye . . . Uncle Ronnie.'

She put the phone down, her heart lightened by the knowledge that Jake was learning to read and write at her instigation. At least her existence was doing someone a bit of good. Perhaps he would leave school and lead a relatively normal life. Annie couldn't envisage any normality in her own future. All she knew was that she would be having a baby in August and that it would be taken from her, probably without her seeing it.

'Best that way,' one of the care assistants told her. 'Then yer don't get too fond.'

'What if I wanted to keep my baby?'

Her query was hypothetical but the answer was abrupt.

'Yer've caused enough trouble, young lady, without causin' any more. Just do as yer told, else yer'll be out on yer ear.'

Annie was a fallen woman before she'd finished being a girl. It wasn't a free passage, all the girls were expected to work. Cleaning, cooking, washing, gardening – Annie didn't mind much, at least she was safe from the clutches of Spode, who was forever in the papers.

'I gather Leonard Spode, MP is yer step-father,' observed the matron one day, over the top of the *Yorkshire Post*. 'There's a bit about him in here. Will he be comin' ter visit yer?'

'I hope not.'

'Nice way ter treat a fine, decent man like that. God knows what the world's comin' to. I can't say as I blame him if he never comes ter visit.'

Annie was constantly conscious of Spode's threat to expose her as an attempted murderer so she said nothing. Not that it would have done any good. Her word against a respectable Member of Parliament's. She was consumed with thoughts of revenge and prolonged bouts of despair at the impossibility of it all. What chance did she have of getting back at him?

Jimmy's new false teeth were the first thing she noticed about him. Pristine teeth in an ancient face. As obvious as a Woolworth's wig, but he used his new dentures to good effect. His gleaming grin drew a rare one back from her.

'That's better, I knew ye had a pretty smile in ye.'

His accent was from the less salubrious part of Glasgow, softened by many years in England. On his occasional visits back to the Gorbals he was considered a posh speaker, much of his guttural Glaswegian having been replaced by a mixture of English vowels he'd picked up on his travels south of the border. He leaned his sweeping brush against the wall and held out a gnarled hand of friendship.

'I'm Jimmy – caretaker and general dogsbody.'

She took his hand. 'Pleased to meet you, Jimmy, I'm Annie Jackson.'

This brought another white gleam to his face. 'Jackson and Johnstone – they sort of go together. Jack and John, see?'

Annie couldn't help but smile at him. He was a scrawny, wizened gnome of a man with deeply corrugated features under a tartan flat cap which, in the time she knew him, she never saw him without.

'How're they treating ye?' he enquired, his expression transforming from comical to caring.

'Like something nasty they've just trodden in.'

The staff at the hostel were, if anything, more antagonistic towards her than Mrs Laycock had been. She'd detected a softness beneath Mrs Laycock's tough veneer, but there were few soft centres here, especially within the matron, who ran the hostel like a Company Sergant Major.

'Aye,' sympathised the Scotsman. 'Much of ma life has been like that.' His blue eyes twinkled out from their deep sockets. 'Ignore 'em,' he advised. 'They're all holier-than-thou bloody hypocrites.'

Annie nodded and hesitated, wondering if it was impolite just to walk away and leave him to it. She didn't want to be rude to him. In the space of a minute he'd lifted her spirits.

'Ye don't have a spare fag on ye?' he asked, hopefully.

'I've got ten Players. Just bought them with my allowance.'

'That's great. Could I have one for me and one for Tom?'

'Tom who?'

'Tomorrer.'

He laughed at his own joke. Annie joined in, happy with her new friend. She gave him two cigarettes.

'I shall return them on Friday, when I get paid,' he promised.

It didn't matter to Annie, who intended giving up. She'd heard it was bad for pregnant women to smoke. Probably an old wives' tale, but it was better to spend her meagre allowance on something else, like the pictures.

The months dragged by and winter turned into spring and then into summer, and her belly bulged embarrassingly before her. The bump she should have been proud of was a cause for great shame. Out in the street was worst. Fingers pointed, tongues wagged and backs turned as though she was carrying a contagious disease instead of a baby. And still no one came to see her. A visit from Miss Bulmer or Movita would have been welcome – or even Jake. But he, being the suspected father, was forbidden to go near her.

'What will happen to me after my baby's been born?' Annie asked the matron.

'You'd be as well not referring to it as "my" baby. It'll never be your baby. And as for what'll happen to yer, it's not up ter me but I reckon yer'll have ter go back where yer come from.'

'What? Halifax Road Prison. I'm not going back there,' Annie vowed. But she might not have a choice.

A doctor had examined her and found nothing amiss except that she needed glasses, which Annie didn't realise until the world around her came into sharper focus when she donned the round NHS spectacles she was prescribed. Such was her jaded opinion of the world around her that she chose to leave the glasses in their case more often than not.

Jimmy came in twice a week, Mondays and Thursdays. Annie had taken to waiting for him with a welcoming cup of tea. He was a comical little beacon who lit up her drab and gloomy life.

'Do you have any family, Jimmy?' she enquired one day.

Normally there was an unwritten taboo about discussing other people's backgrounds in this place, but Jimmy was different. He was neither a child nor a resident. Although his attitude to life almost qualified him as the former.

'None close enough tae speak of, lassie. Ma wife died in childbirth fifty-seven years ago and ma wee boy died on the twenty-fourth of August, 1914, in the trenches at Mons. He was seventeen years old. I brung him up maself – but not tae be killed by them bastards.'

'The Germans killed my dad as well,' commiserated Annie.

'I wasnae talkin' about the Germans, lassie. I was talking about the bastards in charge of the British Army. They placed nae value on ma boy's life.'

They sat in silence, Annie regretting bringing up the subject of his family.

'What about you?' she asked eventually. 'Were you ever in the army?'

'Aye, lassie, Boer War. I fought wi' Kitchener at Khartoum, Redvers Buller at Ladysmith, I fought wi' Lord

Roberts, I fought wi' General George White.' He grinned broadly. 'In fact, I couldna get on wi' anybody.'

Annie laughed loudly. 'What did you do then?'

His eyes lit up. She knew there was a story here.

'As a job, ye mean?'

She nodded.

'I've failed at many things in my life.'

'Except being a father,' she corrected him. 'I expect you were a brilliant dad.' She inwardly cursed herself for returning to that unhappy subject.

He smiled and placed his hand on her arm, pleased with her compliment. 'I did okay.' Then his grin broadened. 'I was highly successful in one occupation. A master of my trade, you might say.'

'What trade was that?'

He learned towards her. 'D' yer know, lassie – there's only two people in the whole world who knew of my occupation. One's me and the other one's dead and buried.'

Her curiosity was aroused. 'What were you?' she joked. 'A secret agent? A spy?'

'Yer on the right lines,' he admitted. 'I was a burglar.'

'Really?'

It didn't seem an adequate response, but what do you say to someone who's just admitted to a life of crime?

'You don't look like a burglar.'

He laughed. 'And what do burglars look like? The only burglars ye've ever seen are the ones wi' their pictures in the paper after they've been caught. Ye'll never see a picture of a burglar who's never been caught.'

'What? You were never caught?'

'Never once,' he said proudly. 'In a career spanning over twenty years.' He leaned towards her as if to reveal the secrets of his clandestine trade.

'I were trained as a locksmith, lassie. A foolish thing for anyone tae do, eh, hen? Train a Glasgow boy tae understand the mechanism o' locks.'

She nodded her agreement to this.

'When ma boy was killed I went off the rails fer a while, lost ma job and ended up beggin' on the streets. An' there's none sae desperate as a Glasgow street beggar.'

'One day I went intae a big hotel at the end o' Sauchiehall Street. Just tae get warm, ye understand. The concierge was bleedin' ignorant tae me – oh, pardon me, lassie.' His hand went to his mouth. 'I'm not used tae talkin' tae decent people.'

'It's okay.'

'He kicked me outae the door – quite literally – his boot up ma scrawny backside. It was quite painful, I might add.'

'I can well imagine,' sympathised Annie.

'So I went round the back tae the fire escape and was back inside in two minutes. I swear I'd only gone back in outa badness because yer man had been sae rude tae me. Anyhow, I saw this old dowager comin' outae one of thae rooms wi' a wee doggie what walked up tae me and peed on ma leg. She must ha' thought I was a maintenance man or something because she looked at me as if I were a piece o' shite and didn't even apologise or nuthin'. An I tell ye, lassie, there's nuthin' so demeaning as tae have a dog come up and pee on yae leg.'

Annie nodded, then anticipated the next bit. 'You broke into her room, didn't you?'

His gleaming grin told her she was right. He held up a single, bony digit.

'One minute and I was in. I smoked a pipe in them days – cheapest way – so I had a pipe cleaner in ma pocket. After that I fashioned my own tools and I could enter any room within half a minute.'

'What did you steal from the old dowager?'

His eyes narrowed, conspiratorially. 'Ah, that's where I was clever. I only took one item – a diamond ring as big as a marble. She'd hidden it among her underwear. All the rest of her stuff was in a box. I left the room as I found it, locked the door and never heard any more about it.'

'What did you do with it?'

'Well, when ye're on the streets ye learn of people who

perform services. People who'll buy certain goods.'

'A fence?' Annie had picked up the term at the pictures.

'Aye, I only ever used the one. When he died I packed the business in. I got fifty pounds fer it, which in those days was a fortune.'

'It's a fortune now.'

'So I bought a train ticket tae London and booked into one o' them big hotels fer a night. I strolled around the corridors dressed like a businessman, waitin' fer someone likely tae come outa their room tae go doon for dinner. The next day I was on the train home wi' a gold watch and a pearl necklace. Over the next twenty years I made many trips tae the Smoke and various other English cities, always taking one or two choice items and always leaving the room tidy. Most folk didn't realise they'd been robbed until they packed tae leave.'

'So you made a good living out of it?'

'Aye, lassie. Kept me off the dole, so in that respect I was an asset tae society.'

'Why did you end up in Yorkshire?'

Jimmy shrugged. 'I used tae lodge in the house I live in now. It was geographically convenient for ma work. Also the Yorkshire people are very much like the Scots – apart from our characteristic streak of generosity. Anyhow, just after ma fence died the house came up for sale and I bought it wi' ma proceeds.'

'And you were never caught?'

He shook his head. 'The secret is tae be tidy, not tae be greedy and tae be many miles away when the theft is discovered.'

'And didn't you feel guilty about stealing from people?'

This question wasn't as easy to answer. 'I always told myself I was getting back at the ruling classes. The people who sent ma son to his death.'

'But that wasn't true.'

He shrugged, sadly. 'I know, lassie. But everyone needs tae gi' themselves an excuse fer behaving badly – an' I was so good at it.'

'I don't blame you,' she decided.
'Thank ye, lassie. That means a lot tae me.'

The matron had become suspicious of Annie's phone calls from 'Uncle Ronnie'. When he was asked to leave a number where she could contact him, Jake made a garbled excuse and put the phone down. He wrote Annie a simple letter, both to illustrate the progress he was making with his reading and writing and to explain why he'd stopped phoning. The letter was intercepted by the matron and not passed on. Jake's new home was notified and dire warnings issued to him not to contact her again.

Annie couldn't quite understand this. Nor could she understand why Movita had stopped writing - even Miss Bulmer, who'd found Annie's story too horrendous to be true, could at least have written. But the thing that hurt most was not hearing from Jake. The glamorous 'running away' adventure they had planned was just a silly dream, she knew that now. Still, she had Jimmy.

Throughout the summer months they'd spend many an afternoon sitting together on the wooden bench outside the hostel as he sucked on his evil-smelling pipe and related fascinating stories of his nefarious career. For all his dishonesty, he had a basic decency that she hadn't seen in many of the people she'd encountered so far in her short life. Without realising it, Annie grew to depend heavily on his cheerful companionship. Despite being vaguely curious, he never once asked her about the circumstances of her pregnancy. That was Annie's business and if she wanted to tell him, she would.

It wasn't until near the end of her pregnancy that the matron grumbled about their friendship. Annie was on her way outside with two cups of tea. The matron followed her.

'You're not to stop him from working,' she complained one morning. 'He's here to work, not fraternise with the residents.'

Jimmy treated the elderly nurse to one of his disarming

smiles. 'See you, Missis, the pittance they pay me wouldnae keep a wee mouse in cheese fer a day. I do this job as a favour tae ye – and I would be verra much obliged if ye'd remember that.'

The matron was aware of the value of Jimmy's cheap labour and walked away. He took the tea from Annie and looked down at her bulging stomach.

'Not long now, hen?'

'Couple of weeks.'

'How about me an' you goin' tae the pictures ternight?'

Annie was taken aback by his invitation.

'Och, now I've embarrassed ye. I'm just a silly old fool thinking a pretty wee lass such as ye might want tae accompany an old gadget like me tae the cinema.'

'I'd love to come to the pictures with you.'

'Tha's great. I rather fancied seeing Doris Day.'

'What? You mean, *Calamity Jane*?'

'The very same, starring Howard Keel and Doris Day – a young lady tae whom I have been proposing on a regular basis but wi' out much success.'

Annie laughed. 'She must be mad, turning you down. Did you send a photograph?'

'Nae, lassie – I didnae want te ruin ma chances completely. One step at a time. I thought tae overwhelm her wi' ma Celtic allure. I can only think ma letters of proposal must have gone astray.'

'Where did you send them?'

He slurped the dregs of his tea and picked up his sweeping brush. 'Doris Day, USA – keep things simple, that's ma motto. Less things can go wrong.'

That evening *Calamity Jane* became Annie's favourite film of all time and she could well understand Jimmy's infatuation with the star, although a fifty-odd-year discrepancy between him and the delightful Doris might have affected his marital ambitions.

She linked his arm on the way home from the cinema, and no one thought it odd. A young mum-to-be out with her grandad, the most natural thing in the world. Annie wore a raincoat which stretched tightly across her bump and Jimmy was enveloped in a ponderous overcoat he'd liberated from an hotel wardrobe one particularly chilly burglary night. He broke into his version of 'The Deadwood Stage' which Annie joined in with gusto, both of them cracking the reins of an imaginary stage coach as they skipped along the road, to amused smiles from passers-by.

They slowed down to a walk. Jimmy was breathing heavily.

'I'm nae longer in the first flush of youth, lassie,' he panted.

She squeezed his arm. 'Rubbish, you're as old as you feel.'

As they walked, Jimmy's curiosity got the better of him.

'What about the father of yer bairn?' he asked, suddenly. 'Shouldnae he be lookin' after ye – or is that a daft question?'

'It's a daft question.'

'Och, sorry. Me an' ma big mouth.'

'It's okay, you weren't to know.'

'Left ye in the lurch, did he?'

Annie could see he wasn't going to let go until she either told him more or told him to shut up about it. She saw no reason not to tell him. He left her to her thoughts for a while, having enough intuition to realise she was about to tell him a secret.

'Nobody believes me when I tell them what happened. Well, apart from two of my friends but I don't see them any more.'

'I'm your friend,' said Jimmy.

They walked on a few paces before she said, quietly, 'My step-father raped me.'

Jimmy made no comment, though it was a bigger secret than he'd been expecting.

'My mother tried to help me and he pushed her down the stairs and killed her.'

Tears had arrived, but Jimmy said no soothing words because they wouldn't have helped. What helped was him listening and understanding and believing her.

'And ye didnae tell anybody?'

There was no hint of disbelief in his question, just curiosity.

'When I realised Mam was dead, I hit him over the head with a vase – I wanted to kill him. I thought I had for a while and I didn't feel a bit sorry.'

'Ye'd nothin' tae feel sorry for, lassie. The bastard deserved tae die.'

'His agent told me to keep quiet about what had happened.'

'Agent?'

'My step-father's an MP,' explained Annie. 'He had this man who helped him get elected.'

'Oh, right – *that* sort of agent. MP, eh? The ruling classes. I can see why ye kept ye mouth shut – very wise.'

'He's threatening to tell the police I tried to kill him.'

'They'd believe him as well.'

'Who do you believe, Jimmy?' Annie stopped walking and turned to him. 'For all you know I could be a stupid girl just making all this up.'

He took her hand in his. 'That's true, lassie. But ye're not making it up, are ye?'

She shook her head.

'And that's plenty good enough fer me, hen,' he said, then added, 'Bide yer time, lassie. It's on your side. One day ye'll get the bastard back when he's least expecting it.'

'I hope so. People shouldn't get away with things like that.'

He walked her back to the maternity hostel like an attentive boyfriend. Annie pecked him on the cheek just as the matron opened the door.

'I should have thought he'd be too old,' she sneered. 'Even for a little slut like you. I hope yer chargin' pensioners' rates?'

Annie could smell the drink on the woman's breath. She folded her fist into a tight ball and hit the matron with all the force she could muster, knocking her flying back into the hallway.

'She came to the door, drunk,' said Annie. 'And accused me of being a prostitute. I'm sorry but I lost my temper.'

The policewoman looked distinctly uncomfortable at having to charge a frail, heavily pregnant young girl with assault on a formidably built woman such as the matron. The police had been called by the live-in care assistant, Mrs Hughes.

'I witnessed the whole thing,' said Jimmy. He pointed accusingly at the matron, who was still dabbing her blood-ied nose. 'She attacked Annie, using foul and abusive language.'

'You bleedin' liar!' roared the matron, rushing at Jimmy who nearly side-stepped her. A male PC held on to the fuming woman.

'See what I mean, officer?' said Jimmy, innocently. 'They've put a mad woman in charge of a maternity home. It's her ye should be arresting, not this young lady.'

Annie's eyes shone with gratitude for her diminutive champion. Up to now she'd always fought her own battles – and in the main she'd lost. It was nice to have someone on her side for a change.

The WPC looked at Annie with the expression of someone who had much better things to do.

'Do you want to press counter-charges?' she enquired.

'Of course she does,' said Jimmy. He foolishly thrust his face into the matron's. 'If she does, it means yer suspended until it's all sorted out, ye old bag.'

The matron head-butted him with some force, knocking him unconscious.

'That's it,' snapped the WPC. 'I'm arresting you for assault, anything you say may be taken down . . .'

She was still reading the matron her rights as she led the

woman out of the door. The constable looked at Annie, then down at Jimmy who was sitting up, nursing a bruised head.

'I'll need to take statements from you both – do you feel up to it, miss?'

Mrs Hughes chipped in. 'Why don't I make us all a nice cup of tea? Now that it looks as if I might be in charge for a while, we might as well get off to a good start.'

'Where will ye live after ye've had the bairn?' enquired Jimmy as Annie bade him a final goodnight. The policeman had gone and the care assistant was busying herself about her new domain.

'I haven't thought that far ahead. Probably back to the Halifax Road Children's Home.'

'If yer ever stuck, I have a spare room at ma house.'

'Thanks, Jimmy, I might just take you up on that.' She pecked his ancient cheek once again and sent him off into the night, happy with the events of the evening.

Annie lay in bed with Jimmy's offer of a room in his house going round in her mind. For the first time in her life she'd been offered a safe option. It made her feel good. After her baby was born she could go there until things sorted themselves out as surely they must. Jimmy wouldn't let any harm come to her. Maybe she could take her baby with her. It was the first time she'd seriously considered keeping it. She dropped off to sleep with a feeling of optimism about her future. An optimism totally dependent on an ancient, retired burglar.

The following day Annie went into a long, uncomfortable labour, its prematurity perhaps brought on by the events of the previous evening. Her baby was born in the early hours of Saturday morning, delivered by a midwife and whisked away before Annie could see it. She could hear her baby crying in the next room, drawing tears from Annie.

'What did I have – a boy or a girl?' she asked Mrs Hughes.

‘The less you know, the less you’ll fret.’ The look on Annie’s face made the woman relent. ‘If yer must know, yer had a little girl.’

‘A little girl,’ repeated Annie. ‘Is she okay?’

‘Right as a bobbin. Six pounds four ounces.’

‘That’s not such a bad weight, is it?’

‘She’s like a skinned rabbit, but everything’s where it should be.’

There was a long pause before Annie’s next question.

‘Can I see her, please?’

Mrs Hughes sighed, she’d been expecting this. ‘Sorry, love, it’s not allowed.’

Love. It was the first time anyone in the place had used a term of endearment when speaking to Annie.

‘I’d like to call her Doris,’ persisted Annie.

‘You can call her what you like, it’ll not make no difference. What she’s called is nowt to do wi’ you.’

‘But she’s my daughter, surely . . .’

‘Don’t make more trouble for yourself, lass. Once you’re out of here your problems are over. You should be thinkin’ about what you’re goin’ to do with yourself then.’

‘I’ve thought about that and I’d just like to see my daughter – just once, please.’

‘Sorry, love. It’s more than me job’s worth.’

‘But I want to see my baby!’ Annie wept.

She swung her legs from the bed, staggered towards the shocked woman and stumbled forward as the strength deserted her.

‘Now look what you’ve done. Get back into bed, I’ll get a plaster for that.’

Annie looked down at the blood on her leg which she’d caught against the iron bedstead. With the help of Mrs Hughes she got back into bed. The care assistant looked up at Annie as she stuck a plaster across the graze.

‘It could really do wi’ a bigger one but it’s all I’ve got.’

Annie smiled, thinly.

‘By heck, lass, you look fair washed out. Which after

what you've just been through you're entitled to. Havin' a baby takes a lot out of you, stops you thinkin' straight. Tell you what, we'll get some grub inside you and start building you up. Then you can put all this nonsense behind you.' She left with a promise to return with Annie's lunch.

Had Annie not taken Jimmy up on his offer of a night out at the pictures her future would have taken a different course. His offer of somewhere to live became an offer of sanctuary for both her and her beloved daughter, whom she had yet to meet. An offer she now intended to grab with both hands. As her tears dried, she thanked God for sending Jimmy Johnstone.

The sound of Mrs Hughes' footsteps disappeared down the stairs as Annie swung her legs out of bed once more. This time she steadied herself against the bedhead until the dizziness went and she felt strong enough to walk. She opened the door quietly and looked along the short corridor which housed the girls bedrooms. Empty – all the girls would be busy downstairs. Scrubbing, washing, ironing, cooking – no way to treat pregnant women.

Breathing noisily from the exertion, she opened the door of the next room. The nursery. Inside were three cots, two of them empty, but the one near the window contained life. Annie's heart surged as she approached and looked down at her daughter, tears of joy blurring her vision.

'Hello, Doris, I'm your mum.'

Her baby's eyes darted around, then stopped on Annie as she leaned over, blocking the light.

'That's right – I'm your mummy. Come here, my darling.'

She picked up her daughter, wrapped in a white cotton gown and grey woollen blanket. There was a helpless warmth about the child as Annie held her gently to her. She looked briefly around then put the baby to her breast, completing a bond which could only be broken by death.

Her daughter sucked away busily as Annie stroked her dark, downy hair.

'I'm taking you away, my darling. We're going to live with Uncle Jimmy. They can't take you away from me if I've got somewhere to live.'

Annie could hear noises from below which told her someone was about to come up. She took her daughter away from her breast and placed her gently back in the cot, replacing the covers as she'd found them.

'I'll be back for you tonight, my darling.' She blew her daughter a kiss.

Mrs Hughes arrived with a bowl of soup and two slices of toast.

'There's been a bit o' bad news,' she announced.

Annie immediately thought it had something to do with the other night's events. 'How is the matron?' she asked.

'It's nothing to do with her, it's old Jimmy. He was found dead this morning.'

'Old Jimmy? You don't mean Jimmy Johnstone?'

'I do, love.' Then she remembered how friendly Annie had been with the old man. 'Sorry, love. You and 'im were quite close, weren't yer?'

It was like a knife going through Annie's heart. She slumped back in bed. The flimsy thread from which her future hung had just snapped. With her track record, why hadn't she seen it coming?

Mrs Hughes snapped her fingers. 'He must have gone like that – best way really. You don't want to drag on when you get to his age. He were well into his seventies.'

'What was it?' asked Annie, quietly.

'Who knows? Heart attack, old age, fed up wi' living . . . take your pick.'

Annie shook her head. 'He wasn't fed up with living. Maybe it was something to do with matron hitting him the other night.'

Mrs Hughes hadn't thought of that. Having the matron locked up would enhance her career prospects. She brightened considerably. 'He were sat in a chair,' she said, 'looking at a photo someone had sent him in this mornin's post. Some film star – you know, one o' them glamour pusses. She'd signed her autograph on it. I've forgotten who they said it was. Anyway, whoever it was sent him love and kisses apparently.'

'It was Doris Day – he was expecting it.' Annie's voice had become lifeless, empty.

'That's her,' said Mrs Hughes, not noticing the sudden emptiness in Annie. 'Well, it got there just in time then. Eat yer soup. You'll need all the strength you can get.'

Although Annie had no appetite, she realised what she had to do – and Mrs Hughes was right. She'd need all the strength she could get. Dipping her spoon into the hot soup. she asked, 'What date is it?'

'Saturday.'

Annie shook her head, wearily. Why couldn't people answer questions properly?

'No – what date?'

'Oh, I don't know. Let's see, August the twenty-ninth.'

'She's a Virgo then.'

Mrs Hughes nodded, then grinned. 'Not like her mam, eh?'

Annie looked away and Mrs Hughes mentally kicked herself. 'Finish your soup,' she said. 'I'll bring you a cup o' tea and a piece o' cake through later.'

Annie stared after the woman who had shown her more kindness than most over the last few hours, but not enough to let her keep her baby. Jimmy's sudden death had destroyed all her plans. She'd felt despair before but not like this. Perhaps she shouldn't have gone to visit her daughter, it wouldn't have been so bad if she hadn't actually seen her, picked her up and fed her. There was an emptiness inside her now, a space devoid of all emotion. She couldn't cope with the enormity of events so she switched them all off and replaced them with a cold calculating logic. She knew what she had to do. The planning had gone on in her mind for months, all the time she'd hoped for a way out, a way not to have to put her plan into operation. Jimmy's kind offer looked to have been that way out, but who had she been fooling? Relying on an old man to save her from the world. Jimmy had made his grand exit, quick and clean and painless. Which was to be envied. She was glad Doris Day had replied in time, but maybe the shock had seen him off.

Still, you couldn't blame Doris for that.

Annie finished her soup and forced both slices of toast down, then reached into a drawer and took out a writing pad she'd bought especially for this purpose and the fountain pen Spode had bought her the previous year. She began to write. Her usually neat handwriting was slightly affected by her weakened condition but it was still better than most, although the ink was smudged in two places by tear stains.

She paused halfway though her writing, deciding whether or not to stick to the accepted majority age of twenty-one or bring it forward a few years. From her perspective, as a fifteen year old, eighteen seemed old enough to take on anything. When she had finished, she folded the letter neatly and placed it in a small brown envelope, on which she wrote:

> To my daughter. Born 29.8.53. To be opened <u>by her and no one else</u> on the 30.8.71 <u>and not before</u>.

She sealed this and put it inside a larger, white envelope which had once contained the birthday card she had meant to send Movita before she had changed her mind with her friend not writing to her any more. The larger envelope was left unsealed, awaiting a second letter.

It was still dark as Annie got out of bed the next morning but the late-summer dawn wasn't far away so she had enough light to get dressed by. They'd given her a more substantial meal the previous evening and her strength was returning. During her time at the maternity hostel her feet had grown out of her shoes and she'd been provided with a pair of old plimsolls which she'd renovated with whitener. She slipped these on and put a green, knitted cardigan over her frock to keep out the early-morning chill. A glance through the window at the fading stars told her the sky was clear and the day promised warmth. That was good, she wanted today to be a nice day for her daughter's sake.

From her bedside drawer she took the envelope containing the letter and placed it in one of her cardigan pockets. In the other pocket she put the writing pad and a pencil. then she picked up the Parker pen and with all her limited strength, she snapped it across the middle, throwing it back into the drawer. It was a beautiful writer but she'd grown to hate it.

Then she checked the contents of her purse. Sixpence. This was where the plan could go wrong. How far would sixpence take her on a bus? She should have saved up more, but how was she to know what lay in store for her? She'd only made up her mind yesterday. Sixpence would have to do.

Her baby was sound asleep as Annie picked her up, noting with some satisfaction that she was now wearing a towelling nappy. There was a pale blue matinée jacket on a shelf which she slipped on to the child, kissing her as she made baby noises in her sleep. A clock in the downstairs hall chimed five o'clock. Would the buses be running at that time on a morning? Something else she hadn't thought of. Never mind. Just get to the stop and wait for the first bus. There was a bench by the bus stop, she could sit on there until the first bus came. She'd be able to spend some time with her daughter. That was good.

Annie and her daughter left the Barrack Road Maternity Hostel without a backward glance. The early-morning bus arrived at half-past five.

The journey back from the church seemed quicker. Annie's mind was a jumble of memories and hopes and fears. Deep down she knew Father Barrett would comply with her wishes to the best of his abilities. She knew she could trust him, despite never having met the man. Doris deserved a better life than the one Annie could give her and this way at least she'd had some influence over who adopted her. It wasn't right to take someone's baby without their permission. People in authority thought they could do just what they liked, no matter whose feelings they hurt. The early-morning chill was being burned away by the sun rising above the trees but it was not enough to thaw the cold deadness within her.

As she walked, Annie somehow managed to cocoon her troubles inside some inner balloon. It housed all the anger and resentment and sadness and despair that were too much for her to cope with. She'd often lain in bed at night imagining a romantic hero who would come along and make everything right. Guy Mitchell perhaps? Jake? No, he was nice but no romantic hero. Her father's misty image cropped up now and again. Maybe he wasn't dead - maybe they'd made a mistake. God! Wouldn't it be wonderful if he was alive? And then her hero had turned up, in the form of an ancient Glaswegian burglar. He might not have been much but he was good and he was real and he was willing to help her. And then they took him away as well.

She was moving like a zombie now. Arms and legs unsynchronised, empty eyes staring into infinity. Everything that had ever mattered to her in life had been taken away. She didn't feel the sun's warmth on her face, nor did she hear the song of the hovering skylark or see the fishermen on the riverbank. All her senses were numbed against the pain which would be unbearable if she didn't keep it bottled up.

Beneath the bridge, the young fisherman was absorbed in attempting to catch his sixth fish of the morning, much to the annoyance of his older companions, some of whom had yet to catch their first. The young man looked up at Annie and their eyes briefly met. He considered abandoning his choice patch on the river to give chase to the now childless young lady retracing her steps. But, sadly, he didn't.

She wasn't aware of the young fisherman's smile. Her mind was enveloped in a dull, grey mist as she stepped across the road and looked down at the water. How inviting it looked. Divine providence, it seemed, had once again stepped in to lend a helping hand. The solution to all her problems was down there flowing beneath her. And then her inner balloon burst. She stepped up on to the parapet and allowed herself to fall limply into the water.

As she disappeared from sight, the young man's eyes were still on the bridge, wondering where she'd gone. Then he saw the flash of a green cardigan preceding a splash on the far side of the bridge.

'Bloody hell!'

'What?' enquired his companion.

'I think she's fallen in.'

The two of them downed their fishing rods and rushed up the bank and on to the bridge. The girl wasn't on the road and she hadn't had time to disappear from view.

'I think you're pulling my plonker,' admonished the older man, who knew his young friend's ways.

'I'm telling yer. She were stood right here an' I saw her fall in.'

'I think he's right, Fred,' confirmed a third, fatter man, puffing with exertion as he climbed on to the road. 'I saw her walk across t' road, then there were a splash. I reckon she's in there. Don't be so bloody stupid, Sam!'

Young Sam had already taken off his boots and jacket and was scanning the river, trying to see where Annie was. He leaped in before his companions could stop him and was immediately grabbed by the fierce underwater currents which swept him away in Annie's wake. Half a mile downriver an overhanging branch saved his life. Another two minutes and he'd have reached the narrow part of the river where it ran fast and deep and would have become another fatal statistic of the waterfall, called

Ackroyd's Drop after an eighteenth-century victim.

'She could be anywhere by now,' said a police frogman, climbing out of the river several hours later. 'She'll turn up somewhere. They mostly always do.'

But Annie's lifeless body would never be found.

She went over the waterfall around the same time as Father Barrett was opening the envelope. His back was to the altar, his attention jumping from the baby lying beside him to the letter in his hands. It was inside the white envelope with his name on.

Dear Father Barrett,

I am the baby's mother. I know you will do your best to place her with a good family who will love her. Please keep the enclosed letter and do not open it or tell anyone about it. Kindly ensure that it is given to my baby and no one else on the day after her eighteenth birthday. She was born in Barrack Road Maternity Hostel yesterday (29 August 1953). This is my last request.

Yours truly,

Annie Jackson

Part Two

Chapter Eleven

Annie's bequest stumbled at the first hurdle. The authorities had turned up and taken the baby away within hours of Father Barrett's finding her. In order not to let Annie down completely he'd baptised her Catherine before reporting his discovery to the police, with half a dozen eager parishioners acting as godparents. He'd agonised over the letters, but they'd been addressed to him so he kept them to himself, assuming responsibility for their ultimate delivery to Annie's daughter. The unworldly priest had no knowledge of the difficulties involved in tracking down an adopted child; he simply considered it was the least he could do. In eighteen years' time he'd be seventy-three. He assumed God would allow him to live that long in order to carry out his duty to the dead mother.

For several months he bombarded the adoption agency with phone calls, demanding that the child should go to a good family. It was ten months before they gave him their assurance that the child had been placed with kind, loving parents – and, no, they weren't allowed to tell him who these parents were. Father Barrett looked at the letters once again and hoped he was doing the right thing. His faith assured him that God would be on hand if he needed help.

July 1954
Mrs Titterington cast an experienced eye over the couple

who came to take Cathy away. She was relieved that they seemed okay because it wouldn't have been up to her to turn them away even if they hadn't. It was up to the 'powers-that-be'. She'd given her babies up to the most unlikely-looking would-be parents, devoutly hoping the 'powers-that-be' knew what they were doing.

Liz and Jim Makepeace seemed decent enough. She looked quite bubbly against her husband's more staid appearance. Funny how opposites attract. Cathy's foster mother would never have had them down for a married couple. Still, it takes all sorts.

'No need to wrap her, we'll eat her now,' laughed Liz as Mrs Titterington lifted the infant from the baby bath and wrapped a warm towel around her.

'Liz! This is a serious business,' scolded her husband. 'We don't want Mrs Titterington to think we're going to take our duties as parents lightly.'

'Don't worry,' smiled the foster mother. 'So long as she's going to a home with lots o' love and laughter, that'll do fer me.'

'Love and laughter's about all we can offer her,' said Liz, taking the baby from Mrs Titterington and hugging the child tenderly. She went quiet as she tried to stem the sudden surge of emotion generated by the warmth of her new daughter. Jim placed an understanding arm around her.

'She won't go short of love, Mrs Titterington,' he assured her. 'And she won't go short of anything else if I have anything to do with it.'

'I can see that, Mr Makepeace. I hope yer'll all be very happy. She's a lovely-natured child.'

'And beautiful,' added Liz.

'Aye, she's a pretty thing all right. As pretty as any we've ever had.'

'Did anyone know who the father was?' enquired Jim.

Mrs Titterington shrugged. 'Not to my knowledge. I've not been told much about the mother, other than she threw herself into a river. And I shouldn't really be tellin' yer that.'

'Well, it was in all the papers,' said Liz. 'Not an easy thing to keep secret.'

'Mebbe,' conceded Mrs Titterington. 'They managed ter keep her name a secret, though. I expect it were for the benefit o' the baby. Mind you, it didn't stop them reporters from snooping round. That's why we had ter leave it so long before putting her out for adoption.'

Do you think they might start bothering us?' said Liz, alarmed.

'If they do, I could lose me job.'

'We wouldn't want that, Mrs Titterington,' said Jim. earnestly. 'We'll keep it a secret as long we think necessary.'

'As far as I'm concerned,' said the foster mother, 'nobody needs ter know that she's not yer own.'

'Well, we're moving into a new house in a few weeks,' said Liz. 'We're moving out to Salterton. No one knows us there.'

'Best thing all round,' agreed Mrs Titterington.

Chapter Twelve

May 1960, Salterton, Yorkshire

Liz Makepeace looked through the kitchen window at her daughter playing happily in the back garden with her dog, Dollop. Some children exude a magical aura. Cathy was one such child, a source of constant joy to her parents who loved their daughter to distraction. In many ways she was what held their marriage together. Liz washed the dishes with her customary lack of enthusiasm as she wondered what course her life might have taken had Cathy not come along. It was hard to see how she and Jim could have stayed together without a common bond. He was a pit deputy and sometimes attempted to bring his authority back into the house with him. Liz had become an expert in deflating this and in an odd kind of way their relationship worked. He was a decent man, honest, reliable – and just a trifle boring. By contrast Liz was bubbly and flirtatious. Her fidelity had been put under serious strain on several occasions, none of which Jim knew about. The crunch had come when she realised she couldn't have children. Had it been Jim's fault it might have been easier, but it made Liz feel incomplete.

A period of conflict had ensued, unnecessary rows, mostly instigated by Liz out of sheer frustration at this empty life she felt she was locked inside. It was Jim who'd suggested adoption.

This had brought an instant change in her. A baby. There

was nothing she wanted more. But adoptive parents needed to prove they had a secure marriage. A deep heart-to-heart had them agreeing that their marriage was worth saving, so when the adoption agency came to do their checks they considered Liz and Jim ideal parent material. They had resolved to make a fresh start. New baby, new house, in a new district. Up to now it had worked, largely because of their extraordinary daughter. Adopting her had been a gamble which seemed to have paid off.

May 1960, Leeds

Leonard Spode snatched the telephone from the girl beside him and clamped his hand over the mouthpiece.

'Never answer this telephone – understand?' he snapped.

Melanie Binns recoiled, startled by a side of his character she'd never seen before. 'Okay, okay, keep yer hair on! Yer were asleep, I thought I was doing you a favour.'

She turned over, petulantly, and dragged the sheets with her. Spode composed himself and put the telephone to his ear.

'Hello?' he said, tentatively.

'Mr Spode?'

'Yes.'

'This is Gordon Robinson. Would you be able to meet with the Prime Minister at six o'clock this evening?'

Spode felt a surge of excitement. His majority in the last general election had increased dramatically. Enough for his seat to be regarded as safe, and he'd been hoping that the rumoured cabinet reshuffle might throw up a junior post for him. He'd served his apprenticeship on the back benches, worked as a PPS for a couple of cabinet ministers he couldn't stand the sight of, and generally kept his nose clean. It was ten a.m. The trains from Yorkshire to London were reasonably reliable.

'If it's inconvenient, tomorrow will do.'

Tomorrow the PM might have changed his mind. Spode committed himself.

'I'll be there.'

'You're sure you can make it for no later than six? The Prime Minister has a busy schedule to get through this evening.'

'Positive,' said Spode. He put the phone down, elated. Although he'd been hoping for such a call he hadn't known what form it would take. It had sounded very informal. *Would he be able to meet the PM?* Can a duck swim?

'Yer shouted at me!'

Melanie's rebuke awoke him from his thoughts, he turned, drew the covers away from her naked body and slapped her lightly on her bottom.

'Time to get up,' he commanded.

'I don't want ter bleedin' gerrup.'

'And you should mind your language,' he reprimanded.

'Yer said we could stay in bed 'til dinnertime.'

'Things to do, people to see – like the Prime Minister.' He looked down at her. 'There may be a job in the offing.'

The girl was totally unimpressed. 'Sounds boring,' she kicked off the rest of the covers and lay there, tantalising him. 'I'm not going ter bleedin' school, if that's what yer think. That's boring as well.'

'Everything's boring to you,' said Spode, pulling on his trousers as he averted his gaze from her naked form. It was a struggle not to jump back into bed with her, but this was more important. 'I don't care what you do with your time. Just don't be here when I get back.'

'Does this mean yer don't want to see me no more?'

'Of course not.'

'Yer'll forget all about me, I know yer will.' She sounded her age now: fourteen.

He took two five-pound notes from his wallet and dropped them on her stomach. 'Here – buy yourself some sweeties.'

The girl scowled. 'Yer don't want to see me no more, do yer? What's this – bleedin' hush money?'

He felt a rush of anger which he controlled immediately.

'Keeping quiet works two ways, young lady,' he retorted. 'One word from me and you'll be in reform school. The police have fingerprints from that poor old lady's home, only they don't know who one set belongs to.'

'I know, I know,' said the girl, quickly. 'I were only jokin'. That's your trouble – yer can't take a bleedin' joke.'

Joke. The word rang a warning bell in his brain. He'd never heard of Gordon Robinson. He was going to Downing Street at the request of someone he'd never heard of. Could be a newspaper with some warped idea of a funny story. It had been tried before. MPs were fair game for jokers within the press.

A few months ago he'd received an invitation through the post to attend the premiere of *The Thirty-nine Steps* starring Kenneth More and Brenda de Banzie. As it fitted in with his Parliamentary duties he'd decided to go. On the morning of his departure to London he'd received a phone call asking if he could open a garden party in his own constituency, in aid of St Margaret's Children's Hospital.

'Depends when,' he'd replied. Opening garden parties wasn't his cup of tea, but needs must.

'This afternoon. Sorry it's last-minute but you'd be doing us an awfully big favour . . .'

'I'd love to have done it but I've got a previous engagement in London. In fact, I'm about to leave right now.'

The following day the *Daily Herald* had run the headline: SPODE SNUBS SICK CHILDREN IN FAVOUR OF A TRIP TO THE PICTURES.

He went downstairs, away from the naked distractions in his bedroom, unwisely leaving his wallet on the dressing table. Melanie swung from the bed and helped herself to another fiver, then reached into her own bag and took out a photograph of herself. She wrote something on the back and stuck it in a zipped pocket in his wallet. In the meantime Spode was on the phone to the Whips' office.

'Harry, who's Gordon Robinson?'

'The PM's Private Secretary.'

'Thanks, Harry.' He made another call.

'Mr Robinson? ... Leonard Spode. I – er – I may be slightly late, I've just checked on the train times.'

'Mr Spode, if you're worried it might be another newspaper set-up, I can assure you this is genuine. I'll mention your vigilance to the PM. It will go in your favour. Can I take it you'll be here at six?'

'Not a minute later.'

Spode bought a paper at King's Cross Station and took it to the taxi rank to read the headlines. CABINET RESHUFFLE – PM TO ACT TODAY. No names, only guesses. He perused the columns. US SPY PLANE INCIDENT THREATENS PARIS SUMMIT.

The PM would have more on his mind today than a cabinet re-shuffle due to the Yanks allowing one of their spy planes to be shot down over the Soviet Union. Kruschev was spitting chips. Spode didn't reckon much to the pilot's chances, his only hope being the worldwide publicity he'd received. Had the US kept a lid on the matter no doubt the pilot, Francis Gary Powers, would be headed for the salt mines by now – or worse.

He looked up from his paper as he arrived at the taxi queue, dismayed to see it snaking back fifty yards, two and three abreast. The train had been forty minutes late which left him fifty minutes to get to Downing Street. It could take him that long to get to the front of the taxi queue. He reluctantly descended the steps into the Underground and stared blankly at the maps on the wall, hoping to spot the words Whitehall or Trafalgar Square. He'd once got hopelessly lost on the Underground and had vowed never to use it again. Westminster was near enough – but how did he get there?

There was an irritated queue at the lone enquiry window, at the head of which was an old man who had apparently been there over ten minutes as the patient attendant explained that it was quicker to walk to Euston Station than go by tube. Spode left the queue as the old man was demanding his money back. It was quicker to walk to Downing Street, much less Euston Station.

He stepped out into the evening sunshine, past the ever-increasing taxi queue, turned right down Euston Road and glanced at his gold Rolex. Quarter-past five. A brisk walk should just about get him there on time, he'd done it before in forty-five minutes. A bit of fresh air after almost five hours on the train would sharpen him up. Someone bumped into him from behind and knocked him to the floor, his briefcase falling from his grasp.

'Sorry, mate, you okay?'

Spode was too confused to take any notice of the face of the man who was pulling him up and handing him back his briefcase.

'My fault, mate, in a bit of a hurry,' apologised the man as he made a half-hearted attempt to dust Spode's coat down before running off.

'Clumsy bastard!' he cursed, but the man was too far away to object.

'Oh, damn!'

His watch had gone – and his wallet. A policeman approached and Spode made to catch his attention, then realised the implications. He just didn't have time to report a theft. He had to walk to Downing Street now whether he liked it or not.

'Good evening, sir,' greeted the constable. 'Everything all right?'

'Fine, thank you, constable,' he replied, banging the dust off his jacket. 'Just had a bit of a fall, that's all.'

'Just as long as you're all right, sir.'

'I'll be fine, thanks.'

Spode was inwardly seething at his predicament. He'd certainly mention it to the PM when he got there. Damn! Why hadn't he just told the policeman who he was and that he needed to get to Downing Street in a hurry? They might provide him with a police car. He turned round but the constable had gone.

Spode scanned the heads of people down the street for the welcome sight of a police helmet. By the time he'd turned left down Tottenham Court Road, crowds were swamping the pavements, making fast walking difficult. And not a helmet in sight. The police knew when to make themselves scarce, and rush hour was such a time. Sweat was pouring down his body as he barged his way through the crowds, swatting people aside with his briefcase, incurring the wrath of many an angry passer-by.

Dodging the traffic, he broke into a trot and ran down Charing Cross Road, skipping into the road now and then to overtake dawdling pedestrians. He stopped to catch his breath outside a jeweller's window, where a dozen clocks told him it was five-fifty. A hand grabbed him by the scruff of his neck and dragged him two hundred yards back up the street to Cambridge Circus where a weeping woman was picking up her scattered shopping. The man who had dragged him was much bigger than Spode and in an obvious temper.

'This is him!' he announced to a crowd of muttering onlookers, some of whom were helping the distressed woman. 'This is the feller what knocked her down. Look, yer broke her eggs – and that bread's no bleeding good now. I fink yer should pay her compensation.'

This met with agreement from the crowd, who were staring menacingly at Spode.

'Look, I'm sorry but I'm in a hurry,' he bleated. 'And I can't give her any money because I've just been robbed.'

He held his coat open. 'Look, if you don't believe me, see if you can find a wallet – and he took my watch.'

There was a murmur of disbelief from the crowd.

'All right, stand aside. What's going on here?'

A policeman had miraculously appeared and was standing over the distressed woman.

'Are you all right, madam?'

The middle-aged constable took out a notebook, around

which was stretched an elastic band holding a short pencil in position.

'All right? Does she look all right?' said the large man, still holding Spode by his collar. 'This geezer knocked 'er down.'

The policeman began to write, decided his pencil needed sharpening, then put the notebook away.

'It was an accident,' protested Spode. He turned to the constable. 'Look, officer, I am a Member of Parliament and I have an important appointment with the PM at six o'clock. I've already been robbed of a gold Rolex watch and my wallet since arriving in London and I'd like to be on my way.'

One person asked what a PM was and the policeman took out his notebook once again and bit at the end of his pencil to uncover enough lead to write a couple of notes.

'Good watches, are they, sir?' he enquired. 'These Rolexes.'

'Only the best yer can get,' said the man holding Spode. 'Wouldn't surprise me if he's making it all up fer the insurance money. He looks like someone what makes stuff up.'

The crowd murmured their agreement, then sniggered as the policeman jabbed his thumb over his shoulder in the direction of the Palace Theatre.

'Are yer sure yer not one o' them actors from over there, sir?'

'Look, officer,' pleaded Spode. 'I'm due at Downing Street at six o'clock. I haven't time for this.'

Big Ben began to strike six, echoing over the traffic noise. The policeman looked studiously at his watch, shook it and held it to his ear. 'If what you're tellin' me is true, sir, accordin' ter Big Ben and my H. Samuel Everight watch, I'd say you're late already, sir.'

'I'm well aware of that, officer,' screeched Spode, whose patience was wearing thin.

'This robbery, sir – do you wish to make a formal report?'

'Yes, but not now. I'm sorry, I just haven't got the time.'

'What did yer say yer name was, sir?'

'Spode, Leonard Spode.'

'Well, Mr Spode. I expect we'll all remember you the next time we cast our votes.'

Spode stood there seething, his collar still firmly in the grasp of the large man. If he told the constable just how little regard this Yorkshire MP had for a Londoner's vote it might land him in serious hot water. With a great effort of will he managed to produce a contrite expression. He looked down at the woman.

'Madam, I'm sorry for any trouble I've caused and if you'd care to send your bill to me at the House of Parliament, I'll make sure you're fully reimbursed.'

The constable looked quizzically at him then shook his head, slowly.

'Well, you'd best be on your way, Mr Spode, while I help the young lady pick up her comestibles.'

The young lady, who wouldn't see fifty again, smiled gratefully up at the constable as the large man reluctantly released Spode. He strode off down the road before breaking into a panicky trot. As Trafalgar Square opened up in front of him he could see Big Ben at the bottom of Whitehall. Ten-past six.

'Hell and damnation!'

It was six-twenty-two when he arrived at Number Ten, breathless and dishevelled. The policeman on the door looked at him, suspiciously.

'I have an appointment with the Prime Minister. My name is Spode, Leonard Spode.'

The door opened in response to a tap from the constable. Spode's face was damp and red as he stepped through the hallowed portals. Gordon Robinson stood in the hallway, his hand outstretched.

'Sorry I'm late,' apologised Spode. 'I . . .'

Robinson held up his hands to stem any further apology.

'No explanation needed. Bit of a flap on over the Spy Plane Affair - we're running desperately late as it is.' He looked at his watch. 'In fact, I doubt if the PM would have been able to see you this evening. I assume you'll be staying overnight?'

Spode nodded miserably, wondering how he would manage without any cash. Then his harrassed mind cleared sufficiently to reach an obvious solution.

'Yes, I'll be staying at Brown's.'

He had his cheque book in his briefcase and knew Brown's would cash him a cheque.

'Capital!' said Robinson. 'I'll slot you in at ten a.m.'

At nine-fifty the next morning Spode was directed into a drawing room and handed a glass of wine to drink beneath chandeliers amongst a group of hopeful back benchers.

The PM took him on one side. 'I thought you might be interested in the Department of Health.'

'I'd be honoured, sir,' said Spode, hoping he didn't sound too obsequious.

'That's settled then. Sir Peter's still Secretary of State. You'll be working for him.'

Spode nodded his appreciation. Junior Health Minister under Sir Peter Foxcroft should open a few doors. Any more rungs up the political ladder and the burdens of state responsibility would far outweigh the rewards. Spode had no such ambitions. Serious jobs were for dedicated politicians. He cast an eye around the room at all the influential people surrounding him. While he was only a junior minister he was no threat to them, and they would cultivate him and want him on their side in all their little subterfuges. He would, of course, oblige the ones who could be most useful to him. Yes, Junior Minister was a prize worth having. It more than made up for the loss of his watch and a wallet with thirty quid in it.

Arthur Stone took his pickings back to his room in Camden

Town. Thirty quid cash was a nice pick up, two weeks' wages for a working man. The wallet itself might fetch another ten bob in the Market Arms and a gold Rolex should fetch a pony at least. Not a bad day's work.

He shook out the contents of the wallet. A return train ticket to Leeds was discarded as useless, as was membership of a second-rate London club and a library card. He unzipped the pocket and took out the photograph of Melanie, taken the year before on Scarborough beach. She wore a Kiss-Me-Quick hat and a one-piece bathing suit that betrayed nothing of the curves just waiting to emerge. Probably his daughter, thought the thief, turning it over. Then he read Melanie's message.

To Leonard from Melanie, the best shag in Leeds – below which she'd written her phone number.

Arthur Stone's lip curled in disgust. 'You perverted old bastard!'

The following day's *Daily Express* ran a picture of the various MPs who had either been moved up, down or sideways in the shuffle. Leonard was among them.

'Why, Leonard Spode.' Stone grinned. 'What would the papers do if they knew what you'd been up to?'

Purely out of curiosity, he went out to the hall telephone and rang the number on the back of the photograph.

'Hello – Mrs Binns speaking.'

'Mrs Binns?' repeated Stone, establishing an immediate familiarity.

'Yes.'

'You don't know me, Mrs Binns, but I'm ringing all the Binns in your phone book to try and track down a girl I met a few weeks ago. All I know is that she comes from Leeds. You haven't got a very pretty daughter about twenty-two with blonde hair, have you?'

'No, sorry, love. There's only our Melanie and she's fourteen and dark. She's a bonny lass though.'

'Sounds a bit young for me, Mrs Binns. Mind you, you sound quite nice yourself – is Mr Binns still around?'

'Yer a cheeky devil, I'll say that fer yer.'

He could sense her blushing and allowed himself a grin of triumph. He could even charm the ladies over the phone.

'You didn't answer my question,' he pressed.

'Well, the answer is, he is still around. Under me feet most o' the bloomin' time – big useless article.'

'So, we have a date then?' Arthur was enjoying himself.

'Gerron wi' yer,' she laughed.

'I might just have to wait for your Melanie then. Still at school, is she?'

'Aye, when she goes, which isn't very often. I'm afraid our Melanie's a law unto herself.'

'Anyway, nice to talk to you Mrs Binns.'

'And you, er ...'

He'd put the phone down before she could ask his name. The grin slowly faded from his face as he realised a Member of Parliament was having sex with a fourteen-year-old schoolgirl. What was the world coming to?

It crossed his mind to be public-spirited and send the photo anonymously to the papers. Instead, he put it in a drawer. You never know when things like that might come in handy.

Chapter Thirteen

February 1971

Cathy stepped warily through the door of the Old Fox, instantly aware of heads turning in her direction.

'I'm not going to get away with this,' she murmured to her companion. 'Everyone's staring at me. They all know I'm not eighteen.'

'They're staring at you because you're so drop-dead bloody gorgeous,' muttered Michelle Duffy, not really meaning to offer a compliment, merely making a statement of fact.

Cathy had deliberately overdone the make-up in order to add an impression of age. She could have been anything between seventeen and twenty-one. The elderly barman smiled as they approached. From his lofty position on the age ladder anyone under twenty-five looked too young to drink so he rarely refused service on the grounds of age. He certainly wasn't going to challenge Cathy. Advanced age didn't stop him admiring much singular beauty. Flashing his National Health teeth, he asked, 'Evenin', ladies, what's it to be?'

Cathy hadn't planned this far ahead. She'd never been in a pub before and she certainly didn't know what to ask for.

'Two rum and peps,' said Michelle, who was two years older and an experienced pub-goer.

'Rum?' whispered Cathy. 'What have you ordered me

rum for? I don't know if I like rum.'

'Well, if you don't, I'll have them both and you can get something else.'

'I'll get these.'

They both turned round. Behind them stood a man in his later-twenties, with a broad, agreeable smile.

'That's a very expensive chat-up line,' said Michelle. 'We're both on rum and peps.'

Their new friend handed the barman a ten-pound note. 'And another two pints, George.' He grinned at the two girls. 'I've just had a nice win on the horses. Plenty to go round.'

Cathy wasn't instantly attracted to him but he was certainly worth a second glance. He had presence, a quality lacking in the few boyfriends she'd had so far. Dave Bywater was a proper man with no remnants of puppy fat, just hard, lean muscles. At least Cathy assumed they'd be hard and lean beneath his dark red sweater. He was pleasant to look at, with long fair hair and an easy charm which contrasted greatly with the excruciating chat-up lines she was getting so bored with. She smiled and said, 'Thanks very much.'

From a fiscal point of view it made sound common sense to let someone buy her the odd drink. She was still at school doing her A levels and money was in short supply.

'You girls grab a seat next to Pete over there.' Dave pointed to a table at which sat another man about his age. 'I'll bring the drinks over.'

He'd taken over within a minute, Cathy had never met anyone who could do that. This was very impressive. She followed Michelle over to Pete's table, still conscious of staring eyes and still convinced these eyes were more accusing than admiring.

'They all know I'm under-age,' she whispered to Michelle. 'I'm just having one drink then I'm going.'

'Please yourself.' Michelle shrugged. 'I'll stick around with Robert Redford.'

'He seems nice.'

'Nice?' echoed Michelle. 'He's a bloody dreamboat! But he's much too old for you.'

Pete wasn't as much of a dreamboat as his pal, so Michelle sat on the seat next to him because from there she'd be making eye contact with Dave. Cathy might have the edge over her in the beauty stakes, but as far as eye contact was concerned, Michelle felt she had something of a gift.

But the dreamboat wasn't remotely interested in her. He brought the drinks across and sat on the bench-seat next to Cathy, directly in the line of fire from Michelle's eyes but totally impervious. Cathy could feel the warmth of his thigh next to hers. She could have moved away slightly, but she chose not to. This man was arousing something within her that none of her teenage boyfriends had ever done.

Michelle got the message and stole a quick glance at Pete, the consolation prize. Plain and dull and not worth a single bat of her seductive eyelashes.

'We're only staying for one drink, aren't we, Cathy?'

'What?'

Michelle leaned forward and spoke in a loud whisper. 'You said you only wanted to stay for one drink, with you being under-age. We don't want to push it.'

Cathy looked daggers at her, but Dave laughed loudly.

'We'd better watch it, Pete, we might get done for cradle-snatchin'.'

Pete grinned, showing a mouthful of dreadful teeth. *Like a row of bombed houses*, as Michelle would describe them later. She grimaced and looked away and Cathy felt some sympathy for her treacherous friend.

'I think we can risk a couple,' she compromised. 'Then I'll have to go home.'

'Why?' grinned Pete. 'Got ter do yer homework?'

He thought he was being witty, then Cathy said, 'Yeah, I've got some calculus to do. What are you like at calculus, Pete?'

'We only did French.' He was being serious.

Dave laughed loudly. 'He thinks it's a language – it's maths, yer brainless bugger!'

Pete stared into his beer, embarrassed. Cathy felt vaguely sorry for him and slapped Dave lightly on his arm. 'Don't be so cruel.'

'You can see why I asked you girls to join me,' he said. 'I was running short of intelligent conversation.'

If Cathy thought this was cruel too she didn't say so. Somehow, she and Dave seemed to have joined forces against Michelle and Pete. It was to be her first lesson in the art of manipulation – and she was in the hands of a master.

Salterton was a pretty village set right on the edge of the West Yorkshire coalfields, midway between Leeds and Castleford. Jim Makepeace's job as pity deputy had afforded him enough money to take out a mortgage on a small terraced cottage, number seven Prospect Row, stone-built with its own garden. A far cry from Grimethorpe, the mining town he and Liz had first lived in. He looked over the top of his newspaper as Cathy came into the room, prior to going out.

'This is the third time this week, young lady. I hope your schoolwork isn't suffering wi' all this gaddin' about?'

Cathy looked in the mirror and wondered, not for the first time, why she didn't look remotely like either of her parents. Deep brown, glossy hair tumbled on to her slim shoulders, framing a stunningly beautiful face. The rest of her, from the neck down, was shapely and equally attractive. She grimaced at herself, wishing her nose was slightly more petite and her mouth not quite so big, and maybe her hair would look better with highlights . . . She spoke to her dad's reflection.

'It's not, Dad.'

'Where yer get the brass from beats me. I could never afford all these nights out when I were your age – an' I were workin'.'

'Leave her alone,' scolded Liz. 'If she's got any sense her young man'll be doing most of the paying.'

'What's he do for a livin', this young man o' yours?' enquired Jim.

'He works in a shop,' lied Cathy. She didn't want to tell them that Dave seemed to live off his wits and the dole office.

'Shop? What kind o' shop?' pressed Jim.

'I don't know. A shop's a shop.'

'Well, I don't want *you* endin' up in no shop. That's why yer doin' yer A levels.'

'Dad, I don't want to work in a shop either, but there's nothing wrong with people who do.'

'And I hope he's not takin' yer into pubs. Yer still under age, yer know.'

'Dad, I know how old I am.'

'I just don't want yer neglectin' yer school work, that's all.'

'For God's sake, Jim! Leave the girl alone. She got nine O levels. That's nine more than me and you put together.'

'They didn't have O levels when we were at school.'

'It wouldn't have made any difference,' retorted Liz, scathingly. 'You'd have still ended up down the pit.'

'I was a deputy before they laid me off. They don't give deputy's jobs ter dummies.'

'Aye, they dress dummies up in fancy uniforms and stand 'em outside hotel doors.'

Their argument was growing heated as they often did lately. Jim blushed at his wife's scornful reference to the only job he could get since losing his job at the closed colliery.

'Stop it, you two,' pleaded Cathy, who hated seeing them arguing. 'I'll be back about eleven.'

'No later,' cautioned Jim. 'It's school in the morning.'

He waited until she'd gone before turning to his wife. 'That was a rotten thing ter say in front o' Cathy. Am I not good enough for yer now I'm only a commissionaire? Are yer ashamed of me or summat?'

'I just don't like you always going on at her, that's all,' retorted Liz. 'You've got to give the girl a bit of slack at her age.'

'Slack? She's got half a mile o' rope at the moment.'

'She's seventeen – have you forgotten what it was like to be seventeen? No, don't answer that. I don't want to hear again how tough it was down the pit.'

Jim sighed and folded up his paper. He couldn't do right for doing wrong. Liz was constantly down his throat for the slightest thing, just like she had been before they adopted Cathy. He walked to the door and watched his daughter walking down the street to the bus stop. For the first time in his life he felt a sense of resentment towards her. Did his marriage depend solely on Cathy? When she left home to go to university, would Liz go too? It sounded daft, but it was a strong possibility.

Whatever tenuous thread had held their marriage together was now at breaking point. He didn't want to be the one to snap it, so he changed the subject as he went back into the room.

'By the way, love, I think we should tell her on her eighteenth birthday.'

Liz didn't need him to explain what he was talking about. It was a subject which had been broached between them many times over the years. The two words 'tell her' always referred to telling Cathy about her being adopted.

'I sometimes wonder if she doesn't know already,' said Liz. 'I mean – where does she think she gets her looks from? Neither of us are oil paintings.'

'I don't know,' said Jim, gallantly. He sat down in his favourite chair. 'She might think she got it from your side.'

Liz laughed and flicked his thinning hair, almost affectionately. 'You can be a real smarmy sod when you put your mind to it, Jim Makepeace.'

Cathy looked at her watch. Half-past ten. 'I'd better be off, I promised my dad I'd be in for eleven.'

Dave's face creased into one of his disarming smiles. 'I used to make promises like that when I was seventeen. Honestly, Cathy, your parents'll think there's something wrong with you if you don't cut loose now and again. That's what being a teenager's all about.'

They were back in the Old Fox and Cathy was feeling quite mellowed by the three brandy and Babychams Dave had bought her.

'How come you know all the right things to say?' she asked, taking a cigarette, another habit she'd picked up since meeting him.

He held up his hands, innocently. 'Hey, I'm just telling the truth, that's all. I'm just telling you what any former teenager will tell you. Seventeen's a great age – you don't want to look back on it and regret missing out on your rebellion stage.'

'Were you rebellious?'

'Me? I was the original James Dean – *Rebel Without A Cause*. Only like all young idiots, I thought I knew it all.'

Cathy laughed. There was an element of unpredictability about Dave that added to his charm. Danger even.

'Where were you thinking of taking me?'

'There's this new nightclub opened in Leeds called Cinderella's. I've been a couple of times – it's great. Do no harm to pay a visit.'

'Nightclub?' queried Cathy. 'I don't want to be too late. I don't want to overdo my first night of being a rebel, my dad'll be waiting up for me.'

'And what'll he do? He doesn't still hit you, does he?'

'How d'you mean, "still". My dad's never laid a finger on me, he's really sweet.'

'And really boring,' guessed Dave. 'Still, you're better off than I was. My old man used to knock seven bells out o' me. At least he did until I outgrew him – then he tried it once too often.'

'Oh? What happened?'

Dave shrugged and said, matter-of-factly, 'I blacked his eye and left home.'

'I'm sorry,' sympathised Cathy. 'It must have been awful.'

'Nah – it was life. It's what happens. Every youngster flies the nest eventually, I just took off a bit sooner than most.'

The two burly doormen nodded their recognition of Dave as they stood aside to allow him and Cathy into Leeds' latest nightclub. She followed him up the spiral stairway that led into a roomful of sound and laughter, seemingly orchestrated by the disc jockey, a young man of Dave's age with long, dark hair and a permanent grin. Pete Stringfellow turned and nodded down to Dave as the two of them passed behind his elevated box.

'That's the third different girl you've brought here this week,' he called out. 'Does your wife know?'

His remark brought more laughter from the crowd. Dave grinned and pushed Cathy through the throng towards the bar. She turned back to face him.

'What does he mean? "Does your wife know"?'

Dave shook his head and grinned. 'Just listen to him for a while and you'll see just how serious he is. If a pretty girl comes within range he'll have a go at the boyfriend.'

The disc jockey immediately proved Dave's point by stopping the music as the dancers were in full flow on the floor in front of him. He leaned over the edge of his wooden pulpit and pointed at a middle-aged man who was vigorously dancing with a much younger woman.

'Excuse me, sir, I've just had a call from the hospital. They reckon you're due back in your iron lung in ten minutes.'

Such happy irreverence was proving highly popular with the young clubbers of Leeds. Dave sat Cathy down in a seat just vacated and went off to the bar. Pete Stringfellow was offering a bottle of champagne to the first person who could shout out the name of Hopalong Cassidy's horse.

'By heck, Cathy! You moved in there quick, didn't you?'

Cathy looked to see Michelle standing over, drink in her hand and her other arm linked with that of an insignificant-looking youth. 'This is Gordon,' she said.

'Pleased to meet you, Gordon.'

Michelle leaned down towards her. 'Apparently Gordon knows Dave – and he says you've to watch him. Bit of a wrong 'un apparently.'

'Really?'

Cathy didn't ask her friend to elaborate as she didn't believe a word of it. Michelle wasn't beyond spreading a bit of malicious gossip if it suited her own ends. Dave arrived behind them with drinks in his hand, nodding his vague recognition of Gordon.

'It's true,' said Michelle, nodding knowingly at Cathy before walking away.

'What's true?' enquired Dave, sitting down and placing a glass of sparking wine in front of Cathy.

'Girls' gossip,' said Cathy. 'Nothing you'd be interested in.'

'So it wasn't about me then?'

'Why, is there some guilty secret you're worried about?'

'I've got many guilty secrets, but I can't say that I'm worried about any of them.'

'Aha! Tell me more,' said Cathy, more intrigued than worried.

Jim was now glancing at the clock every five minutes. Liz had already gone to bed leaving him with strict instructions not to 'go on' at Cathy when she came in.

'She's a young woman now, Jim. She's only doing what we all did at her age.'

'I just hope she's all right, that's all. She should have been back over an hour ago.'

'Come to bed, love. She's got her own key, she can let herself in.'

'No, I just want ter be sure she's in safely.'

He was asleep in his chair when Cathy tiptoed past the

living room and went upstairs to bed. Her mother was standing on the landing.

'Don't try this on too often, love.' Liz's tone was reproving but also contained an element of sympathy. Cathy kissed her on the cheek.

'What have you been drinking? That's not just lemonade on your breath.'

'Mum, I'm nearly eighteen.'

'For God's sake, don't let your dad find out you've been drinking.'

Liz went downstairs and shook Jim by the shoulder.

'Are you coming to bed or what?' she asked.

He looked at the clock. Half-past one.

'Cathy's fast asleep upstairs,' said Liz. 'I thought you'd have followed her up.'

Jim's relief at his daughter's safe return just outweighed his annoyance at her disobeying him.

'I'll speak to her in the morning,' he decided, following his wife upstairs.

But Jim needed to be at his post outside the Metropole Hotel at eight the following morning and was long gone when Cathy came downstairs. Her head was pounding, her mouth furry and she was too bilious to want any breakfast. She looked pleadingly at her mother.

'I really don't feel like going in to school today, Mum.'

'Cathy, you don't need my permission any more, you're a big girl now.'

'I know, but I want your blessing.'

'My blessing?' laughed Liz. 'Don't even think about it, lady. You've just learnt one of life's cruel lessons – self-inflicted illnesses get no sympathy. Get a pint of water down you and get yourself off. And think yourself lucky your dad's not around.'

'Don't tell me – you're being cruel to be kind.'

'How did you guess?'

Over the following weeks Cathy negotiated a later 'coming in' time of midnight, which meant she could stretch it to half-past twelve without too much fuss, especially as she'd cut down her nights out to Friday and Saturday.

Her relationship with Dave had been unusually chaste at first, just the usual doorstep groping. Cathy began to wonder if he was actually sexually attracted to her. In truth, during the week he was relieving his carnal frustrations with two other girls, keeping Cathy on tenterhooks, wondering if it would ever happen between them. When the time came he wanted her to be the one to make the move. Then he'd think about ditching the other two girls and concentrate all his attentions on her. Michelle Duffy brought events forward somewhat.

She occasionally stopped for a chat with Jim Makepeace as he stood on the steps of the Metropole Hotel in the uniform of the Royal Corps of Commissionaires.

'Morning, Mr Makepeace.'

'Hello, Michelle.' He'd been hoping she'd pass by. 'I don't suppose you'll see much of Cathy, now she's got this new boyfriend.'

'I don't actually.'

Michelle paused. She didn't want to be bitchy but felt Jim should know certain things, for Cathy's sake. 'Have you met Dave yet?' she enquired, pretty sure of the answer already.

'I haven't actually . . . why? He hasn't got two heads or anything, has he?'

Michelle shrugged, not quite knowing what to say. 'Just thought he was a bit old for her, that's all.'

Jim frowned. Cathy had told him Dave was twenty-one, which he considered a bit old but he'd had to bow before Liz's better judgement. 'Most twenty-one-year-old lads aren't as mature as Cathy,' she'd assured her husband.

Jim nodded down at Michelle, happy to have found someone who agreed with him on the subject. 'I gather he works in a shop.'

Michelle shook her head. 'As far as I know he doesn't

actually work anywhere. I've often wondered where he gets all his money from. He never seems to be short.'

'Twenty-one and not working,' remarked Jim. 'Does he come from a well-to-do family or something?'

Michelle would have laughed at this had it not been a serious enquiry. 'He's a bit older than twenty-one, Mr Makepeace. *I think he's nearer thirty.*' She took a step nearer to him to ensure no one overheard. What she told him was enough to set events in motion. Jim was waiting for his daughter as she came in from school. Liz had tried to placate him, but was finding it difficult to take her daughter's side. There were things they definitely needed to know about this Dave character.

When Cathy came into the room Jim was standing with his back to the fire, like a Victorian father. She dropped her schoolbag on to the floor before flopping down into a chair. Jim's eyes followed her every move. Liz came in from the kitchen, to act more as referee than inquisitor.

'Tell me about this Dave character.'

Cathy looked up, taken aback by Jim's sudden question. Then she looked at her mother and realised there was a problem. She immediately went on the defensive.

'What about him?'

'Well, for a start, you told me he was twenty-one years old and works in a shop.'

Jim was trying to maintain his self-control but could feel himself rapidly losing it. Liz was eager for her daughter to give a plausible explanation, but suspected she'd be unlucky. Cathy's complexion paled under her father's glare. How much did he know about Dave? Did he know something she didn't?

'That's what he told me,' she lied.

'So, a thirty-year-old man tells you he's twenty-one and you believe him?'

'He's not thirty, he's twenty-eight!'

Liz's heart sank. She'd been hoping Michelle would be

proved wrong. It was likely the rest of her story would be true.

'I suppose you're going to tell me he's not a car thief as well!' thundered Jim.

'Steady on, Jim,' cautioned Liz. 'He's never been convicted of any of this.'

'Not yet. He probably thinks he's too damn' clever for the police.'

Cathy genuinely knew nothing of this. 'I don't know who you've been talking to, but they're lying.'

'There's only one person in this room that's been lying and that's you.' Jim's breath was coming in short bursts as he suddenly realised what Liz already suspected.

'I suppose you're sleeping with him as well!' he roared.

Tears of anguish and anger rolled down Cathy's face as she withered under her father's verbal onslaught. 'No, I haven't,' she protested. She looked at her mother.

'I haven't, Mum, honest.'

Liz looked away. It was hard to believe a beautiful girl such as Cathy wouldn't have been seduced by such a man.

'You don't believe me, do you?' she shouted, turning defence into attack. 'You'd rather believe *him* than me.'

'Why should she believe you?' fumed Jim.

'Because I'm telling the truth, you stupid old sod!'

Whatever self-control Jim had flew straight out of the window. He raised a clenched fist at her for the first time in her life. Cathy didn't flinch.

'Go on, hit me,' she shouted. 'You've been dying to hit Mum for the last few months, but you're too scared she might leave you.'

Jim lowered his fist. This situation was totally beyond his control. 'Just get upstairs to your room and don't come down until you can show us some respect.'

'You can't treat me like a child, I'm nearly eighteen.'

'I can treat you any way I damn' well want.'

'Jim . . .'

He turned on his wife, tears of anger and frustration

spilling from his eyes 'You stay out of this. It's . . . it's because of *you* she's like she is.'

'Because of me? What the hell are you talking about?' fumed Liz. 'Don't you bloody start on me. It's *her* you should be shouting at.'

'Her?' screamed Cathy. 'I'm not a *her*, I'm your daughter. Or have you forgotten?'

Jim wagged an irate finger in her face. 'If you *were* our daughter you'd behave with a damn' sight more respect than you are.'

'How do you mean, *if* I was your daughter?' blazed Cathy. 'I *am* your daughter – although you wouldn't know it by the way you treat me, you – you stupid man!'

'Oh, is that what you think?' blustered Jim. 'You think I'm stupid, do you?'

'Jim,' hissed Liz, seeing the anger on his face. 'Don't you dare! Not now.'

Cathy looked from one to the other. 'Will someone please tell me what's going on?

Jim's self-control had deserted him at a crucial moment. 'I'll tell you what's going on,' he exploded. 'You're *not* our daughter – that's what's going on. Your real mother left you in a flamin' church when you were one day old – an' I can see now why she did!'

There was a frozen silence as he realised what he'd said. He laboured for breath, still upset by his daughter's insulting behaviour, but he knew he'd gone too far. 'I'm sorry – I didn't mean that last bit,' he said quietly.

'What's he talking about, Mum?'

Liz took a step towards her but Cathy backed away. 'Please, just tell me what you're talking about.'

'Look, love,' said Liz. 'This isn't the right time . . .'

'Right time? Right time for what?'

Liz looked daggers at her husband, who was staring at a point above her head, at a loss what to do or say. This wasn't his fault. He'd been trying to do his best by his daughter and he'd been driven to this.

'We meant to tell you when you were eighteen ...' began Liz.

'Tell me what, Mum?'

Liz sighed deeply. This was the worst possible way to tell her but it had to be done.

'Cathy, we adopted you when you were a baby.'

Cathy began to shake with emotion. 'You did what?'

'We adopted ...'

'I heard what you said.'

'Sorry.'

'Sorry?' exploded Cathy. 'You tell me I'm adopted and then you say you're sorry? This is just bloody brilliant! I mean ... why the hell didn't you tell me? Why did I have to find out like this? With him using it against me like he has.'

Jim banged his fist on the table in frustration. 'I'm not using it against you, Cathy. Don't talk so damn' stupid ...'

Liz cut him off before he did any more damage. 'Cathy, he didn't mean it. It was said in the heat of the moment.'

'Didn't mean it? Of course he meant it. He's been waiting for our first big row so he could use it against me.' She took a step towards Jim. 'Haven't you? Haven't you – you lousy pig!'

Jim's chest was rising and falling. His insides were torn with conflicting emotions: his love for Cathy, his rage at what she'd done and what she'd been saying to him, his anger at his wife for turning on him and forcing him to blurt out something he shouldn't have. And most of all anger at himself for losing his self-control and finding himself in this terrible mess.

Cathy dashed from the room and ran upstairs. Jim followed her to the door. 'Catherine! Come back here.' He jabbed a finger at a spot beside his feet, like a man calling his dog to heel. 'We need to sort this out.'

'Oh, for God's sake, Jim, let her go,' screamed Liz. 'She's right, you are a lousy pig!'

He cracked then. Lashing out, more in frustration than

malice, he hit Liz full in the face, knocking her across the room. He stood there, open-mouthed, more shocked than she was. In all the time he'd known her, he'd never so much as raised a finger to her.

'Oh, God, love – I'm sorry. I didn't mean to . . .' He knelt beside her but she pushed him away, then touched her lip and examined the blood on her finger.

'Just leave me alone, Jim. You've done enough damage for one day.'

'I know. I'm sorry – I don't know what's happening to me.'

Jim got to his feet then sank into a chair with his head in his hands. Neither spoke for several minutes, trying to regain control over their emotions, Liz succeeding better then her husband.

Cathy surveyed the scene from the door as she stood there with a change of clothes stuffed hurriedly into a suitcase.

'I'm leaving this awful house,' she announced between sobs.

Jim looked up. First at Liz, then at Cathy whom he still blamed for the whole mess.

'If you go out of that door, you'll never come back,' he threatened.

'Cathy, take no notice,' pleaded Liz.

Cathy shook her head hopelessly and left the house as Liz laid into Jim with a ferocity that had him retreating from the room.

It was probably the emerging rebel inside Cathy that made her head for the Old Fox. She knew Dave would be there, it was his second home. He was standing at the bar when she walked in. The barman spotted her and said something to him. She didn't hear Dave whisper, 'Oh, shit,' under his breath as he turned to greet her.

'Cathy. What are you doing here at this time?'

Tears weren't far below the surface and Dave seemed to spot it. He took her suitcase from her.

'Look, I've got a car outside, why don't we go somewhere quiet?'

Cathy nodded, still not having said a word. She didn't trust herself to speak. There was too much spinning through her mind. She was adopted. They weren't her parents. Why the hell hadn't anyone told her before now? Who were her real parents? Did she care? How had her mum got blood on her face? Had *he* hit her? Dad had never been violent in his life but what else was she to believe? Christ, what a mess!

A minute after they'd left a woman arrived. Leggy, blonde, lived-in face, revealing sweater and a skirt up round her backside.

'Have you seen Dave?' she asked the barman.

'Been and gone, love.'

'Well, sod him! He was supposed to be taking me out tonight. Give us a gin and tonic, George, I've bloody had it with him!'

'I've left home,' said Cathy suddenly.

They'd been driving in silence for ten minutes. Dave felt she needed some time. Cathy appreciated this.

'Well, that would explain the suitcase,' he said.

'It's like living with the Gestapo, living with my dad.'

Dave pulled into a lay-by and switched off the lights of the Volvo. It was dusk and they were out in the country. He turned on the radio and ran through the stations until he found something soothing, Frank Sinatra singing 'All The Way'. It seemed appropriate for what he had in mind, although he had the sense not to mention it.

'Why don't we sit in the back and you can tell me all about it?' he suggested. There was no hint of seduction in his voice, only what sounded like genuine friendship. And right now she needed a friend.

They sat in the back and Cathy laid her head on his chest as she poured out her troubles. He stroked her hair and kissed her, lightly.

'It'll be all right,' he soothed. 'It's normal for parents

and kids to fall out at some stage.'

She began to sob.

'What is it?' He lifted her chin. 'What?' he asked.

'Apparently they're not my parents.'

'Apparently? How do you mean, apparently? Either they are or they aren't.'

'I've just been told I'm adopted.'

'Oh – that's why you're so upset. It's understandable, I suppose.' He was wondering whether to postpone his carnal ambitions to a more suitable time but she put her arms around him and squeezed him.

'Hold me, Dave.'

He obliged.

'It's the way he told me.' Cathy looked up at him, her eyes flooded with tears. 'We were in the middle of an argument and he used it against me – like some sort of weapon. What sort of person would do that?'

Dave shrugged. He knew better than to blacken a parent's character. It could easily backfire. Families were something you didn't interfere with.

'He probably regrets it now.'

'Oh, Dave, you're such a nice person. Come here.'

She pulled him down to her and kissed him. He responded, gently at first, then ran an exploratory hand inside her blouse. Meeting no resistance, he expertly unhooked her bra. Briefly illuminated by passing headlights, he slowly undressed her until she lay naked beneath him, scared, but determined to go through with it. She would give herself to him, not out of desire but for revenge on her dad. Dave had never seen anyone or anything quite so lovely.

'My God, Cathy – you're beautiful.'

'I'm also a virgin,' she whispered, defiantly.

At first, Dave was as gentle as he could be, practising a self-restraint he didn't know he had, employing all the expertise at his disposal. But it deserted him as they came to a mutual noisy climax, rocking the car on its springs. A passing motorist hooted, well aware of what was going on inside.

Cathy had gone through fear and pain to be rewarded with an esctasy she'd never known, a sensation which would tie her to this man for longer than was sensible.

Chapter Fourteen

Cathy stood in front of the clothing factory and gazed up at the large sign above the door: Spode Fashions Ltd. Over the past ten years it had grown into one of the biggest clothing companies in the West Riding, second only to Montague Burton's.

Beside the door was parked a Jaguar XJ6, its nose almost touching a sign on the wall indicating this to be the personal parking spot of the managing director. A handsome, middle-aged man emerged from the factory and smiled at Cathy before climbing into the car.

'Was that him?' she asked the girl on reception.

'Mr Spode? Yeah. Can I help yer, love?'

'I've come for a job – I'm supposed to see Mrs . . .' she took a piece of paper from her pocket. 'Mrs Greenhalgh.' She said it slowly, looking up at the girl to check she'd got her pronunciation right. The girl made no adverse comment so it must have been okay.

'Through the double green doors, first right. Just knock and go in.'

'Thanks.'

Mrs Greenhalgh looked to be teetering on the verge of retirement. She gave Cathy a welcoming smile, which turned to a slight frown.

'Is there something wrong, Mrs Greenhalgh?'

'No . . . it's just that you bear a remarkably strong

resemblance to – er – to someone I know.'

'Oh, right.'

Cathy stood there, slightly self-conscious under the woman's keen gaze.

'Before you sit down, Miss Makepeace, I need to ask you one question which might save us both a lot of time.'

'Oh?' Cathy knew what was coming.

'Are you pregnant?'

Cathy took a deep breath. She could hardly deny it, the evidence was beginning to stick out in front of her for all the world to see.

'I only wanted a temporary job, Mrs Greenhalgh, just for a couple of months. I lost my last job because of . . .' She pointed to her bump.

'When's the baby due?' Mrs Greenhalgh's tone was kindly but not encouraging.

'I'm four months gone.'

The older woman sighed and looked at a sheet of paper in front of her for Cathy's first name. 'Look, Catherine . . .'

'Cathy.'

'Cathy. It's just not practical. There's a lot of training required. By the time you start to become useful you'll be leaving us.'

Cathy shook her head, then slowly nodded her acceptance of the situation. It was more or less what she'd expected, let's face it. She'd been trying it on, hoping the woman wouldn't see the bump beneath her coat. But Cathy's normally slim figure betrayed it too easily. As she turned to go, Mrs Greenhalgh's eyes remained glued to her, amazed at the resemblance.

She left the factory and walked out into the July drizzle, turning up her coat collar as she headed for the bus stop. Her life definitely wasn't turning out as she'd planned. She'd been bound for a university degree in engineering, not one of these prissy arts degrees, then a proper job with a civil engineering company.

She stood at the bus stop alone with her thoughts as the fine rain made her dark hair cling to her pale face. As things had turned out she was an unemployed, pregnant, trainee sewing machinist – living in a run-down squat with a man who was becoming increasingly abusive. And the people who'd been her parents all her life had turned out not to be her parents after all.

Even if she'd got the job, no way would she have given Dave most of her money as she had in her last job. What her dad had said about his being a car thief was true, only right now he was having to keep a low profile, as he called it. The police had been sniffing round a bit too close for comfort so they'd been living off her earnings and his meagre pickings, most of which he spent on drink and horses. Only pride prevented her from going home, that and her reluctance to tell her parents that she was pregnant.

It had been a hell of a shock to the system finding that out, she was only just coming to terms with it herself. On odd occasions she felt quite maternal, stroking her tummy and waiting for the first kick.

Leaving school before she took her A levels had been a calculated risk, but she'd figured she could go back at a later date and take them. Cathy was bright enough and time wasn't exactly of the essence, not at her age anyway. Dave had convinced her of that.

At first, life with him had been quite exciting, especially the physical side. Her hitherto schoolgirl fumblings had hardly prepared her for Dave, who knew many unusual ways to stimulate a girl. Unfortunately he could also be a complete prat, especially with a drink inside him. A man who was very free with his fists. Over the past few months, since she'd run away from home and gone to live with him, he had changed out of all recognition. He was no longer the handsome charmer with money to burn, more an unshaven, down-and-out, jumping every time he heard a knock at the door. She'd tried to talk him out of his thieving lifestyle, but he had a way with him. A way of creating a shield around himself which couldn't be penetrated by words of reason. Dave was a law unto himself. At least he was until the police started looking for him. The two of them did a very hurried moonlight flit from his flat, causing Cathy to leave most of her clothes behind. Rather than allow her to go back, Dave had bought her new stuff. But the money soon ran out.

To begin with, a pal of his had put them up, until it became obvious that they'd outstayed their welcome. The squat was to be a temporary measure, just for a couple of nights until he'd 'sorted something out'. That had been three months ago and getting something sorted out seemed further away than ever, especially with Cathy losing her job. The bus arrived and she hesitated before boarding. Across the road another bus was pulling to a halt. A bus which would have taken her home to her mum and dad.

Her bus stopped at the end of the bleak street that she and Dave called home but Cathy couldn't bring herself to get off and face an inquest from him about why she hadn't got the job. She stayed on the bus as it set off towards the centre of the city. Below her was a newsvendor's placard which said a bomb had killed thirteen people in Belfast. She felt a wave of incredible sadness sweep over her. Why did people have to be so cruel to each other? What's wrong with just being nice? She fingered a swelling on the side of her head, concealed by her hair. A legacy of her last altercation with Dave. Then she remembered the last time she'd seen her mum, kneeling on the carpet with blood on her mouth. Was there a man alive who could keep his fists to himself? Had she been unreasonable in threatening to leave Dave if he ever hit her again? The bus stopped outside the Odeon Cinema where there was a short queue waiting to see an early showing of *Fiddler on the Roof*.

For the next three hours she sat in a sparsely inhabited corner, right at the back of the cinema, sucking a quarter of Mint Imperials and totally engrossed in the film.

By the time she emerged on to a bright Headrow, the

rain had gone and the late-afternoon sun was drawing steam from the tarmac road. Cathy felt refreshed by the gentle optimism of the film. The bus conductor smiled at her as she stepped on, humming 'Sunrise, Sunset'.

'By heck! Somebody's cheerful.'

Cathy shrugged and handed him her fare. She had nothing to be cheerful about but it didn't take much to get her back on track. Something she'd inherited from her mother, if she did but know it.

Dave was there when she got back.

Their home comprised a single room on the first floor of an empty house in a seedy street. The furniture was a mattress on the floor, an armchair with stuffing escaping from several holes and an ancient dining table on which stood a small transistor radio to which Dave was listening with increasing dejection as an excited commentator called out the names of the first three horses past the post. None of these names was on Dave's betting slip. He looked up at Cathy.

'Well?' he asked. 'Did you get it?'

'Never mind that, how much did you just lose?'

'What? Oh, not much.'

Her voice went hard with annoyance. 'You said you weren't going to bet any more. How much, Dave?'

He threw his betting slip at her. She snatched it from mid-air and examined it.

'Two pounds each way – that's four pounds you've just thrown away.'

'You can add up, I'll give you that.' He got to his feet.

'It's as well I didn't get the job,' snapped Cathy. 'I'm not slaving away all day just to finance your gambling. Why don't you get a job?'

'You know why – I've got no qualifications. I've always lived off my wits.'

She surveyed her surroundings. 'And look where your wits have got us. Dave, we're having a baby in five months, we can't live like this.'

He walked to the window and looked out at the dismal street beyond the dirty pane, thumbs hooked into the pockets of his fashionably flared jeans.

'Yer've bloody trapped me with this baby,' he grumbled. 'Under normal circumstances I'd be long gone from here, operating somewhere where they don't know me. Maybe even down in London. I could do well down there,' he mused. 'Teach them soft Southerners a thing or two about nicking motors.'

'Oh, yes,' said Cathy, sarcastically. 'And what would you have done for money? Had it not been for my wages we'd have starved. That's it, isn't it? You only wanted me while I was useful to you.' She walked up behind him and tapped him on his shoulder. 'So, Mr Wonderful, what are you going to do now? Now that I can't support you any more.'

He swung round on her, sudden anger in his eyes. 'Why the bloody hell didn't you take something?'

Cathy shook her head and stood her ground. 'Oh, no, I'm not going through all that again. The pill costs money – we didn't have any money. You knew that at the time.'

He took a few steps towards her. 'I only know what you tell me – how do I know it's the truth?'

It was suddenly apparent to Cathy that he'd been drinking. Up until now she hadn't been able to differentiate between the smell of his breath and the usual dank odour of the room.

'How much have you had to drink and where'd you get the money from?'

Dave decided to answer with a drink-inspired question of his own. He prodded at her stomach.

'How do I know it's my bastard in there?' he sneered. 'How do I know you haven't been having it off with somebody else?'

Cathy was too shocked to answer immediately. It was a ridiculous accusation. At the time of conception they'd been in each other's company practically twenty-four hours a day.

'You lousy pig! You know that's not true.'

He held out his hands and shrugged. 'How do I know? Tell me that. How do I know you haven't had it off with some other bloke?'

Cathy pushed him away, angrily. He retaliated by cuffing her around the head.

'You're good at hitting women, aren't you?' she shouted through emerging tears. 'Funny how I've never seen you hitting men.'

He hit her again, harder this time, making her stagger back to the door. 'This isn't hitting you,' he snarled. 'This is chastising you.' He smacked the side of her head once again, then, as she brought up her hands to protect her face, he punched her hard in the stomach.

'*That's* hitting you.'

'You're hurting my baby,' she sobbed.

'Ah! *Your* baby. I'm glad you said your baby, because it sure as hell isn't *our* baby.'

He hit her full in the face. 'You've been lying to me, haven't you, you slag? Whose baby is it?'

Cathy was in pain now, with blood streaming down her face. Dave was out of control, pushing and punching her back through the room door, out on to the narrow landing.

She felt herself overbalancing backwards and windmilled her arms in an attempt to regain control. Dave gave her a contemptuous push which sent her tumbling down the stairs. She lay there, unconscious, for several minutes before another resident took the trouble to go down the street to ring for an ambulance. Dave had returned to the room to catch the last race.

Four hours later Cathy gave birth to a stillborn son whom she called Marcus though she never saw him. Dave came to visit, consumed with remorse and unable to apologise enough. But the shock of losing her baby had opened Cathy's eyes.

'Dave,' she said, 'just go away and don't come back.'

‘Are you sure?’ There was relief in his eyes.

‘Absolutely sure.’

‘Are we okay? I mean, are you . . .?’

‘No, Dave, I’m not going to report this to the police. I told the doctor I fell downstairs. If you don’t clear off now I might just tell them the truth.’

He leaned over and attempted a farewell kiss, which she turned away from. Dave shrugged and said goodbye, nodded at a pretty nurse and walked out of the ward. He thought he was being let off the hook, no charges would be made against him for assault, which was a relief. Nicking cars was one thing but assault on a woman – he didn’t fancy doing time for that.

Cathy rang the police anonymously from the hospital. They were waiting for him when he got back to the squat, and arrested him for car theft. At least that was something. People shouldn’t get away with things. Cathy had a thing about people not getting away with things.

Her next call was to her mother.

Chapter Fifteen

'I told your dad you were in hospital,' said Liz. 'And why.'

'How did he take it?'

Liz paused before answering. 'Not too well, I'm afraid. Words to the effect of you making your bed and now you've got to lie on it.'

'I can just picture him saying it,' said Cathy. 'So I'm not welcome back then?'

'As far as I'm concerned, love, you can come home with me right now. Sod him and his daft ideas.'

Cathy lay back on her pillow. She was due to be discharged as soon as the doctor had done his rounds and given her the final all clear.

'I don't want to go where I'm not wanted. I know what he'll be like. He'll look upon me as some sort of spoiled goods.'

'No, he won't, Cathy. Your dad's a good man, he . . .'

Cathy interrupted her. 'I know all about that, Mum. But I'm right, aren't I?'

Liz shrugged, then nodded. 'If you came back you'd have to put up with him – that is, until he gets over it.'

'*He* gets over it? Does he know what *I've* just had to get over? I've just lost my baby.'

Liz didn't say what came into her head. She didn't mention what Jim had said about their desperately wanting a child of their own and having to adopt being the next best thing. How he'd said it wasn't fair that someone not fit to have a baby had become pregnant then lost the child through her own negligence and stupidity. If she'd told Cathy all that she'd have lost her forever.

'He'll come round. Just let me work on him. In the meantime you'd better have this.'

Liz gave her an envelope which obviously contained money. Cathy stared at it for a while then realised she had no option but to take it.

'Thanks, Mum. I'll go back to the bedsit and stay there until I sort myself out.'

The Leeds Central Lending Library carried a comprehensive slide record of local newspapers dating back to before the war. It took the assistant librarian just five minutes to come up with a slide copy of the *Yorkshire Evening Post* for Monday, 31 August 1953, two days after Cathy's birthday.

'There wasn't a paper on the thirtieth,' explained the librarian. 'It was a Sunday.'

Cathy placed the slide into the viewer and manoeuvred the first sheet into place.

A Hunslet youth had been arrested in connection with a series of burglaries which had been baffling the police for weeks. Olivia de Havilland had got divorced and the French were having trouble in Cambodia. She saw what she was looking for at the bottom of column five. A minor headline read: BABY FOUND IN CHURCH.

'*A parish priest getting ready for Mass found a new-born baby lying in front of the altar. More on p. 3, col 2.*'

Cathy frantically moved the slide around the viewer trying to find page two. She looked across to the librarian for help.

'I can't find page two.'

The woman came over and expertly positioned the required page in the centre of the screen. 'Is there anything in particular you're looking for?'

'There's something about a baby found in a church.'

Cathy's voice was trembling with emotion.
'There,' said the librarian, pointing to an article.

Cont. from page 1.
A newborn baby was found on the altar of St Catherine's Church, Beckhall, by the parish priest as he was preparing for Mass. It is believed that the mother of the baby is the same person seen falling into the nearby River Wharfe. Despite intensive searching, the woman has not been found. A young man narrowly escaped death attempting to rescue her. Police have released no details of the identity of the missing woman but say that foul play is not suspected. The search was called off late last night.

Cathy clasped her hands together in unconscious prayer as she realised she had just read about the death of her own mother. A woman she'd never known, who had abandoned her at birth. She knew her real mother was dead but she didn't know the circumstances. Liz probably did but there was no point in tackling her about it.

Cathy looked up at the librarian who was concerned by the shocked look on her face.

'Are you okay, love?'

She gave a wan smile. 'Actually, no. I don't suppose I could borrow a pencil and paper, could I?'

The woman went to her desk and returned with a biro and a sheet of memo paper. Cathy wrote down the few details contained in the article and handed the woman back her pen.

'I don't suppose you know where Beckhall is?' she enquired.

'Out towards Selby, I think.'

'Thanks ever so much, you've been very kind.'

Chapter Sixteen

Cathy's eighteenth birthday had come and gone without much celebration, just a drink with Michelle and a chicken chow mein at the Kee Hong. Finances were low. The benefit people frowned on youngsters who left home of their own accord and then tried to live off the State. Cathy had made a half-hearted application before telling the patronising man behind the counter where he could shove his form. Liz helped out when she could and Cathy supported herself by doing bar work.

She had no idea what she hoped to gain by paying a visit to St Catherine's Church. She'd made a few cursory enquiries about her biological parents but had hit a brick wall at every turn. Her enquiries were treated sympathetically but apparently she had no right whatsoever to find out who she really was. It was the way of things and on balance it generally worked, despite the frustration it caused. Without knowing it, she travelled the same bus route as her mother had and asked for the bus to stop as soon as she saw the church spire rising above the trees.

Father John Barrett absent-mindedly buttoned up his rugby shirt, then loosened the top button as it had always been too tight for him. In many ways so had his dog collar. Too restricting for a free-thinking priest such as he. A recent heart attack had reminded the man of his mortality.

Although he was still living in the presbytery, he'd had to hand over his parish to a younger, fitter priest. He still conducted Mass now and again as well as hearing the odd confession, although he sometimes wished for a more inner-city clientele with interesting sins to assuage the boredom. A recent adultery had brightened up his week, especially as he had a good idea as to the identity of the adulteress, despite her muttered confession. She was Mrs Dunsford, a stalwart of the Union of Catholic Mothers and a woman usually quick to condemn such acts in others.

The old priest managed to fix her with a baleful gaze as he stood in the pulpit relating the gospel of St John concerning the woman taken in adultery by the scribes and the Pharisees. With particular reference to Jesus's answer when it was put to Him that Moses had laid down a law commanding that she be stoned.

'He that is without sin among you, let him cast the first stone at her.'

Majorie Dunsford, seated next to her pious husband, lowered her eyes and got the message. But would it stop her little game?

Father Barrett knew it was time to do something about the letter he'd had for eighteen years. Time to hand it over to the child before it was too late. Child? She'd be a young woman by now. But how? In his quest to find her he'd been afforded the same amount of co-operation as Cathy herself, but without the sympathy. He'd worn his dog-collar, but it counted for nothing before the Registrar of Births, Marriages and Deaths. He'd tried praying, hoping the Good Lord might drop everything to step in and lend a hand, but this was a bit much to ask considering all the other problems in the world. As a last resort he had decided to go higher up the clerical ladder and enlist the help of Monsignor Devlin. They'd been ordained at the same time, only Bernard Devlin had kept his nose clean and still harboured hopes of a bishopric. He hated asking Bernard for favours as he knew he'd first have to endure a pious sermon listing his shortcomings.

John Barrett actually had the phone in his hand as Cathy rang the doorbell. He replaced the receiver and annoyed his housekeeper by just beating her to the door. The girl's radiance impressed even an old celibate like him. His eyes twinkled in appreciation of her presence.

'Come in, young lady,' he said, without asking what she wanted.

Cathy stepped across the threshold, sniffing for incense or something, and was surprised at the smell of baking drifting from the kitchen. It smelled like a normal house.

On the wall was a crucifix, a print of the Sacred Heart and a framed Leeds Empire poster advertising Gracie Fields and a host of supporting artists including Arthur Askey. There was a reassuring incongruity to it that made a visitor feel at ease. Perhaps that was the idea.

He led her into a spacious living room that could have been furnished around the time the house was built, over a hundred years previously. The ceiling was high and elaborately corniced and in the centre was an equally elaborate plaster rose from which hung an ugly chandelier. Almost every available inch of floor space was taken up by furniture of Gothic design. A heavy rosewood writing bureau had its sliding top jammed open by a mountain of papers; a huge Victorian sideboard supported a host of framed black-and-white photos of clerical faces and a tantalus holding three crystal bottles, all half-full. At the side of this stood a plant-stand supporting an out-of-control aspidistra. Beneath an ornate gilt mirror stood an upright piano with a song book open at 'Love Me Tender', and on the top stood a silver-framed photograph of Pope Paul VI.

Father Barrett motioned her to sit on a worn velvet drop-end sofa, whilst he made himself comfortable in one of the two squashy armchairs. Heavy brocade curtains hung from the high window behind him, through which the sunlight reflected on the crockery jammed inside a huge mahogany china cabinet.

'Tea?' he asked.

'That would be lovely.'

He picked up a bell from the small table beside his chair and rang it vigorously. Time drifted back a hundred years as the black-and-white-clad elderly housekeeper bustled in and asked, with a complete lack of reverence, 'What is it? I'm busy.'

'The young lady and I wish to take tea – a selection of your cakes would be nice.'

'I'm sure it would.'

She whirled about and disappeared in the same huff she'd arrived.

'She's a treasure,' Father Barrett assured his bemused guest. 'Been with us since time immemorial.'

Cathy nodded, not at all sure if they'd be getting tea and cakes. The old priest rubbed his hands together.

'Right, where were we?'

Cathy was forced to smile. 'You haven't asked who I am yet.'

'Haven't I? How remiss of me. Let's put that right immediately. Who are you?'

'My name's Catherine Makepeace – my friends call me Cathy.'

'Then I shall call you Cathy.' He leaned forward and shook her hand.

'Father Barrett,' he said. He saw her eyeing his rugby shirt. 'I'm off duty at the moment,' he explained.

'Right.'

Being off duty didn't seem to fully explain why a seventy-odd-year-old priest should be wearing a green-and-blue-hooped rugby shirt and tennis shoes.

'Are you a Catholic?' he enquired.

'No.' There was a hint of apology in her voice.

'Splendid – then you're allowed to call me John.'

Cathy felt herself instantly taken to this old priest and desperately hoped he could help her.

'How can I help you, Cathy?'

He flashed her a smile, revealing long, nicotine stained teeth. Tufts of hair sprouted from his ears and his bushy, grey eyebrows almost concealed his twinkling blue eyes. His hair was sparse and left to its own devices as a comb wouldn't really have improved matters. But all in all he had an amiable face.

'I'm not sure you can, actually. You see, I was adopted and I'm trying to find out who my mother is.'

'Ah, you have my sympathy there. I've been trying to track down a certain person myself for the past few weeks . . .' He stopped and frowned. 'What made you think I could help?'

'Well, this is where I was found when I was a baby.'

'Good Lord!' The old priest crossed himself and glanced upwards, nodding his thanks. He knew for certain there'd been some sort of divine intervention here. This was no coincidence.

'What is it, John?'

'Nothing. Just the Good Lord moving in one of his mysterious ways again.'

'Oh.'

'Your name's Catherine?'

'Yes, but my friends call me Cathy.'

'You were born on the twenty-ninth of August 1953?'

'You know about me, don't you? I knew someone here would know about me, that's why I came.'

'Know about you?' exclaimed the priest. 'It was I who found you. It was I who baptised you and named you after this church.'

'Baptised me! You mean, I'm a Catholic?'

'Well – yes. I just did it as a precaution.'

'Before the opposition could get their hands on me, you mean?'

'Before the devil could get his hands on you. You looked a bit under the weather. Had you popped off, at least you'd have died in a state of grace and gone back to where you came from with no harm done.'

Cathy was incredulous. 'And you actually believe all that, do you?'

The priest nodded. 'I've devoted my whole life to believing all that, as have thousands of people much more intelligent than me.'

'I'm sorry, John. I assume I can still call you John?'

'Please do.'

'It's just a bit of a shock to discover I've been a Catholic all my life without knowing it.' Cathy grinned mischievously. 'I've missed out on a lot of school holidays.'

Father Barrett returned her grin, then admonished her gently. 'There's a bit more to it than holidays, my child.'

'I'm sorry, John, I wasn't trying to disparage your beliefs.'

He dismissed her apology with a wave of his hand. 'Our faith is easy to disparage . . . but enough of this ecumenical stuff, we're here to talk about you. I've been looking forward to meeting you for eighteen years, this is like a dream come true.'

They got to their feet simultaneously and without really knowing why, hugged each other. Father Barrett relaxed his hold first, feeling slightly awkward at the proximity of such a beautiful young lady. Ten years ago, when his sap was still rising, he'd have felt more than awkward.

'When I said I was trying to track someone down,' he said, 'I think I can safely say I've found you.'

'Really? Why did you want to track me down?'

'I can perhaps best explain by showing you something.'

The priest went to the writing bureau, took a key from his pocket and opened one of the drawers then crossed himself once again. He'd been waiting for this moment for so long and knew it had been God's hand that had delivered her to his door.

'This is my own personal drawer,' he explained over his shoulder. 'I bequeathed the rest of the clutter to my successor, Father Edmunds.'

From the drawer he took out a large, birthday-card type

envelope, from which he took another, smaller envelope which he handed to Cathy. She turned it over in her hand a couple of times then looked up, questioningly, at him.

'What's this?'

'Read what it says on the envelope.' Then, scarcely able to control the emotion in his voice, he added, 'It's a letter to you from your mother.'

'My mother?'

Cathy looked down at the envelope then back up at him, not understanding. He handed her the letter from the larger envelope on which Annie had written her instructions to him.

'Perhaps if you read this first, it might explain the situation more clearly.'

Cathy read it carefully, then looked back up at him, holding the envelope.

'Do you know what's in this?'

'Oh, no, that letter is for you and you alone.'

She sat down again, expelled a long breath, then carefully tore open the envelope and took out her mother's letter.

Barrack Road Maternity Home
Leeds
29 August 1953

My darling Doris,

I am your mother and I am writing this on the day you were born. You are probably not called Doris because it's not up to me to give you a name but that's what I call you – after Doris Day in *Calamity Jane*. I'm not supposed to see you because they say they're going to take you away from me, but I have seen you and you are beautiful. You should have been eighteen yesterday which is three years older than I am now (I am fifteen), so Happy Birthday for yesterday, my darling.

I did not want to spoil your birthday so I've arranged for you to read this the day after. There is something you need to know and something I would like you to do for me.

I am sorry to tell you that you were conceived when my step-father, Leonard Spode, raped me on the night he was elected an MP. He also killed his wife (my mother, your grandmother, Olga Jackson), when she tried to get him off me. Your granddad, Alan Jackson was a war hero who was killed in 1945. I have only told four people about this. Movita Lunn who was at school with me only she moved to Sheffield, knows most about the things that happened to me. Also Jake Parker a very good friend who was in the Halifax Road Children's Home with me, Jimmy Johnstone another friend of mine who died this morning and Miss Bulmer who was my form teacher at Brookland Park High School. Miss Bulmer did not believe my story because Spode got to her first, but she is a nice woman.

If your father, Leonard Spode, is dead when you read this I hope he is rotting in hell. If he is still alive I expect he will have risen to an important position in politics or something and I would like you to try and expose him for what he is. If you are like me you won't like people getting away with things like that even if he is your father. In the morning I am going to get you from the next room and take you somewhere really nice where you will be looked after properly by people who love you, instead of being adopted by any Tom, Dick or Harry.

Hope you have a lovely life.
Your loving mother,
Annie Jackson

A tear which had been making its way down Cathy's cheek finally dropped on to the page, causing a smudge to match the one left by her mother's tears all those years ago. She folded the letter up and looked at the priest who was dying to see what was in it.

'Good Lord, Cathy,' he said. 'You look as though you've seen a ghost. Can I get you a brandy or something?'

'Yes, please, John. I think I need one.'

'Am I allowed to see the letter?' he asked.

Cathy was deep in thought. The man in charge of Spode Fashions was an MP. Wasn't his name Leonard? Could it be him? God! She'd nearly gone to work for him. He could be her father. This was all just too much to take in.

'Cathy?'

She looked up. 'Pardon?'

'The letter, I was wondering if I could read it.'

But she didn't want to share her mother's letter with anyone, not just yet. 'Sorry – I'd rather you didn't. It's very personal.'

'Oh, I understand.'

The priest opened the tantalus, took out a bottle of brandy and waved away his housekeeper who had just arrived with a tray full of tea and cakes. Cathy didn't notice the look of intense annoyance on the woman's face. She was miles away as the implication of what she'd just read began to sink in.

Father Barrett sat quietly, allowing her to be alone with her thoughts although he felt cheated at not being able to see the letter which he'd been conscientiously guarding for eighteen years. Had Cathy been a Catholic he might have considered pulling rank and insisted on seeing it. She absentmindedly turned the folded paper over in her hands and looked up at him.

'My mother's name was Annie Jackson.' Her voice was small, like that of a child.

'I . . . er . . . I actually knew what her name was.'

'She called me Doris – after Doris Day.'

'Did she really? I like Doris Day. If I'd known I could have baptised you Doris.'

'I prefer Catherine.'

'So do I.'

'She was only fifteen.'

'Yes, I heard she was very young. It was a terrible tragedy.'

'Did she die far away from here?'

He went quiet. Her eyes forced an answer from him. 'The er – the river's about half a mile away. You'll have crossed it on your way here. I'll walk down with you, if you like.'

'I'd like that.'

'She fell in. It was a tragic accident.'

'John, she probably committed suicide.'

'No one knows that.'

Cathy squared her shoulders, brushed away her tears and expelled a long breath.

'Can I see where you found me, please?'

'Of course you can, my child.'

It was a Monday and St Catherine's Church was deserted apart from an old woman in a front pew, her head bowed reverently, quietly reciting her rosary. She looked up from her devotions as the old priest walked past with Cathy and stepped over the communion rail. He turned and invited her to follow him, then recognised the old lady who was smiling at him.

'Good afternoon, Mrs Delaney. Still trying to get Terence into Heaven with your prayers?'

'Yes, Father. If he hadn't been such an old divil I could have been at der Bingo by now.' Her Dublin accent echoed around the empty church.

'I hope he appreciates it, Mrs Delaney.'

'Oh, I'll make sure he does, don't you worry about dat, Father. Terence Joseph Delaney will get a piece of my mind when I get up dere. He's been more of a nuisance dead than ever he was alive. The trouble is, Father, just when I tink I've got him safely behind der Pearly Gates, the verger tells me about another bad ting he's done.'

'You're a credit to him, Mrs Delaney.'

The old woman bowed her head and resumed her prayers as the priest pointed to the floor in front of the altar.

'That's where I found you,' he whispered.

Cathy looked at the carpeted spot where she and her mother had parted company and gave a shudder. The priest placed his arm around her shoulder.

'Do you know how to pray?' he asked gently.

She nodded and clasped her hands together. Together they recited the Lord's Prayer, the priest saying 'Amen' as Cathy ended with 'For Thine is The Kingdom, the power and the glory, forever and ever. Amen'.

The Irishwoman looked up. She'd never heard the Anglican ending used in a Catholic church and wasn't sure it might not be some sort of blasphemy.

Father Barrett stepped back, allowing Cathy a few minutes on her own, then held out his hand to help her back over the rail. Cathy's eyes darted around the church, knowing she was retracing her mother's last steps.

'Can we walk to the end of the lane? I'd like to see where she . . .'

John Barrett understood her need. 'I'd like to show you something else first,' he said.

It was a warm, early-autumn afternoon as he led her to the young mountain ash in the south-east corner, its leaves now turning gold and lilting to the ground in ones and twos, borne on a vague breeze. Taking her arm, he pointed to a wooden plaque, surmounted by a crucifix, beneath the narrow trunk. She looked at him, questioningly. He squeezed her hand.

'It's your mother's tree. I planted it when it became apparent that she'd never be found. I thought one day you'd want somewhere to come . . .'

Cathy looked at the flourishing tree, then back at him. 'You did this for my mother? But you didn't know her.'

'She wanted me to arrange your adoption, but it was taken out of my hands and I felt I'd failed her. This was the least I could do.'

'Failed her? John, I hardly know you, but I doubt if you've ever failed anyone in your life.'

Some people have a happy knack of saying the right things. Cathy was one of them. He suspected her mother had been the same.

'Thank you for that.'

Side by side they looked at the memorial to the girl neither of them had ever met, but who was having such a profound effect on their lives. An effect which would soon spread to the lives of other people. The inscription on the plaque was simple: *This is Annie Jackson's tree. Requiescat in pace.*

'I've kept it varnished and weather-proofed but I can arrange for a stone plaque, if you like,' John offered.

'No, it's perfect as it is.' Cathy looked up at the tree, and brushed one of its falling leaves from her hair. 'She couldn't have a more beautiful memorial than this.'

The priest walked away as Cathy knelt down and began talking quietly to the mother she'd never known.

'I got your letter, Annie. Don't ask me to call you Mum or Mother or anything, I'm three years older than you.' She paused and clasped her hands together, allowing the inevitable tears to flow unchecked.

'What you did was a bit drastic, you know, throwing yourself into the river. Still, having read your letter, I can't begin to imagine what you were going through.'

She suddenly leaned forward and thumped the ground angrily. 'Why did you do it, Annie Jackson? Why did you leave me?'

She lay there, prostrate, for a few seconds before pushing herself back up and looking over to where the priest was standing. He glanced away quickly so as not to embarrass her. Cathy got to her feet.

'Sorry, Annie,' she said. 'You did what you thought you had to do. Anyway, I'm here now and I know what needs to be done. He won't get away with it, Annie. I'll come back here when it's finished.'

She turned and walked over to where the priest was talking to the verger.

'I wish you'd stop filling Mrs Delaney's head with stories of her late husband's wrongdoings,' he was saying.

'Nay, it's the only bit o' fun I get, Father.'

'Did you actually know the late Mr Delaney? To my recollection he didn't attend Mass too often.'

'Well, I only knew him by sight, Father. But I heard many stories about him.'

'It's wrong to speak ill of the dead, Verger,' said the priest, sternly. 'Especially if you're not sure of the facts.'

The verger dropped his head, contritely. 'You're quite right, Father. It was very remiss of me.'

John Barrett took Cathy's arm and walked on, happy in the knowledge that his authority as a priest was still intact.

'What are you smiling for?' enquired Cathy.

'Just remembering. I can still recall the day the old reprobate died.'

'Reprobate? So they weren't just stories then?'

John shook his head. 'Terence Delaney was a villain, but he didn't have an evil bone in his body. His problem was that he couldn't take life seriously. He made a joke out of everything. His wife worshipped him, as did the four children he owned up to.'

'The original likeable rogue?'

'Something like that. It's no excuse for his behaviour, but the world would be a friendlier place if all the villains were like him.'

Spode sprang immediately to Cathy's mind. 'It would indeed, John. Maybe Mr Delaney's philosophy was right and the rest of us are wrong. Maybe life *is* just one big joke.'

The priest gave this possibility some consideration, rather than dismissing it out of hand.

'I went to see Terence on his deathbed,' he remembered. 'He'd asked if I'd hear his confession, but when it came to it, his memory didn't go back far enough. I told him I'd settle for his renouncing the devil, but he said he'd rather not.'

'And why was that?' asked Cathy, curiously.

'He said under the circumstances it was a bad time to start making enemies.'

Cathy laughed and linked her friend's arm. 'I'd like to walk down to the main road now, John. I've had a chat with my mother.'

The priest clapped his hand to his head. 'Oh, bugger!' he exclaimed.

Cathy was mildly shocked.

'I knew there was something else I had to tell you,' he said.

'What's that?'

'A few weeks ago I had a phone call from a solicitor in Leeds asking me if I knew the identity of the baby found on the altar. I told them I was currently looking into it as I had something to give her on her eighteenth birthday – apparently they've got something for you as well. Don't ask me what because they wouldn't tell me. Other than that it was to your advantage.'

'Sounds intriguing.'

'Shall I put them in touch with you?'

'Why not? You know, John, this is turning out to be a most interesting day.'

'Really?' He sounded pleased. 'I don't have interesting days any more. You will come and see me from time to time, won't you?'

'Try and stop me.'

They stopped by the bridge where just one lone fisherman was trying his luck. Sam had been coming here since he was a boy and Monday was his day off, so he fished alone. Scarcely a day's fishing had gone by in the last eighteen years without his looking up at the bridge and wistfully remembering the young girl so fed up with the world that she'd jumped into the river. Sam often cursed himself for not being there for her. If only a fish hadn't taken his hook at that particular moment he'd have gone up the bank to talk to her. He often fantasised about how he might have made a difference to her life had he managed to save her. How he could have made her happy. He looked up and smiled at Cathy and Father Barrett.

'Nice day for it,' he shouted.

Chapter Seventeen

Mary Dawson looked up at the street sign and shook her head for what seemed the hundredth time. This was where her life had begun. They'd named her after this street for want of something better to call her. Somewhere beyond this sign was a past cloaked in darkness, illuminated only by occasional flashes of awfulness. When these came she tried to shut the black door in her mind through which they were trying to force themselves. But somewhere, in the tiny spaces between these vile intruders, were friendlier faces. Loved ones who wanted to get through to her but couldn't without letting the evil through first.

And she didn't want that.

'Ring any bells, Mary love?'

Mary smiled at her companion and shook her head. Nurse Jeanette Hargreaves took her gently by the arm and guided her up the street towards the shops. It was a weekly ritual which had been going on for years. Mary always stopped and gazed up at the sign saying 'Dawson Street' and tried her best to remember. But she knew deep down that whatever was locked away was too dreadful for her to bring back. Maybe she was just a coward.

The bad images almost always came at night. A man behind her in bed, doing despicable things to her. And stairs . . . Horrible things happened to people on stairs. In eighteen years she'd neither gone up nor down more than two steps – any more would constitute a staircase – and how amazingly inconvenient that had been. Woolworth's only had one step to negotiate, so that was her favourite.

Nurse Jeanette always accompanied her on these outings. Someone had to do the talking. Mary hadn't spoken since the day the police found her, late at night, beneath the street sign. At first glance they'd thought she was a prostitute and had stopped their car to move her on, but her mute distress soon put paid to that notion. Dried mud clung to her hair, her clothes were filthy and her eyes were empty as if all the life had been drained out of her, leaving just a shell. Both arms hung uselessly by her sides, deeply lacerated and caked with congealed blood and mud. The police took her to hospital, from where she was transferred to a psychiatric wing and thence to a mental hospital.

The police had tried to identify her, to the extent of running a photograph in the local paper, the *Hull Daily Mail*, but no one recognised her.

It soon became apparent that apart from her lack of speech and memory, she wasn't mentally sub-normal. But her injuries had robbed her of the use of her hands, on top of which she had no identity, so her options were limited. During the day, especially bright sunny ones like today, she sensed the good images behind the door and was sorely tempted to reach out and open it. The soft, downy head of a newborn baby. A lady whose face was blurred but who loved her. The baby's trusting eyes, looking up at her. An old man with a funny accent, singing as he walked beside her, making her smile. Smiles which some people took to be a sign of madness, but these people were wrong. And a final image of a young man fishing. Somehow this always came last.

She told no one of her inner turmoil because she had neither the words nor the will nor the wherewithal to do so. Her existence was based on the certain knowledge that one day things would be better. There was someone behind that door who would see to that. Being called Mary didn't feel right but she didn't mind. It was a nice enough name.

But it didn't feel right.

Then sometimes, mostly at night, a dark chill would close over her head and she couldn't breathe. She was scrambling to get back up to the light but beyond the light was *him* and she didn't want *him* near her. Being near *him* was the worst place in the world to be. She'd wake up screaming and sucking in deep lungfuls of air as the nurses fought to control her and calm her down.

Mary loved the bustle of the Saturday afternoon street. The cheerful chatter of people going by, the buses, the newspaper vendors, the funny man illegally selling cigarette lighters and the way he miraculously snapped his suitcase shut as a policeman's helmet approached.

'Annie.'

Someone shouted out the name from across the street and Mary instinctively turned to see who. But, to her odd disappointment, the shout wasn't directed at her.

Chapter Eighteen

Graham Forber sat down at his desk and glared with distaste at the mountain of files laid there by his secretary. A twenty-one-day Caribbean cruise had its drawbacks. His partner in the law firm, Peter Weaston, had done the absolute minimum to keep Graham's clients at bay. Graham would do the same for him now that he was away. The file on top had a note attached to it.

'*Father John Barrett rang to say he had located the young lady. She is Catherine Makepeace, 7 Prospect Row, Salterton.*'

As it looked to be the easiest way to start the day he picked up the file and pressed a buzzer that brought his secretary's voice on the intercom.

'Yes, Mr Forber?'

'Eileen, who's Catherine Makepeace?'

'I believe she's Annie Jackson's daughter.'

'Right . . . Eileen, who's Annie Jackson?'

'Mr Weaston asked me to locate her, the details are in the file.'

'Is she one of Mr Weaston's clients?'

'No, sir, she's one of *our* clients. At least she will be once we've got proof of her identity.'

Eileen hated this division of labour between the two of them, it made her job that much harder.

'Right – er, I'll leave that one up to you, then.'

'Very good, Mr Forber ... *you bastard!*' She delayed saying the last two words until after she'd put down the receiver.

'These walls are very thin, Eileen,' shouted her boss.

She winced as she placed a sheet of A4 in her Remington and began to type a letter to Cathy.

Cathy Makepeace sat opposite Graham Forber. The solicitor took a ribbon-bound sheaf of papers from a file and examined it carefully.

'The Register Office has confirmed your identity,' he said, tapping a pencil between his teeth as he turned over a few more pages.

'It's good to have an identity.'

He looked up. Cathy smiled to emphasise that she wasn't being serious. He returned his attention to the file.

'It's not normal practice for them to do this, you see.'

'Do what?' she asked.

'Reveal the true identity of an adopted child.'

'I suppose they have their reasons.'

'Quite. They only did it because we already knew – and just needed their official confirmation in order to proceed.'

'Proceed with what?'

The solicitor continued his tooth-tapping, setting Cathy's own teeth on edge. He stopped a split second before she asked him to.

'Have you ever heard of a gentleman called James Johnstone?' he asked.

Cathy gave a puzzled frown and shook her head. 'Don't think so.' Then she remembered. 'Jimmy Johnstone. My mother mentioned a man called Jimmy Johnstone in a letter to me. He was a friend of hers. Apparently he died the day I was born.'

Graham rifled through the file and picked up a death certificate.

'Died twenty-ninth of August 1953.' He looked up at her to check the date.

‘That’s the day I was born.’

He nodded as he read on. ‘In his will he left everything to your mother, and in the event of her death to her first-born child when said child reached the age of twenty-one.’ He looked up at her. ‘That’s you.’ He smiled.

There were so many questions in Cathy’s mind. Who was Jimmy Johnstone? What was his connection to her mother? How did he die? Was his death in some way connected to her mother’s suicide? Had her mother been in love with him? Her mind had been jumbled with these questions and many others ever since she’d read the solicitor’s letter.

‘I expect you’re wondering how much he left you?’

‘Who was he?’ she asked.

Graham Forber was slightly taken aback by her lack of interest in financial matters. ‘We actually know little about the man other than that he made out his will in this office the day before he died of a heart attack. Odd that, don’t you think?’

‘Heart attack? How old was he?’

The solicitor did a mental calculation. ‘Seventy-eight,’ he said.

‘So he wasn’t my mother’s boyfriend?’

The solicitor smiled. ‘I’d say not. Although he did leave her – sorry, you – almost nineteen thousand pounds after costs.’

‘What?’

‘Eighteen thousand nine hundred and sixty-two pounds forty-eight pence.’ He examined some figures on a type-written sheet in front of him. ‘As executors we sold his house and effects and placed the money in our clients’ account where it has been gathering interest for eighteen years.’

‘So, in three years I’ll inherit nineteen thousand pounds?’

‘Plus another three years’ interest.’

‘Wow!’

He picked up a bulky parcel up off the floor and placed it

on the desk. 'There are some effects which weren't considered saleable.'

'What's in it?' enquired Cathy.

'No idea. But I see no reason why we can't hand these over now. That is, if you want them now?'

'Er – yes.' Cathy was still trying to come to terms with her windfall. Nineteen thousand pounds was more than her mum and dad's house was worth.

Graham Forber pushed the parcel towards her. 'If you'd care to sign this receipt, Miss Makepeace, our business is concluded – for the time being at least. Unless, of course, you require our advice on any other matter.'

'Er, no – that is, not at the moment.'

'We have your address, we'll contact you in three years. I assume you'll let us know if you move anywhere else?'

'Yes, definitely.'

Cathy picked up the parcel and left the office. As the door closed behind her she shuddered. It was as if her mother was reaching out to her from beyond the grave, helping as much as she could.

Annie hadn't known about the will. That much was obvious to Cathy. Had her mother realised she had such wealth she would surely not have taken such a drastic action. Jimmy Johnstone's other effects amounted to a couple of photo albums, a signed ten by eight photo of Doris Day, some letters to and from his wife when he'd been serving in the Boer War, and a most revealing set of notebooks in which he'd recorded the events of his life. Excluding nothing. The final page mentioned Annie. It was dated 29 August 1953.

> Yung Annie Jackson is the finest yung lady I ever clapped eyes on sinse my Mary dide. At last I have somwun to leeve my house to insted of it going to the guvermant. If she dusent survive the birth like my Mary dident then I hav left my stuf to her wee baby. This is wat the solissitor advizd. This morning Doris Day sent

me her foto sayin to Jimmy with love on it and kisses. I have a pane in my arm so I will continnu tomorrow.

Cathy shook her head, sadly. Tomorrow, for Jimmy Johnstone, never came.

According to Jimmy's notebooks, she'd just inherited the proceeds of a life of crime and she wasn't sure how she felt about that. However, it was all tied in with her mother who'd been a victim of a far worse unpunished crime. There was a swings and roundabouts sort of justice here that assuaged Cathy's conscience.

On the way back, the bus passed the expansive playing fields of Brookland Park High School. Football and hockey were being played on neighbouring pitches and Cathy smiled as she imagined the boy/girl banter crossing the adjacent touchlines. More than likely her mother had played on that very pitch. Suddenly she developed an urge to be one of them. Back where she should be, taking her A levels. Purely on a whim she got off the bus and made her way to the school gates.

Chapter Nineteen

Brookland Park High School had increased in size in the nineteen years since Annie had been a pupil, from five hundred to eleven hundred pupils, accommodated in extensions which were architecturally hideous but nevertheless necessary. Jim and Liz Makepeace had deliberately steered their adopted daughter towards another of the city's grammar schools. They knew her mother had been a pupil there.

The Headmistress seemed the obvious person to approach. Cathy knocked on the door with a certain amount of trepidation.

'Come in.' The voice was pleasant and put Cathy at her ease before she'd opened the door.

Behind a busy desk sat a grey-haired woman of around fifty who looked up and smiled at her visitor, glad of a diversion. She gave a quizzical frown.

'Are you a new student? Don't seem to recognise you. I pride myself on knowing everyone's name but some slip through the net, especially new students. I expect it's my age. Do sit down. How can I help you? Would you like a coffee?'

Cathy smiled at this pleasantly garrulous lady. 'I'd love one, thanks.'

The Headmistress thrust out a welcoming hand. 'Silvia Scatchard – Scrapyard to the pupils. Beyond this door you'll have to call me Mrs Scatchard, which seems a bit ridiculous, I know, considering you're practically an adult yourself.'

She heaved her ample frame from her chair and moved stiffly over to a simmering coffee percolator. A pencil was stuck through the hair twisted into a bun on her neck, presumably for safe-keeping.

'My only vice,' she remarked over her shoulder. 'I tell myself that the caffeine gives me the edge over the enemy without.' She inclined her head towards the door.

'Do you mean the pupils or the teachers?' laughed Cathy, who had taken an instant liking to this odd woman.

'Both. I need to keep my wits about me to cope with them all.'

She handed Cathy a cup of steaming coffee. 'Help yourself to milk and sugar.'

The Headmistress plonked herself back down in her chair and laced her fingers together across her stomach. 'There, let that cool for a while as we talk.' She looked expectantly at Cathy. 'What did you say your name was?'

'Catherine Makepeace – and I'm not actually a student.'

'Ah! That explains it. My memory hasn't betrayed me.'

'But I wondered if I might become one?'

Cathy accompanied this with a pleading look. Mrs Scatchard gave the vaguest shake of her head, obviously disappointed to be saying no.

'We're halfway through the term. Even if I could agree, I doubt you could catch up.'

'It wouldn't be a problem, I've . . .'

Mrs Scatchard held up a hand to stop her. 'Sorry, it's just not on, I'm afraid. If I push any more students on to my teachers I'll have a rebellion.' She picked up her coffee, took a tentative sip to test the temperature, then followed it with a deep gulp.

'Where were you before? Couldn't they give you a place? I mean, it's actually a bit late in the year to be starting A levels.'

'I was at City Girls' High. I was actually halfway through my second year when I had to leave through, er, circumstances beyond my control.'

'Ah – I've come across those circumstances myself from time to time.'

Cathy doubted this but smiled anyway.

For no apparent reason the Headmistress donned a pair of half-moon glasses which had been hanging on a black cord around her neck, and looked at Cathy over the top of them. 'And they won't take you back. Typical of them.'

'To be honest, I haven't asked them. My mother was a pupil here – I just thought it would be nice.'

'Your mother? She recommended us, did she?'

'Not really, she died the day I was born.'

'Oh dear,' said Mrs Scatchard, 'how sad.'

'Perhaps you knew her?'

'I doubt it, I wouldn't have been here then. What was her name?'

'Annie, Annie Jackson.'

Mrs Scatchard ran the name over in her mind. 'You know, that name rings a bell. Now, who used to talk about Annie Jackson?' She shook her head. 'Sorry, can't remember. There was something special about her, what was it?'

'Among other things, *me*,' said Cathy. 'You see, she was only fifteen when I was born.'

'Ah . . . Unfortunately it all happened long before I arrived here, so I never actually knew her.'

'Pity,' said Cathy. 'You see, I don't know much about her myself. I was adopted and I've only just found out about her . . .'

The Headmistress removed her glasses to tend to the tears welling up in her eyes as Cathy gave an abridged version of recent events, ending with her losing her baby but not including anything about Annie's letter.

'You know, I'd love to help you,' said Mrs Scatchard. 'But as far as giving you a place here . . .' she thought about it for a second. 'I really can't.' She drained her coffee and went to the percolator for a refill. 'Gloria Elliot!' she exclaimed. 'I'm sure it was Gloria. She was here around that time. She's left now, but I can give you her address.' She nodded her head as she poured milk into her cup. 'Yes, it was definitely Gloria Elliot – or Gloria Bulmer, as she was then. She'll tell you about your mother.'

Gloria Bulmer. The name rang a bell in Cathy's mind. Annie had mentioned a Gloria Bulmer in her letter. 'That'd be great. I'd love to talk to her.'

'She lives in Haverford Close. I know this because I've been there once or twice. She's a school governor now.'

Cathy had no clear plan in mind as to how she was going to even things with Spode, but she felt it would help if she began to fill herself in on her mother's background. A chat with Gloria would be a good place to start. Then perhaps she could track down the other people Annie had mentioned in her letter.

She counted the houses down the Street as her taxi cruised into Haverford Close.

'Last on the right,' she instructed.

She stood at the gate and looked up at the three-bedroomed semi housing her mother's former teacher, a universally popular design in the sixties with its dormer windows and built-in garage. She rang the bell, listening to ensure it was working.

Gloria Elliot had lived with her guilt at rejecting Annie Jackson for over eighteen years, always wondering if the girl might have lived had she shown a bit more compassion. Sadly, throwing herself into a river hadn't added in any way to the veracity of the girl's story, she could still have been lying about her step-father raping her and simply have killed herself out of sheer despair. Gloria's husband kept convincing her that this was the case and that she had nothing to feel guilty about. Her guilt had subsided over the years but was resurrected when Cathy appeared on her doorstep . . .

*

'Mrs Elliot, my name is Cathy Makepeace – my mother was one of your pupils and I wondered if I could come in and have a chat with you about her?'

It didn't ring an immediate bell with Gloria Elliot. 'Oh dear,' she said. 'I wasn't aware that any of my pupils had grown up daughters. You've suddenly made me feel quite old.'

Cathy laughed. 'There's no need, Mrs Elliot. My mother had me when she was fifteen.' She looked directly at the woman and added. 'My mother's name was Annie Jackson.'

Gloria Elliot stared at Annie.

'Oh dear God!'

She now knew beyond a doubt that Annie had been telling the truth all along. She'd seen Spode on television only the night before, being interviewed about the way he'd dealt with a recent problem at his factory. Some of his workers had gone on strike because of a job demarcation dispute and Spode had marched out to the picket line and given them all their cards. The *Evening Post* had picked up the story and run it with a photograph of him. He was still a handsome man despite his fifty-seven years and Cathy had too strong a look of him for it to be a mere coincidence. Gloria took a step back to steady herself and Cathy's smile of greeting turned to a look of concern. She darted forward to catch Gloria before she fell and lowered her mother's former teacher to the floor. She knelt beside her.

'Are you okay, Mrs Elliot?'

Gloria smiled ruefully. 'Yes, sorry about that. But the sight of you took me by surprise.'

'Could you tell me what you mean by that, Mrs Elliot?' asked Cathy. She'd also seen photographs of Spode and was conscious of a similarity.

Gloria didn't know what to say. She'd no idea why Cathy was here and even less idea if she knew how she came to be conceived.

'Were you thinking I looked like someone?' pressed

Cathy. 'Someone my mother accused of being my father, only no one believed her, not even you?' Her question came out with a belligerence she hadn't intended, especially in the present circumstances.

'Sorry, Mrs Elliot, that sounded awful. But I would like to know.'

Gloria stood up, shakily, and shook hands with her. 'I'm delighted to meet you, Cathy – and please call me Gloria. Your mother was one of my favourite pupils. Seeing you standing there, proving her right and me and everyone else wrong, was such a shock, even after all these years.'

'So you do think I look like him – Gloria?'

'I'm afraid so. The similarity is startling.'

'Good.'

Cathy had already considered the implications and had decided the advantages outweighed the disadvantages.

'I can't begin to tell you how sorry I am,' said Gloria.

'Why be sorry? He's quite a good-looking man.'

'Oh – well, I suppose there must be a bright side to everything,' said Gloria, slightly taken aback by the girl's attitude.

'And it does prove he raped my mother.'

Gloria said nothing.

'Doesn't it?' pressed Cathy.

'I suppose so.'

'There's no suppose about it, Gloria.'

'No, sorry, you're right. Forgive me, I'm finding it hard to accept that I failed your mother when she needed me most.'

Gloria beckoned for Cathy to follow her into the living room where she sat down and buried her head in her hands. Cathy sat and allowed her time for tearful contemplation, fighting an uncharitable urge to add to her grief by reminding her that Annie had been deserted by everyone – and had resorted to delegating her revenge to her baby daughter. As Gloria sobbed, Cathy was more determined than ever to be the one person in the world that Annie Jackson could rely on.

She left two hours later, well aware by then why her mother liked this woman so much. Much of her time had been spent reassuring Gloria, trying to assuage her guilt, telling her that her mother understood why her favourite teacher hadn't believed her.

'In her letter she said you were a good woman.'

'Letter? You say she left you a letter?'

Cathy nodded.

'Can I see it?'

Cathy studied Gloria, briefly wondering whether to enlist her help in bringing Spode to book. But only briefly. Gloria Elliot was a good woman but that was no qualification for helping with what lay ahead. She was happily married, with a family and responsibilities. And a tendency to faint when suddenly shocked.

'I'm sorry, it's sort of private. I haven't shown it to anyone.'

'Oh – I understand. At least I think I do,' said Gloria.

'I'm trying to trace a former pupil called Movita Lunn,' said Cathy. 'She moved to Sheffield but was at Brookland Park High at the same time as my mother.'

'The name rings a bell. So many children pass through one's hands that it's only possible to remember the ones who stood out for some reason. Annie Jackson was outstanding in many ways.'

'It's okay. I didn't really expect you to know where she was. I'm just trying to find out as much about my mother and the circumstances surrounding her death as I can. If you think of anything else, would you give me a ring?'

'Of course, Cathy. I want to help.'

It would have been nearer the truth had Gloria said, 'I need to help.'

Tracking down Movita wasn't as straightforward. She'd moved from Brookland Park to Hallamshire Girls' High in

Sheffield, but there the trail dried up. The address the school had for her no longer existed. The whole district had been pulled down to make way for an estate of insubstantial-looking town houses with communal lawns littered with old cars, barking dogs and motor-cycling youths. Cathy returned to Leeds disappointed but not disheartened. Avenging her mother wasn't going to be easy. This was a minor setback. She knew there'd be other, not so minor ones.

She placed advertisements in the Leeds and Sheffield local papers enquiring as to Movita Lunn's current whereabouts. The phone rang the night the advert appeared in the *Yorkshire Post*. Cathy picked up the receiver, expectantly.

'Hello, Cathy Makepeace.'

'Yer were asking about Movita Lunn,' said a voice of indeterminate sex.

'I was,' replied Cathy, excited. 'You're not her, are you?' But somehow she knew this uneducated voice didn't belong to her mother's best friend.

'Me? Nah. I know where she went ter live, though.'

There was a pause as Cathy waited for the caller to elaborate.

'Hello?' said the voice.

'Hello – I'm still here,' said Cathy.

'Is there any money in it? A reward like?'

Cathy was slightly taken aback. She was also wary lest this was a crank caller simply trying to extract money she didn't have in exchange for worthless information.

'Possibly,' she hedged. 'Depends on how good your information is.'

'Right. Well, she went ter live in Sheffield.'

Cathy nodded, at least this wasn't a crank caller. 'I actually know that much,' she said. 'I tracked her down to Hallamshire Girls' High School but the address they gave me doesn't exist any more.'

'Oh,' said the caller, disappointed. 'I didn't know that.'

'So you don't know where she's living now?'

'Er, no.'

Cathy was about to end the conversation when an idea struck her. 'Do you mind if I ask how you knew Movita Lunn?'

'Mind – why should I mind? She used ter live near us. I went ter t' same school as her. Same primary school anyroad.'

Cathy felt a lurch of excitement. 'Lowtoft Road?' she asked.

'Yeah.'

'Did you know anyone called Annie Jackson?'

'Annie Jackson – yeah, I knew Jacko all right. She got hersen up t' stick and killed hersen.'

Cathy felt a surge of anger at this callous description of her own conception and her mother's death.

'Annie was my mother,' she said angrily, almost slamming the phone down.

'Sorry,' said the caller, quickly. 'How were I ter know?'

'Look,' said Cathy, 'can I meet you for a chat? I'm willing to pay for your time.'

She seemed to have said the magic words. 'Fair enough. Where d'yer want ter meet me?'

'I'll come to you,' decided Cathy. 'Which is your local pub?'

'Ashley Arms probably. I could see yer there at dinner-time tomorrer.'

'Right, shall we make it twelve-thirty? Oh, what's your name?'

'Brenda Bacup. I'll be in t' tap room. I've got ginger 'air.'

The following day, Cathy was checking her purse and trying to estimate what Brenda Bacup might consider her time to be worth when her phone rang.

'Are you the person who's looking for Movita Lunn?'

'Yes, I am.'

'Do you mind if I ask who you are and why are you looking for her?'

Reasonable questions. The caller sounded far more articulate than Brenda Bacup.

'She knew my mother. There are things I need to know about her.'

'And who is your mother?'

'My mother's dead, her name was Annie Jackson. Who is this, please?'

'You're Annie's daughter? The one . . .?'

Cathy filled in the awkward pause. 'I'm the one she left in the church before she killed herself,' she said quietly. 'Who are you?'

There was another long pause. 'I'm Movita Lunn – or I was. I'm Movita Steadman now.'

Cathy felt her heart lift. 'Movita – this is great! My name's Cathy. I wonder if I could talk to you about my mother?'

'I'd love that. Your mother was a dear friend of mine.'

Not dear enough, thought Cathy, uncharitably. 'Where are you ringing from – Sheffield?'

'No,' said Movita. 'I've been living back in Leeds since I got married thirteen years ago. Where are you?'

'Salterton. Look, I'm coming into Leeds this lunchtime to meet another of my mother's old friends. Perhaps you'd like to join us? I'm meeting her in the Ashley Arms.'

'Anyone I know?'

'Er, yes, I expect you will. Someone called Brenda Bacup.' Cathy didn't hear the gasp at the other end. 'Do you know her?' she asked.

'Yes, I do,' said Movita. 'She said she was one of Annie's old friends, did she?'

'Well, yes – er, well not in so many words. They were at school together, I just assumed . . .'

'Look,' said Movita, 'I've got a little part-time job but I can see you in my lunch hour. I think it might be as well if you and I had a little chat before you meet Brenda – just to let you know what you're letting yourself in for.'

'Really?'

'Really,' confirmed Movita. 'What time are you meeting her?'

'Twelve-thirty.'

'I'm in a blue Mini. I'll be in the car park at twenty-past twelve.'

'So will I.'

'I assume you're . . .' Movita did a mental calculation. 'Eighteen?'

'That's right,' confirmed Cathy. 'Old enough to buy you a drink. I'm looking forward to seeing you, Movita.'

Brenda Bacup stared at herself in the full-length wardrobe mirror, searching for redeeming features and finding none, unless National Health teeth could be considered a redeeming feature. The last of her own crooked teeth had been extracted during her time in jail. Perhaps she'd been hoping that the advent of middle age might have moulded her face in such a way as to give her a motherly appeal, although she wasn't a mother and was never likely to be. Not for any gynaecological reasons, simply because prospective fathers couldn't be persuaded to do the necessary. After coming out of jail she'd tried a variety of occupations, even prostitution. But not one single client had taken her up on her free introductory offer. Brenda Bacup was a terminally ugly woman.

Her size and strength kept all the many insults aimed at her well out of her earshot, so she did have that in her favour. When Brenda counted her blessings she didn't use many fingers, although she could count being above average intelligence. Not *way* above, but enough to set her ahead of most people. It was a combination of these two assets which led her to the King Street Collection Agency where she was the star performer. Her fifteen per cent commission on all debts collected provided her with a good income and a certain contentment at having at last found a niche in her life. Few debtors gave Brenda Bacup much hassle. She was also able to figure out the hopeless cases.

The people so skint they couldn't pay back no matter how much you hassled them. Brenda never wasted time on hopeless cases.

But despite her fulfilment in her occupation there was still an unfulfilled need to right the wrong she had been done when Her Majesty had deprived her of seven years of her life.

She'd been out for more than ten years now but the hurt was still there. It wasn't like when Annie Jackson had locked her in the bogs all those years ago. In a tit-for-tat way, maybe she'd deserved that. She'd even admired Annie for it and had decided against risking her revenge ever again. People with imagination make the most formidable of foes. She smiled at the memory of her old adversary and wished they could have been friends. Any friend would have done.

As a child, Brenda had never been exposed to love and as a consequence had never developed a capacity for love herself. Her standards were set by the people around her. In her childhood home violence, hatred and abuse were the norm. For many years, friendship was an alien concept to her. There wasn't a single person in the world she could call a close friend, not even her brothers, neither of whom she had seen or heard of since the day she'd been arrested. Her mother had grudgingly visited her a couple of times, each visit ending in an argument. Cancer had taken her, just six months before Brenda was released. She had been allowed home for her mother's funeral, which was just as well because her brothers didn't manage it.

Yes, a friend would have been nice. A friend like Annie Jackson. She picked up the paper and once again read the notice in the Personal Column.

'*Would anyone knowing the whereabouts of Movita Lunn, a pupil of Brookland Park High School, Leeds, in 1953, please contact Salterton 45372.*'

Movita Lunn. She'd been Annie Jackson's friend. Brenda had never been struck on Movita, she wasn't made of the same stuff as Annie. Mind you, few girls were.

Brenda had a last grimace at herself in the mirror before she went off to meet Annie's daughter.

The Ashley Arms was a brick and concrete edifice, built in the 1920s and growing uglier by the day. Movita looked at it and decided that the face-lift it had undergone since she'd last seen it had served no purpose. Years of industrial grime had been sand-blasted away along with the mortar joints which had been badly re-pointed. Leaded lights, its only redeeming architectural feature, had been replaced by plate-glass windows in an attempt to bring more daylight into the dismal interior, which had also been altered. The four original rooms were now just two, a concert room and a bar. Fruit machines and a juke-box now restricted the idle chatter of the drinkers. Another nail in the coffin of civilisation.

Cathy spotted the Mini straight away. There were only four cars altogether. The Ashley Arms catered mainly for the pedestrian trade. She tapped on the window, disturbing Movita's daydream as Harry Neilson sang 'Without You'.

'Movita Lunn?'

'Movita Lunn as was. I got married.'

'Sorry, you did tell me.'

Movita turned off the radio, then leaned across and opened the passenger door as Cathy walked around the front of the car. They shook hands formally. The age gap didn't seem like a generation, Movita was wearing well. She was a lot prettier than Cathy figured anyone called Movita had a right to be, fair-haired and slim with a bright smile. Had her mother lived she probably wouldn't have looked any older. The thought saddened Cathy.

'Look,' began Movita, 'before we talk about anything else, what do you know about Brenda Bacup?'

Cathy shrugged. 'Nothing – apart from she used to go to school with my mother.'

'That much is true,' confirmed Movita. 'She wasn't

exactly a friend of your mother's, though. In fact she was a very unpleasant bully.'

'People change as they grow older – don't they?'

'I'm not sure Brenda changed much. She killed her dad when she was about seventeen. Got sent to prison.'

'Wow!' said Cathy. 'I'm not sure I should keep my appointment with her.'

'I just thought I'd warn you,' said Movita. 'We could go somewhere else for a natter.'

'Why did she kill her father?'

'Not sure,' replied Movita. 'I think he was abusive and Brenda sort of lost it. She hit him with a chair – several times apparently. There were mitigating circumstances but she blew any chance she had of a light sentence by jumping over the dock and thumping the prosecuting barrister. It went down badly with the judge. She got ten years, although I believe she got out after seven.'

Cathy sat there for a while, wondering what to do. She turned to Movita. 'I must say, I'm curious to meet her.'

Movita was opening the car door before Cathy had finished. 'So am I,' she said. 'I haven't seen her since I was a kid.'

Brenda was halfway down a pint of Guinness when Cathy and Movita walked in. She turned and gave them a cursory glance, then looked away. She was expecting a young woman on her own, not a couple of obvious dykes. Prison had contaminated Brenda's already jaundiced view of people.

Cathy found the sight of her intimidating. Close on six foot tall and pushing fifteen stone, Brenda had a mop of short, wiry red hair sprouting from her head in all directions, like an old lavatory brush. Her face was mean and freckled as she finished off the remaining half pint in one go. She thrust the glass towards a nervous barman.

'And again,' she ordered. 'Clean glass.'

Cathy walked up beside her with Movita in her wake,

playing second fiddle just as she had to Annie all those years ago.

'Brenda Bacup?' enquired Cathy.

The large woman turned round and glared at them.

'Who wants ter know?'

The menace she exuded made Cathy catch her breath, as did Brenda's acute body odour. She took a step back but it wasn't enough. 'Er – my name's Cathy Makepeace. We spoke on the phone?'

Brenda's sorry attempt at a welcoming smile was let down by her ill-fitting teeth. 'Oh, right. I thought yer'd be on yer own.' She looked suspiciously at Movita who was hovering at Cathy's shoulder.

'Hello, Brenda,' said Movita. 'Long time no see.'

Brenda stared at her for a while then shook her head. 'I don't know yer,' she concluded.

'Movita Lunn – Annie Jackson's friend.'

The big woman nodded, then looked at Cathy.

'So yer found 'er then? I don't suppose yer'll be needin' me.'

'Look, shall we grab a table?' suggested Cathy. She took a five-pound note from her bag, all the money she had in the world. Brenda's time would have to be cheap. 'What are we all drinking?'

The three of them sat down, Cathy and Movita on the opposite side to Brenda, and waited in awkward silence for the barman to bring their drinks to the table, a service not accorded to mere mortals, only the likes of Brenda. She gave Movita a surly glance as she took out a packet of cigarettes. She put one in her mouth and seemed to remember her manners at the last minute. Offering the packet to the others, she asked, 'Smoke?'

Movita shook her head and Cathy said, 'No, thanks, I'm trying to give them up.'

'I've been tryin' since I were ten,' said Brenda. 'Managed it for a while then prison got me started again. Yer can pick up some bad habits there.' Then, realising what she was saying, she added, 'I suppose yer'll know all about me bein' locked up?'

Movita nodded. 'We know what you did.'

'Maybe you had good reason,' chipped in Cathy.

'Maybe I did,' said Brenda. 'Maybe 'e were a drunken bastard what knocked us about once too often.'

'I know the type,' sympathised Movita. 'My dad was handy with his fists when he'd had a few. Mind you, my mother was handier.'

Brenda almost sneered at her. 'You? Yer've no idea what it were like. Me dad were a bloody psycho after a few drinks. He treated us like shit. Killin' 'im were the best thing I ever did. It saved me mam's life, I can tell yer that for nowt, not that she appreciated it. I did seven years for 'im, but it were worth every bloody day.'

'My mother had a step-father who probably made your dad look like a saint,' said Cathy. 'He raped her and caused her to commit suicide.'

She found herself crying as the words came out. Brenda's face softened to a friendly scowl as she laid a beefy hand on top of Cathy's. 'It's all right, love – they're bastards are men. Every last one of 'em.'

Movita felt like giving her an argument in defence of her own husband, but turned instead to Cathy.

'Your mother told me all about Leonard Spode. The abuse had been building up for a while before he actually raped her.'

Cathy listened intently to Movita's detailed recollection of her talks with Annie. Of how he beat Olga, Cathy's grandmother, and interfered with Annie in the bath. Of the psychological cruelty he inflicted on the two of them during the short time he'd been married to Annie's mother. Her voice dropped to not much more than a whisper as she related how Spode had raped Annie and killed her mother.

'The worst part as far as I was concerned was that we'd moved to Sheffield by the time she found out she was pregnant. They stuck her in this maternity hostel which sounded a right hell-hole. We used to write to each other regularly, but towards the end it became obvious they weren't passing my letters on to her.'

'They'll have been reading 'em before they gave 'em to her,' said Brenda. 'Yer must've said summat they didn't like.'

Movita nodded. 'The thought occurred to me. In one of my letters I'd suggested she went to the papers with her story. In her next letter to me she didn't mention it. Not long after that she stopped writing to me. I kept meaning to visit her, but by the time I got round to it, it was too late . . .' Movita was close to tears as she took a sip of her drink. 'She'd hit Spode with a vase. He was threatening to have her locked up for attempted murder.'

'She'd 'ave got mebbe five years,' concluded Brenda. 'Ten if she'd topped 'im.'

'It might have been worth it,' said Movita. 'He was an absolute animal.'

'Yer don't know what yer talkin' about,' sneered Brenda. 'Somebody like Annie wouldn't o' lasted two minutes in the shit'ole they put me in. Good-lookin' lass like 'er, they'd 'ave 'ad her fer breakfast.'

'She was fifteen,' pointed out Movita, inwardly angry at Brenda's uncalled for attitude. 'She'd have been put in a juvenile detention centre.'

'Aye, for a couple of years mebbe. After that . . .' Brenda shook her head.

'I didn't come here to listen to you two arguing about something that didn't happen,' said Cathy, sharply. She was forced to smile at the sudden contrition on the faces of the two older women.

'You're right, sorry,' apologised Movita.

'Sorry,' echoed Brenda, who couldn't remember the last time she'd used the word. There was something about Cathy.

'What is it you *do* want, Cathy?' asked Movita.

She didn't know whether to let them into her confidence,

especially Brenda. She stared at them in silence for a while, a silence broken by the big woman.

'If Leonard Spode married yer grandma, what does that make him then, yer step-granddad? Bugger me! Fancy yer granddad bein' a bleedin' millionaire!'

'He's not my granddad,' corrected Cathy. 'He's my natural father.'

The tears she then dissolved into had been threatening since the day she'd read her mother's letter. Her two companions watched with sympathy. Brenda's meaty hand pressed down on Cathy's once again.

'Yer know, lass, everybody thought I were in t' wrong for what I did ter me dad. But I weren't, yer know. He got what were comin' to 'im. I'll not go into details but in 'is own way 'e were just as bad as Spode – if not worse. I got away wi' manslaughter because I were a girl. Mind you, I could 'ave got off wi' a lighter sentence.' She grinned. 'I lost me temper in court. I reckon it cost me another two years.'

'I heard about that,' said Movita. 'What happened, exactly?'

Brenda finished her pint and looked at it ruminatively, as if waiting for it to fill itself up. But neither Movita nor Cathy had any intention of going to the bar until Brenda told her story.

'Well, it were all over bar the shoutin' – and I knew I were gonna be found guilty so I didn't see no need for 'em ter blacken me character any more than they already 'ad. Anyroad this prosecutin' barrister were doin' his summin' up. He suddenly pointed at me an' asked the jury ter tek a good look at me. "Take a good look at the accused," he said. Yer know, in that supercilious bloody way these pillocks 'ave. "Do you see anything but evil in that face? Ladies and gentlemen of the jury, that is the face of a killer."' Brenda picked up her pint and swallowed the dregs. Cathy signalled the barman to bring another as the big woman continued:

'I'm tellin' yer, I've never felt so useless in all me life.' 'I'd 'ad years o' me dad batterin' me about an' then this bastard starts on me. I mean, it's bad enough 'avin' ter walk round wi' a face like a camel's arse without folk goin' on about it. I lost me temper and jumped on him.' She laughed out loud. 'I broke 'is nose before they got me off 'im.'

Brenda's story-telling had a self-effacing humour about it that had Movita smiling. It was a side to Brenda she had never seen as a child. She was shocked by Cathy's next remark.

'Brenda, your face isn't at all like a camel's arse, but I'm afraid you do smell like one!'

Every muscle in Movita's body went on red alert, ready to dive for cover. She looked at Cathy in horror. Her late friend's daughter was smiling sweetly at Brenda, who was looking totally bemused at this sudden attack on her personal hygiene.

'It's a common medical complaint, the sufferer's always the last to know,' went on Cathy. 'Because people are always too embarrassed to tell them, which I think is a bit silly because it's easily cured.'

Brenda lifted an arm and sniffed under her armpit. Movita recoiled in disgust.

'Yer right, love,' she admitted. 'I do smell a bit ripe.'

'There's stuff you can buy to get rid of it,' advised Cathy. 'A friend of mine had it. I told her straight away – it was either that or keep her distance.'

'I can well believe it,' said Movita, who could see a lot of Annie in this young lady.

Cathy regarded Brenda with an innocent smile which totally disarmed the older woman.

'You're not offended or anything are you?'

'No, love. I'd like ter know how ter get rid of it, though.'

'I'll give you a ring as soon as I get back,' said Cathy.

She then subjected Movita to the same scrutiny she'd

given Gloria Elliot the day before. Was it fair to burden her with this? Another happily married woman. She suspected that Movita might feel honour bound to help, but would her heart be in it? Maybe. After all, she'd been Annie's best friend. Cathy's hand went to the letter in her pocket.

'Have you any children, Movita?' she enquired.

'Two.' Movita smiled. 'Both boys – a real handful.'

That settled it. Cathy brought out her hand, minus the letter, and looked at Brenda, applying the same scrutiny to her. Don't be silly, Cathy, she told herself. Your mother hated Brenda. She's a bully, a killer, and the most intimidating person you've ever come across. Smelly as well.

Movita looked at her watch. 'That's me,' she said. 'Back to the grindstone.' Her mother's old friend held out a hand to Cathy. 'It was lovely to meet you, Cathy.' She handed her a card. 'This is where I work. If you need any help at any time you just have to ask. Perhaps we can have a more leisurely drink sometime.'

Cathy stood up to say goodbye, Brenda remained firmly in her seat.

'Nice to see you, Brenda,' said Movita, flatly.

'Aye, you an' all, lass,' returned Brenda, with equal insincerity.

Cathy sat down again, watching Movita walk out of the pub.

'Nice lady,' she said to Brenda.

'Oh, aye, one o' the best,' agreed Brenda, unconvincingly.

Cathy looked at her and felt an odd affinity with this mountainous woman. For reasons she couldn't explain to herself she made the decision to show her mother's letter to her. Brenda read it in silence, then shook her head in disbelief.

'By 'eck, Annie lass,' she remarked. 'I were a bit scared ter cross yer when yer were alive. Yer've been dead eighteen years an' yer still at it.'

She looked up at Cathy and related the story of Annie

locking her in the school lavatories on scholarship day. Cathy didn't know whether to smile or be sympathetic.

'I'd probably o' passed an' all,' grumbled Brenda. 'There were only yer mam an' one or two others what ever beat me in t' tests.'

Cathy felt a pang of guilt. Her mother's revenge must have seriously affected Brenda's education.

'I suppose I asked for it,' she conceded. 'It were revenge, yer see. I – er – I 'adn't been very nice to her.'

'What do you mean, you hadn't been very nice to her?'

Brenda felt embarrassed, a novel emotion for her. She grimaced, making Cathy recoil slightly. When Brenda grimaced it had that effect.

'Well, I suppose I were a bit of a bully.' She nodded to herself. 'Actually, I were a lot of a bully.'

'And you bullied my mother. Why?'

Brenda inserted a sausage-like finger into her right ear and wiggled it about as if trying to trigger off some inspired answer.

'I don't know. Mebbe I were jealous of 'er.'

Cathy was trying to understand. 'Jealous of what?'

Brenda examined the product of her ear-probing on her fingertip, making Cathy wince. 'She were pretty an' I weren't.'

'Pretty. You bullied her because she was pretty?'

'Not just that – people liked 'er. Not because she were pretty an' clever but because she were one o' them people what people liked.'

'What about you, did you like her?'

'Me?' said Brenda, surprised at the question. 'I 'ated 'er. Yer see, no one liked me. There were them what hung about wi' me because I were tough an' all that. But they were mostly prats, not worth botherin' about.'

Cathy shook her head, not understanding. 'So you hated my mother because no one liked you? Am I missing something?'

Brenda shrugged. 'I'm not sayin' what I did were right.

Not that there were any sense to it, which there weren't. I gave over bullyin' her after she got me back. Mind you, I bleedin' got more than I deserved. She were a bugger for gerrin' 'er own back were your mam.'

'She needs to get her own back on Spode,' said Cathy.

Brenda took a pint off the tray the barman had brought to the table and swallowed a good half of it.

'I can see that.' She grinned. 'Your mam'll never rest till that bastard gets 'is comeuppance.'

'You liked her really, didn't you?' said Cathy, accusingly.

Brenda dropped her eyes and gave a non-committal shrug. 'There were summat about her that I've never seen in anybody before or since.' She looked up at Cathy. 'Until now,' she added.

It was probably the finest compliment anyone would ever pay Cathy. It turned the tide of her opinion of this daunting woman.

'Brenda, will you help me?' she asked suddenly. Then qualified this request with, 'I'm afraid I won't be able to pay you if you say yes.'

Brenda's face gradually creased into the most fearsome smile Cathy had ever seen.

'Keep yer brass, lass. I've probably got more'n you any road.'

'Well?'

Brenda ruminated for a few seconds then looked up. 'D'yer know, I think I might like that,' she said. 'Aye, I might like that a lot. Yer'll need a bit o' muscle an' I'm not as daft as I look.' Then, taking a further step into the realms of self-congratulation, she added, 'There's a lot more ter me than meets the eye.'

Cathy didn't think this possible, but didn't say so. Instead she said, 'If you'd managed to take your scholarship I reckon you'd have done okay.'

Brenda grinned. 'Nay – I wouldn't 'ave lasted two minutes at grammar school. I'd 'ave been expelled.'

She looked across at Cathy, the daughter of the only person for whom she'd ever had any real respect – and by the cut of her, Cathy deserved the same. Helping her might purge the injustice Brenda herself had suffered at the hands of the law. She held out a hand which completely enveloped Cathy's.

'Right, Cathy lass,' she said, 'where do we start?'

Chapter Twenty

As the minute hand on the wall clock shuddered over to nine o'clock, the stragglers of Form 4b drifted into the classroom. It was six weeks into the Christmas term and already they'd seen off one form teacher. He'd refused to teach such unwilling and unruly pupils. A new teacher had arrived to take his place.

The usual bunch took up occupancy towards the back of the classroom. No one argued with them, especially with Rodney Cole. They looked up with a mixture of expectancy and curiosity as the new teacher casually strode in and sat on the edge of his desk which was elevated several inches above theirs. The two minutes he spent looking around at his charges, his eyes resting on each pupil for a few seconds, had a slightly unnerving effect on the boys. The girls viewed him favourably. He was a vast improvement on the recently departed form master.

There was an athleticism to him which added to his overall attractiveness. He was tall, dark, and not to put too fine a point on it – handsome. He also had a bamboo cane in his hand which aroused a certain amount of curiosity and apprehension.

'Good morning, class,' he said, eventually.

They shuffled in their seats, uncertain how to react.

'When I say "Good morning" I expect you to respond,' he said. 'We'll start again. Good morning, class.'

'Good morning, sir,' came back a unified chant, mainly from the front. The boys at the back exchanged knowing glances.

'Not bad,' he said. He looked slowly around the room once again, causing unease among some of the children who didn't like being stared at.

'My name is Parker,' he announced. 'To you I am either Mr Parker or Sir. Behind my back you will no doubt wish to refer to me as Nosey, but not within earshot or I will punish you for being so unoriginal. Do I make myself clear?'

'Yes, sir.'

'I am here to teach you English and Physical Education. And by the look of you, I've arrived not a moment too soon.'

Some of the children smiled at this. His cane hammered down on the desk like a firecracker. His face was like thunder.

'Smiling without asking permission is not allowed!' he roared.

The smiles instantly disappeared, even from the back row.

'Under my guidance you will become fine physical specimens and acquire an unquenchable thirst for further knowledge of our mother tongue.'

He pointed his cane directly at Rodney Cole. 'You, boy, do you know what our mother tongue is, boy?'

The youth was taken aback. He knew the answer but was confused by this madman.

'Er . . . er . . .'

'Don't just say "er", boy. I want no people in my class who say "er". Does anyone know the answer?' he asked, looking round at a sea of waving hands.

'English, sir.'

The response was unanimous, leaving Rodney feeling a bit stupid.

'Of course, English. You will learn to appreciate

Shakespeare and Coleridge and regard John Keats as an even greater poet than John Lennon – but not as good as our finest living poet.'

He pointed his cane at a young girl in the front row. 'And who is our finest living poet, young lady?'

'John Betjeman, sir?'

'Wrong. Anyone else?'

'John Masefield, sir.'

'Wrong – he's dead. Anyone else?'

He looked around the silent class, satisfied that he was now in total control. They were both scared and in awe of him.

'Our finest living poet is, of course, Spike Milligan,' he said. 'You now have permission to laugh.'

They obliged, nervously at first, then seeing him laughing with them they let themselves go. A bond of respect had been forged between teacher and class that he would maintain with ease throughout the school year.

'One last thing before we begin our lesson,' he said. 'I have heard a disturbing rumour that you are harbouring a bully or two in your midst. I do not believe rumours until they are proved to be true. But if these rumours prove to have any substance to them, I will deal with the bullies myself and it will not be pleasant for them. I myself can be something of a bully. So if any of you is a victim of these people or sees them bullying other pupils, you will not hesitate to come to me. Do I make myself clear?'

'Yes, sir.'

There was markedly more enthusiasm from the front of the class than the back.

Rodney Cole glanced shiftily from side to side, hoping no accusing eyes were looking in his direction. He returned his gaze to Jake and was perturbed to see the teacher staring straight at him.

'What is your name, boy?' asked Jake, who already knew the answer.

'Er – Cole, sir.'

'Er Cole. Is this a foreign name? Do we have a foreigner in our midst?'

'Er – no, sir.'

'You're not a bully are you, Er Cole?'

'No, sir,' lied the boy, now squirming in his seat.

'Well, Er Cole, you appear to have an uncomfortable chair so you will exchange with one of the people sitting at the front. In fact, that goes for all the boys sitting at the back. You will now occupy these front desks throughout the whole of the school year.'

There was a slight hesitation as the boys in question looked at each other for mutual support. Each had mutiny on his mind but wasn't prepared to make the first move. The cane came crashing down once again.

'I meant today, not some time next week!'

Within a minute the exchange had taken place. The bullying which had been building up for the last three years stopped there. None of them wished to be the first victim of this lunatic.

It was lunchtime two days later and the staffroom was crowded. A cloud of stale tobacco smoke hung in the air and when Jake entered he headed straight for the window. As he made to open it to allow fresh air into the room, a shout from behind stopped him in his tracks.

'Leave it shut, Nosey. We'll tell you when to open it.'

The buzz of conversation dropped several decibels as Jake turned round. He looked at the man who had spoken. Ted Mallinson was older than him, maybe mid-forties. He exercised to its fullest extent whatever authority he had as deputy head.

'Leave it shut.' Ted smiled, the cigarette dangling from his thin mouth dropping ash on to his waistcoat. 'There's a good lad, Nosey. It gets draughty when it's open.'

'My name isn't Nosey.'

'It is now. With a name like yours you'll hardly be able to avoid it. Best get used to it, lad.'

Jake returned his grin. 'From what I've heard so far,' he said, 'the kids seem to be doing you an injustice. I got the impression you were a shy sort of individual.'

'Shy, lad? I don't think anyone's ever accused me of being shy.' Ted grinned around the room in search of support, which wasn't forthcoming. 'What makes you say that?'

Jake shrugged. 'I must have got it wrong then. It's just that I could have sworn I heard some of the kids refer to you as Shy Ted.'

The laughter had Ted reddening with annoyance. Jake turned to open the window. 'Tell you what, Ted,' he suggested, 'I won't call you Shy Ted if you don't call me Nosey.'

He chose an unoccupied table by the now open window and opened his *Daily Mirror* which he bought for the sport and Andy Capp. If he felt the need for edification he'd borrow someone's *Times*. A shadow fell across his newspaper.

'Is this a non-smoking table?'

Jake looked up at Silvia Scatchard.

'Not entirely, I smoke myself occasionally.'

'Me too. May I join you?'

'Be my guest.'

'I promise not to call you Nosey,' she said. 'If you promise not to call me . . .'

Jake beat her to it. 'Scrapyard?'

'You've heard it already.'

'I guessed, actually. It's a bit obvious.'

They passed a congenial half hour, mainly with Silvia filling Jake in on all the school background and gossip. 'Ted's a bit of a prat,' she said. 'But he's harmless.' She leaned her head to one side. 'You know,' she said, 'I thought I knew all the nicknames at this school but I've never heard Ted's before.'

Jake grinned. 'I made it up,' he admitted. 'It's called fighting fire with fire.'

'More like fighting fire with napalm. He'll never live it down if the kids get hold of it.'

'The kids here can't have much imagination,' said Jake. 'In my day they'd have christened him that on day one. It's a sad reflection on the decline in educational standards.'

Silvia laughed at this, completely charmed by him. If only she were ten years younger.

'How long have you been here, Silvia?' he asked suddenly. He figured her to be in her late-forties so she might just have been here when Annie was a pupil. Perhaps she remembered her.

'Twelve years.'

'Oh.'

She spotted his slight disappointment. 'Why?' she enquired.

'Oh, nothing. It's just that I knew a girl who went to school here, but she left seven years before you started. She's dead now.'

A bell rang in Silvia's head, but two enquiries in the space of a few days about the same girl had to be too much of a coincidence.

'She made a huge difference to my life,' went on Jake, vaguely. 'When I was fourteen I couldn't read or write. It was she who encouraged me to learn. Up until then, no one else had taken an interest in me.'

'She sounds an extraordinary young lady.'

'She was that all right.'

'Did she, by any chance, die while she was at school?'

'Well, just after she'd left, actually. She had a baby.'

Silvia shook her head in disbelief. Jake's last four words pretty much confirmed the girl's identity. 'You're talking about Annie Jackson, aren't you?'

He looked at her, surprised. 'How on earth did you know?'

'Her daughter came to see me a couple of days ago.'

'Her daughter? You mean the one she had by . . .' He stopped just short of mentioning the name Leonard Spode.

'What did she want?'

His heart was pounding. Annie's death had hit him harder than anyone. The fate of her child had remained cloaked in secrecy. He knew about her being found in a church but that was all.

'She was enquiring about doing her A levels here. I had to turn her down.'

'Pity. If she's doing English I could have squeezed her in. I owe her mother one or two favours.'

Jake thought about Annie. No one else in his life had had such a profound effect on him. How he wished he could have been there to protect her when she needed someone. But he'd backed off, had foolishly obeyed people who knew nothing about Annie. All his life he'd regretted it. His memory of her had even drawn him to this school.

'Do you have an address for her?'

Silvia nodded, wishing the look in his eyes had something to do with her. 'Her name's Cathy – Cathy Makepeace.'

'Cathy Makepeace,' he repeated. 'Is she pretty?'

'I think the word is beautiful.'

'Her mother was beautiful.'

It didn't take much intuition to prompt Silvia's next question. 'You loved her, didn't you?'

Jake gave this some consideration. 'Yes, I loved her – but I wasn't "in love with her", if you know what I mean. We were only kids.'

'Kids can fall in love. I know I did.'

'She was more like a sister – although we did kiss once,' reminisced Jake. 'They split us up because they thought I was the father.'

'And you weren't?'

'No, I wasn't. But I know who was.'

Gloria Elliot was running her last meeting with Annie through her head, wishing for the umpteenth time she'd offered the girl some help. Had that agent chap she was talking about backed her story up it might have been a different matter. Odd that he was killed just a few days later. What was his name? She racked her brains, trying to think of it. Strange sort of name, began with an 'I' – or did it? No matter, it was a detail Cathy would be able to sort out. She picked up the phone and dialled the number the girl had given her.

If Gloria didn't know his name, she was fairly precise about the date of Malcolm Lindis' death. Last week in January 1953. It took Cathy less than half an hour scanning through the newspaper archives in the library to come up with his name. A name that was so individual it took her only one phone call to locate Malcolm Lindis' widow.

'I never remarried, as you can see,' said Mrs Lindis. 'I was nearly forty when Malcolm died, pretty much on the shelf.'

'What was he like?' enquired Cathy. 'Apart from his being Spode's agent, I don't know much about him.'

Margaret Lindis lived alone in the marital semi-detached, a modest house which she and her late husband had planned to leave at the earliest opportunity. But fate had dealt her a cruel hand and she was now a fifty-eight-year-old grey-haired widow with no children and nothing to look forward to. Losing her husband had sucked the spirit out of her. His being well insured might not have been the blessing it was supposed to be because he'd left her without the financial need to work. Without a reason to get up on a morning.

Cathy would never allow that to happen to her. No matter how old she got there would always be something to live for. Even if she took up parachuting in her old age.

'He was a good husband to me,' said Lindis' widow. 'But he could be a bit ruthless in his ways. You had to be in his job. "Politician's Labourer", he called himself.'

'And you never had any suspicions about the manner of his death?'

Mrs Lindis looked curiously at Cathy. 'What do you mean by that?' she asked, pointedly.

'I mean, were you entirely satisfied that it was an accident?'

There was a long pause as Mrs Lindis considered the implications of Cathy's question.

'Not entirely, no,' she said. 'But the police said he was over the legal limit for alcohol and lost control of the car.'

'So why aren't you entirely satisfied?' pressed Cathy.

Margaret Lindis got to her feet. 'Do you mind if I put the kettle on? It'll take some thinking about will this.'

With a cup of steaming tea in front of her, Margaret had had time to gather her recollections.

'Somebody from the Rotary Club came round, I forget the man's name. He came to offer condolences from everyone, usual stuff. You don't actually take it all in at the time – it's the shock, you see.' She sipped her tea, reflectively. 'Then on his way out he said an odd thing – would you like a biscuit, love?'

Cathy accepted a biscuit just to encourage the woman to continue with her story.

'He asked me if the police had checked on a patch of oil or something where Malcolm's car had been parked. He said he thought it could be brake fluid.'

'And did the police check on it?' asked Cathy.

'I mentioned it to them. They said it was possible that his brakes were faulty, but under the circumstances it wasn't worth pursuing. It was an accidental death no matter which way you looked at it.'

'So what makes you unsatisfied about all this?'

Margaret looked at her in surprise. 'If you'd known my Malcolm you wouldn't be asking that question. Car maintenance was his hobby. If he saw a drop of oil leaking from his car he was on to it like a shot.'

Cathy took all this in but didn't quite know where it was leading. 'What about Leonard Spode?' she asked. 'How did your husband get on with him?'

Margaret gave a dry laugh. 'Get on with him? I don't think anyone actually "got on with" him. My Malcolm tolerated him – but you can't tolerate people forever. There's a limit to everything.'

'How do you mean?' enquired Cathy.

'They had a falling out. I've no idea what it was about, I never got involved in that sort of thing. Head cook, bottle washer and unpaid chauffeur, that was me. Typical dutiful wife.' She gave Cathy a warning look. 'Never fall into that trap, love. Your life's not your own when you give in to that sort of thing. Still, he was a good husband for all that. I do miss him.'

Cathy allowed the imminent tears to subside before continuing. She drank her tea, slightly guilty at reviving upsetting memories for this obviously pleasant lady.

'Mrs Lindis, just a couple of things before I go. This falling out between Malcolm and Spode ... How long before the accident did it take place?'

'Not long. The day before, I think. Mind you, Leonard came to the funeral, in fact he was a big help to me at the time, so I didn't hold it against him.'

'Mrs Lindis – do you remember my mother, Annie Jackson?'

'I do, love. And your grandma, Olga. Liked a drink did Olga. Mind you, from what I gather she only took to drink after she took up with Leonard. You can make of that what you like.'

'Did your husband mention Annie Jackson? What I mean is – at the time of him and Spode arguing can you remember if my mother's name was mentioned?'

'Well, I didn't actually hear them arguing, love. I only know what Malcolm told me. He did mention Annie's name to me but he didn't go into details.'

The memory of the incident caused her face to crease with sorrow.

'I remember him saying Spode wasn't going to screw him like he screwed Annie Jackson. I remember because I told him not to be so crude. In fact, I gave him a bit of a telling off. I don't like that sort of talk, you see. Telling him off was the last thing I did before he went out that night.'

Margaret looked forlorn as she glanced up at Cathy. 'You know, I do wish I hadn't – it was such a petty thing for me to pick on him for.'

Cathy leaned forward and took her hand. 'It's okay, Mrs Lindis. I'm sure he'd have forgotten all about it by the time he reached the pub. Men thrive on being told off by us women.'

Malcolm Lindis' widow wiped her eyes and smiled at her young visitor. 'Talk about an old head on young shoulders. You're dead right, of course. He'd have forgotten about it before he got into the car, knowing my Malcolm.'

Cathy left the house with the conviction that her adversary was much more ruthless than she'd originally thought. Leonard Spode was a killer, of that she had little doubt. The fact that he was her father counted for nothing. Faced with the task her mother had placed before her, she had no time for such irrelevancies.

Chapter Twenty-One

The woman who knew herself only as Mary Dawson stared out through the window. Ten years ago she'd been given a small room of her own as it was thought that mixing too much with the other, more obviously mentally ill patients would slow her progress. But for eighteen years she hadn't spoken or shown any sign of interest in what was going on around her. She responded well to questions and instructions and it was obvious that the brain behind those blank blue eyes was functioning perfectly well. It was thought she was now in her mid-thirties and if somehow they could stoke up the dying embers within her, she might yet become a pretty, even vivacious, lady. There was something inside her, something wanting to get out.

The physiotherapist came into the room for her weekly visit and knew her task was as hopeless as it had been last week and every week since she'd started at the hospital. But she was paid to go through the motions. She pulled a chair in front of her patient and took her hands.

'Now I want you to squeeze me as hard as you can.'

Mary's eyes flickered. She gave one of her endearing half-smiles and returned her gaze to the window where pleasant images had been occupying her thoughts.

'Mary, just for me. Just one tiny squeeze.'

Mary obliged with a tiny squeeze. The squeeze which allowed her to turn door handles and pick up a spoon. She knew she had to admit to being able to do that, or her life would be impossible.

'Good, now a big squeeze.'

Mary dropped her hand away as if the tiny squeeze had taken all her strength. A big squeeze would only encourage the woman. If Mary gave her a big squeeze she'd be back for a bigger squeeze and so on ad infinitum. Soon they'd have her picking up a pen and wanting her to write. Demanding proper communication. She couldn't cope with that. Perhaps they'd give up. Like she had. At least until one of the friends in her head came to put things right.

The physio, having done her duty, stood up to leave. 'I'll call back next week.' She made for the door, then turned round. 'I know you can do it, Mary. I'm not stupid.'

That makes two of us, thought Mary.

Evil images had arrived behind the black door, pushing aside her friends. Bad that, they didn't often come during the day. Mary quickly slammed the door shut and, with a great effort of will, switched off that part of her mind. As she got to her feet, her arms dropped uselessly by her sides. If she couldn't use them to open the black door then what good were they?

The images first began eighteen years ago, only Mary didn't know it was eighteen years. Time had become a dimension accelerated by the deep black holes infesting her mind. A whole winter would suddenly become spring without her noticing its passing. Then she'd have lucid intervals, some longer than others, when time moved along at its normal rate. It was during these intervals that she saw the images, as clear to her now as they were when they first appeared.

Chapter Twenty-Two

'Cathy Makepeace?'

'Speaking.'

'My name is Jake Parker. I was given your number by the secretary of the school where I . . .'

'Jake Parker! I've heard of you,' she interrupted, excitedly. 'And I'd love to meet you.'

'Oh, right.'

He couldn't for the life of him figure out how she'd heard of him. 'I'll . . . er . . . I'll come to you, shall I? I've got your address as well.'

'Would now be too soon, Mr Parker?'

'Now suits me fine. It's Jake by the way. I'll be there in an hour.'

Jake knocked on the door tentatively. He had an inherent shyness of the opposite sex which, paradoxically, made them even more attracted to him. Now thirty-three years old, with a broken marriage and a couple of ill-advised relationships behind him, he trod very carefully in female company.

His ex-wife had enjoyed the reflected glamour of being married to a professional sportsman and when his career came to an abrupt end, so did his marriage. Their parting was as amicable as these things can be. Thankfully they'd had no children to complicate matters and she soon found a boyfriend whose presence accelerated the divorce.

Jake's eyes widened imperceptibly as Cathy opened the door. Mrs Scatchard's description of her was accurate. She was beautiful.

'Jake,' she said, her smile dazzling him. 'How lovely to meet you.'

He stood there, awkwardly. He was no match for women like this, no matter how young they were. 'I . . . er . . . I was a friend of your mother's.'

'I know you were. Would you like to come in? It's a bit messy, I'm afraid. My – er – room-mate's just moved and I'm trying to get rid of all the stuff he left behind.'

He stepped in and surveyed the room. Much like his own, only she had an excuse to be messy. 'You seem a bit young to have flown the parental nest.'

'I did that some time ago. I wasn't getting on with Dad so I jumped out of the proverbial frying pan into the fire. Ended up with an abusive boyfriend – hence the mess.' She saw the look of concern on his face. 'Don't worry, he's safely locked up where he can't do me any harm.'

Jake almost said something about abuse running in her family, but stopped himself in time. Being abused was nothing to joke about. He of all people knew that.

'I'm pleased to hear it,' he said.

It was a time to exchange traditional pleasantries with this man she'd only just met. But Cathy hated small talk.

'I gather you know who my real father is?'

Jake was taken aback. 'Do I? Er, yes, I suppose I do. I'm amazed you do, though. In fact, I'm amazed you know who *I* am.'

'Annie told me,' she said, without further explanation.

There was an awkward moment as they stood in the cramped confines of the room she'd once shared with Dave. It didn't seem right, having this nice man in the same space.

'Why don't we go for a walk?' she suggested.

'Suits me.'

Jake had harboured a long-term hatred of the man who'd ruined Annie's life so despicably. He'd planned Spode's downfall many times in his imagination, frustrated by the knowledge that this was as far as he would ever get.

'Are they good people?' enquired Jake. 'Your adoptive mum and dad.'

'Dad can be a bit of a pain, but they're okay.'

'Believe me, you're lucky.'

Cathy didn't press him on this. It sounded as though his life had been a lot tougher than hers.

'I suppose so,' she conceded.

'It's what Annie . . . your mother . . . would have wanted.'

A picture of Liz crouching on the floor with blood on her mouth passed fleetingly through Cathy's mind.

'Well, apart from a few ups and downs they've given me a good life, which is exactly what Annie wanted me to have.'

Her second reference to her mother puzzled Jake but he didn't press her on it. They were strolling through a nearby park, watching the bright afternoon sunshine picking out the brown and gold leaves as they flickered down from the trees. Cathy said 'Hello' to a couple walking a dog and pointed out an ancient bandstand where she and her friends once went for an illicit smoke.

'Gave it up within three minutes of starting,' she remembered. 'I threw up all over the steps. Mind you, I started again. I'm in the process of giving up again as we speak.'

'So you don't want one of these then?' said Jake, taking a packet of John Player Specials from his pocket.

'Annie never mentioned anything about you being cruel,' complained Cathy, tongue-in-cheek. 'Maybe it's a side of you she never saw.'

She was at it again, pretending her mother had somehow spoken to her from the grave.

'How can Annie have mentioned anything at all to you?' he asked, as he lit the cigarette.

A noisy game of three-a-side football disturbed them, catching Jake's attention. There was an autumnal nip in the air and Cathy drew her loose coat around her, wishing it was his arm. She felt comfortable in his company, there was something safe and reassuring about him. She'd ascertained his marital status within a few minutes, her heart lightening at the news that he was available. Then she admonished herself for such thoughts: Stop it, Cathy, he's much too old for you. Even older than the dreadful Dave.

Before she showed Annie's letter to Jake she needed to know he was ready for such a burden. She wanted his help more than anything, but Spode was a ruthless man and she didn't want a half-hearted accomplice.

'Tell me about yourself, Jake,' she said. 'All I know is that you were a friend of my mother's and that you were at the same children's home as her.'

The football came flying their way. Jake trapped it neatly under his right foot, flicked it up in the air, headed it half a dozen times, then volleyed it with tremendous force straight past the hapless goalkeeper standing between two coats.

'I'm impressed,' said Cathy.

He grinned, self-consciously. 'So you should be – I used to be a pro.'

Cathy waited for him to continue what was obviously an interesting story. Everything about this man was of interest to her.

'After Annie died,' he went on, 'I had a stroke of luck. I was pretty good at football and I'd had trials with a couple of clubs. Anyway I ended up signing for Huddersfield Town.'

'You must have been good.'

'Well, yes, I suppose I must have been. Apart from a couple of years' National Service I spent the next ten years earning a good living from football. Then I broke my leg playing against Tranmere in the Cup.' He turned and grinned at her, ruefully. 'Never played again,' he said. 'Not at that level anyway. They had a testimonial for me which paid off my mortgage ...' His voice tailed off. 'Then I made up my mind to do something that Annie had encouraged me to do. I went back to school.'

'Back to school? I don't understand.'

'Well,' he explained, 'when Annie found out I couldn't read or write she offered to help me ...'

'Couldn't read or write? How old were you?'

'Fourteen,' he said, smiling at her reaction. 'My home life had never been idyllic. In many ways it was worse than Annie's – insofar as she had a mother who loved her.'

Cathy didn't pursue this, it sounded too painful. One day she'd ask him.

'You were saying she helped you to read and write?'

'Not exactly. As things turned out she wasn't in a position to help, but she gave me the confidence in myself to learn. I persuaded one of my teachers to give me extra tuition.'

'It takes a special kind of kid to do that.'

'I think I did it for Annie. At one point I nearly gave up, but she made me promise to stick at it. When I heard she'd died, that promise was the only thing I had to remember her by. There was no way I could ever go back on it.'

One of the footballing youths tapped the ball over to him, knowing he wouldn't be able to resist it. Jake grinned, flicked the ball on to the youth's head then turned his back on any more action, giving Cathy his full attention. She was feeling more and more drawn to this man who had apparently achieved so much against all odds and yet was totally without conceit.

'So,' he went on, 'by the time I signed for Huddersfield I could read and write as well as any of the other lads in the club – better than most. You've no idea what a difference it made to my life.'

'And after you packed in football you went back to school?' she prompted.

'That's right. You see, Annie said I was bright enough to go to university. At the time I took it as one of her jokes, but I promised I'd give it a go. It'd been preying on my conscience all the time I was playing football. Maybe breaking my leg while I was still young enough to learn was a blessing in disguise.'

'It's one way of looking at it.'

Jake grinned. 'I took adult classes at first, to get some O and A levels, then I got a place at Durham University.' He grinned ruefully. 'Lost my wife but I got a BA.'

'Was it a good swap?'

'It was a bargain.'

He stopped and stared into the middle distance, then looked round at Cathy and smiled.

'When I was a kid I was kicked around a lot, never encouraged to learn anything. Everybody thought I was thick. Everybody but your mother. She was a very special person was your mother, very special. If my own mother had been half as special I might have had a decent childhood.'

His brow furrowed as he set off walking again, Cathy close by his side.

'Whatever I am today, I owe to Annie Jackson,' he said. 'Your mother – you should be proud to have a mother like that.'

'I've yet to hear anyone say a bad word about her,' said Cathy.

'I'd flatten anyone who did.'

'I can well imagine.' Cathy took his arm and stopped him walking. 'What do you know about Leonard Spode?' she asked, quietly.

'Spode ...' Jake almost spat the name out, then gave Cathy a look of concern. 'You know what he did, don't you?'

She nodded. 'I've only just found out, but yes, I know about him. I know he's my biological father.'

'How do you know I know about him?' queried Jake.

'Let's just say Annie told me. Now you tell me what you know about him.'

Jake stopped to think for a second. Cathy's answer puzzled him, but he let it go.

'I only know what Annie told me,' he said. 'About him raping her. After she died the only thing that stopped me going out and killing him was me being scared of the death sentence. Maybe I've mellowed a bit now but I reckon I'd still kill him if I thought I could get away with it.'

They approached a wooden park bench. Cathy took a couple of quick paces towards it and swept away a few leaves with her hand, sitting down and gesturing for Jake to do the same. Her decision was made. She took an envelope from her pocket.

'You were wondering how my mother could talk to me,' she said.

'Something like that,' he replied. 'It doesn't matter. I don't wish to pry into your personal thoughts. Everyone has their own way of dealing with things.'

Cathy laughed. 'I wasn't imagining it – she really did leave me a message. I think you should read this,' she said, handing him her mother's letter. 'It's from my mother – Annie Jackson.'

Jake reached out and held it between finger and thumb with Cathy still holding on to the other side. Their eyes met, the letter creating a tangible bond between them. He took it gently from her and read it with a touching reverence, then kissed the paper and stared at the writing, shaking his head.

'My God, Annie. I should have been there for you. What must you have thought of me?'

'She thought you were a very good friend.'

'Not good enough,' he said, returning the letter to her. 'What are you going to do?'

'I'm my mother's daughter,' replied Cathy. 'What do you think I'm going to do?'

'Not on your own, you're not. I've got a right to help you.'

She didn't reply immediately. Her emotions were

running riot. Maybe it was the way he'd kissed her mother's letter. Maybe it was the pleading in his soft, brown eyes when he insisted on helping her.

'You can't do it on your own,' he went on. 'He's a powerful man.'

'And an evil one, Jake,' she added. 'My grandmother isn't the only person he's killed.'

She went on to tell him about her visit to Mrs Lindis. Jake's face hardened when she came to the part about the brakes.

'That settles it,' he said. 'It's him against the two of us.'

'Three of us, actually,' said Cathy. 'There's someone else you need to meet.'

The three of them met in the Ashley Arms, mainly because it was within walking distance for Brenda who couldn't drive.

'By the time I push the seat far enough back ter get me fat arse behind the steering wheel, me feet won't reach the pedals,' she explained.

Cathy and Jake both admitted they hadn't thought of this. He looked across the table at their third partner with considerable apprehension. He'd been noted for his aggression on the football field, never backing away from a fifty-fifty ball, even against opponents very much bigger than him. But he'd never come up against anyone as intimidating as Brenda Bacup.

As she went off to the bar to replenish their drinks he leaned over and whispered to Cathy, 'I assume they've let her out for the day so they can clean her cage out.'

'Don't be so rotten. It's not her fault she looks like that.'

'Sorry.' Jake's contrite expression turned into a grin. 'I'm glad she's on our side, though.'

'She's actually quite bright when you get to know her,' said Cathy. 'She's cleverer than she looks.'

Jake was thinking this wouldn't be too difficult but he didn't say as much to Cathy for fear of another reprimand.

‘Right,’ said Cathy after Brenda had brought the drinks back, ‘our aim is to bring Leonard Spode to book for what he did to my mother. Anyone got any bright ideas?’

Jake handed his cigarettes round and all three of them lit up, Cathy having abandoned her attempt at giving up until all this was over. Brenda sent out a smoke ring, to the envy of Jake who’d practised all his life and never managed it.

‘I think we should start by forgetting about proving he raped Annie,’ she said, blowing a second ring through the expanding centre of the first.

‘Why’s that?’ enquired Cathy. ‘I thought that would be our main aim.’

‘Because we’d be wasting our time,’ explained Brenda. ‘Annie’s dead an’ the only bloke who could ’ave pointed the finger at Spode was Malcolm Lindis who’s also dead.’

‘I agree,’ said Jake. ‘We’ve got to approach it from a different angle. Spode was – and probably still is – a paedophile.’ He paused and looked down into his drink. ‘I’ve had personal experience of such creatures.’

Brenda opened her mouth, but her question was stopped by Cathy’s warning finger. Jake looked up and went on.

‘He wouldn’t have given it up just because of what happened to Annie. That’s not how these people operate. He may well have abused other young people in his time, probably boys as well as girls – it’s all the same to these vermin. Most of his victims will be grown up by now.’

‘And ready to help us?’ suggested Cathy.

‘Possibly,’ said Jake. ‘Or just wanting to forget about it.’

‘Like you?’ suggested Brenda.

‘Brenda!’ scolded Cathy. The other woman shrugged, wondering what the problem was.

‘Yes, like me,’ agreed Jake. ‘I was abused by blokes who got away with it. Somehow I managed to put what they did to me to the back of my mind, but I could never do the same with what happened to Annie. Odd that. I could forget about my own abuse, but not hers.’

'So,' summed up Cathy, 'you don't think these people will come forward?'

'I didn't say that,' said Jake. 'Some might want to see him brought to book. Some might want to forget about it. Some might have been scared into silence by Spode.'

'They could always be scared into opening their mouths again,' suggested Brenda with a certain amount of relish, hoping to be assigned such a job.

'If we're going to frighten anyone,' warned Cathy firmly, 'it's going to be those who deserve it. Not people who have suffered enough already.'

Disappointment clouded Brenda's pudgy face for a second until Jake added, 'I suspect you'll have plenty of opportunity to display your unique talents, Brenda.'

The big woman nodded. Anything he said was okay by her; she'd be dreaming about him tonight. With Jake blissfully unaware of this, Cathy reached across the table and took his hand.

'Thanks,' she said. 'For being on our side. Mine and my mother's that is.'

'It's my pleasure.'

Their eyes met for a brief second. Cathy turned to Brenda. 'And the same goes for you, Brenda.'

Jake looked at the two women, opposites in every respect apart from their common objective.

'You know, if Spode learned what was going on he'd be quaking in his boots,' he said.

Chapter Twenty-Three

An executive jet soared from the runway at Leeds and Bradford Airport and headed west towards Dublin where Leonard Spode was expanding his business empire. He looked down upon the city of his birth.

Leeds Town Hall passed under the port wing, latticed in scaffolding as a major cleaning operation was currently underway. Spode looked down and remembered the time he was dragged before the Court for thieving clothes from a stall in Leeds Market and how, years ago, he'd had to sweet talk a certain corrupt senior policeman into removing that particular entry from his file prior to his going into local politics. He laughed to himself. Sweet talk? Blackmail would have been a more accurate word. He'd made it his business to 'know' things about people. The more you knew, the more power you had. And people had good reason to fear him. He'd already seen off his wife and Malcolm Lindis. Olga was more of an accident but the Lindis killing had been a classic. How easy it had been, like swatting a fly. Lindis had got in Spode's way and he'd been eliminated. Apart from a group of curmudgeonly employees who'd recently led a strike at his Leeds factory it had been a long time since anyone else had tried to cross him. Pity that. He'd like to take on another worthy adversary before he went soft.

There had been a time when Spode had thought nothing

could stop him going right to the top in politics. And perhaps he could have – but he soon realised that there is a stage in political life where the material rewards aren't sufficient recompense for the effort and dedication required. Politics is a selfless occupation and Spode was anything but. Some years ago he'd agonised over a cabinet post he'd been offered. It would take him away from his business and alienate certain people who had up to that time been willing allies in his schemes. Turning the post down had relegated him to the back benches, which in many ways suited his purposes better.

A pretty stewardess brought him coffee which he placed on the table in front of him. 'Anything else you'd like, sir?' she enquired with due deference. He waved her away with a smile.

That's what he enjoyed most about his position in life, the deference. Most of them were sycophantic bastards, but he was accorded respect.

His return to the back benches was okay insofar as politics didn't eat into his working hours quite as much, but he still needed a higher public profile. When the presidency of the British Children's Society became vacant he pulled sufficient strings for the post to be offered to him. He then fulsomely expressed his surprise at such an honour coming right out of the blue and vowed to carry out his duties to the utmost of his abilities. He would make his first speech as President at the forthcoming annual fund-raising dinner at the Queen's Hotel in Leeds. Because of the presence of celebrities from the worlds of showbusiness, politics and sport, there would be press and TV coverage and Spode's business could only benefit.

It was all part of his single-minded resolve to become the biggest clothing manufacturer in the north of England. Even his 'little friends', as he chose to call them, had faded into the background as he channelled his energies into business. He restricted his sexual activity to holiday times, apart from inviting Melanie Binns round now and again.

But she was no longer 'little' so it wasn't the same.

The factory was running smoothly once again after the minor hiccup caused by the abortive strike. All his workforce, bar the twelve he wanted rid of, had slunk back when they realised they couldn't win. One of the twelve had tried to burn the place down. Pity that had failed. The insurance money would have come in handy.

As the plane flew over the northern suburbs, before turning west along its allotted flight path, Spode peered down and tried to identify his street, but the world from ten thousand feet up is a totally unrecognisable place.

It would have taken a powerful pair of binoculars to have spotted Cathy walking up the street towards his house.

Chapter Twenty-Four

Cathy peered up at the house with the same sense of unease her mother had felt when she and Olga first moved in, nineteen years ago. It was outwardly respectable and unpretentious, the only addition a high boundary wall to keep out any intruders and a pair of solid wooden gates, as high as the wall, painted dark green and decorated with a recently daubed piece of graffiti: *Judy H shags like a rattlesnake*. A curious analogy but at least the spelling was correct. Spode could afford a better house in a better area, but why bother? He had a villa in the West Indies where he spent discreet holidays entertaining a string of Caribbean juveniles, all of whom hid their distaste of him as they accepted his money.

The gate was open as Cathy approached to find a stooped gardener pruning the roses around the front lawn.

'Good morning,' she called out brightly.

The old man looked up and returned her smile. Hers was a difficult smile to ignore.

'Morning,' he returned. 'Sorry about t' gate. Only he didn't get me no paint ter paint it over. He said he would, but he didn't. He's like that. Thinks I'm a miracle worker.'

She walked up the path. The gardener waited until she'd passed him before calling out.

'He's at work, love. He's allus at work at this time.'

'Are you sure?'

'I should be – I've worked for 'im for over eighteen years.'

Cathy already knew Spode was out, that was why she'd left it until late morning. She didn't want to bump into him. Just knock at his door, then, on getting no reply, she could have a look through his windows and maybe in his dustbin, which was round the back and out of sight. She didn't know why, but you've got to start somewhere. Brenda had suggested breaking in and having a good look round, but this seemed a bit drastic to both Cathy and Jake. Fortuitously bumping into Spode's gardener seemed somehow too good an opportunity to pass up. An idea clicked into Cathy's brain. She turned, annoyance on her face.

'Can you believe that man?' she snorted.

The gardener shrugged. He hadn't a clue what she was talking about.

'I distinctly told him eleven o'clock.'

'I told him ter get me some paint, but he didn't,' countered the gardener as if not wanting to be outdone. 'He's like that.'

'What time do you make it?' Cathy asked.

He laboriously drew a fob-watch from his waistcoat pocket, squinted at it, then tried to shake it to life.

'T' bugger's stopped again. It's allus doin' that. I 'ad it presented, yer know. Twenty-five years wi' Wilkinson's – and now t' bugger's stopped.' He viewed his timepiece with disgust. 'I 'aven't 'ad it two bloody minutes.'

'Eleven o'clock,' said Cathy, checking her own watch. 'Straight up.'

The gardener returned his watch to his pocket then took a startlingly white handkerchief from another pocket and blew his nose, as if in mourning for his defunct timepiece.

'I might as well chuck t' bugger away,' he grumbled. 'It's never been right since it were presented.'

Cathy got the impression that he was keeping the watch out of some sort of duty because it had been 'presented'.

'I've got an old watch at home you can have if you like,' she lied. 'It keeps good time.'

'I'd 'ave ter pay yer for it. I'll not be beholden ter nobody. I'm like that, me.'

'Tell you what,' suggested Cathy, 'I came to interview Mr Spode for the *Evening Post* – perhaps you can help me. I can pay you for your time with the watch.'

He weighed the proposition in his mind for a few seconds. The prospect of owning a reliable watch was very tempting.

'What are yer, some kind o' reporter? I'm not so struck on reporters.'

He didn't seem the type who would have had much to do with reporters, but Cathy let it go.

'We're doing a feature on Leonard Spode. We'd be grateful for any background information.'

'Is it about them what he sacked?' Then, without waiting for an answer, added, 'He might sack me an' all – he's like that.'

'No, it's nothing to do with the strike. It's more a personal profile of him.'

The gardener looked uncertain, but he was weakening. He took another look at his watch.

'Of course he won't know who gave us the information,' pressed Cathy. 'That's standard practice as you probably know.'

'Oh, aye, I know all about that, lass.' He rubbed his chin. 'Yon Spode can be a rum bugger when he wants, yer know.'

'Can he really?' She smiled. 'In what way?'

'Is this it, then?' he asked. 'Is this what yer payin' me for?'

She held out her hand. 'Shake my hand and we have a deal.'

He took her hand and shook it gently.

'What do you mean when you say he's a rum bugger?'

'I mean he 'asn't got a wife or nowt, but I reckon he's

'avin' it off wi' a young woman what's young enough ter be his daughter.'

'It wouldn't be someone called Judy, would it?'

The old man grinned as his eyes flickered towards the gate.

'Nah – well, not as far as I know.'

'How young would you say she is?'

'Not much older than you.'

'Oh.'

Cathy was disappointed. This information wasn't worth the trouble of buying him a second-hand watch. He sensed her disappointment and knew the deal was in jeopardy.

'I'll tell yer summat else an' all.'

'What's that?' She held out no hopes of this 'summat else' being of any interest.

'T' gardener afore me thought he were a rum bugger an' all. That's why he left.'

'Really?'

She turned to go, he'd have to make do with his old watch.

'Aye – he were only a young lad an' all.'

'Young? How young?'

The gardener sensed her interest. 'It were a while ago. I'd just retired from Wilkie's. That's them what presented me wi' this crap watch.' He tapped his pocket. 'That were over eighteen year ago.' He paused, waiting for her to ask him how old he was and congratulate him on his eternal youth. Cathy wasn't even curious.

'How old was he?'

'What, the lad? He were still at school. Thirteen, mebbe fourteen. He packed it in about a year afore I started.'

'Did you ever meet Mr Spode's wife?'

'Just afore me time, all that business. Never knew the woman – an' I've never 'eard him talk about her neither. Nor that young lass of hers what did hersen in. He's like that.'

Cathy was slightly taken aback at hearing her mother

described as a 'young lass what did hersen in'. It was a somewhat dismissive obituary considering the glowing reports everyone else had given her. But this man never knew her, so perhaps it was understandable.

'What? In all the years you've worked for him he's never mentioned them once?'

'Never a once – he's like that. He's a rum bugger is yon.'

'Tell me about this boy, this other gardener?'

'Nowt much to tell. He came round ter see me one day and told me Spode 'ad been messin' wi' him.'

'Messing? How do you mean, messin?'

The old man shrugged once again. His young predecessor hadn't gone into details.

'Do you know what they call this boy?'

The old man's eyes brightened. A new watch was becoming a definite possibility.

'He's norra boy no more,' he said. 'He's a milkman now. Ronnie Sykes. He works for t' Craven Dairies.'

'Do you know where he lives?'

'No idea.' A grin lit up the old man's face. 'But he delivers my milk.'

'And where do you live?'

'Am I gerrin' a watch?'

'Of course you are, that's the deal.'

'Quarry Hill Flats. Number sixty-three, Priestley House. Yer'll have ter get there early doors ter catch him. Six o'clock mebbe.'

The phone was ringing in his flat as Jake walked in from school. It'd been a pig of a day. He'd had to haul Rodney Cole in front of Mrs Scatchard who had been amazingly severe with the youth, suspending him for two weeks with a threat to expel him if he was found bullying again. On top of which Jake's car had just broken down and he'd had to walk half a mile in the rain. He dropped his briefcase on the settee and picked up the phone. His spirits lifted when he heard Cathy's voice.

'Ah, Miss Makepeace, I hope you're ringing to cheer me up.'

'Ah, Mr Parker – and why would you need cheering up?'

'Bad day at work. Car broken down. Soaked through with rain. Usual stuff.'

'Is the car fixable?' She had a vested interest in his answer.

'Probably. There were no loud banging noises or anything, it just stopped. And before you say anything, no, I didn't run out of petrol. I think it's something electrical.'

'I've got a job at the Crown and Anchor. Start next Monday. I thought I might invite you out for a drink to celebrate.'

'Cathy, you've got yourself a deal.'

'Right, Crown and Anchor at eight. Bring plenty of money, I'm skint.'

'Me too – I'll bring a couple of straws, we can share my half of bitter.' He paused, then asked, 'Any news on the Spode front?' Simply saying the man's name took the cheer from his voice.

'That's one of the things I want to talk to you about,' answered Cathy. 'I might need your help with something. But you'd need your car.'

'No problem. I'll be ringing the RAC as soon as I've finished talking to you.'

She didn't fancy hanging about Quarry Hill Flats at six o'clock in the morning waiting for a milkman. Jake had a car. They could wait together in comfort. Just the two of them. She could ask him about his A level English course. Maybe he could fit her in. She'd like being taught by him.

Ronnie Sykes looked much older than his thirty-one years. His early life had seen to that. Fatherless due to a German mortar shell, he'd been brought up by a feckless mother to whom he'd felt he couldn't turn for advice on Spode's unwelcome advances. The money Spode had lavished upon him had been snatched from Ronnie's hand the minute he walked through the door. Never once did his mother question why he was being paid so much. He'd always pitied the girl who'd moved in along with Spode's new wife. Their fate had come as no great surprise to Ronnie. But all this was past history. His mother was now dead and he had a wife to endure and three children to love. All that remained of his past was a simmering hatred of Spode. A hatred he could do nothing about. His former abuser was a million miles from his thoughts as he went about his work.

The Quarry Hill Flats estate was falling into decay. Built just before the war to house almost two and a half thousand people, it had become a seven-storey concrete monstrosity, and currently the setting for a television series called *Queenie's Castle*. It was six-thirty when Ronnie stopped his electric milk float beside the television unit vehicles and banged on the door of the catering truck. Diana Dors, the star of the series, popped her blonde head out of a caravan door a few yards away.

'Have you got a spare pint for me, Ronnie darling?'

He grinned and took her a bottle, his eyes drawn to the expanse of cleavage protruding from her dressing gown.

'Good for building you up,' he commented. 'Seems to be doing the trick with you.'

'Don't be so cheeky!'

Ronnie grinned. This was the nearest he got to glamour. His plain wife wouldn't have appreciated his having a bit of banter with a famous actress, so he never mentioned it to her. He climbed back on his vehicle and headed towards Priestley House.

'Are you Ronnie Sykes?'

The question came from behind him as he was leaning over his float, loading empties into a crate. He turned round and caught his breath at the sight of Cathy. She was obviously with the television people. No one as beautiful as her would be seen dead around here without good reason. Especially at this time on a morning.

'If yer want some milk just grab a bottle,' he said.

'Are you Ronnie Sykes?' Cathy repeated the question and held out her hand.

The milkman shook it. 'Aye, I'm Ronnie Sykes.'

'My name's Cathy Makepeace.'

'Pleased ter meet yer.'

'Jake Parker,' said Jake, extending his own hand.

'Pleased ter meet you an' all. Are you with that lot?' He inclined his head towards the TV unit.

Cathy followed his gaze then looked back at him. 'No – oh, no. They're nothing to do with us.'

'What's all this about, then?'

'Look, we're sorry to waylay you at this time on a morning,' said Cathy, 'but this was the only way we knew of finding you. Leonard Spode's gardener lives here and he told us you delivered his milk.'

Ronnie froze at the sound of that name. 'Spode? What's he got ter do with owt?' He almost spat the words out.

'Are we to understand you don't like Mr Spode?' enquired Jake, disarmingly.

'I hate him if yer must know. Look, what's this all about?'

'We won't take up much of your time,' said Cathy. 'But we have cause to hate him too, and we wondered if you might tell us what you know about him.'

Ronnie melted under her smile. 'I don't really know nowt – and ter be honest, I'd just as soon never have nowt no more ter do with him. It were a long time ago.'

'But you still haven't managed to lay your hatred to rest,' she observed.

'Happen not,' accepted Ronnie grudgingly. 'Happen it's summat yer can't forget easily.'

'Would you like to see him get his comeuppance?' asked Jake.

'I'd like nowt better. But he's a wealthy man – and wealthy men aren't easy ter get at.'

'Depends who they're up against.' Cathy smiled.

Jake watched admiringly as she easily won over a new recruit.

'Can we meet somewhere to discuss it?' she asked.

'I knock off at twelve. I can see yer in t' Ashley about half-past, if yer like.'

'It's a date,' said Cathy.

She linked arms with Jake as they strolled back to his car.

'He wouldn't have done it for me,' Jake commented. 'You know that, don't you?'

'Maybe not. A woman would, though.'

'Really?'

'Definitely.'

Ronnie Sykes was unconsciously tapping his feet in time with The Who blasting out from the jukebox as Jake and Cathy walked into the pub.

'Don't get up,' insisted Jake. 'What can I get you?'

Ronnie swallowed the dregs of his pint and handed Jake the empty glass. 'Bitter, please.' He'd been there since ten-past twelve, wondering what all this was about. Cathy sat down beside him as Jake went to the bar.

'It must be good to have a job that leaves you most of the day to yourself,' she said, brightly.

'Gerrin' up at five o'clock's not so good, though.'

Cathy tried to imagine getting up at five every morning. It wouldn't be so bad.

'I bet the streets are quiet,' she said. 'It must be nice to have them all to yourself.'

'Aye – there is that about it,' agreed Ronnie. 'There's not many folk about at that time of a morning.'

Cathy forced the small talk along until Jake returned, balancing three glasses between his hands.

'Here, take that before I drop it, Ronnie.'

He gingerly eased one of the pint glasses from Jake's grasp and sipped the froth off the top before wiping his mouth clean with his sleeve.

'Right,' he said. 'Yer'd better tell me what this is all about.'

'It's about Spode,' said Cathy. 'He was responsible for my mother's death.'

'And he killed her grandmother,' added Jake.

They now had Ronnie's full attention. 'Did I know yer mother and yer grandmother?' He asked the question as if he already knew the answer.

'Probably,' agreed Cathy. 'My mother was Annie Jackson.'

She'd confirmed Ronnie's suspicions. He stared at her, long and hard.

'What?' she asked.

'Nowt. Well, yer remind me o' somebody.'

'Do I have to guess who that someone is?'

'No, I reckon yer know.'

'I look like Spode, don't I?'

Ronnie sent out a long sigh and nodded. 'I reckon yer do.'

'There's a reason for that,' said Jake.

Ronnie looked at Cathy. 'What happened?'

She swallowed. 'Spode raped my mother,' she said. It wasn't an easy thing to say.

'Is that why she killed hersen?'

Cathy nodded. 'She had no one to turn to.'

Jake felt the guilt arriving, but Cathy took his hand. 'None of her true friends could get to her,' she added, for his benefit.

There was a short silence as each of them assessed the situation. Which way to go from here. Ronnie went first.

'So,' he said, 'what do you need me for?'

Cathy treated him to one of her smiles and Jake knew his solidarity with them was assured. 'I think Spode abused you when you were a boy.'

Ronnie coloured. 'Don't be embarrassed,' added Jake. 'The same thing happened to me. Not with Spode, but with other blokes.'

Ronnie half nodded. They'd entered an area of his life he'd locked away in his mind.

'Well?' pressed Jake, gently.

Cathy sat back. Here were two men with similar experiences. Jake was the best one to deal with this.

Ronnie nodded slowly and hung his head as he spoke. 'I didn't think he were abusing me at the time. He paid me, yer see. I thought I were as bad as him. Worse even.'

'That's what they like you to think,' said Jake. 'I bet he threatened to have you sent away somewhere, if you told anybody.'

Ronnie looked up at him, relieved to have found a confidant after all these years. 'He did an' all. He told me I'd get locked up in a reformatory. I were scared ter death of him. That's why I did what I were told.' He looked at Cathy. 'Then when Annie and her mam moved in, he didn't want nowt no more ter do wi' me.' He grinned at them. 'Best day of me life, that.'

'It appeared he transferred his affections to my mother,' said Cathy. 'And I was the end result.'

Ronnie's head dropped again. 'I'm sorry – I didn't mean it like that.'

'Please, don't apologise,' she said. 'We're on the same side.' She glanced across at Jake, then back at Ronnie. 'Both Jake and I have reason to hate Spode. We want to bring him to justice for what he did all those years ago. And we need your help.'

Ronnie nodded his head. Bringing Spode to justice would help to lighten a dark corner of his soul. 'What do you want me ter do?'

'Mainly, we need you on our side. As a witness if it goes to court – and to help us track down anyone else he might have abused.'

'I'll help you all I can,' said Ronnie. 'But I don't know no one else.' He thought for a minute. 'Apart from that Melanie Binns bird. He's been knockin' her off since she were fourteen. Still is for all I know.'

'Melanie Binns?' Cathy's eyes lit up. She looked at Jake and saw a faint smile of triumph on his lips. Turning back to Ronnie, she asked, 'Do you know where she lives?'

'Have yer gorra pencil? I can write it down if yer want.'

Chapter Twenty-Five

Ronnie's meeting with Cathy and Jake had raked up a memory that he'd been trying to obliterate from his thoughts for almost twenty years. And now, it seemed, was the time for retribution. Time for Spode to get his come-uppance. But did Ronnie really want this to happen? Did he want the whole world and his brother to know what had been done to him when he was a boy? People would look at him and think their thoughts, all with differing opinions. Some sympathetic, others wondering why he'd let it happen, and others having a more cynical opinion altogether. Had he perhaps been a willing victim?

Ronnie had always hated himself for being too cowardly to stand up to Spode. Too cowardly to say, 'No! Leave me alone, you filthy pig, or I'll tell the police.' It was this shame that had held the secret secure within him. No one knew, not even his wife, definitely not his kids. But soon they would. Cathy wouldn't keep his involvement secret now, even if he wanted her to. Why the hell had he let her talk him into this? She had a freshness and beauty that had mesmerised him – and something else, something special he couldn't put his finger on. Maybe if she'd been an ugly cow with breath that could strip pine his secret might still have been safe.

His wife listened to his story with the blood draining from her face as the tears ran down his. He unburdened himself completely, giving her chapter and verse before sitting back to await her verdict. She didn't criticise his submission to Spode as he had feared she might but neither did she display that ounce of the compassion he needed. She wasn't impressed by Cathy's meddling either. Perhaps she was annoyed that another woman had somehow wormed a deep secret out of her husband – a secret he'd kept from her, his own wife, all these years.

'You go straight to the police before she twists everything to her own advantage,' she insisted, harshly.

'Give over,' he protested. 'What's the use o' that without proof?'

'I'll tell yer what's the use o' that! It'll let everyone know what a bloody pervert he is.'

'Not without proof it won't.'

'Yer don't need proof to accuse someone o' summat.'

'Suppose t' papers get hold of it, what'll we do then?'

'I'll make damn' sure they do get hold of it,' she fumed. 'Then it's up ter them what they print. There's no law against accusin' someone o' summat. Mud sticks. Other folk he's done it to'll mebbe read it. Yer never know what'll happen.'

Spode's housekeeper answered the door. 'I'll see if Mr Spode's in, sir,' she said, leaving the reporter on the step like a door-to-door salesman. She returned within a minute and invited the young man inside. Spode was drinking his morning coffee. He looked at his watch, then at the reporter.

'I can give you a minute. I start work at eight and I'm never late.'

'Thank you for seeing me, sir.' The reporter looked at the housekeeper. 'It's rather a delicate matter.'

Spode indicated for his housekeeper to leave with a curt inclination of his head. She closed the kitchen door behind her. Spode waited a few moments, then got to his feet and yanked the door open to reveal her hovering behind it.

'Do that again, Mrs O'Hagan, and you're fired!'

He shut the door and smiled at the reporter. 'Loyalty's hard to find nowadays. Everyone wants a slice of the cake.'

'I'm not sure I follow you?' said the reporter.

'I'm a high-profile figure,' explained Spode. 'Not front-page material, but always worth a few lines of gossip somewhere. The staff find it tempting to disclose the odd titbit here and there in return for a few quid. Then they cry foul when I sack them.'

'Ah,' said the reporter.

'Ah, indeed.' Spode smiled. 'Have I spiked your guns before you even begin to fire at me? If so I apologise. What is it? Heartless employer? Ruthless businessman?' He leaned forward and held the reporter in his steady gaze. 'You're embarrassed. That can only mean one thing – sex.'

The reporter's silence made Spode smile. 'I'm right, aren't I?'

The reporter shrugged.

'So what am I now? A sex maniac? A raving queer? I live on my own with no obvious outlet for my sexual requirements. What's the latest gossip?'

'Well,' stammered the reporter, 'it's not actually gossip. A woman rang up to say her husband once had sex with you.'

Spode laughed uproariously. 'And you've actually taken the trouble to come round here to check on it?'

'It's a story, sir.'

'It's not much of a story if it's not true.' Spode finished his coffee and got to his feet. 'Look, I don't know who you're talking about, but I can assure you that I've never had sex with a man in my life.'

'He wasn't a man at the time, Mr Spode. He was a boy! Apparently he worked for you.'

Spode had his back to the reporter so the young man didn't see the worried expression on his face. 'A boy? And does this boy have a name?'

'I'm not allowed to disclose my sources.'

'Of course not,' said Spode through a fixed smile. 'Look, I'm not even going to dignify this accusation with a denial. If you have proof, go ahead and print.'

'So you're not going to make a statement, sir?'

'Only to my solicitor if you print this rubbish.' Spode's composure was beginning to crack. 'A damaging article like this would cost your newspaper thousands unless you have concrete proof, which of course you haven't with it not being true.'

'So I can take this as a denial?'

'You can take yourself out of my house before I kick you out,' snapped Spode.

Jake called at Cathy's bedsit on his way to school.

'Morning, Cathy. It crossed my mind this morning that Ronnie might jump the gun and go to the papers or the police. Or at least his wife might if he tells her what he told us.'

Cathy nodded sleepily. 'Fancy a coffee while I get dressed?'

Jake didn't particularly want a coffee but the sight of Cathy in a red silk dressing gown which ended way short of her shapely knees had him stepping through the door.

'Just a quickie.'

She raised an amused eyebrow at his unintended double-entendre.

'Now then, Miss Makepeace, less of your smutty thoughts,' he scolded.

She wiggled her backside at him and disappeared behind a screened-off sleeping area. Jake caught his breath, then mentally chastised himself for having such thoughts about her.

'Put the kettle on,' she called out. 'I'll not be a minute. I'll walk you to school. Do you think we should go back and have another word with Ronnie?'

'No,' he decided. 'You see, I've been thinking.'

'Not again.'

Jake ignored her. 'An article in the papers might flush a few of Spode's other victims out.' He spoke to the top of her head, the only bit of her he could see behind the screen.

'Yeah,' she agreed. 'It's just that I was hoping to hit him hard and catch him off guard. Oh, make it in the cups. Black, no sugar for me.'

Cathy was suddenly conscious of being completely naked and standing only a few feet away from him. She could see his reflection in the wardrobe mirror, which meant he'd be able to see her. If only he would turn round! With a deliberate lack of haste she pulled on her panties.

Jake spooned coffee into two cups, oblivious to the treat he was missing. 'It probably won't happen,' he mused. 'Ronnie's word against his and all that. Would a paper take such a risk?'

'Probably not,' she agreed. 'He could go to the police, though.'

'Same difference – he'd still need proof. I doubt if they'd touch it.'

'So what do we do?'

'Play it by ear,' said Jake, half turning. His gaze rested momentarily on Cathy's half-dressed reflection. Their eyes met before Jake averted his. She wondered if he'd seen her earlier and didn't mind in the least if he had.

'I, er, I was thinking of tracking this Melanie Binns down,' he said.

'I'll go and see her on my own,' decided Cathy. 'Try and get something out of her. Let the water go off the boil for a minute – I never make coffee with boiling water.'

'Hmm,' said Jake, pouring boiling water into his own cup and wishing he'd looked in the mirror a bit sooner.

'It's something I heard,' she explained. 'Makes the coffee taste better.'

'Oh, right.'

She appeared from behind the screen wearing jeans and a baggy, white sweater which would have looked ordinary on ninety-nine percent of women. But not on her. 'You can pour mine out now.' She smiled.

Jake did as he was told and handed her the cup. 'You think Spode's fancy woman might open up to you, do you?'

'I wouldn't quite put it that way,' said Cathy, sipping her drink. She sat on the arm of a worn easy chair and beckoned Jake to sit on the other. 'Woman to woman, she might let something slip, especially if she doesn't suspect who I am.'

'I should wear dark glasses,' advised Jake. 'If Spode's fancy woman can't spot the similarity, no one can.'

Spode drew his Jaguar up behind the milk float and waited for Ronnie to return with a crate of empties. Ronnie did a double take as he arrived, taken aback when he recognised his visitor. What the devil was happening? First those two, now the man himself? Spode got out of the car and confronted the wary milkman.

'So you thought you'd go to the papers with your lies, did you?'

'I don't know what yer talkin' about.'

Spode looked a lot older than when he'd intimidated Ronnie into those disgusting antics. Ronnie was on his guard but not scared. He filled another crate with bottles as Spode hovered behind him.

'I'm warning you . . .'

Ronnie turned around to face his tormentor. 'Warning me about what? Yer don't want me ter tell the truth about yer – is that what yer warning me about?'

Spode jabbed a warning finger into Ronnie's chest. 'I'll destroy whatever miserable existence you've made for yourself. You need proof, you see, or hadn't you thought of that? What proof have you got to back up your lies?'

Ronnie pushed him away. 'I don't need proof – I know things about you.'

'Oh, yes?' Spode frowned. 'What things?'

'I know people yer've done it to.'

'You know nothing,' sneered Spode.

'I know Melanie Binns for a start!' blurted Ronnie.

'Never heard of her,' growled Spode as he got back in his car.

He drove away with his mind racing. He hadn't been worried until Ronnie had mentioned Melanie Binns. If the two of them ganged up on him, it could make life awkward. Perhaps persuade a few other skeletons to come out of various cupboards. Skeletons who, at the moment, thought they had no allies. Ronnie's knowing about Melanie Binns was a real problem. Who else could he possibly know about? Spode ran through the possibilities as he drove. None came to mind. Melanie was almost certainly the only one.

There were two different solutions to this problem. One a bit more final than the other, and much less expensive. He turned into his factory gate. A phone call to Melanie should set the ball rolling. He'd take it from there.

The *Daily Express* picked up the story of Spode's election to President of the British Children's Society and ran it on page one, with the only photograph of him they had, taken during his early years in Parliament. That evening, his face almost leapt off the page as Mary Dawson spotted the paper lying on the day room coffee table. It was *him*. She'd never been able to put a name to *him* but there was no doubt about it. He'd obviously emerged from her troubled thoughts with the singular intention of coming for her. Of that she had no doubt. Silent tears of fear coursed down her pale cheeks as panic struck. The black door exploded open in her face and all the vileness within engulfed her, choking her into terrified oblivion.

Nurse Hargreaves found her comatose on the floor. Saliva was running from her bloodless lips, her body was in spasm and Jeanette Hargreaves thought she was dead.

Arthur Stone picked up the newspaper from the seat beside him as he waited for his haircut.

'Here – I know this dirty bastard!'

A picture of Spode looked back at him, above the heading: *YORKSHIRE MP TAKES OVER PRESIDENCY OF CHILDREN'S SOCIETY.*

'I did time for this bloke,' he exclaimed. 'The dirty bastard!'

'Watcha moanin' about now, Arfur?' enquired the barber.

Stone stabbed his finger at Spode's picture. 'This bastard.'

He held up the paper for the barber to see. The customer peered into the mirror, trying to read the reflection back-to-front.

'I turned him over when I were goin' through me villain phase,' explained Stone. 'Held me hands up for it later – had it taken into consideration when they nicked me for a burglary. But I never was a dirty bastard like him.'

'Why? What's he done?' asked the barber.

'He's been messin' wiv little kids.'

'The dirty sod!' said the barber. 'An' look what they've put him in charge of. They ought ter casterate blokes what do that.'

'It's not bleedin' right,' grumbled Arthur. 'I done time for a lot less than what he done – the dirty bastard!'

'Blokes like that,' commented the barber as he snipped away, 'allus get away wiv it. I mean, what can yer do about it? Nuffin' – that's what yer can do.'

'It's allus the bleedin' same,' grumbled Arthur. 'I got an incriminating photo of one of his birds. Christ! She were only fourteen. I should've handed it over when they pulled me in. Serve the bastard right.'

'Why didn't yer?'

'I 'ad other things on me mind, didn't I?'

'It's never too late, Arfur,' said the barber. 'Sorry, sir!' He wiped a speck of blood off the customer's ear.

Arthur gave it some thought. 'Nah, it's a long time ago. The bastard'd just deny it.'

'I'd blackmail the bastard,' said the customer.

That evening, Arthur dug out the picture of Melanie Binns, on the back of which was her mother's telephone number. It took several frustrating minutes arguing with first the operator and then with Directory Enquiries before he found Mrs Binns' new, up-to-date number.

'Hello, Mrs Binns?'

'Yes.'

'Could I speak to Melanie, please?'

He was fairly certain she wouldn't be there, but past experience told him that people were more ready to part with privileged information if they weren't asked direct questions, such as 'Could you tell me your daughter's phone number, please?'

'She's not here, love.'

'Oh, right.' He sounded disappointed. 'Can you tell me what time she'll be back, please?'

'She doesn't actually live here.'

'Oh, right. Er, look – sorry to have bothered you . . .'

'I can give her a message if yer like. Who is it?'

'Arthur,' said Stone. 'I – er – I knew her from school, before we moved down south. There's no message, I just thought I'd give her a ring. I've just moved back up here, you see. She probably won't even remember me. Tell you what, I'll leave it.'

'I'll give you her phone number if yer like.'

'Honest, it's all right.'

'Listen, lad. Yer sound a lot more decent than the idiots she usually knocks about with. You just give her a ring.'

A minute later Stone was staring at Melanie's address and phone number, wondering what to do with them.

Cathy knocked on the door of Melanie's second-floor maisonette and glanced at Brenda with some apprehension. There was an eye-watering smell of disinfectant on the landing which was preferable to the smells which had assailed their noses on the way up. Cathy had no plan of attack and was hoping she'd be able to think on her feet. She adjusted her dark glasses as Melanie's blurred outline appeared behind the frosted glass door.

'Who is it?'

It seemed a reasonable question in this neighbourhood.

'My name's Cathy Makepeace.' She had a friendly voice which usually disarmed people of either sex. But not always.

'An' who's Cathy Makepeace when she's at home? If yer from t' Social, yer can just piss off.'

'I work for Leonard Spode.'

There was a moment's silence from the other side, then a bolt was drawn and the door pulled open. Loud music blared out from within as Cathy stood face to face with Spode's lover. She had estimated Melanie to be in her mid-twenties by now and was surprised to see a young woman who had obviously looked after herself, a condition totally at odds with her grim surroundings. She either took regular exercise or had been blessed with one of those rare physiques that look good no matter what. Her face, although not unattractive, had a pinched meanness around the eyes, her hair was bottle-blonde and a cigarette hung from dark-painted lips.

'What's he sent yer for? I told him what the deal were yesterday. If he thinks he's gonna gerroff wi' owt less, he's got another think com ... Jesus!'

Brenda appeared around the door, doing her best not to look intimidating. Melanie took a step backwards, positioning Cathy between her and Brenda.

'Look, I don't want no trouble. I'm here on me own wi' three bairns.'

Cathy felt guilty. 'It's all right. We're not here to harm you.'

'What's she doin' here, then?'

'She's a colleague.'

'What? She works for Leonard as well, does she?'

'Yes,' lied Cathy. 'She's his ... er ...'

'Troubleshooter,' put in Brenda.

'I shouldn't think he gets much trouble then,' observed Melanie. 'Yer'll not get none from me, I promise yer. What have yer come for?'

Cathy's brain was racing to keep up. What was the 'deal' Melanie had with Spode? 'Mr Spode's been called away on urgent business and he wanted us to call round to check that everything was all right with regards to the deal.'

'Why shouldn't it be? That's why yer've come, in't it? Ter try an' knock me price down. The tight sod!'

'He seemed to think you were asking for too much money,' said Brenda.

'How come he lets you in on all his private business?' asked Melanie. 'It's supposed ter be between him an' me.'

'I handle things for him,' said Brenda.

'So do I.' Melanie grinned.

Brenda laughed. The two of them seemed to have things in common.

'I told him a thousand an' he agreed,' said Melanie.

Brenda shrugged. 'Fair enough,' she said. 'I told him I'd try, and I have. Yer right about him bein' a tight sod.'

'He wants ter think himself lucky,' grumbled Melanie. 'It's in all t' papers about him becoming president o' that Children's Society.'

'It's a bit ironic, I must admit,' said Cathy, who'd been discussing the news with Brenda on the way over.

'It's a bleedin' joke, that's what it is,' sniffed Melanie. 'Still, each to his own. He's never done me no harm.' She grinned at Brenda. 'I tell yer what – I can't believe Ronnie Sykes had the bottle ter go ter t' papers. He were allus a snotty-nosed wimp when I knew him.'

'Maybe it was his wife?' suggested Cathy.

Melanie nodded. 'More likely. Anyroad I told Mr High an' bloody Mighty that t' papers'll get nowt from me so long as he keeps payin'.'

'He'll be relieved to hear that,' said Cathy.

They were all standing in the cramped hallway. Melanie

treated them to a smile that lacked a top tooth.

'Fancy a cup o' tea?'

'That'd be lovely, thanks,' said Cathy.

Melanie stepped back, allowing Cathy and Brenda to go through into the living room. Loud music came from upstairs, not quite drowning arguing children. Melanie went to the bottom of the stairs and shouted: 'Shut yer bloody racket, you lot.' It had no effect.

'How many children did you say you'd got?'

Melanie gave her another gappy grin. 'Three,' she said.

Cathy wondered if any had been fathered by Spode, and shuddered at the thought. Some of the children here could be her siblings. They followed Melanie through to an untidy living room smelling of stale tobacco and wet nappies. A small ginger-haired child waddled towards them, its face smeared with chocolate from the half-eaten biscuit clutched in its podgy hand.

'Bloody 'ell, Dale! Have you peed yersen again?'

Despite her language there was no harshness in Melanie's voice, she obviously loved this child – and the two upstairs. Brenda would have swapped Melanie Binns for her own mother any day. Melanie looked at Cathy and frowned.

'Is there summat wrong with your eyes?'

'Oh, you mean the dark glasses? I've got a touch of conjunctivitis.' Cathy had looked up the complaint before she came out. It satisfied Melanie.

'Park yer bum if yer can find somewhere ter sit.'

Cathy picked up a pile of magazines from a chair and laid them, as neatly as she could, on the floor before sitting down. Brenda sat on a dining chair and watched with interest as Melanie picked up Dale, checked his nappy, laid the child on a rug and proceeded to change him.

'He's a grand little lad,' said Brenda. 'I wouldn't mind a little lad like him.'

'He's a bloody nuisance,' said Melanie without a hint of malice. 'But I wouldn't be without him.'

'I should think not,' said Brenda.

A wave of sadness hit Cathy as the memory of her recent loss came back to her. Then it occurred to her that this child could be her only living relative, apart from *him*.

'Does his father have red hair?' She was fishing.

'No idea.' Melanie smiled. 'He didn't take his cap off.'

Brenda howled with laughter and Melanie joined in. Cathy sat there with a broad smile on her face, still curious as to the truth.

'Yeah,' said Melanie, at length. 'His dad had ginger hair. He were a bit of a shit, but not bad-looking.'

Her expert hands pinned Dale's clean nappy on in a few seconds. Pulling the child into a pair of plastic pants, she looked up at Cathy. 'By the way, in case yer thinkin' – none of mine have owt ter do wi' Spode.'

'It never crossed my mind,' lied Cathy, hoping the relief on her face wasn't too obvious.

The noise from upstairs increased. Someone sounded to be in pain.

'Jesus! I'll bloody swing for them two.' Melanie looked at Cathy. 'Would yer keep an eye on him, love, while I go clatter the pair of 'em?'

Without waiting for an answer she handed the child to Cathy and marched purposefully out of the room, banging up the stairs with an exaggerated tread designed to intimidate. The phone beside Brenda rang, adding to the overall cacophony. Her hand automatically reached for it, then withdrew, undecided.

Melanie's voice bellowed from above, 'Get that forrus, will yer, love? Tell 'em I'll ring 'em back.'

Brenda picked up the phone and blotted out the row with her free hand.

'Hello?'

'Could I speak to Melanie Binns, please?'

'Speaking,' said Brenda. She held her hand over the mouthpiece and whispered 'Yer never know' to a bemused Cathy.

'You don't know me,' said Arthur Stone. 'But I've gotta a photo of you what I nicked off Leonard Spode.'

'A photo?' said Brenda. 'What sort of photo?'

'A photo of you when you were a kid in a swimsuit.'

'Oh, that photo.'

'I thought you'd remember. I bet he nearly wet himself when he lost it. He's lucky I didn't try to blackmail him.'

He paused, waiting for some reaction. Brenda mimed for Cathy to be quiet. She shrugged and sat back, listening warily for sounds of Melanie coming back down. She seemed to be in full flow, delivering an almighty roasting to her now bawling children.

'What's the matter?' asked Stone.

'Telly,' said Brenda. 'What's wrong wi' a picture of me in a swimsuit?'

'You've forgotten, haven't you?'

'Forgotten what?'

'What you wrote on the back.'

'What did I write on the back?'

Stone paused, suddenly embarrassed. 'Enough to tell me he were havin' it off with you. An' I know for a fact you were only fourteen.'

Brenda stuck her thumb up to a bemused Cathy.

'Who are yer an' where are yer ringing from?' she asked Stone.

'Me name's Arthur and I'm in London.'

'Right, Arthur – now what's all this leadin' up to?'

'I can let you have the photo back if you make it worth me while.'

'Oh, aye – an' why should I want to make it worth your while?' enquired Brenda. Stone seemed put out.

'What about him, then?' he asked. 'With him bein' made President of this Children's Society. He won't want the papers to get hold o' this photo.'

'No, I don't suppose he will.'

'Mebbe you should have a word wiv him?'

'Mebbe I might. How much do yer want?'

'I reckon it's worth a long un.'

'What's a "long un" when it's at 'ome?' enquired Brenda.

'Hundred quid. Don't you speak English up there?'

'So if I bring a hundred quid down, you can let me have the photo?'

Stone was relieved that he wouldn't have to travel up to Leeds. 'King's Cross station,' he said. 'Three o'clock, day after tomorrow. I'll be standing under the destination board.'

'See you then,' said Brenda.

'How will I know you?'

'I tend ter stand out in a crowd.'

Stone looked down at the photo and allowed his imagination to wander. 'I imagine you probably do by now.'

Brenda put the phone down as Melanie came down the stairs.

'Who were on the phone?' she asked, entering the room and taking Dale from Cathy's arms.

'Someone called Arthur,' said Brenda. 'I told him to ring back. He didn't say what he wanted.'

'Right.' Melanie didn't even bother to toss the name around in her mind. She doubted very much if the caller had given his real name, they usually didn't.

'Look, we'll have ter get off,' said Brenda, making silent signals to Cathy.

She frowned, not ready to leave, but Brenda seemed adamant.

'Strikes me yer've got enough on yer plate,' said Brenda. 'Without us bothering yer.'

'Yer weren't botherin' me, love,' said Melanie. 'So it's as we agreed then?'

'What is?'

'The money – it's still a thousand?'

'No problem,' said Brenda. 'I'll tell him we tried us best but yer wouldn't budge.'

'To be paid by twelve o'clock on Thursday?'

‘Not a minute later,’ agreed Brenda.

‘Well,’ said Cathy as they went down the steps, ‘I’m not sure we made much progress there. Who was on the phone? What’s all this about a hundred quid? Why did you want to leave in such a rush? I was thinking we might get to work on her. Make her see the error of her ways and blow the whistle on Spode.’

‘Woah, woah,’ said Brenda, gripping her arm. ‘That bloke on t’ phone thought I were Melanie.’

‘Not an easy mistake to make.’

‘Don’t be so bloody cheeky. He’d seen Spode’s photo in t’ papers – an’ listen ter this . . .’

‘What?’

‘He’s gorra photo o’ Melanie what he thinks’ll drop Spode in t’ shit if t’ papers get hold of it.’

‘So that’s why you arranged to meet him?’

‘Correct,’ said Brenda.

‘And we’re giving him a hundred pounds for it?’ said Cathy, doubtfully. ‘I haven’t got a hundred pounds.’

‘Don’t you worry about that. I’ll negotiate further when I see him.’

Chapter Twenty-Six

'How is she, doctor?' asked Nurse Jeanette Hargreaves.

'There's no way of knowing until she wakes up.'

The doctor was shining a light into Mary Dawson's eyes. He switched it off and checked her pulse. 'Physically she's all right.' He tapped his patient's head, gently. 'But who knows what's going on in there? Does anyone have any idea what triggered it off?'

The nurse shrugged. 'She was on her own in the day room. I found her on the floor . . .'

The doctor sighed. 'All the great advances we've made over the last hundred years and we still haven't a clue what goes on between the ears.'

'Maybe it's better that way,' remarked Nurse Hargreaves. 'There are times when I wouldn't want the world knowing what's inside my mind.'

The doctor looked at her over the top of his glasses. 'I reckon your thoughts are worth a damn sight more than a penny.'

Jeanette reddened. She had a thing for the doctor, but he was happily married. Weren't they all?

They left the room as Mary's fingers twitched. She had come out of the coma and was now simply sleeping. Dreaming. He was behind her again, pressing himself into her. Hurting her. And this woman was screaming. This woman. Her mother. It was her mother, she hadn't known that before.

The two of them were falling away from her. Down and down, mile after mile, she could hear them but not see. Now she could see them. They were a long way down, an unreachable distance, maybe a hundred miles, but she could see them clearly. Standing beside him now but he wouldn't die. No matter how hard she hit him, she simply wasn't strong enough to make him die. Oh! and how he deserved to die. Please give me the strength to make him die. To make him go away. Forever.

He was looking at her, surrounded by words. That same face. She screamed and was sitting bolt upright when the doctor and Jeanette came dashing back in. They stood to either side of her, waiting for her desperate breathing to subside. For her eyes to stop dancing as if witnessing some inner catastrophe. Then she suddenly became calm. The beast disturbing her had left. But not for good. She knew that. He never left for good. Jeanette reached out and took her friend's hand.

'It's okay, Mary. You've had a bit of a fall but you're okay now. Is it all right if the doctor takes a look at you?'

Mary remained stock still at first, as if the nurse's words hadn't immediately registered. Then she gave a half smile and nodded. Jeanette looked at the doctor.

'I think she's back to normal, doctor.'

'Whatever normal is, in her case.'

Mary could have said something, but she didn't. She might have started something she couldn't finish. Her silent, cloistered world was all she could cope with. While ever *he* was around.

Meanwhile, Spode was checking his face in the rear view mirror and pulling the hood of his duffle-coat further down over his head before stepping out of his Jaguar. He'd parked it almost quarter of a mile away to avoid anyone making a connection. As he walked, he tried to set aside all thoughts of the purpose of his visit until the moment arrived. The duffle-coat was in keeping with the chill weather and wouldn't arouse any suspicions. They were ideal garments for this sort of work. He must start making them himself. Start a come-back. Why they'd gone out of fashion in the first place had been a mystery . . .

Melanie had asked for a thousand pounds. How long before she'd be asking for another thousand, and another? Despite her limp denials, he knew she was on the game. Last year she'd taken her tribe on holiday to Benidorm and you don't do that on dole money. It could turn to his advantage. Prostitutes often met with sticky ends at the hands of their clients. If she'd simply promised to keep her mouth shut for old time's sake he'd have given her a grand. But her whole attitude when she rang him up had put him on his guard. The silly bitch thought she was in the driving seat, giving him a deadline. Noon on Thursday or else. Who the hell did she think she was?

The concrete maisonettes all looked alike, built only six years ago, in what sixties architects considered to be balanced and aesthetically pleasing quadrangles, with young trees, play areas and walkways. The trees had been early victims of junior lumberjacks who had made good use of them on Bonfire Night. The lawns were grassless and littered with parked cars and the only vegetation grew profusely between the uneven concrete flags of the walkways. Graffiti was obscene and mis-spelt and there was a general air of dereliction around him as Spode identified the unedifying cube of concrete in front of him as Gaitskell Court.

He allowed his rage to mount as he climbed the four flights of urine-reeking steps, his right hand clasped firmly over the steel poker hidden in his deep pocket. Melanie's blurred outline appeared behind the glass panel in the door.

'Who is it?'

'Me, Leonard.'

Spode leaned towards the glass, perspiring freely now as reality hit him. He was about to commit a murder. His voice was little more than a nervous croak as he checked the landing either side to ensure no one else could see or hear him.

The bolt was drawn and the door unlocked. Melanie stood back to allow him through, but he politely motioned for her to go first. Ladies before gentlemen. As she turned her back on him he struck her with all his strength, over the back of her head. Time and time again. Beating her to the floor, and continuing to beat her until he was absolutely sure there wasn't a spark of life left in her. As he put the bloodied poker back in his pocket he found himself looking into the eyes of Dale, who was standing at the living room door. For a brief moment Spode considered doing the same to the baby and was halted only by the sound of other children playing upstairs. If he did one he'd most likely have to do them all. Too messy all that. Breathing heavily from his exertion and the shock of what he'd just done, he hurried out of the house, leaving behind a wailing child and a silent, blood soaked mother.

The oldest of Melanie's children was only six and hadn't figured out how to open the self-locking Yale. The three of them sat around their dead mother, clutching each other's hands, waiting for their mum to open her eyes and tell them everything was all right.

The following morning, a curious paper boy heard whimpering behind the door and looked through the letter box on to a sight which had him retching over the balcony.

The television was on mainly to cheer the place up. Cathy wasn't watching it as she paced up and down the grubby, worn carpet. She didn't hear a local news item about a mother of three small children having been found battered to death. They didn't give her name as the next-of-kin hadn't been informed.

Cathy kept looking at her watch, the one Liz had bought her for her birthday. The card had said 'From Mum and Dad,' but she knew better. Ten past six. The door opened and Dave strode in, throwing his jacket on the chair as he always did.

'Put the kettle on, love.' He'd been drinking.

She stood transfixed for a moment. He looked up at her. 'Put the bloody kettle on. How many more times do I have ter tell yer?'

Automatically she moved to the kitchen area and filled the kettle from the tap. Her heart was pounding.

'How come you're out?'

'Served me time. Me case came up this mornin'. I got six months, less time off for good behaviour, less time on remand. Here I am.'

'If I'd know I'd have moved my stuff out.'

'No rush.' He leered at her and made a lewd mime with his hands. 'I've gone without for four months – seems me luck's in.'

'Not with me it's not.'

Cathy's courage was returning. She knew he wouldn't dare try anything or he'd be straight back inside. There was a long uncomfortable silence as she waited for the kettle to boil. How on earth could she get out of this? Why hadn't she moved out of this dump with all its bad memories? Dave got to his feet and came towards her, hands outstretched, palms held innocently upwards.

'Come on.' His speech was slightly slurred. 'We might have had us differences but we were good in bed, yer've got to admit that.'

'Dave, come one step nearer and I'll hit you with this kettle. I suggest you go out and come back in an hour. I'll be gone.'

'Go out? How d'yer mean, go out? This is my home.' He was swaying and she realised his sense of reason had deserted him. In this state he had no fear of going back inside. His only thoughts were of her and what he wanted to do to her. She took the kettle off the cooker where it was beginning to simmer.

'I'm warning you, Dave. Back off or I'll hit you with this.'

He stopped in his tracks, his eyes on the kettle, steam drifting from the spout. A grin appeared on his face as he began to move sideways. She turned to keep him in front of her, kettle at the ready.

'You wouldn't dare,' he challenged.

'You don't scare me, Dave. You're a thief, you live off other people. Why should I be scared of you?'

Anger flashed in his eyes and she mentally kicked herself for provoking him. This wasn't the right way to go about things. Calm him down, that was the way.

'It was you who shopped me, wasn't it?' Before she could say anything he added, 'Don't bloody deny it, I know it were you.'

Her eyes flashed defiantly, her plan to calm him down instantly forgotten. 'If I'd wanted to shop you to the police, I'd have had you done for assault and the murder of an unborn child! Your child. You had a son, did you know that? You killed your baby son.'

The anger in his eyes vanished, replaced by drunken sullenness.

'It weren't my baby.'

'Make your sick excuses all you want. You know whose baby it was, and you killed it.'

'How do yer know it were a boy?'

Cathy was crying now, the awful memory coming back to her. 'He was fully formed, you idiot.'

He took another step towards her, his carnal intentions perhaps forgotten, but she still didn't want him near her. She drew her arm back. Water spilled from the spout of the kettle.

'Are you all right, Cathy?'

Brenda didn't wait for a reply. She opened the door and took in the little cameo at a glance. Her good friend Cathy was being threatened by a man. No questions needed to be asked. Dave's expression turned to horror as she advanced on him and took him by the throat.

Cathy looked on, making no pleas for clemency on Dave's behalf as Brenda dragged him backwards, choking, towards the door. They disappeared from view and Cathy winced at the sound of several loud thuds followed by the screams and howls of someone falling down the stairs. Brenda came back in and smiled.

'Put the kettle back on, love. I reckon we've time for a cuppa.'

The tension building within Cathy was suddenly released like a dam bursting. She flung her arms around Brenda and sobbed it all away. Brenda patted her friend's head, pleased she'd been able to help.

'Why don't yer move back to yer ma an' dad's? It's got ter be better than this.'

'I'm not grovelling to my dad. I'd rather stay here.'

'Now, why doesn't that surprise me?' said Brenda.

Chapter Twenty-Seven

'Nice day for it,' shouted the lone fisherman as Father Barrett walked across the stone bridge. He'd crossed this bridge a thousand times since that fateful day but he never crossed it without thinking of Annie, the girl he'd never met. He'd also heard this greeting many times before and had usually responded with a polite touch to the brim of his cap. This time he stopped. At his time of life there were many unanswered questions and the time for getting answers was running out.

'Nice day for what?' he called back, accompanying his question with a smile.

The man returned his smile with fifty per cent interest. 'Fishing, walking – owt yer want.'

John Barrett looked up at the dark, grumbling sky. 'I wouldn't say it was a nice day. Looks like rain to me.'

'All days are nice if yer enjoying yerself.'

'I suppose they are,' conceded the priest. He walked down the bank to join the fisherman, who was opening a packet of sandwiches.

'Salmon,' he said. 'Made 'em meself.'

'You didn't catch them yourself, did you?'

The fisherman laughed. 'Not round here I didn't. No, it's out of a tin. Actually I prefer tinned salmon, but don't tell anyone.'

'Your secret's safe with me.'

Sam held out two hands, one offering a sandwich, one for John Barrett to shake. 'My name's Sam,' he said. 'Want one?'

'Thank you, you're very kind.' The priest took a sandwich and shook his new friend's hand. 'My name's John.'

The rain came, heavy and noisy, livening up the river with a violent blur of staccato splashes. Sam hurriedly put up a large dark green umbrella for them to huddle beneath.

'You can't see your float for all the splashing,' observed the priest.

'I let the fish off when it's like this.'

'God's way of giving the poor creatures a break,' said John, who thought fishing was a bit cruel.

'Don't you agree with fishing?' asked Sam.

John shrugged. He didn't feel strongly enough about it to upset his new friend. But Sam wouldn't let it go.

'I thought God was a fisherman,' he said.

'That was his son,' said John. 'And you know what kids are like.'

Sam grinned at his clerical friend and they talked until the rain cleared and the skies gave way to a clear, winter chill. John spent a whole entertaining afternoon in this man's company and it wasn't until he was about to leave that he realised just how much they had in common.

'Are you from that church where that girl left her baby?' enquired Sam.

'You mean Annie Jackson?' replied John. 'That was a long time ago. Yes, it was I who found the child.'

'I nearly got drowned trying ter save her.' There was no hint of a boast in Sam's voice, only sorrow.

'Really?' recalled the priest. 'I seem to remember something about that. Weren't you given some sort of bravery award?'

'Yeah. They gave me a citation. They should have given me a certificate of insanity.'

'Not at all. You did a brave thing. I never met her, you

know. I wish I had. By all accounts she was a special kind of person.'

'Do yer know,' said Sam, 'I always thought that – and I only saw her from down here. I shouted at her and she smiled at me. I can still remember that smile.'

'I bet you shouted, "Nice day for it",' laughed the priest.

'Probably. It wasn't a very nice day for what she had in mind, though.'

'It's never a nice day for that,' agreed John.

He watched with some fascination as Sam teased a fish out of the water and brought it up wriggling on the end of his line until he unhooked it and tossed it into his keep-net.

'What will you do with them?' enquired John.

'Lerrem go,' grinned Sam. 'It's only a game.' He opened his bait-tin to reload his hook and said, 'I never thought she drowned, yer know.'

'Pardon?'

'That girl, Annie Jackson. I always thought they were a bit quick off the mark declaring her dead like they did.'

'It was assumed she'd been swept out to sea.'

'They can assume all they like. If they knew this river like I do, they'd know that was a load o' bollocks – sorry, John.'

'That's okay. It's quite a versatile word. In fact, it'd be my favourite if it weren't for this.' He tapped his dog-collar. 'So you think she's still alive, do you? Now there's an interesting thought. You see, I've always harboured doubts myself.'

'I don't know about still alive,' said Sam. 'But I'm willin' ter bet she were never drowned. She'd have been found, I'd bet my mortgage on it.'

The light was fading as John looked at his watch. Four p.m. 'I'd like to have a little chat about this,' he said. 'Exchange theories. When are you here next?'

'Tomorrow,' said Sam. 'I'm on nights – I'm a bobby,' he explained.

'Ah, I see. Well, we must put your detective skills to good use.'

'I'm not actually a detective, just a uniformed constable.'
'The ones who do all the work, eh?'
'If yer could explain that to my sergeant I'd be much obliged. I'll meet yer here tomorrow – one o'clock. I'll not bring me tackle, we'll have a walk down the river instead. You'd best bring a pair of wellies.'
'Excellent,' said John. 'I shall look forward to it.'

It was a crisp and clear afternoon as the priest and Sam set off walking. The trees were mainly devoid of summer leaves and the low, winter sunshine penetrated the bare branches and danced along the quickening river as it narrowed on its approach to Ackroyd's Drop. John had found a pair of old Wellingtons in the gardener's shed. They were a couple of sizes too big and one of them wasn't entirely waterproof, but they were marginally more robust than his shoes.

Sam pointed out an overhanging tree on the far bank. 'That tree saved my life. That and me mates who were running after me. I were convinced I'd had it.'

'It wasn't your time,' said the priest, philosophically.

Sam looked at him. 'What I'd like ter know,' he said, 'is was it Annie Jackson's time? They dragged all this part of the river and never found her. If she'd been washed over the waterfall she'd have more than likely got stuck on the rocks, and if she'd got past them there's a weir further down. She'd have got stuck against it.' He shook his head. 'I think about this nearly every time I come fishing.' Grinning at John, he added, 'Nowt else ter think about, yer see. That's the beauty of fishing. It's just you and yer thoughts and them little beggars yer trying ter best.'

'I might come and join you some time,' said the priest. 'Providing we throw them all back.'

'Hey! Don't tell me I've got a convert,' laughed Sam.

They arrived at Ackroyd's Drop and Father Barrett shuddered as he looked at the water cascading sixty feet down a sheer rock face into a churning black pool, beyond which it battered its way past a menacing array of large and jagged rocks before disappearing round a bend about two hundred yards away.

'See what I mean,' said Sam. 'Even if she went over she'd more than likely get caught up among them rocks. And even if she got past them there's a weir about a mile further down. The river's a lot wider there and the water barely trickles over.'

'What do you think happened to her?' asked John.

Sam grinned and held up a finger. 'I've been giving this a lot of thought. It's only a theory, mind – but there's summat I'd like to have a look at first.'

With the old priest panting in his wake he pushed his way through the damp undergrowth along a path of sorts so narrow and overgrown they had to walk in single file. After ten minutes they arrived at a canal on which a colourful narrow boat called *Hilda B* was sitting patiently, above her own reflection, waiting for her owner to open the lock gates. John sat down on a low, stone wall and removed his left boot. His sock was soaking wet. Sam looked up and down the canal.

'I thought so,' he said.

'Thought what?' asked John, squeezing the grey water from his sock.

'There's only one path from the river and it leads here.'

'So?' puzzled John, putting his damp sock back on.

'So it's possible she somehow managed ter get out of the river after she'd gone over Ackroyd's Drop. If she did, she'd end up here.'

'She might have got out the other side,' said John, examining his boot to locate the leak.

'Yer can't get out of the river the other side.'

'So you think she survived the waterfall?'

'It's theoretically possible,' said Sam. 'And it would explain a lot.'

'It wouldn't explain why she seemed to disappear off the face of the earth.'

'Hey!' protested Sam. 'It's only a theory.'

John nodded. 'Right. So she got this far. What happened then? Why did she disappear?'

'She could have easily climbed on a barge while they were doing the lock gates. This canal was a lot busier then. Yer can go anywhere in the country on a barge from here.'

'Maybe she hid herself?'

'Stowed away,' agreed Sam.

John had his boot back on. He stamped his feet to compare the dry foot with the wet one. 'If we're assuming she survived going over the waterfall,' he said, 'I think it's reasonable to assume she was injured. Then we have to assume she somehow made her way here and got on a barge.'

'That's a lot of assumptions, isn't it?'

'We have to make assumptions,' pointed out the priest. 'In the absence of facts, they're all we've got. What we must do is ring all the hospitals in all the major towns within say a fifty-mile radius along the canal network and ask if they have a record of an injured girl answering Annie's description – about eighteen years ago. We should get on to it straight away.'

'As simple as that? I'm beginning to realise why they declared her dead so quickly.'

'You think it might be too difficult?'

'Depends. If she travelled west she could have ended up anywhere. Leeds, Manchester, Liverpool – possibly down south. Birmingham or London even.'

'After going over the waterfall, I think we can safely assume she was injured,' decided John. 'She probably couldn't stand a long journey.'

'That's another assumption. They're mounting up, these assumptions.'

John ignored him. 'So, how far would a barge travel in, say, twelve hours?'

'Not sure,' said Sam. 'Thirty or forty miles?'

'And supposing she went east instead of west. Where would she end up?'

'If we assume she travelled east, her destinations are pretty much limited to Goole or Hull.'

'That's where we must start looking,' decided John. 'We'll divide our labour to cut down time.'

'I know someone in Hull Police,' said Sam. 'He'll help, he's a good bloke.'

'And I'll pray for a miracle.'

Sam couldn't help but grin. Miracle or not, the odds were shortening.

Chapter Twenty-Eight

'You've got a bloody nerve comin' here!' snapped Mrs Sykes. 'Our Ronnie's scared ter death.'

'I'm sorry, Mrs Sykes,' said Cathy. 'But I don't understand why you're blaming us.'

'I'll tell yer why I'm blamin' you!' she snapped. 'It only started when you two started askin' my Ronnie about Spode. Next thing we know, Melanie bloody Binns is dead. I never had no time for her, but I wouldn't wish that on her. Not in front of her kiddies.'

Ronnie came to the door and stood behind his wife.

'Morning, Ronnie,' said Jake. 'Bad business this.'

'It were Spode what did it,' said Ronnie. 'He were round here t' other day threatening me.'

'You could go to the police,' suggested Cathy.

'Oh, aye,' sniffed Mrs Sykes. 'An' say what, exactly? I told t' papers about what Spode did ter my Ronnie when he were a lad and what good did that do?'

'*You* told the papers?' said Cathy.

'That's what I said, in't it? Next thing we know Spode's threatenin' my Ronnie. An' now this.' She shook a copy of the *Yorkshire Evening Post* in Cathy's face. It featured the story of Melanie's grisly murder. 'If you ask me we're as well keepin' quiet.'

'You say Spode threatened you, Ronnie?' said Jake. 'What exactly did he say?'

'He knew we'd gone ter t' papers,' muttered Ronnie. 'An' he weren't so pleased. I stood up to him – I weren't scared or nowt.'

'Oh, I'll bet yer weren't,' said his wife, scornfully.

'I weren't,' said Ronnie. 'I asked him why he should be frightened of me tellin' t' truth. He said I'd need proper proof and I hadn't got none.'

'Well done, Ronnie,' said Cathy. 'It's about time someone stood up to him. What did you say then?'

'I told him I knew people other than me he'd done it to.'

'Did you mention any names?'

Ronnie went quiet. His wife turned to look at him. 'Ronnie, yer never told him you knew about him an' Melanie?'

The implication of his actions suddenly hit Ronnie. 'Oh, my God!' he said. 'It were me, weren't it? It were me what put him on to her.'

'Sod this! I'm ringin' the police.'

'No, Mrs Sykes,' said Cathy. 'Like you said, you're as well keeping quiet. Spode will have covered his tracks. He's a very clever man.'

'He's also a Member of Parliament,' added Jake. 'Without proper proof, he's untouchable.'

'We're after him, Mrs Sykes,' said Cathy, coldly. 'We need him to think he's beyond suspicion.'

'You realise that Melanie Binns' murder was as much my fault as Ronnie's, don't you?' said Cathy as they drove away. 'If we hadn't gone round to see him, his wife wouldn't have gone to the papers.'

'If you start thinking like that, everybody and his brother's to blame,' said Jake.

'I suppose so,' she conceded. 'What do we do now?'

'To be honest, I've no idea. Maybe we've been going at things like a bull at a gate.'

'I don't think we have,' said Cathy. 'And maybe that's where we're going wrong. Maybe we should be a bit more direct.'

Jake looked at her and suddenly felt worried. 'Oh, heck!' he said.

Jake nodded his head in agreement with the voice on the other end of the phone. 'Tell me about it. I was in children's homes for seven years. These reforms haven't come a minute too soon ... yes, well, that's why I'm ringing. No, not me personally, I'd bore them to tears in two minutes. What you need is someone to make everyone sit up and take notice and I know just the person ... yes, no problem. Right ... if the bloke I'm thinking of is in, he'll ring you straight back. I promise you, you won't be disappointed.'

He put the phone down and stared at it for a moment, then he looked up at Cathy. 'They're going for it,' he said.

'Good.'

'I said I'd get Father Barrett to give them a ring.'

'Do it now.'

Jake picked up the receiver and dialled John Barrett's number.

Chapter Twenty-Nine

'I think we might have tracked her down,' said Sam, excitedly. 'It's taken my pal some time but he reckons there's a mental hospital in Hull where there's a mystery woman who turned up eighteen years ago. She seems to fit Annie's description.'

'Mental hospital?' said John, switching the phone to his good ear. He already had mixed feelings about Sam's news. A mental hospital didn't sound too promising. 'Really?'

'Yeah, it really sounds promising. I've already had a chat with them. They call this woman Mary Dawson, but I gather it's just a name they gave her. She turned up the day after Annie disappeared.'

'When can we go?' enquired John, impatient to get on with it.

'It'll have to be tomorrow. I'll pick you up at your church. One o'clock.'

Mary Dawson tugged at the curtains to shut out the rain. She didn't like rain or any kind of water, especially in large quantities. They'd once taken her on a trip down to the docks to see the ships and the first sight of the sea had sent her into a fit of shivers. As she turned away she caught a glimpse of herself in the mirror. That was something else she shied away from, looking at her own image. This time she allowed her glance to linger for a while. Was she pretty? Mary sometimes wondered. Once upon a time she'd been told she was pretty but she couldn't remember who'd told her. One of the people in her head probably. She went to the door and looked up and down the corridor to see if anyone was about. Then, satisfied, she closed it and picked up a Gideon Bible, the only book in the room. She sat down on the bed and in little more than a whisper read to herself.

'"... they mourned for Aaron thirty days, even all the house of Israel.

'"And *when* king Arad the Canaanite, which dwelt in the south, heard that Israel came ..."'

She took particular care to emphasise the words written in italics, knowing they must have a special meaning. She read not to enhance her religious knowledge but to keep her brain working. Over the years she'd read the Bible several times, always in secret, always in a whisper. The hospital had large grounds and sometimes she'd walk out to a spot where she knew she wouldn't be heard and talk to herself in a normal voice. No one must know she could do this or they would put pressure on her. She could barely cope with the images inside her head, let alone anything else. Footsteps approached along the corridor. She put down the Bible and rested her hands on the bed as though she'd been sitting like that for hours. It was Nurse Hargreaves.

'Mary, you've got visitors.'

She got to her feet obediently and walked to the door.

'Two men, one's a priest. They think they might know you.'

Her words meant little to Mary.

John and Sam were more than a little curious to see the woman who had, in different ways, affected both of their lives.

All Sam had in his memory was an ephemeral image of a pretty girl on a bridge. A girl who'd had a special quality – something about her. Into the room walked a mousy-haired, hollow-faced woman in her thirties. She was slim and wearing a housecoat in pale blue to match her wide eyes.

Was it her? He didn't know. Was there something about her? He didn't know that either. She stood there with her hands hanging loosely by her sides. The two of them had been forewarned not to put any pressure on her. John smiled and held out his hand.

'I'm John,' he said. 'And this is Sam.'

Mary looked at the nurse for guidance. Jeannette smiled.

'It's okay, Mary. You can shake his hand.'

Mary held out a limp hand for the priest to shake. Sam extended his hand, then allowed it to fall away as Mary didn't seem interested.

'Sit down, Mary,' instructed the nurse.

Mary obeyed, like an automaton, sitting in a high-backed chair opposite the two men. There was an awkward silence as John worked out how to begin.

'We've come from Leeds and we think we might know who you are.'

His words frightened Mary who didn't want anyone to know who she was. She wasn't sure she wanted to know herself. Knowing who she was might be too much to cope with. John waited for some reaction. He looked at Sam, who gave a slight shrug.

'I'm sorry, gentleman,' said Jeannette. 'You should have been told. Mary doesn't talk – or communicate in any way. I'm afraid you're in for a one-sided conversation.'

'Ah,' said the priest, scratching his head and looking once more at Sam for inspiration. Another shrug. John frowned at his friend's unhelpfulness.

'Mary,' he began, 'does the name Annie Jackson mean anything to you?' His eyes were fixed on hers as he spoke and he was sure he detected a flicker of recognition.

Mary allowed the name to sink into her thoughts. She knew this name, it was a good name. A name she recognised.

'We think it may be your real name,' continued John.

Mary shook her head, confused. She turned to Jeannette for help.

'I'm not convinced that this approach is a good idea,' said the nurse. 'Especially as you're not sure of your facts.'

'You're quite right, nurse,' agreed Sam, who thought the priest had been a little blunt. 'Do you have any idea where she came from?'

'None at all. I've taken her back to where she was found dozen of times but I can't jog her memory.'

'We need to bring someone along who knew her as a girl,' suggested Sam. 'Someone who can properly identify her.'

The old priest took Mary's hand and said, 'My name's Father John Barrett. If you're who we think you are, you left me a letter to pass on to your baby daughter. You'll be pleased to know I've done that. She's a beautiful young woman now.'

Images were conjured up in Mary's mind, good and bad, clearer than ever before. He'd said baby. She could see a baby – and lots of black water, choking her, and black rocks, hurting her hands. And *him*, sneering at her. He'd come back to get her – she'd seen his face not long ago. Tears streamed down her cheeks as she looked helplessly at the nurse.

Jeannette led her from the room, leaving John and Sam feeling guilty at the grief they'd just caused. Sam secretly blaming John's lack of tact, but not saying so.

'That was Annie Jackson, all right,' said John. 'My words wouldn't have had such an effect if it wasn't her.'

The nurse returned after a while and before she could issue any words of rebuke, he said, 'We're convinced she's Annie Jackson. I'd like to come back with someone who can properly identify her.'

'Pity you didn't bring someone today,' sniffed Jeannette.

'We're not sure who we can bring as yet,' retorted the priest. 'But now I'm fairly sure it's her . . .'

'*Fairly* sure? You'd better be absolutely sure before I let you upset her anymore.'

'That's why we need to bring someone who knew her,'

explained Sam, stepping in front of John to prevent an exchange of harsh words. 'We'll ring you to let you know we're coming, hopefully tomorrow. Perhaps you can prepare Annie . . . er . . . Mary.'

'For a priest you're a bit lacking in tact and diplomacy,' said Sam, testily, as they drove back to Leeds. 'We'll be lucky to get past that nurse next time.'

'Never mind her,' said the priest. 'I want Cathy's friend Jake to take a look at this woman. He knew her before she . . . I'm seeing him and Cathy tonight. I think we should bring them both along. Get this thing settled once and for all.'

'For God's sake, don't get the girl's hopes up too high. Where are you seeing them?'

'They invited me out to dinner.'

Chapter Thirty

Jake took a sharp breath as Cathy opened the door to her bedsit. She was wearing a simple black halter-neck dress, full-length but cut to display every delightful curve of her body, including more cleavage than he had seen on her up until now.

'What?' she asked of his unspoken question.

'Nothing. I was just taken back by your – er – décolléte.'

She looked down at herself. 'Do you thing it's too much?'

'For a bloke with a weak heart, yes. But I think they'd be happy to take the risk.'

'Is that a compliment, Jake Parker?'

'It's as near as you're going to get, Miss Makepeace.'

'You scrub up quite well yourself, Mr Parker,' she said, eyeing his dinner jacket which looked to be a generous fit.

'Borrowed it from a bloke at work. He's a bit bigger than me.'

'It'll leave room for your dinner.'

'I doubt if I'll be eating much.'

'Nor me,' said Cathy. She slipped into a pair of gold high heels. 'I bought this lot today.' She grinned. 'On the never-never.' Then she picked up a string of outsize pearls and held them to her neck. 'Help me with these, Jake.'

He went around the back of her and examined the fastener. 'I assume they're not real?'

'If they're not, I've been swindled out of nearly three quid,' laughed Cathy. 'They're to draw attention to my – er – attributes.'

'Your attributes don't need any help in drawing attention to themselves.'

'There you go again, paying me compliments.' She gave a shiver of excitement at the touch of his hands on the back of her neck.

'Are you cold?' he asked, naively.

'No, just nervous. It's a big night tonight.'

Jake snapped the clasp shut then stood in front of her, one hand on each of her shoulders. 'Cathy,' he said, looking deep into her eyes, 'after tonight you can get on with your life.'

She nodded, wondering, *Will you be a part of it, though?*

'Hey! Guess what?' she said. 'I'm moving back in with Mum and Dad. He rang me today, full of apologies.'

'I'm glad.' Jake smiled.

'In fact, I've packed an overnight bag if you can drop me off there afterwards? I don't want to spend another night in this dump.'

'Cathy, have you mentioned Spode to them?' he asked, curiously.

'Not yet. That's a complication I can do without. They'll find out soon enough.'

'They'll find out tomorrow.'

'I know. That's why I'm moving back tonight.'

'Shrewd girl.'

Leonard Spode examined his reflection in the full-length mirror on his bedroom wall. The evening suit was brand new, as was the ruffled silk shirt and dark red cummerbund. He placed his chain of presidential office around his neck and pinned the MBE just below his top pocket. A knighthood wasn't far away. Wheels had been oiled and set in motion. Sir Leonard Spode, MBE, MP, had a nice ring to it.

His greying hair showed off a tanned face. All in all he exuded an air of affluence and success. He would look good on television as he made his speech. They'd probably show it all. They always did if the President was any good. Then they'd show clips of the funny man's speech at the end and odd interviews with the celebrities. But *he* would be the star. That's what this was all about, self-promotion. Nothing else mattered. Self-promotion would be converted into business success if tackled properly, and no one knew how to do that better than Leonard Spode.

He glanced through the window at his chauffeur, leaning against the brand new Bentley. His next step would be to move out of this house and into a mansion in North Yorkshire. His household staff there would be hand-picked and discreet and he would be able to indulge himself as never before. The thought of being the President of the British Children's Society made him smile. It proved one thing: anything was possible if you put your mind to it. Melanie Binns' killing had excited him, but there it must stop. Her death had served a purpose. It had been useful. To kill again, just for the sake of it, would be an indulgence too many. He was a businessman, not a serial killer. But if anyone else got in his way . . .

Father Barrett was waiting on the steps of the Queen's Hotel when Jake and Cathy arrived.

'John, this is my friend Jake,' she said. 'You spoke to him on the phone.'

'Nice to put a face to the voice, Jake.'

'And you, Father Barrett.'

'You can call me John, if you like.'

'I feel more comfortable calling you Father.'

'Once a Catholic, eh?'

'Once,' admitted Jake. 'Until disillusionment set in.' He sensed an argument forming in the priest's mind, so he changed the subject. 'It's handy, you being a priest. You don't have to wear one of these penguin suits.'

'No, it's my lot to wear a dog-collar every day of the week,' laughed John as they joined the noisy throng inside the foyer.

'The first time I met him, he was wearing a rugby shirt,' said Cathy. 'You mustn't believe everything he says, just because he's a priest.'

'*Especially* because I'm a priest,' said John. 'I took the vows of poverty, chastity and obedience. Not telling lies was never mentioned. Who's that chap over there? He seems to know you.'

'It's Jack Charlton,' said Jake, acknowledging the famous man's wave. 'I used to bump into him from time to time at work.'

'Jake used to be a professional footballer,' explained Cathy.

'Really?' Father Barrett was impressed.

Children's charities always attracted a liberal sprinkling of sports and showbusiness personalities, which was one way of ensuring press and television coverage. A Yorkshire Television cameraman followed Richard Whiteley through the crowd as he picked out celebrities to interview. At each interview, a clutch of grinning non-celebrities would gather behind the interviewee's shoulder, in view of the camera, elbowing each other out of the way to claim their moment of fame.

The buzz of conversation was polite and reserved. The ladies in their evening gowns smiled and hoped not to see a dress identical to theirs as they wondered if the jewels around them were actually real. The immaculately suited men wore a variety of chains and medals of office and rank. Jake wore his baggy dinner suit and John Barrett his dog-collar and shiny black jacket. But they weren't bothered, because they knew the third member of their trio outshone everyone.

'By the way,' said John, taking a glass of wine from a passing tray, 'I'm still not sure why I'm here.'

'You're here because you were invited,' said Cathy,

taking his arm and leading him into the banqueting suite.

'There's something I need to discuss with you,' he said. 'Something rather important.'

'Can it wait until later?' said Cathy.

'Of course it can.'

Spode cleared his throat as the red-coated toastmaster introduced him.

'My Lord Mayor, Lady Mayoress, Lords, ladies and gentlemen. The next speaker this evening is the incoming President of the British Children's Society. Pray silence for the Honourable Leonard Spode, MBE, MP.'

Spode got slowly to his feet, conscious of the television camera being pushed towards him to get a better shot. He turned to face it and smiled.

'My Lord Mayor, Lady Mayoress, honoured guests. Tonight I feel incredibly humble to be addressing an audience of such eminence . . .'

Cathy's skin began to crawl as he oozed his way through a speech of such blatant hypocrisy and lies that she felt physically sick as the audience applauded him.

'. . . it is our bounden duty to protect our children from such wickedness. I believe in this great society with every fibre of my being . . .'

She switched off his words until they became a distant echo in her mind. This was the man who had raped her mother, murdered her grandmother, Malcolm Lindis and Melanie Binns.

'. . . ladies and gentlemen,' concluded Spode, 'would you do me the honour of joining me in a toast to that most worthy charity of all . . .' there was a shuffling of chairs as five hundred people got to their feet '. . . the British Children's Society!'

There was a murmur of response from the audience as they all repeated the toast before sitting down and applauding Spode's speech. Cathy couldn't look at him. Her heart was racing with hatred and apprehension as the toastmaster banged on the table with his gavel. Someone positioned a table microphone in front of her. The Secretary of the society looked across at Father Barrett and nodded his appreciation of the priest who had warmly recommended this next speaker, then at Jake who had made the initial suggestion.

'My Lord Mayor, Lady Mayoress, Lords, ladies and gentlemen,' called out the toastmaster, 'our next speaker is a person who was raised in children's homes since she was one day old and found on the altar of a church.' John cringed a little at the white lie he had condoned. It wouldn't have been so bad if Jake had told him why. A murmur went round the audience as they looked at the back of menus to see what this person was called. 'Pray silence for Miss Catherine Makepeace.'

Cathy stood up to a polite ripple of applause and took a deep, nervous breath. The audience went completely silent and all eyes were now on this extraordinarily beautiful young lady.

'My Lord Mayor,' she began, determined to comply with the etiquette of the occasion, 'Lady Mayoress, Lords, ladies and gentlemen ... You must excuse me because I have never spoken in public before.'

'Well, don't bother with the speech, love. I'm happy enough just looking at yer.'

The audience exploded into laughter at Les Dawson's wisecrack, meant to put Cathy at her ease. The laughter subsided as all eyes focused on her once again, sitting at the top table, three places from Spode. Her face had a familiarity about it that no one could put their fingers on. Glossy, dark brown hair tumbled on to her slim shoulders. She took a deep, controlled breath, causing her breasts to push firmly against her evening gown.

'Ladies and gentlemen, in 1952 the new President of this society,' she turned to look at Spode who smiled back at her benignly, 'married a woman called Olga Jackson. My mother was her daughter, Annie Jackson.'

There was a murmur of surprise from the audience. Spode sat forward in his seat, his smile frozen now. Cathy fixed her eyes on his bemused face as she continued.

'In November of that year, just before my mother's fifteenth birthday, Leonard Spode won his first Parliamentary seat and, in the early hours of the morning after the election, he celebrated his victory in a unique fashion.'

Spode's mind was racing. He definitely remembered the night in question. The night Olga had died. But the precise details had been fogged by drink and a blow to his head. He well remembered Annie accusing him of raping her and making her pregnant, and vowing to get him back. The words: *I will get you back for what you did. Just you wait and see*, were imprinted on his memory. The more he tried to forget them, the more indelible they became. But what the hell did this girl know about that night? And who was she? If she was Olga's grand-daughter, as she claimed, then she must be . . . Oh, hell! He could *see* himself in her face. Cathy opened her handbag and took out Annie's letter.

'I can best describe what went on that night by reading out a letter left to me by my mother . . .'

She began to read, fighting back the tears. This was the moment her mother had been hoping for. This was the legacy she'd inherited from Annie. This was their moment.

'"*Dear Doris . . .*"'

She gave a half-smile and looked up at her puzzled audience.

'She – er – she wanted to call me Doris, but no one knew.'

There was a sympathetic '*Oohh*', mainly from the women as Cathy read on. Her voice trembled with controlled emotion as she spoke her mother's words. It carried through the speakers to every part of the vast room. Jake and John were at a table not far from Cathy. The old priest was leaning forward, resting his elbows as he listened intently to every word of the letter he'd guarded so carefully for eighteen years, shaking his white head in disbelief as the terrible story unfolded.

'"*. . . I am sorry to tell you that you were conceived when my step-father, Leonard Spode, raped me on the night he was elected an MP. He also killed his wife (my mother, your grandmother, Olga Jackson), when she tried to get him off me . . .*"'

There was a stunned silence in the room, eventually broken by angry mutterings and people shushing the mutterers into silence. No one wanted to miss a word Cathy had to say. All eyes moved from her to Spode as he visibly shrank in abject horror as her words of condemnation poured out.

'"*. . . If your father, Leonard Spode, is dead when you read this, I hope he is rotting in hell. If he is still alive I expect he will have risen to an important position in politics or something and I would like you to try and expose him for what he is. If you are like me you won't like people getting away with things like that even if he is your father . . .*"'

Cathy read on until the end, then looked straight into the television camera. 'I realise that this is a terrible accusation,' she said, quietly. 'But I am the living proof of this awful crime. The striking similarity between me and Leonard Spode is no coincidence.'

The people at the tables nearest to her gasped and nodded to each other as they spotted the likeness, as would millions watching later on television. Spode was welded to his seat with shock. The muscles in the sides of his neck began to twitch uncontrollably. To either side of him, the Society hierarchy were mentally distancing themselves, unspoken curses on their lips. Their eyes glazed over as in their minds they tried to formulate plans of escape from this awful débâcle in which they wanted no part. Cathy turned and directed her gaze at Spode. Her face was now glistening with tears and her voice was cracking. But she hadn't finished.

'Over here, Cathy,' called out a voice.

She turned and looked into Jake's reassuring face. He pointed at his eyes and mimed '*Look at me*'. Cathy nodded and fixed her gaze on him as she said, 'My mother then killed herself.'

The audience gasped and Spode began to hyperventilate. A St John's ambulanceman ran up to the top table to attend to him. Cathy stared at Jake, drawing strength from his smile. How she loved this man.

'Shortly after the rape ...' the audience was straining now to hear her trembling voice '... Malcolm Lindis, Spode's agent, found out what had happened to Annie and broke off his association with Spode.'

Jake was on his feet, openly encouraging her to continue. Her eyes never left his as she went on.

'The following day, the brakes mysteriously failed on Mr Lindis' car and he was killed. In 1960, Leonard Spode was robbed on a visit to London. The thief found a photograph of a fourteen-year-old girl in his wallet.'

She took the photograph from her bag. 'This is the photograph. On the back it says, "*To Leonard from Melanie, the best shag in Leeds*".' With her eyes still on Jake she handed the photograph to the shocked Secretary of the Society, sitting beside her. Jake was nodding his encouragement. Just one last thing and it was done. Cathy nodded back.

'Melanie Binns was subsequently paid by Spode to keep quiet. She could have ruined him had she spoken out. A few days ago she was battered to death in front of her children. The police don't know who did it. Ladies and gentlemen, I think we do.'

She unclipped the microphone from its stand and walked up behind Spode. The St John's ambulanceman was holding a brown paper bag to the stricken man's gasping mouth.

'Ladies and gentlemen, this man, in my opinion, is the foulest creature ever to walk the face of the earth. He is a murderer and a paedophile and yet he has been elected President of the British Children's Society.'

Cathy leaned forward, picked up a full glass of red wine from the table and poured it over Spode's head. The paper bag opened and closed even quicker as he tried to rid himself of the excess oxygen he was gasping into his lungs. With his eyes bulging, hair plastered to his face and shirt stained red, he was helped from the table by the St John's ambulanceman, who was showing little sympathy for his patient. A uniformed policeman appeared from nowhere and followed in their wake. The room was hushed, the guests too dumbfounded to speak.

Cathy returned to her seat and sat down, exhausted, as Jake knelt beside her with his arm around her. He allowed her a long moment to herself before he spoke.

'Well done, Cathy. Annie would have been so proud.'

'Pity she couldn't have been here,' said Cathy through her tears. 'God! I wish she could have been here.'

'God moves in mysterious ways, Cathy,' said John, taking her hand as she got to her feet. 'I suggest you have a stiff drink to settle your nerves.'

'A stiff drink sounds good to me, John. But not here.'

'We'll find a quiet pub,' said Jake. 'This young lady needs to unwind.' He looked at the priest. 'Didn't you say you had something important you wanted to discuss with Cathy?'

'I have – but under the circumstances . . .'

'I don't want to discuss anything tonight, John,' said Cathy. 'I just want a quiet drink then to go home – to Mum and Dad.' She looked at Jake and smiled. 'We did it, Jake, didn't we?'

'You did it, Cathy. The rest of us just tagged along for the ride.'

'It's been an interesting ride,' commented John. 'So far anyway . . . Could we meet up tomorrow somewhere? I'd like Sam to be there as well. I think he deserves to be there.'

'I'll arrange it,' said Jake, puzzled. Cathy was still too high on adrenalin to be puzzled by anything.

The crowd watched from their tables with a mixture of sympathy and awe as the trio made their way to the door. As they were leaving, the Secretary stopped them. 'The police would like a word, Cathy,' he said.

'Not right now,' said Jake. 'Give the coppers that photo to be going on with. We'll sort it all out tomorrow. She's had enough for one day.'

'I'll tell him she's already left,' said the Secretary. 'It was a bad do tonight, I hope it hasn't done too much damage.'

'It could have been a lot worse,' said Jake. 'I could have given a speech about my experience in children's homes.'

'Maybe I'll book you for next year,' said the Secretary. 'I was in children's homes myself. You can't tell me anything I don't know.'

Chapter Thirty-One

After John and Sam had left, Mary sat on her bed trying to make sense of the cloistered world she now inhabited and the images which inhabited her turbulent mind. The name Annie Jackson rang very loud bells but she didn't know whether they were good or bad. The priest was a good man, though, she could tell that – and his name rang a distant bell. Father John Barrett, DD. He hadn't said DD so where did those letters come from? The turmoil inside her head was worsening. She curled up under the blankets and refused to respond when the nurse came to call her for afternoon tea.

'I'll leave you to come round in your own good time,' said Jeannette. 'It's a shame those people had to come, upsetting you like that. I'll get rid of them if they come back.'

Although she wouldn't admit it to herself, the nurse didn't want her patient's identity revealed. Mary would go away if this happened and she'd grown fond of her over the years. Mary had been a friend and a mute confidante, perhaps the best kind. One to whom you can unburden yourself without fear of their ever offering advice.

The smell of cooking coming from the nearby kitchen brought Mary from her bed the following lunchtime. She walked through the day room on her way to the dining room and saw the *Hull Daily Mail* on a coffee table. The headlines jumped off the page at her: LEONARD SPODE ARRESTED AT CHILDREN'S SOCIETY DINNER.

She circled round the table like a stalking animal, twisting her head to read the story. *His* picture was there. He had been dramatically exposed as a child molester, with worse charges to follow. He was locked up somewhere, bail was unlikely to be granted. The person who had exposed him was his own daughter. Daughter? Bells were ringing in her head and she didn't know why. But these were good bells.

The door in her mind began to open and *he* wasn't there. He was somewhere where he couldn't harm her. People knew about him now. Him and his evil ways. There were happy people occupying her thoughts now. People whose names and faces she couldn't quite make out. Then the happiness clouded over as quickly as it had come and confusion reigned. These people have been shut out for too long, much too long. Maybe they were dead as well. She sat down and began to cry bitter tears as she ripped the newspaper into tiny shreds. An orderly summoned Nurse Hargreaves, who took Mary back to her room, comforting her on the way.

'It's all right, Mary love. If they upset you again, I'll give 'em the bum's rush. You get into bed and I'll bring your meal to your room. How's that? Room service. Not bad, eh?'

But Mary knew they'd be coming. In a reluctant corner of her mind she'd been waiting for this and now she was afraid. Her world was about to be invaded and she didn't know what to do. Was she safe, now that *he* was gone? She didn't feel safe. Why was that? How could she stop these people? Suddenly she made up her mind and marched out of her room to find her friend, her only friend.

Jeannette was having a quiet smoke in the garden when she became aware of a presence behind her. She smiled to herself.

'Hello, Mary.'

Mary wasn't aware of the aura she exuded. The aura that alerted people to her proximity. She simply thought these people were cleverer than her.

'I don't want to see them.' These were the first words she'd spoken to another human being for over eighteen years. Jeannette had never heard Mary's voice so she didn't know it was her who had spoken. She turned round to find only Mary standing there, coatless and shivering in the winter chill.

'Who said that?'

Jeannette turned a complete circle to ascertain that she'd missed nothing or no one. 'Did you hear that?' she asked.

Mary shrugged and repeated, 'I don't want to see them.'

'It was you! You can talk. How long . . .?'

'I don't want to see those people again,' said Mary for a third and final time.

'No, of course not,' Jeannette assured her. 'Mary, you can talk! This is wonderful.'

'You mustn't let them take me away from here. I'm very frightened.'

Tears were welling in her eyes and Jeannette's heart went out to her. She threw away her half-smoked cigarette on the grass and held Mary in her arms.

'No one will harm you, my darling. I promise you that.'

'You must promise you won't let them take me away,' pleaded Mary.

'I promise.'

Mary walked back to the shelter of her room.

Leeds Town Hall clock was striking two when Jake walked through the doors of the Jubilee. John was at the bar, halfway through a pint of beer and in earnest discussion with a young man about the chances of Leeds United winning the FA Cup. The old priest wore a flat cap and an old Crombie overcoat, beneath which poked out the collar of a rugby shirt. Jake grinned.

'Afternoon, Father,' he called out across the pub. John

turned and smiled, then finished off the pint and wiped his mouth with his sleeve

'Hello, Jake. Just in time to buy me a drink.'

Jake joined them. The priest's young companion looked at him. 'You his lad, then?'

'Me? No.'

'Oh, I thought I heard yer call him dad.'

'No, I called him Father – he's a priest.' Jake grinned. 'You wouldn't think it, would you?'

'No, yer bloody wouldn't,' agreed the young man, moving rapidly away from them.

'What did you do that for?' protested John. 'We were getting along fine. He thinks Leeds have got no chance of winning the cup.'

'I hope he's wrong. I've got a tenner on them at six to one.' Jake caught the barman's eye. 'Two pints of bitter, please.'

'I got seven to one,' gloated the priest as he looked down the long Victorian bar. 'Handy this, the bus dropped me off right outside.'

'That's why I chose it. Handy for everyone. Cathy's still down at the cop shop. I had to give a statement myself.'

'Oh?'

'Well, I was one of the people Annie confided in about what had happened to her.'

'I know, it was in the letter. You and a few others.'

'The police are trying to track them down. There's a bloke in London they're wanting to talk to as well. They're opposing bail – it looks as if they're definitely going to nail the bastard. Oops! Sorry, John. I keep forgetting.' Jake took a drink from the barman and handed it to the priest. 'I'm worried about how Cathy's bearing up,' he said.

'She's a very strong-minded young lady,' said John. He looked keenly at Jake. 'You love her very much, don't you?'

Jake looked away. 'Father, don't be silly. I'm much too old for her.'

‘Not from my end of the age spectrum, you’re not.’

Hurriedly changing the subject, Jake asked, ‘Anyway, what’s this meeting all about?’

‘It’s better discussed when we’re all here. Ah, here she is now . . .’

He waved to Cathy as she hurried through the door, closely followed by Sam. They arrived at the bar together, each wondering who the other was.

‘You two don’t know each other,’ said John. ‘Cathy, this is Sam. He’s the person who tried to save your mother from drowning.’

Cathy’s eyes shone as she took his hand. ‘Sam – how lovely to meet you.’ She kissed him on the cheek. Sam gulped. He wasn’t ready for someone as beautiful as Cathy.

‘I think he’s a bit overwhelmed,’ commented John wryly.

‘Pleased to meet you, Cathy,’ said Sam at last. ‘Blimey, John, you never warned me about this. I’d have had a bath if I’d known!’

‘You look fine to me,’ laughed Cathy.

‘If only I was ten years younger,’ lamented Sam.

Cathy laughed. ‘Pity you’re not then.’

Jake took this as a pointer to how she felt about older men. Sam was about the same age as he was, give or take a couple of years. Jake held out a hand to him.

‘Jake Parker. I was one of Annie’s friends.’

The introductions over, Jake pointed to a table in the corner. ‘Grab that table and I’ll get you two a drink. What’ll it be?’

From somewhere beyond the stained-glass pub window a Salvation Army band struck up with ‘Oh, Come All Ye Faithful’. John peered through the coloured glass and looked across the Headrow to where the band stood playing in the square outside the art gallery, their enthusiasm barely dampened by the grim weather.

‘I wouldn’t have minded joining the Sally Army,’ he said wistfully. Turning to Sam, he added, ‘I can play the trumpet, you know.’

'No, I didn't know.'

'Oh, yes, I played in a band once.'

The priest sang along in Latin for a while until he forgot the words. Memories of his youth crept into his thoughts. He could have told Sam about the girl with whom he'd fallen in love and she with him. Until the piano player moved in.

'I like brass bands because they don't have pianos. Can't stand pianists.'

His memories were of a jilted, unworldly young man who took to the cloth to hide his broken heart. Initially a rash move, but having sampled some of the delights and most of the disappointments of the secular world, he'd decided on balance that he had a true vocation.

'You know, there are so many drawbacks to being a Catholic priest, I do hope He makes it worth my while eventually.' John glanced upwards and smiled at his own cheek.

'Maybe He'll let you join a band,' quipped Sam.

'Oh, I want to join a big band when I get up there. I want to play the trumpet with the Joe Loss orchestra.'

'They'll have to call it the Dead Loss orchestra,' laughed Sam.

Cathy's face broke into a broad smile at the banter between the two of them. Jake arrived with the rest of the drinks, pleased that John was cheering her up.

'I hope you're not telling smutty jokes, Father.'

'Heaven forbid! What would I know about such things?' John's face became serious then as his eyes met Sam's. 'Look, I might as well get straight to the point.'

All eyes were on him as he began.

'I – or rather – we – have a story to tell you,' said the priest. 'A story which began a short time ago when I first met my good friend Sam here.' John took a sip of his drink as he collected his thoughts. 'You see, Sam is a policeman . . .' Jake and Cathy looked at Sam with interest. 'And as such,' continued John, 'he has a very suspicious mind. You see, he could never understand why Annie's body was never found. He knows that part of the river as well as anyone and figured her body would be found well before it was washed out to sea. So we got to thinking, didn't we, Sam?'

Sam nodded and took up the story. 'We got to dreaming up various scenarios whereby Annie might not have drowned – and we came up with one whereby she survived the drop over the waterfall and managed to climb up the riverbank. It's highly unlikely, of course, but there again it was highly unlikely that her body should just disappear.'

'Where's this leading to, John?' asked Cathy. The previous night had drained her of patience. 'You said you'd get straight to the point.'

Sam looked at John and sighed. He'd wanted to break the news gently but it was no use. The priest took her hand.

'Cathy,' he said gently, 'we think we may have found Annie Jackson. We think your mother is still alive!'

Cathy sank her head into her hands. After last night's events, all this was too much to take in. There was a long silence, broken only by the sound of the band outside. Jake became annoyed.

'You say you *think* she's alive. *Think*'s a very inadequate word to use under these circumstances. You can't just make a statement like that without being absolutely sure of your ground.'

'I'm sorry, Jake,' said John. 'Personally I don't think there's much doubt that it's her, or I wouldn't have brought Cathy here.'

'We should have got Jake to go and see her with us before we told Cathy,' murmured Sam. 'I knew this was a bad idea.'

'Where exactly is she?' frowned Jake.

'She's in a hospital in Hull,' John told him.

'Hull?' said Cathy. 'John, are you absolutely sure it's my mother?' Her voice was cracking with emotion. 'I mean, it can't be.' She turned to Jake. 'Can it?'

Jake looked accusingly at John, who hesitated, wondering now at the wisdom of telling Cathy before he'd confirmed Annie's identity. 'I'm ninety per cent sure – call it ninety-nine per cent. We've been tracking her down for a while now.' He looked to Sam for help.

'We thought of one scenario whereby she could have got out of the river and travelled as far as Hull. We thought she might have gone there on a barge,' Sam explained.

'A barge?' said Jake. 'How did you work that one out?'

'Because of the canal. It's not far from the river. It would have been her only likely means of transport.'

'And so you figured she went to Hull?'

Sam shrugged and took a swig of beer. 'Well, we hoped she'd gone in that direction. Had she gone west, we'd never have found her. Too many possible destinations, you see. Anyway, through my police connections we found out about a mystery woman who'd turned up in Hull the day after Annie disappeared. She's the right age and seems to fit Annie's general description.'

'And what does this woman have to say for herself?' asked Jake. 'Surely she knows who she is?'

'That's just it,' said John, 'she doesn't. She's lost her memory and is unable to communicate in any way.'

His story was becoming more believable by the second. Cathy was unable to take in the enormity of what she was hearing. Jake took her hand and squeezed it. She looked at John, her lips trembling as she asked, softly, 'Have you actually seen her?'

'Yes, Cathy, we saw her yesterday,' replied the priest. 'There was something about the way she responded to my questions about Annie Jackson. They seemed to provoke an emotional reaction.'

Jake still looked sceptical. He glanced at Cathy. 'Do you want me to go on my own? It sounds as though it could be a wild goose chase and after all you've been through . . .'

'I'm coming,' she said flatly, and smiled at Father Barrett. 'I've got a lot of faith in this man. He's never let me down yet and I don't think he's going to start now. John,' she asked him, 'do you honestly think it's my mother?'

'Yes, Cathy. I honestly think it's her.'

'Can we go today then?' She turned to Jake. 'You can take us, can't you?'

Worried, Jake took her hand. 'I'm not sure the car's up to a trip to Hull, but . . .'

'We'll go in my car,' volunteered Sam.

'I'll make the arrangements,' said John. 'Is there a phone in here?'

He was rebuffed by Nurse Hargreaves when he rang to tell her they were coming.

'Mary spoke to me today,' announced the nurse.

'Spoke to you?' said John. 'Why, that's wonderful. It must have been triggered by our visit. What did she say?'

'She said she didn't want to see you.'

'She's obviously confused.'

'Maybe – but until she becomes more stable I intend to respect her wishes.'

'But you can't! We're bringing her daught—'

The line went dead and the priest cursed mildly under his breath.

'You should have let me speak to her,' said Sam when John told them what had happened. 'Your old-world charm seems to go into reverse at times.'

John grimaced. 'The good news is that she's started talking. Obviously our turning up triggered something off in her.'

Cathy's eyes blazed angrily. 'If this is my mother, that woman's got no right to refuse me!' Turning to Jake, she said, 'Well? What are we waiting for?'

'What? You want to go now?'

'Wouldn't you, if it was your mother?'

Jake wouldn't have crossed the street to see his own mother but didn't say so. He looked pointedly at Sam and

John. '*We'll* go in this time,' he said. 'You two had better wait outside.'

John felt a bit put out at this. After all, had it not been for them . . .

'You're right,' said Sam. 'We might make things worse.'

'You mean, *I* might make things worse,' grumbled the priest.

Cathy hugged him. 'John Barrett, stop feeling sorry for yourself. You've made such a difference to my life.'

Chapter Thirty-Two

Mary's whole world seemed to be changing. The images in her mind had gone from horror to confusion. *He* was no longer a threat, but had been replaced by something equally disturbing: a sense of not knowing what was going to happen now. The threat *he* represented had been the only real thing in her life for so long. It was something she'd learned to handle, to control – and at times to beat. At these times, when, through sheer strength of mind she'd made him go away, she'd felt a sense of triumph. But now he was gone for good.

So what now?

Nurse Jeannette knew her secret so it wouldn't be long before everyone knew. It had been a big secret, a secret worth having. To know something that they didn't. They who thought they were so clever. But now they would know.

She would run away to somewhere where people didn't know her secret. Where she could live a life of peace and not be troubled by people who said they knew her. No one really knew her. She didn't know herself.

A cold shiver ran through her body as Nurse Jeannette said those dreaded words, 'There's someone here to see you, Mary. If you don't want to see them, I can send them away.'

Mary nodded her eager assent to this suggestion.

'It's not the same people,' explained Jeannette. 'It's a young woman and a man about your age. He says he knew you when you were younger.'

'Please tell them to go away.'

Jeannette hesitated for a second, then walked out of Mary's room.

Cathy held on to Jake's arm as they waited in the day room. Other patients wandered in and out, some staring blankly ahead, others subjecting them to intense scrutiny. Cathy was dreading what state she'd find her mother in.

'Do you think she'll be like these people?'

Jake shook his head firmly. He couldn't believe that the Annie he'd known would allow herself to degenerate into this state.

The nurse returned. 'She doesn't want to see you.'

'Really?' Cathy exclaimed.

'Really,' said Nurse Jeannette, implacably.

'Would the fact that I'm her daughter alter the situation?' asked Cathy, sharply. 'Don't you think she might want to see her only daughter – and don't you think I have a right to see my mother?'

Jeannette opened her mouth to speak but Cathy continued; 'If you don't let me see her, we'll simply go to whoever's running this establishment and kick up a stink until we get what we want.'

Jeannette sighed heavily. The rights of patients in this hospital were minimal but the Nursing Supervisor wouldn't thank her for allowing a scene to start.

'I'll get her.'

'Thank you, nurse,' said Jake, who saw no reason to provoke her hostility.

Mary was already out of the window, running across the expansive lawn. The day was chilly but bright and she was wearing a coat, but her flimsy shoes were no match for the long damp grass. By the time she reached the wall her feet were soaking. She hated having wet feet. Hated having wet anything. The wall was old and weathered and provided ample footholds. She clambered to the top and realised the drop at the far side was further than she'd thought. A memory returned. A memory of standing on a stone wall with rushing water below. Someone not far away shouted to her, 'Nice day for it.'

She'd heard that voice and those words before. How long ago she couldn't tell. It was yesterday and it was a lifetime ago. Why was that? The events of the past few days had taken her to the brink of recollection and those four words had been the final trigger. Suddenly her fragmented memory of that long-ago day began to slot together like a jigsaw. She vividly remembered the church and her baby and why she'd gone there. Then the horror of falling over the waterfall and being hammered against the rocks. She was reaching out in front of herself to protect her face, and her hands became wedged so tight that she couldn't free herself. The water was thundering past her head, breathing was difficult and she was sure she was going to drown. Then the pain went from her hands and she tore them free and pulled herself out of the torrent, leaping from rock to rock until she lay on the bank, heaving water out of her choked lungs. She lay there until some of her strength returned, then in the distance she heard voices and a wailing siren and knew she must get away from here or they'd be along to get her.

Jumping into the river hadn't worked, she was still alive, so she must get far away so they couldn't find her. The sharp branches scratched at her as she crawled along the path. Her breath came in great sobbing gasps. And there was a boat. Divine providence again. A boat to take her away. She hid between the wood piles and stayed there until dark. Then she climbed off and walked until she could walk no further and arrived at a place called Dawson Street.

And now she was here, standing on a wall. What the hell was happening to her? Shards of memory littered her mind.

Spode was no longer an image of horror, he was a real person. An evil man who'd done her and her mother untold harm. But he couldn't harm her now, somehow she knew that much. Events from her childhood rushed through her brain like an express train hurtling through a station when you wanted it to stop so you get on board and slow things down but the memories wouldn't stop, there were just too many of them.

Mary swayed on the wall, to Sam and John's consternation. They'd parked in a lay-by, having dropped Jake and Cathy off. Mary's sudden appearance on top of the wall had taken them by surprise. Sam had wound down the window and called out the first greeting that came into his head. He got out of the car and rushed towards her.

Now she knew she was Annie Jackson. She would never be Mary Dawson again. A man was running towards her. Should she go back? Run away from him?

'Annie!' he shouted.

Whoever he was he knew her – and he looked okay. He seemed concerned. He didn't want her to hurt herself. Behind him was a priest. She didn't remember who they were, but it was only a matter of time. The train rushing through her head was scattering random memories like confetti.

'I'm Annie Jackson,' she breathed.

Sam stood below her as the priest came panting up beside him.

'Watch yerself, love,' warned Sam. 'Yer could do yerself a nasty injury jumping from that height.'

'I'm Annie Jackson.' She spoke louder this time, announcing herself to the world.

'Yes, love, I reckon you are. Look, love, lower yourself down. You can stand on my shoulders.'

She did as she was told. Old habits die hard. Sam reached up and took her hands to steady her and for a brief, isolated flash of memory she was four years old again, standing on her daddy's shoulders. She giggled and sat down. Her dress enveloped Sam's head.

'Hey up!' he shouted. 'Who turned the lights out?'

John stepped forward and lifted her dress back over Sam's head, restoring his vision and her modesty. Annie hadn't laughed for over eighteen years and she seemed to be making up for it now. Sam strode down the road towards the hospital entrance with John by his side and a happy passenger on his shoulders. Annie pulled gently on his hair. He stopped and twisted his head round.

'I don't really remember either of you,' she said. 'Should I know who you are?'

'Not by name, love,' said Sam. 'John never actually met you and I only saw you from a distance – and that was a while ago. There's someone here who does know you, though.'

'I don't know what you mean?'

'Someone called Jake Parker.'

The name sparked a reaction in her. 'Jake ...' She mulled the name over for a few seconds. 'Is he okay?'

'He's fine,' said the priest. 'He wants to see you.'

'And I want to see him. They blamed him, you know.'

'Did they?' said John, who didn't know what she was talking about.

'They thought he was the father.' She was intriguing herself as much as them with all these revelations. 'It wasn't, though, it was Spode.'

'We know all about Leonard Spode,' said Sam heavily.

'They've got him, haven't they?'

'Yes, Annie,' confirmed John. 'They've got him. He'll never hurt you any more.'

'I think you'd better let me down,' she said. 'I'm not a child anymore. I'm practically a grown woman.'

Sam turned and caught John's eye, hoping the priest wouldn't say anything tactless. John beamed up at Annie. 'How old are you now, Annie? Or is it a rude question to ask a young lady her age?'

'Well, it *is* a rude question, but seeing as it's you – I'm fifteen.'

With John's help, Sam eased Annie to the ground. She stood between them, poised between two worlds. One a vague, but returning memory, the other confused and yet familiar.

'I don't know what's happened to me,' she said, and looked at John. 'Do you know what's happened to me?'

'Yes, Annie. But it's a long, long story.'

She nodded. It was good that someone knew what had happened to her. She sensed she'd been waiting for that someone for a long time.

Cathy, Jake and Jeannette appeared at the gate. Cathy didn't need telling who the woman was. Her eyes misted over as John held up his hands to stop any questions. 'This is Annie Jackson,' he said. 'And her memory's coming back.' He turned to Annie. 'How old did you say you were, Annie?'

'Fifteen.'

John nodded at the trio to indicate the point he was making, telling them to be careful not to confuse her.

Cathy was having difficulty controlling herself. She wanted to rush forward and take her mother in her arms. Her shoulders were shaking. Jake put his arm around her.

'One step at a time, love,' he whispered. 'We've found her.'

Jeannette stepped forward. 'Mary, do you know who I am?'

'What sort of a question's that?' asked Annie. 'Of course I know you. You've been looking after me. But my name's Annie – you didn't know that, did you?'

'Do you know how long you've been here?' enquired the nurse.

Annie frowned, then shook her head. 'I can't remember.' She stared at Jake. 'Who are you? I know you. You look a bit like someone.'

'Jake?' he suggested.

She hesitated. 'Yes, Jake. Jake Parker. He was my friend.'

Jake looked at the priest, not knowing what to do, then back at Annie.

'Annie,' he said, 'I *am* Jake.'

'Don't be silly. You're too old to be Jake.'

'You haven't seen me for a long time, Annie.'

She became confused, began to shake. 'I don't understand. I'm frightened . . .'

Jake held her in his arms. 'There's nothing to worry about, Annie. You're safe now. Everything's all right. You're with friends.'

She buried her head in his shoulder. 'I had a baby,' she said, her voice high with fright. 'I called her Doris.'

'I know, Annie. You left her with Father Barrett.'

John placed a hand on her hair and ruffled it gently. 'Annie,' he said, 'I'm Father Barrett.'

She looked up from the security of Jake's shoulder. Cathy could scarcely breathe.

'Father John Barrett, DD?'

He nodded.

'Did you find my baby?'

'I did.'

There was a long silence as everyone anticipated the next question. Jeannette thought Annie needed time to assimilate everything, but Cathy had her own ideas.

'Annie,' she said, moving slowly towards her mother, 'your daughter's all grown up now.' Jake let Annie go and stood back, allowing the two of them to come together. Cathy took Annie's hand. 'You've been ill . . . for quite a lot longer than you think.'

Annie's eyes darted all over Cathy's face. 'I know your face, it's . . .'

'It's like my father's face. My father Leonard Spode.' Cathy touched Annie's face and kissed her forehead. 'Annie,' she said, 'you're my mother.'

Realisation hit Annie, sending her into a faint. Cathy couldn't hold on to her and Annie dropped to the ground. Jeannette was beside her charge in a flash.

'Stand away from her!' she ordered. 'You shouldn't have done this. It's too much for her. Give her some air.'

The five of them stood around the prostrate Annie, each of them with a different reason to love her though one of them was only just realising it. Annie's faint lasted a couple of seconds only. She used the rest of the time to sort out her thoughts. They'd all be there when she opened her eyes again. How long had she been in this place? It had only seemed like a few . . . a few what? She didn't know what. Weeks, months, years? She had no concept of time any more. If these people were telling the truth it must have been years. And this must be Doris. God, she was beautiful. What should Annie say to her? Her eyes flickered open and she gave a smile that told Sam all he needed to know. It was the smile he'd seen on the bridge all those years ago. Annie looked up at Cathy.

'I called you Doris,' she said. 'After Doris Day.'

'No one knew,' explained Cathy. 'I didn't know until I opened your letter. Father Barrett called me Catherine, after the church you left me in.'

'You got my letter? You weren't supposed to open it until you were eighteen.'

'That's right,' said Cathy, softly. 'And I didn't.'

'Oh,' said Annie. She didn't understand but she did have faith in these people. What they said was probably true, even if it didn't make sense to her.

'Everything's taken care of,' Cathy reassured her. 'Just like you asked. Spode can't hurt you any more.'

'Thank you . . . Catherine,' said Annie. 'Catherine. I thought they might call you that.' She reached up and ran her hand through Cathy's hair. 'Hello, Catherine,' she said.

'Hello, Mum.'

Chapter Thirty-Three

May 1972

Annie had elected to stay in the hospital with Nurse Hargreaves until she had become acclimatised to her new self. Mentally she was still fifteen, with all the newness of adult life still to be discovered. The warm, spring sunshine and discovery of her true self had brought a bloom to a face still largely unwritten on by life. The loss of eighteen years was difficult to take in. Eighteen of her best years.

'You'll just have to make the next eighteen years count double,' advised Jeannette, now reconciled to the imminent departure of her friend and patient. Jimmy Johnstone's bequest had legally reverted to Annie, and a small flat had been found for her in Leeds.

Sam and Cathy had visited every week and would shortly be taking her back to Leeds. Father Barrett had been a couple of times when he could cadge a lift. Jake had been on his own several times and on his last visit had told her of a job he'd been offered in the Middle East. They were walking through the hospital grounds, her arm linked through his, comfortable with each other.

'The money's great,' he said. 'And I fancy seeing a bit of the world before I get too old. Anyway, there's nothing keeping me here.' It sounded as though he was trying to convince himself.

'There's either nothing keeping you here,' said Annie,

innocently, 'or something you're running away from.'

'Such as? I've got no ties – and you've obviously got a thing about Sam, so I've got no chance with you.'

Annie blushed. She liked Sam. Just how much she liked him she'd yet to figure out. Jeannette had become her self-appointed moral guardian in such matters.

'It's like choosing a new coat,' she'd advised. 'You need to shop around before you find one that suits you. You don't buy the first coat you try on. What about Jake? Now *there's* what I call a man.'

But to Annie, for all his physical attributes, Jake was just Jake. A friend. She didn't sense any chemistry between them.

'Do you fancy me, Jake Parker?' she teased.

'Well,' he admitted, 'you're the first girl I ever kissed.'

'And look at the trouble *that* got you into!'

'I know.' He grinned ruefully and went quiet for a while. 'There is someone but . . .'

'But you think you're too old?' guessed Annie.

They walked a few paces in silence before he answered. 'You know, don't you?'

Annie laughed. 'Jake, of course I know. I saw it the first time I met you both.' She squeezed his arm with hers.

'Jeannette seems to think I can sense things about people. For instance, I'm pretty sure Sam thinks he's in love with me.'

'And how do you feel about him?'

'I think he's lovely. But I'm not ready for that sort of involvement yet. I've enough to cope with.' Her eyes glistened as she spoke. 'Do you know he never married because of the memory he had of me? And he only saw me for a couple of minutes.'

'A couple of minutes of you is usually enough.'

'I'll take that as a compliment.'

They walked in silence. He looked at her pale hand, tucked under his arm.

'How are the hands?' he enquired.

She withdrew the one he'd been looking at and examined them. Lumpy scar tissue disfigured both wrists. 'I can just about manage a knife and fork,' she said. 'I should have exercised them as soon as the damage healed up, but apparently I wasn't interested then. According to the physio it's going to be a long, hard road.'

'You'll get there.'

'I know.' She said it without conceit, just a statement of fact. 'Since my reincarnation I've become the beneficiary of Jimmy Johnstone's will. I offered to split it with Cathy but she wouldn't hear of it, so I intend having a bit of a fling.'

'I'm not sure the public are quite ready for the world's oldest teenager,' laughed Jake.

She sat down on a wooden bench and looked back at the hospital.

'You know, this has been my home for most of my life,' she said. 'And yet there's so little of it I can remember. I know my way around it, but more by instinct than from memory. Can you imagine that?'

Jake sat down beside her. 'There's a lot about your life I find hard to imagine, Annie. For instance, I find it hard to imagine how you've managed to survive – and yet, knowing you, it hasn't surprised me.' A thought struck him. 'Did Cathy tell you about Brenda Bacup?'

'She brought her to see me,' said Annie. 'I got the shock of my life when Brenda walked in the room. It's the most unbelievable thing. We hated each other when we were kids.'

'Yet by the sound of it, you were the only person she ever had any respect for – until Cathy came along.'

'She had a funny way of showing it!'

Annie went on to relate all the stories of her clashes with Brenda. Jake laughed out loud when she came to the one where she'd locked her old adversary in the toilets on scholarship day.

'But for all her bullying, you always knew where you

stood with Brenda. She was the genuine article. There was nothing sneaky about her – and she certainly came through for me in the end.'

'Pity there was no one about like her when you really needed them.' Jake wasn't excluding himself from this and Annie sensed it. She placed her ruined hand on his.

'You'd have been there for me if they'd let you. I always knew that.'

Jake shrugged. He'd always thought he could have done more.

'People are being so good to me now,' said Annie. 'Especially Jeannette, and do you remember me telling you about Movita? Well she's been a couple of times. Apparently the people in the maternity home didn't give me her letters. I can't believe people can be so cruel.'

'I can.'

She squeezed his arm. 'Gloria's been trying to fill in the gaps in my knowledge of recent history, including her own. She's Mrs Elliot now.'

'A lot's happened,' agreed Jake. 'England won the World Cup in '66, did she mention that?'

'No, that must have slipped her mind. Is that cricket or something?'

'Football.' He couldn't tell if she was teasing. 'You must have heard of football, coming from Leeds. They won the FA Cup last week. I won sixty quid on them.'

'I know,' laughed Annie. 'Father Barrett told me. He won seventy.'

'He likes a gamble does Father Barrett,' agreed Jake. 'He gambled on you, in a way.'

'He did. He believed I was still alive when no one else did.'

'Except Sam,' corrected Jake.

'Ah, Sam.' She spoke the words with obvious affection.

Jake looked at her. 'You like him a lot more than you care to admit.'

Annie chose to change the subject then. 'I seem to have

missed out on so much,' she said lightly. 'The Beatles, Elvis Presley, mods, rockers, hippies, drugs, all that stuff. Jeannette gave me a Rolling Stones record. They're okay but I prefer Guy Mitchell.'

'They're an acquired taste – you'll acquire it,' Jake prophesied, confidently.

Annie's mind was jumping with all her recently acquired information. 'And men have been walking on the moon, and all this trouble in Ireland, and the war in Vietnam . . .' She looked at him. 'Where's Vietnam?'

'Somewhere near China.'

'Did you have to go?'

'No, it's an American thing.'

Annie gave a deep frown. 'There's so much I don't know. Gloria's persuaded me to get some O levels. She's enrolled me at Park Lane College, I start in September.'

'Just like you encouraged me, eh? It's only because of you that I became a teacher.'

'You could teach me,' she suggested.

'Somehow, Annie, I don't think I could teach you anything.'

Annie's fluttering mind sent her in a different direction. 'My writing's improved – I wrote to Liz and Jim.'

'About Cathy?'

'Yeah. I told them I wasn't ready to meet them just yet. They sent me a really nice letter back. I think she wrote it. What's she like?'

'She's nice – he can be a bit strait-laced, but they both think the world of Cathy.'

'She was better off with them than with me.'

Jake didn't agree but he didn't argue. Annie needed to justify to herself her actions of eighteen years ago.

'I'm going on holiday with her.'

'With who?'

'Gloria. We're going to Majorca. Have you ever been?'

'I was a pro-footballer, remember. Majorca was practically compulsory during the summer.

'I'm glad you went back to studying,' she said. 'I always knew you had a good brain.'

Jake put a friendly arm around her shoulders and kissed her cheek. 'Annie Jackson, there's something really bloody special about you. Did I ever tell you that?'

She smiled and shrugged off the compliment. 'What about Cathy?' she enquired. 'Do you think there's something really bloody special about her?'

'Yes, as a matter of fact, I do.'

'But you think you're too old for her?'

'It's not just that.'

'Oh, what else is there?'

Jake considered her question for a while. 'Probably you,' he said at length. 'You're her mother. You and I were friends. For God's sake, Annie, I was even accused of being her father! It puts a . . . I don't know . . . a seedy perspective on things. Does that make sense?'

Annie laughed. 'Oh, Jake. You're such a decent person. Can't you see how unhappy Cathy will be if you go away?'

'Really?'

'Jake, she's besotted with you and she knows you've got feelings for her. She can't understand why you haven't done anything about it.'

'She's told you that?'

Annie let out an exasperated sigh. 'Not in so many words, but I don't need her to spell it out for me. For heaven's sake, Jake, it's *me* who's supposed to have the mind of a fifteen year old, not you.'

'And you wouldn't mind if she and I . . .'

'I'd be delighted. You're my two favourite people in all the world.'

'So, you think I should tell her?'

'Unless you want me to?'

He was giving her offer some serious thought when she interrupted him.

'I was joking,' she said, gently. 'Cathy and Sam are picking me up to take me to Leeds tomorrow. When she gets here I want to see a big silly smile on her face, and I want *you* to have put it there.'

'Right, I'll tell her tonight then,' he said. 'She can only turn me down.'

'I wouldn't bet on it.'

Liz answered his knock.

'Is Cathy in?' enquired Jake.

'Yes, she is. But she's not in the best of moods.'

'Oh?'

'I gather you're leaving us?'

'Yes, I've been offered a job in Abu Dhabi.'

'Sounds a long way away.'

'United Arab Emirates – Persian Gulf.'

Jim appeared behind his wife and shook Jake's hand.

'Cathy's been in a state ever since she heard you were leaving,' he confirmed.

'So it's my fault?'

Jim hesitated, awkwardly. 'She's got a bit of a crush on you.'

'It's a bit more than a crush!' said Liz.

'Could I talk to her in private?'

'You can have the house to yourself if you like. We're going out for the evening.' Liz gave her husband a commanding look. 'Aren't we, Jim?'

Within seconds they had their coats on and were calling, 'See you later' to Cathy who was in the living room pretending to read a book. She'd heard Jake's voice and was putting on a brave display of indifference. He entered the room apprehensively. He'd never been so stuck for words in his life.

'I've ... er ... I was ... er ... I was talking to Brenda Bacup the other day ...'

'Were you?' said Cathy, politely. 'She came round here last week. She was concerned about Melanie Binns' children. They're going into care, apparently.'

'That's what she rang me about. She's apparently made it

abundantly clear to the people at the care home that she'll be monitoring the children's progress.'

'Can she do that?'

'Would you like to be the one to stop her?' Jake grinned. 'She reckons she's going to keep an eye on them until they're old enough to look after themselves. Apparently she's signed up as a volunteer worker for the British Children's Society. Maybe that'll give her some clout.'

'Brenda doesn't need any more clout,' observed Cathy.

'True – I wouldn't have minded having someone like her to turn to when I was a kid.'

There was an awkward silence, broken by Cathy. 'I've just heard your news,' she said.

'About me going to Abu Dhabi?'

'Is that where you're going? It sounds very exciting. I'm so happy for you. You deserve the best.'

He cleared his throat. 'I wouldn't exactly call it the best. It's good money and all that . . .'

'I'll miss you.'

She was looking up at him now and his heart was lurching with dread at the thought of her turning him down. He was going away and she was happy for him. Happy for him to go away. What was he to make of that?'

'I'll miss you, Cathy. I'll, er, miss you quite a lot as a matter of fact.'

'Then why are you going?' Her question sounded rhetorical. The expression on her face silently adding, *As if I didn't know.*

'It's just something I've always wanted to do. Itchy feet and all that.'

'Itchy feet?'

'Yes.'

'Liar!'

'What?'

'You're going because you think you're too old for me.'

He didn't answer. The situation still wasn't as clear to him as it would have been to most people. Cathy was on her feet now, standing only inches away from him. Flirting with him, her arms on his shoulders, her nearness causing him to swallow, hard.

'What are you doing?'

'I'm about to kiss you, Mr Parker. It's something I should have done a long time ago.

She pressed her lips to his and stepped into his embrace. The kiss might have lasted ten seconds or ten minutes. Neither would be able to remember. It was a kiss that told Jake he'd finally arrived where he wanted to be. There was a warmth about her, an affection he'd never felt from anyone. Cathy kissed him with a fierce love she'd never know or need to know again. He was hers and she had the means to keep him. Jake had no say in the matter. They pulled apart to draw breath.

'By the way,' she enquired, 'why did you come to see me? Was it to say goodbye?'

'Actually, no.' That kiss had given him all the courage he needed. 'As a matter of fact, I popped in to tell you that I love you.'

'Really?'

'Well . . . yes.'

'And then you were going to Abu Dhabi?'

'Well . . . no. I mean, it sort of depended on what you said. I wasn't sure how you felt about . . . you know.'

'So – you want to know how I feel about you?' She was teasing but he was still nervous. Things looked promising but the situation wasn't fully resolved.

'Tell you what, I'll give you a clue,' she said, leading him by the arm into the hall. 'Apparently Mum and Dad have gone out for the evening. Which was considerate of them, don't you think?'

'They seem like very considerate people.'

'They might not have been so considerate if they knew what I'd got in mind.'

Jake followed her up the stairs, needing no further seduction. Cathy stood with her back to the bed, cheeks slightly flushed as she flicked undone the buttons of her blouse. He held her in his gaze and undid his shirt, matching her, button for button. It was a game. A game with two players and only one possible outcome.

They were naked now and standing inches away from each other, hearts thumping, not touching but feeling the warmth of the other's passion. He moved towards her and held her until they could feel every part of each other. She closed her eyes and trembled slightly beneath his touch, then she pulled him back on to the bed. He knelt above her, stroking her and feasting his eyes on her. Never had he seen anyone so beautiful and so desirable and with so much love for him. Cathy placed her hand around his neck and brought him down to her, whispering urgently, 'Now, my darling. We can have our playtime later.'

It was like the first time for them both. In love and making love, that sweet and rare cocktail, tasted only by the very fortunate. They began slowly and exploratively, moving rhythmically together, eyes fixed on each other. Jake's widening slightly as he desperately tried to delay his own gratification so their moment, when it came, would coincide. It wouldn't be long. Cathy's mouth opened and her eyes squeezed shut as they clung together and moved into each other with increasing greed until it all ended in a mutual spasm of violent beauty that left Jake collapsed and gasping for breath on top of his damp-faced and contented lover. They lay there in happy delirium as the moment ebbed away. The best moment of their lives.

'It doesn't get better than this,' he said. 'I couldn't take it if it ever got any better than this.'

'I hope you can, this was only the starter.'

'Good grief!' he groaned. 'And to think I was worried about you being too young and inexperienced for me. I think it's the other way round . . .'

Cathy pressed her finger on his lips. 'Whatever went

before doesn't count,' she said, softly. 'Everything was just a rehearsal for this. This is the real thing. And just for the record – I love you, Jake Parker.'

Chapter Thirty-Four

In the distance, Spode could hear the Sunday service coming from the prison chapel, discordant voices singing an unrecognisable hymn.

The case against him had strengthened over the months. The unrelenting wave of incriminating evidence now included a mounting number of former victims who had been abused by him in his pre-Parliamentary days. People of both sexes, some of whom had been as young as twelve at the time. Reluctant to come forward in isolation, they now realised they weren't the only ones and that their stories would be believed: Ronnie Sykes, a girl who'd delivered Spode's papers, the daughter of one of his factory workers, and many others who had been seduced by his deviant charm and frightened by his threats of what would happen to them if ever they told on him.

Annie had become an obsession with him. She had been special, worth going to a lot of trouble for. He hadn't planned on raping her, he'd always hoped that once he'd got her in his lair, she'd succumb to his charms. She would become his Lolita. Marrying her mother to achieve this had been a stupid idea. From the recesses of his mind once again emerged Annie's last, chilling words to him . . .

. . . I'll get you back for what you did. Just you wait and see!

And now she'd come back from the dead. It was as if

she'd been waiting for her daughter to destroy him before she had the courage to return. He was too weak in body and spirit to summon up any hatred for Cathy. Or was this because she was so obviously his own daughter? The suddenness of his fall from grace had shocked his system to its foundations and he hadn't recovered. There'd been a long way to fall and he'd plunged the full distance in the space of a short speech from Cathy. Few people had sunk so far, so fast. Spode was in his sixth and final month of remand in Armley Jail. His case was listed to be heard the following week. Ever since that terrible night in the Queens Hotel his past life had been crawling out of the woodwork. Many of his crooked business dealings had been uncovered, including the school uniforms scam, which had led to the arrest of his erstwhile business partner Michael Rawnsley.

He was now helpless and powerless. Even the most junior of the prison officers treated him with utter disdain. A recent chronic bowel infection had been only the latest in a long string of ailments to hit him since his incarceration. Periodic migraines, an abscessed tooth, which had been painfully removed, and a bout of shingles had added to his discomfort. His hair was lank and colourless and his permanent suntan long gone, replaced by prison pallor. He was thinner by two stones, lessened in both body and spirit, and just like Annie all those years ago, he had no one to turn to. His humiliation and degradation were now complete. Almost.

His mouth twitched into the nearest he could muster to a smile. The bastards thought they'd got him but they hadn't. Oh, no – they hadn't enough proof to charge him with any of the murders, and it was his word against Annie's that he'd actually raped her. He'd admitted to having sex but not to rape. If he could beat that, then what was left? He'd serve time for messing with the kids – but he hadn't assaulted or raped any of them. Sex with a minor, that's all it was. And he might get time for the school uniforms scam – but that wasn't theft, just underhand business tactics or whatever they chose to call it. So what would he get? Could be as little as eighteen months according to his solicitor, less six months remission, less time already served. His grin widened, showing dark teeth behind cracked lips. He'd be out in six months. Take his money abroad, that's what he'd do. He had more than enough to retire on. He looked at his watch; his Rolex had been confiscated, perhaps for the best. Too much of a temptation in this Godforsaken place. His housekeeper had sent him one of his cheaper time pieces, one not worth stealing. It was time for room service.

His cell door opened but Spode didn't accord the visitor so much as a glance. All part of his game. His way of preserving his sanity and self-respect. Meals had been delivered to his cell three times a day ever since the severe beating he'd taken on his first morning inside. His meal, such as it was, had been thrown to the floor by fellow inmates and his tray repeatedly smashed over his head as a way of persuading him to lick up the food like the animal he was. The warders had arrived on the scene very late.

The game was everything now. It was the only thing that kept him sane. He'd show them he didn't care about them or their opinions of him. Act as though the world around him didn't exist. Never let them get to him. Compared to him, all these people were nothing. Once he got out he'd be able to buy and sell the bloody lot of them, and no doubt exact the odd spot of revenge here and there. Every night he lulled himself to sleep with visions of sweet and vicious retribution and he took comfort from the fact that he knew he was capable of it.

His nose twitched, trying to detect what foul concoction was on today's menu, but he smelled nothing. He glanced sideways, his eyes still low. The boots he saw weren't the warder's. He gave a violent shudder of fright as he looked up.

Framed in the open door was the monster from the top landing. A vicious and unrepentant armed robber who wasn't supposed to move around unescorted. Behind him, almost hidden by his bulk, were others. The same expression on each face. Brown-toothed grins beneath empty eyes, exuding evil and menace. The stench from their bodies suddenly pervaded the cell and Spode retched with terror.

'We've heard yer do it ter kiddies.' The monster's icy voice came from somewhere deep inside his bowels. 'We don't allow perverts like you ter live.'

Spode's eyes swam with tears and urine ran down his trouser leg as he whimpered for mercy. The party moved inside his cell and closed the door behind them.

Cathy took the call from the Chief Inspector dealing with Spode's case.

'You won't be needed as a witness, Miss Makepeace. Leonard Spode was found dead in his cell this morning.'

She felt nothing. Or did she feel a sense of relief? 'How did he die?' she asked, flatly.

'You don't want to know.'

Epilogue

September 1972

Annie wanted to set off at dawn, just as she had before, but the first bus wasn't until seven-fifteen. There were ghosts she had to lay and most of them lay ahead of her. This time her daughter wasn't wrapped up in a blanket but sitting beside her in a sheepskin coat to keep out the cold. The fare had gone up as well.

'Two to Beckhall Lane end. That'll be thirty-two new pence,' said the conductor, who wasn't fully reconciled to decimalisation.

Annie did a mental calculation as Cathy handed over the fare. Sixteen pence each, that was about three and twopence. More than six times what she'd paid the last time. Cathy looked at her.

'Are you absolutely sure you want to do this, Annie?'

She squeezed her daughter's hand. 'I'm not sure of anything, Cathy. But I think I need to do it. There are too many things I'm frightened of. I'm having too many nightmares. I need to confront my past. I need to beat the bogeymen.'

'We'll beat them together,' Cathy assured her. 'We're a team.'

'Always have been,' said Annie.

The bus rumbled on. Empty at this time on a Sunday, as it had been last time. They passed a placard carrying last night's news about the eleven Israeli athletes who had been murdered at the Munich Olympics and Annie wondered once again why the men of violence hadn't learned any lessons from the last war.

'Spode's solicitor contacted me, you know,' said Cathy. 'He died intestate, would you believe? A man with all that money.'

'He had no one to leave it to,' said Annie.

'Apparently, if I can prove I'm his daughter, I get the lot.'

'Shouldn't be too hard,' said her mother. 'Do you want his money?'

Cathy shuddered. 'No, thanks. Just the thought of having any of his money gives me the creeps.'

'Tainted money eh?'

Cathy nodded.

'What about Jimmy Johnstone's money?' asked Annie. 'Should I have taken that?'

Cathy laughed. She'd heard all about Jimmy's escapades. 'Well, *I* was going to take it, I must admit. I wish I'd met him.'

'Oh,' said Annie, her eyes misting over at the thought of her old friend, 'you'd have fallen in love with him. I know I did.'

'I'll just have to make do with Jake.'

'He's not a bad substitute. Jake was a good friend to me – still is.'

'He's asked me to marry him.'

'And?'

'And I'm nineteen years old. I don't want to become an old married woman just yet.'

'He won't wait forever.'

'I won't ask him to. Two or three years maybe. I want to go to university.'

'You could give the money away,' said Annie, her thoughts fluttering like a butterfly. 'Maybe the children of that woman he murdered?'

'Melanie Binns?' mused Cathy. 'Yes, I could go along with that. We could spread it around a bit. Children's homes, stuff like that. I'll ask Jake, he'll help. Did you hear about Brenda becoming their self-appointed watch-dog?'

'Whose?'

'Melanie Binns' kids.'

'Yes, Jake told me,' said Annie. 'How is he, by the way?'

'Jake's fine. How's Sam?'

'How would I know?'

'I thought you and he were – you know,' teased Cathy.

'He's a good friend. I don't need any more complications in my life right now.'

'Sorry. I just thought he was more than a friend. I think Sam's good for you.'

Annie didn't take the bait. She and her daughter were more like sisters, with Cathy being the older and wiser one. The conductor was a younger man than last time and highly impressed by his passengers. The blonde, sun-tanned one was probably more his age, late-twenties, early-thirties. Not a bad looker but not in the same league as the younger brunette.

'How did the holiday go?' enquired Cathy.

'Oh, we had a great time,' laughed Annie. 'God help Gloria if her husband ever finds out what she got up to.'

'Never mind Gloria. What did *you* get up to, Annie?'

'Nothing!' she said, sharply. 'I didn't get up to anything.'

Cathy sighed. Perhaps Annie was right. Perhaps she wasn't ready for a relationship with Sam – or with any man for that matter. Apart from anything else, Annie had the morality of a fifties girl. The swinging sixties had passed her by.

The church steeple came into view and Annie's heart began to race. Cathy sensed her trepidation.

'Annie, this time there's nothing to worry about.'

'I know, I'm okay.'

As they got up, the conductor rang the bell and the driver looked in his mirror, surprised to see anyone getting off here at this time on a morning.

It was a chilly morning. The early sun lit up the horizon and tried to break through the distant sky but was thwarted by heavy clouds. The sign pointing to the village was different; made of metal and devoid of obscene alteration. Annie pulled her coat around her and looked up, aware that something was missing. The skylark.

There were no potholes in the road. Patches of darker tarmac indicated where they'd been filled in. The hedges were lush and showing signs of changing colour. Annie clung to Cathy's arm as they marched in step up the centre of the road, the mother taking strength from her taller, stronger daughter. The church bell began to strike and Annie counted the bongs. Eight. Two more than last time. The bridge came into view and she suddenly wanted to see him. She wanted him to be there like he had been then. They stopped and Annie peered along the line of fishermen, deliberately not looking over the other side of the bridge. The side where her ghosts lurked.

'Sam isn't there,' she said, trying to hide her disappointment.

'Did you think he would be?'

Annie shrugged. 'Well, he was last time. He told me he still came here.'

'Maybe he'll be along later.'

'Maybe.'

Annie turned and took the few steps necessary to get to the other side of the bridge. 'This is where I jumped in.'

'I know.'

She stared down at the water for a long time, trying to expurgate the feeling of ultimate despair she'd known the last time she was here and to replace it with a feeling of hope. Cathy stood silently by her side, unable to understand what her mother was thinking. Then she noticed a smile creep across Annie's face. She looked round at her daughter.

'My God, you really got him, didn't you, Cathy?'

'He can't hurt you now, Annie.'

'I know. I hope you're burning in Hell, Spode!'

The fishermen looked up, but couldn't see who was shouting. Annie turned to her daughter again. 'Is it sinful being happy that someone's dead?'

'Not someone like Spode,' Cathy assured her. 'He forfeited his right to live the night he attacked you.'

Annie took her hand. 'Come on, we'll go to the church.'

As she stepped off the bridge, a weight was lifted from Annie's shoulders. She'd been back to the scene of her lowest moment and looked down at the water. And she'd survived unscathed this time. The demons in her mind couldn't hurt her now.

The rickety bench on which she'd breast-fed Cathy hadn't survived. It had been replaced by another which was already showing its age. The branches of a nearby tree now overshadowed it and the seat was dotted with bird droppings.

'I sat on that and fed you,' said Annie. Then she noticed the carving. *In Memory of Edna Grovehall*. 'No, it's a different one. The other one said, "*In Memory of Wilfred Eames*".'

Her recollection of such detail amazed Cathy who suggested, 'Unlike the birds, I think we should give Edna Grovehall's seat a miss. Unless you're tired?'

Annie shook her head. 'No, I'm not tired any more. I was tired that day. Tired, terrified, alone.'

'You weren't completely alone. I was there.'

Annie looked at her, not wanting an argument. 'Cathy, I've come here as much for your benefit as mine. I want you to understand why I did what I did.'

'I do understand, Annie.'

'You see, they hurt me and they lied about me and took everything away from me. I had no mother, no possessions, no dignity, no self-respect, no friends . . . no one to turn to. And they took away the most important thing of all. They took away hope. Without hope there isn't anything left.'

'It's all right, Annie.'

'I had you and I had sixpence. That's all I had in the world, just you and sixpence . . . and I spent the sixpence on the bus fare . . . and I was fifteen years old. For God's sake, Cathy, I *still am* fifteen years old!'

'No one's condemning you, Annie, especially me.'

'So I just stepped off the ride. But I left you in good hands.' She looked at her daughter. 'Didn't I?'

'You did – and thanks for that.'

Annie stood there, silently. No tears came. She'd cried all her tears long ago. Then she said, 'Do you really mean that?'

'Yes, I do. You don't have to justify what you did. We couldn't have survived together. You did the right thing.' Cathy suddenly grinned. 'Mind you, jumping off the bridge was a bit drastic.'

Annie nodded. 'As far as I was concerned, I was already dead. The miracle was, I've never been much of a swimmer. The currents kept bringing me back to the surface. When I went over a waterfall and got jammed between two rocks, I suppose my survival instincts took over. That and Divine Providence.'

'Hello there!'

Annie's bitter memories were curtailed by the sight of John Barrett, standing by the lych-gate. The two women looked across at the priest who had changed their lives.

'What brings you here?' he called. 'Are you coming to Mass? Do I see a couple of converts? A couple of lost sheep returning to the flock? Shall I alert the Pope?'

Cathy laughed and walked over to him. 'We believe in you, John,' she said. 'If that's any good.'

'It's good enough for me.'

'Is everything still the same inside the church?' called out a cautious Annie, still at the other side of the road. She wanted at least something to be exactly the same as before.

'Practically down to the flowers and the same fag burn on the baptismal font,' he assured her.

'Can I go in on my own?'

'You can.'

They stood back as Annie walked past them and into the church. John was right. Everything was exactly as she remembered it, even down to the beams of coloured sunlight filtering through the stained-glass window. Quiet and safe. And she recalled how empty she had felt at having to say goodbye to her baby. She recalled the peace and the pain of that morning. But as she stood at the end of the aisle looking down towards the altar she sensed no recrimination being directed at her. If the church had ever condemned her for leaving her baby here, she was now forgiven.

So that was okay.

It was brighter when she went back outside. The clouds were rolling back, allowing the low sun to light up the sky. A sparrow twittered in the eaves above her before flying off. No trapped birds today.

'There's something we want to show you,' said Cathy. 'Something very few people get to see.'

They took her to the south-east corner and Cathy pointed at the mountain ash, its slender leaves as green and full as they'd ever be, rippling in the light breeze.

'There,' she said.

'What am I looking at?'

'That's your tree. John planted it for you when he thought you were . . .'

Annie finished her sentence. 'When he thought I was dead?' She went closer and looked down at the plaque.

This is Annie Jackson's Tree. Requiescat in pace.

There was a long, uncomfortable silence as Cathy and John looked at each other and questioned their wisdom in bringing her here.

'Well, I was never much good at Latin,' said Annie at length. 'But I'm fairly sure what it means. And you're right about its being something very few people get to see – their own memorial.'

'Oh, I'll be removing the plaque, of course,' John assured her. 'God willing, you won't be resting in peace for quite some time.'

'No, no,' protested Annie. 'John, this is the loveliest thing.' She looked at Cathy. 'Isn't this the loveliest thing?'

'He's a lovely man,' agreed Cathy.

Annie took the embarrassed priest in her arms and smothered him in kisses to the amusement of the verger who had just arrived. His exaggerated version of the scene would soon be working its way around the parish. Annie let him go and took Cathy's hand. The engraving on a nearby headstone took her eye.

Vengeance is Mine; I will repay, saith The Lord.

'I prefer, "An eye for an eye",' said Annie.

'Each to his own,' said Father Barrett.

Annie kissed him again. 'There's just one more thing I have to do – and I need to do it on my own.'

'You're going back to the bridge?' guessed Cathy.

'That's right. Then it's all done. But I need to go alone.'

'I understand,' said Cathy. 'At least, I think I do.'

The sun was out now. There was no warmth in it but the light was cheerful and reassuring and Annie's step was confident and determined. All her fears had been confronted and she now had a lot more to live for than most. Retracing her final steps entirely on her own was just a formality. She stopped in the middle of the bridge and looked to her left, to the spot where she'd recently stood hurling abuse at Spode. That no longer mattered to her. He was a diminishing speck in her memory. She walked to the other side and sat on the parapet wall, from where she could look down at the fishermen. When she'd sat there last time there were several coping stones missing. They had been replaced now. Everything was mended. Just as it should be. Perfect, in fact, because Sam was down there.

He'd arrived late and had claimed his usual pitch, nearest the bridge. Annie wanted to ask him where the devil he'd been, disappointing her like that. Then her life suddenly made sense. All the happiness she needed was down there, trying to catch a fish. Sam was concentrating on his float which had just dipped out of sight. This was a big one, a fighter. A grin lit up his face as he reeled it carefully in. The others were watching from the corners of their eyes. Jealous as hell. Wondering how he did it. Annie knew little about the niceties of fishing.

'Nice day for it!' she shouted.

Sam looked up into her face and time moved back some nineteen years. Nineteen years of cursing himself for letting her go. But no one gets a second chance, do they?

'Stay right there,' he shouted. 'Annie Jackson – don't you dare disappear again.'

The line slackened and Annie laughed as the fish escaped and Sam's rod dropped into the river to be swept away downstream, out of sight beneath the bridge. He didn't care. He was already halfway up the bank.